Jim Henson's™

FRAGGLE ROCK™

JOURNEY TO THE EVERSPRING

Jim Henson™
THE JIM HENSON COMPANY

ARCHAIA™

**JIM HENSON'S FRAGGLE ROCK: JOURNEY TO
THE EVERSPRING, AUGUST 2015.** Published by Ar-
chaia, a division of Boom Entertainment, Inc. © 2015 The Jim Henson Company. JIM HENSON's mark & logo, FRAGGLE ROCK, mark
& logo, and all related characters and elements are trademarks of
The Jim Henson Company. Originally published in single mag-
azine form as JIM HENSON'S FRAGGLE ROCK: JOURNEY TO THE
EVERSPRING No. 1-4. ™ & © 2014, 2015 The Jim Henson Company.
All Rights Reserved. Archaia™ and the Archaia logo are trademarks
of Boom Entertainment, Inc., registered in various countries and
categories. All characters, events, and institutions depicted herein
are fictional. Any similarity between any of the names, characters,
persons, events, and/or institutions in this publication to actual
names, characters, and persons, whether living or dead, events,
and/or institutions is unintended and purely coincidental.

BOOM! Studios, 5670 Wilshire Boulevard, Suite 450, Los Angeles,
CA 90036-5679. Printed in China. First Printing.

ISBN: 978-1-60886-694-6, eISBN: 978-1-61398-365-2

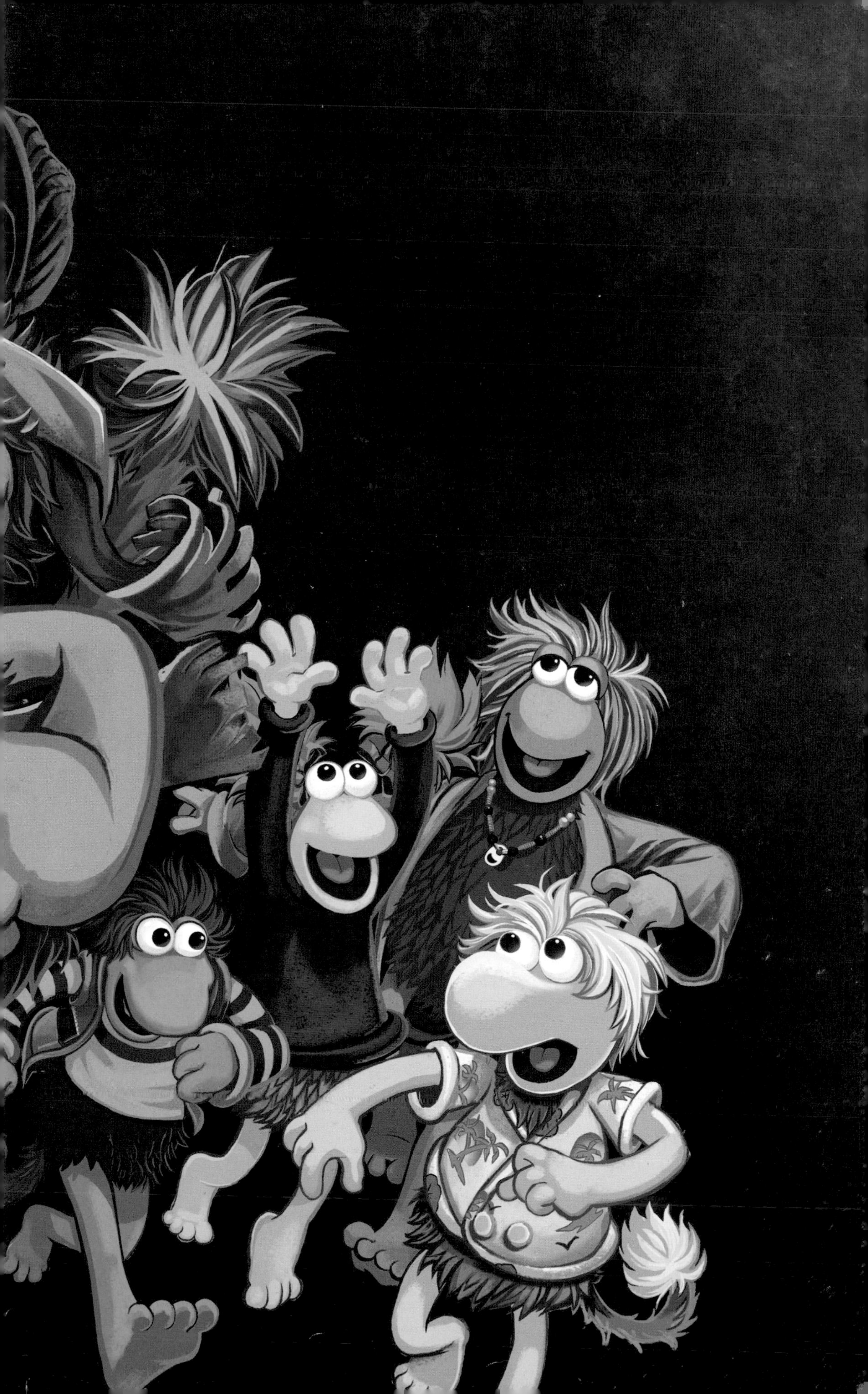

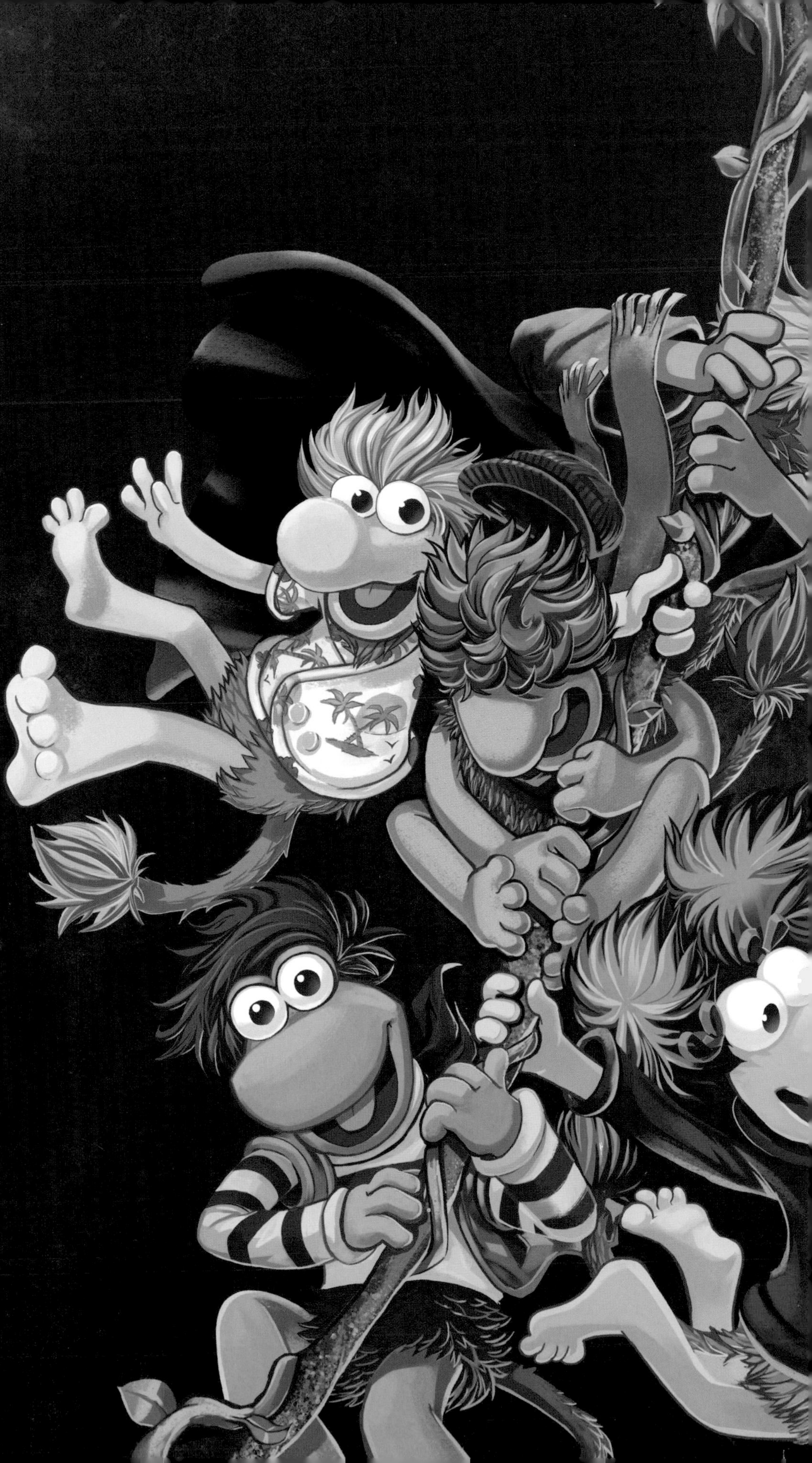

JIM HENSON'S FRAGGLE ROCK™

JOURNEY TO THE EVERSPRING

WRITTEN BY **KATE LETH**
ILLUSTRATED BY **JAKE MYLER**
LETTERED BY **COREY BREEN**

COVER BY **JAKE MYLER**

DESIGNER **KARA LEOPARD**
ASSISTANT EDITOR **CAMERON CHITTOCK**
EDITOR **REBECCA TAYLOR**

SPECIAL THANKS TO BRIAN HENSON, LISA HENSON,
JIM FORMANEK, NICOLE GOLDMAN, MARYANNE PITTMAN,
CARLA DELLAVEDOVA, JUSTIN HILDEN, JILL PETERSON,
KAREN FALK, AND THE ENTIRE JIM HENSON COMPANY TEAM.

DANCE YOUR CARES AWAY

CHAPTER ONE

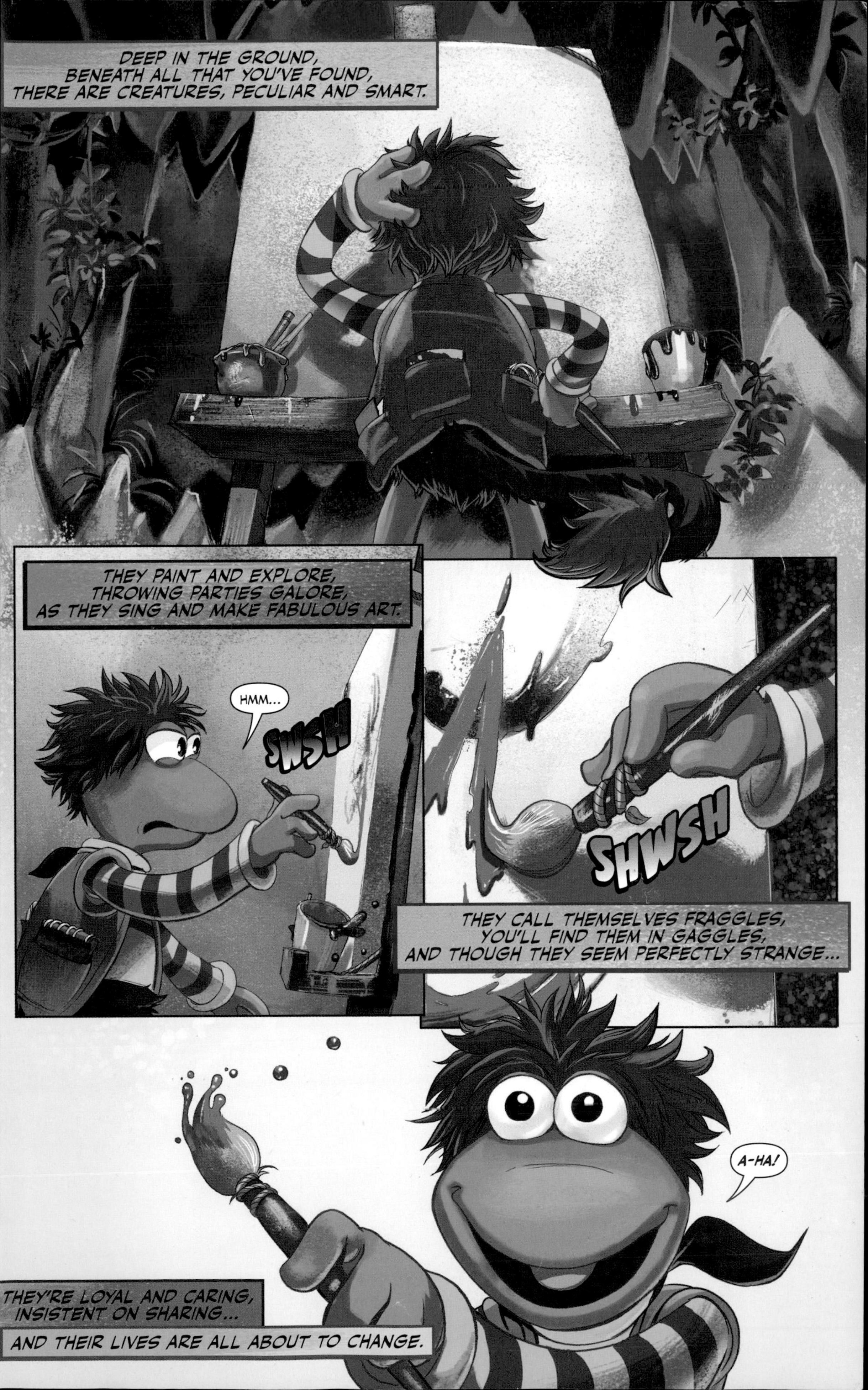
DEEP IN THE GROUND, BENEATH ALL THAT YOU'VE FOUND, THERE ARE CREATURES, PECULIAR AND SMART.
THEY PAINT AND EXPLORE, THROWING PARTIES GALORE, AS THEY SING AND MAKE FABULOUS ART.
HMM...
SWSH
SHWSH
THEY CALL THEMSELVES FRAGGLES, YOU'LL FIND THEM IN GAGGLES, AND THOUGH THEY SEEM PERFECTLY STRANGE...
A-HA!
THEY'RE LOYAL AND CARING, INSISTENT ON SHARING...
AND THEIR LIVES ARE ALL ABOUT TO CHANGE.

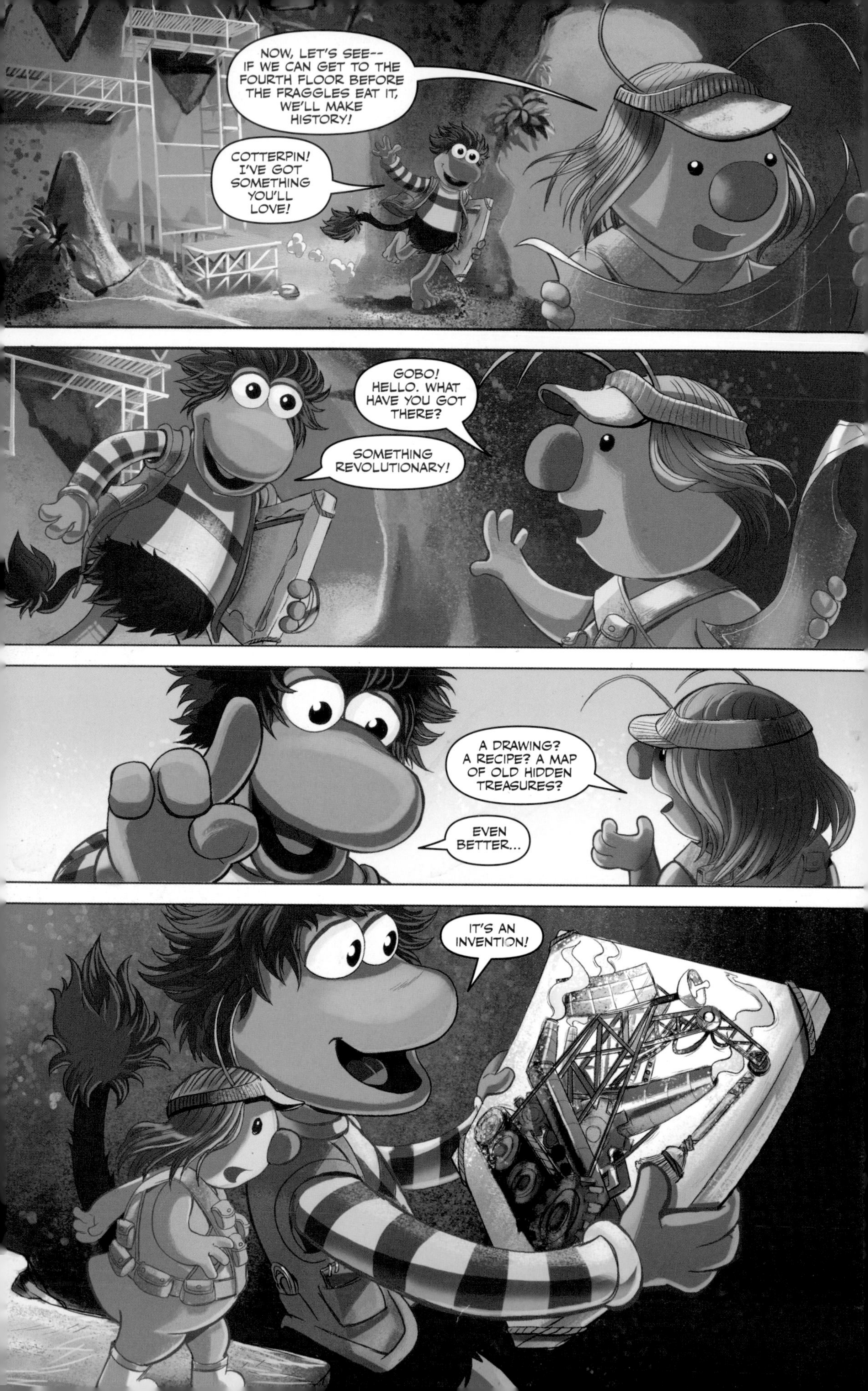
NOW, LET'S SEE-- IF WE CAN GET TO THE FOURTH FLOOR BEFORE THE FRAGGLES EAT IT, WE'LL MAKE HISTORY!
COTTERPIN! I'VE GOT SOMETHING YOU'LL LOVE!
GOBO! HELLO. WHAT HAVE YOU GOT THERE?
SOMETHING REVOLUTIONARY!
A DRAWING? A RECIPE? A MAP OF OLD HIDDEN TREASURES?
EVEN BETTER...
IT'S AN INVENTION!

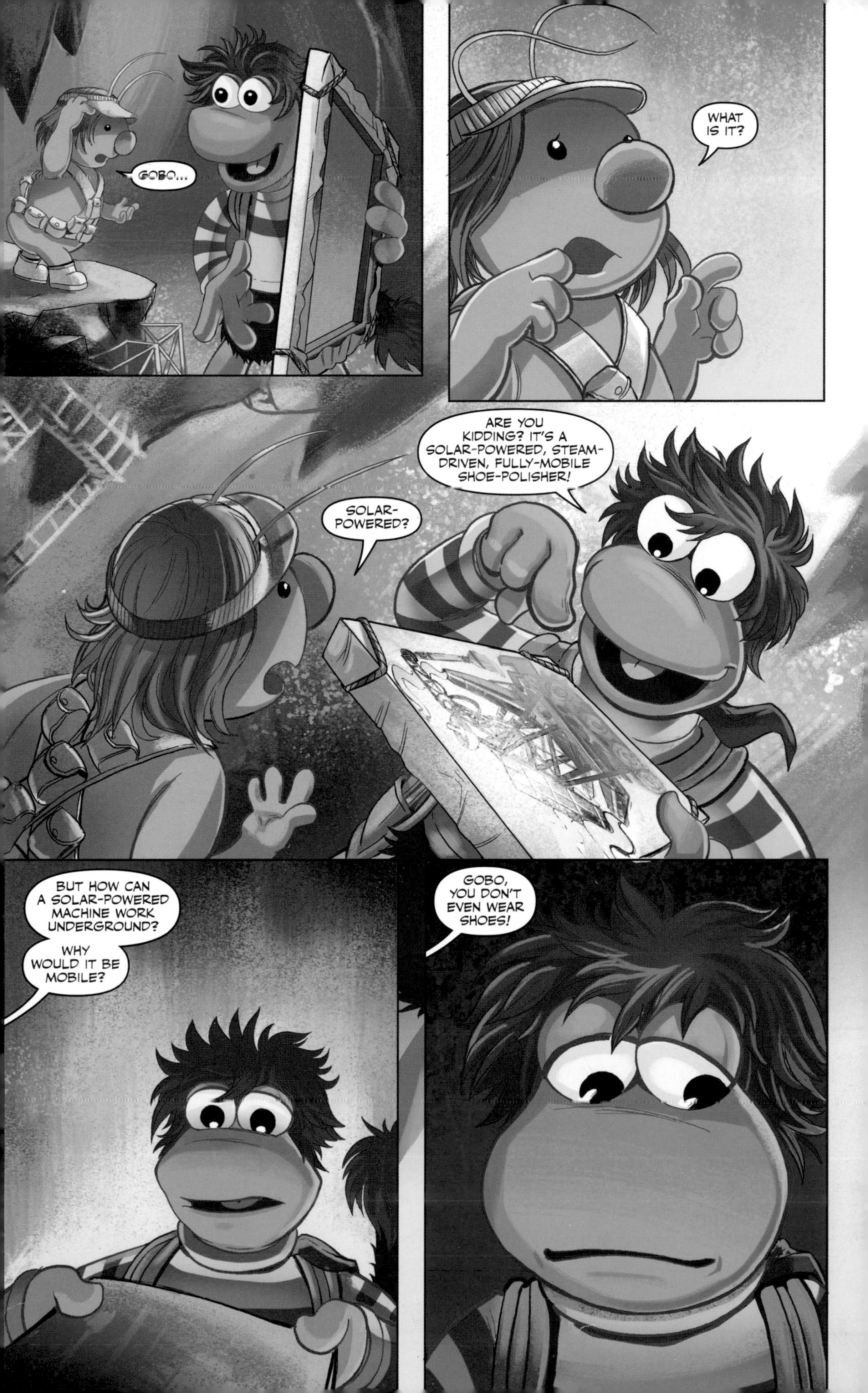
GOBO...
WHAT IS IT?
SOLAR-POWERED?
ARE YOU KIDDING? IT'S A SOLAR-POWERED, STEAM-DRIVEN, FULLY-MOBILE SHOE-POLISHER!
BUT HOW CAN A SOLAR-POWERED MACHINE WORK UNDERGROUND?
WHY WOULD IT BE MOBILE?
GOBO, YOU DON'T EVEN WEAR SHOES!

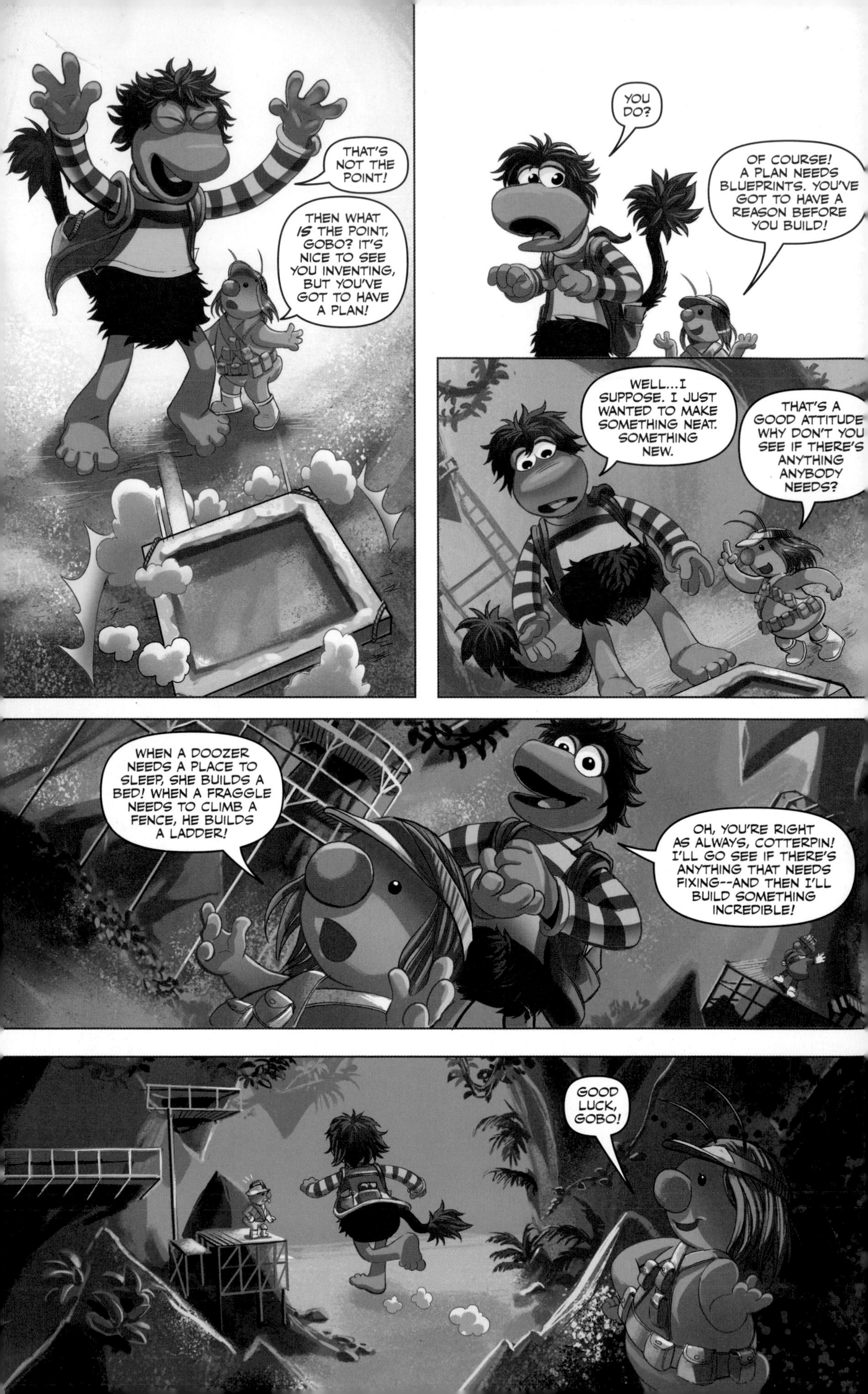
THAT'S NOT THE POINT!
THEN WHAT *IS* THE POINT, GOBO? IT'S NICE TO SEE YOU INVENTING, BUT YOU'VE GOT TO HAVE A PLAN!
YOU DO?
OF COURSE! A PLAN NEEDS BLUEPRINTS. YOU'VE GOT TO HAVE A REASON BEFORE YOU BUILD!
WELL...I SUPPOSE. I JUST WANTED TO MAKE SOMETHING NEAT. SOMETHING NEW.
THAT'S A GOOD ATTITUDE WHY DON'T YOU SEE IF THERE'S ANYTHING ANYBODY NEEDS?
WHEN A DOOZER NEEDS A PLACE TO SLEEP, SHE BUILDS A BED! WHEN A FRAGGLE NEEDS TO CLIMB A FENCE, HE BUILDS A LADDER!
OH, YOU'RE RIGHT AS ALWAYS, COTTERPIN! I'LL GO SEE IF THERE'S ANYTHING THAT NEEDS FIXING--AND THEN I'LL BUILD SOMETHING INCREDIBLE!
GOOD LUCK, GOBO!

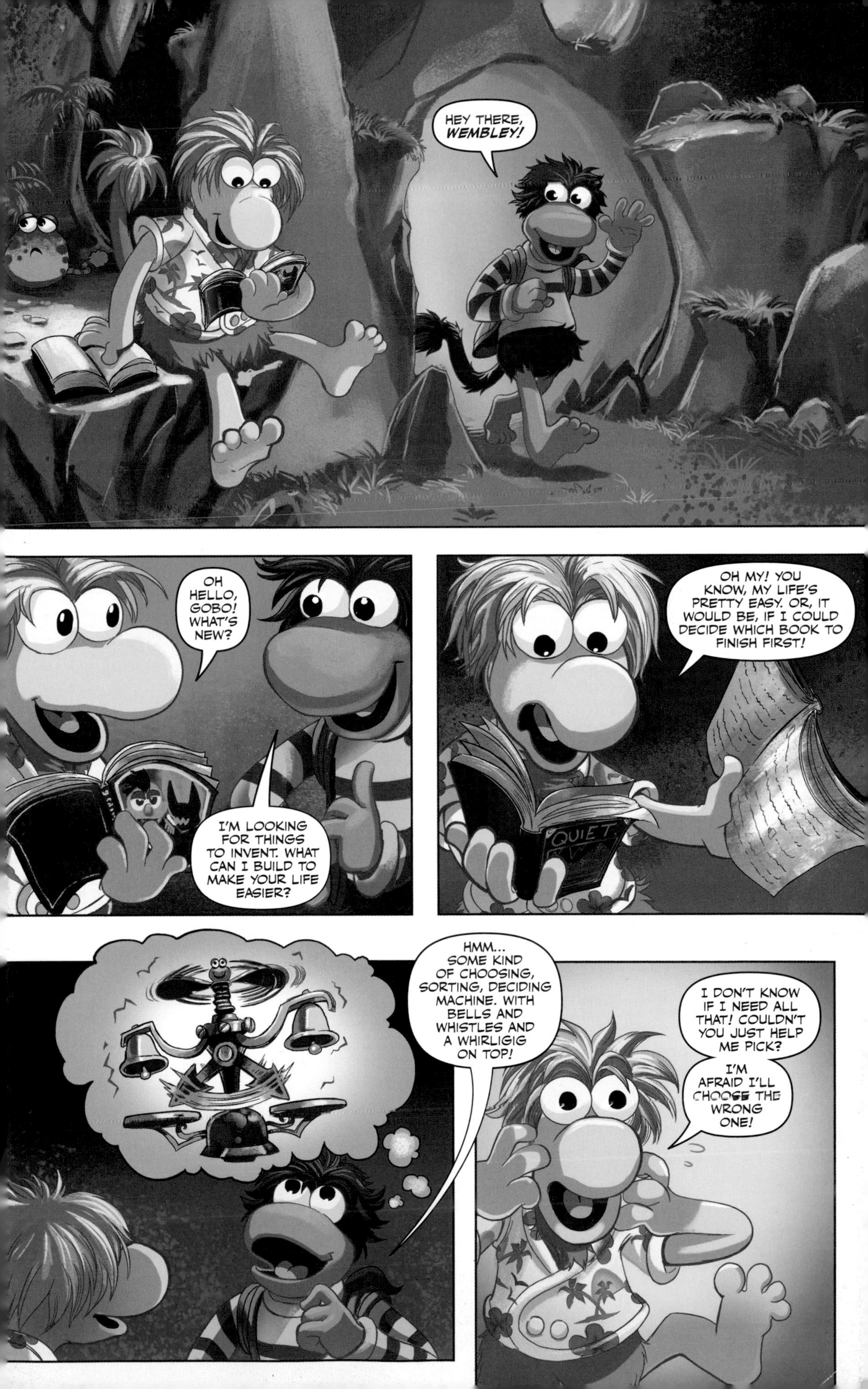
HEY THERE, *WEMBLEY!*
OH HELLO, GOBO! WHAT'S NEW?
I'M LOOKING FOR THINGS TO INVENT. WHAT CAN I BUILD TO MAKE YOUR LIFE EASIER?
OH MY! YOU KNOW, MY LIFE'S PRETTY EASY. OR, IT WOULD BE, IF I COULD DECIDE WHICH BOOK TO FINISH FIRST!
QUIET
HMM... SOME KIND OF CHOOSING, SORTING, DECIDING MACHINE. WITH BELLS AND WHISTLES AND A WHIRLIGIG ON TOP!
I DON'T KNOW IF I NEED ALL THAT! COULDN'T YOU JUST HELP ME PICK?
I'M AFRAID I'LL CHOOSE THE WRONG ONE!

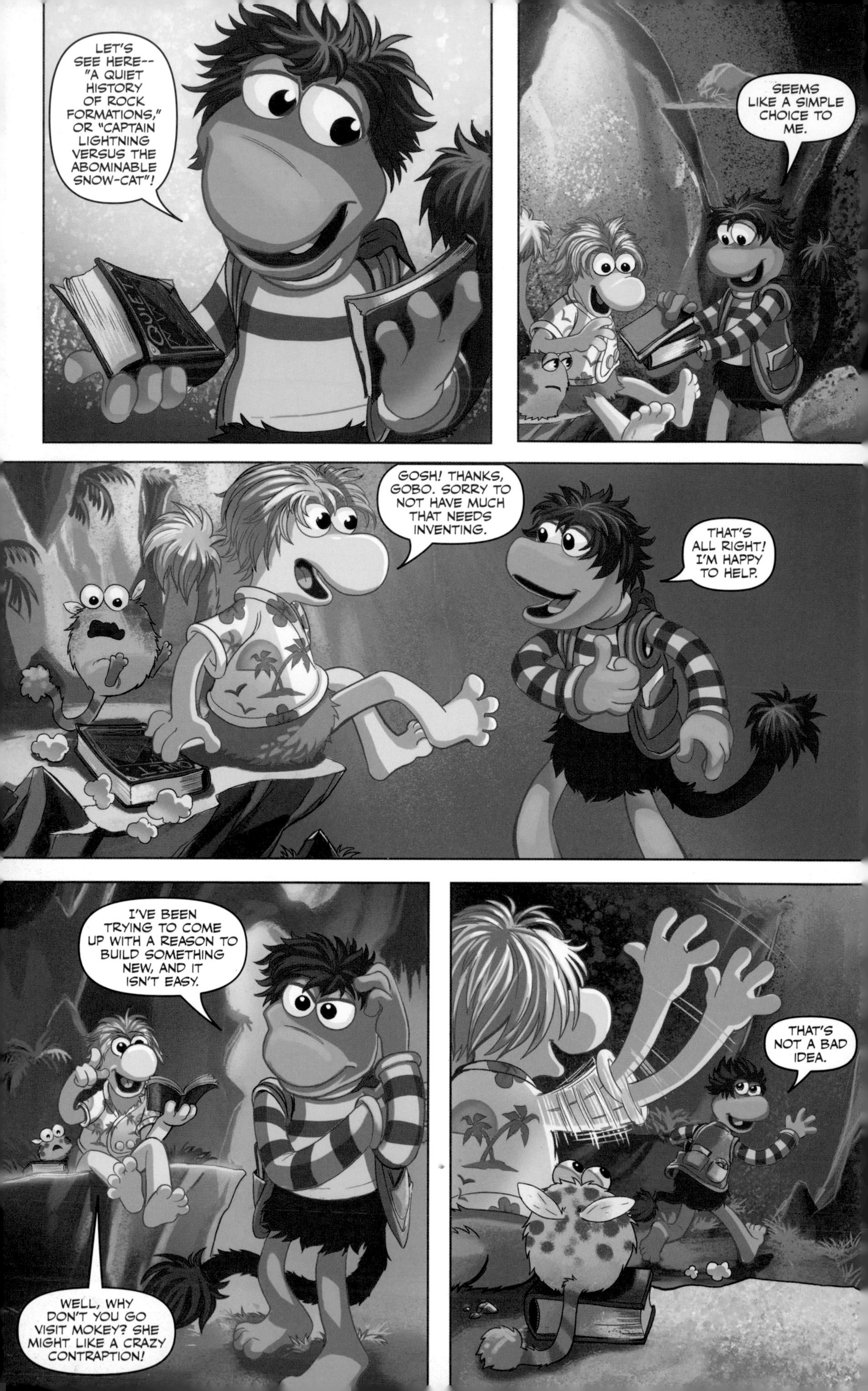
LET'S SEE HERE-- "A QUIET HISTORY OF ROCK FORMATIONS," OR "CAPTAIN LIGHTNING VERSUS THE ABOMINABLE SNOW-CAT"!
SEEMS LIKE A SIMPLE CHOICE TO ME.
GOSH! THANKS, GOBO. SORRY TO NOT HAVE MUCH THAT NEEDS INVENTING.
THAT'S ALL RIGHT! I'M HAPPY TO HELP.
I'VE BEEN TRYING TO COME UP WITH A REASON TO BUILD SOMETHING NEW, AND IT ISN'T EASY.
WELL, WHY DON'T YOU GO VISIT MOKEY? SHE MIGHT LIKE A CRAZY CONTRAPTION!
THAT'S NOT A BAD IDEA.

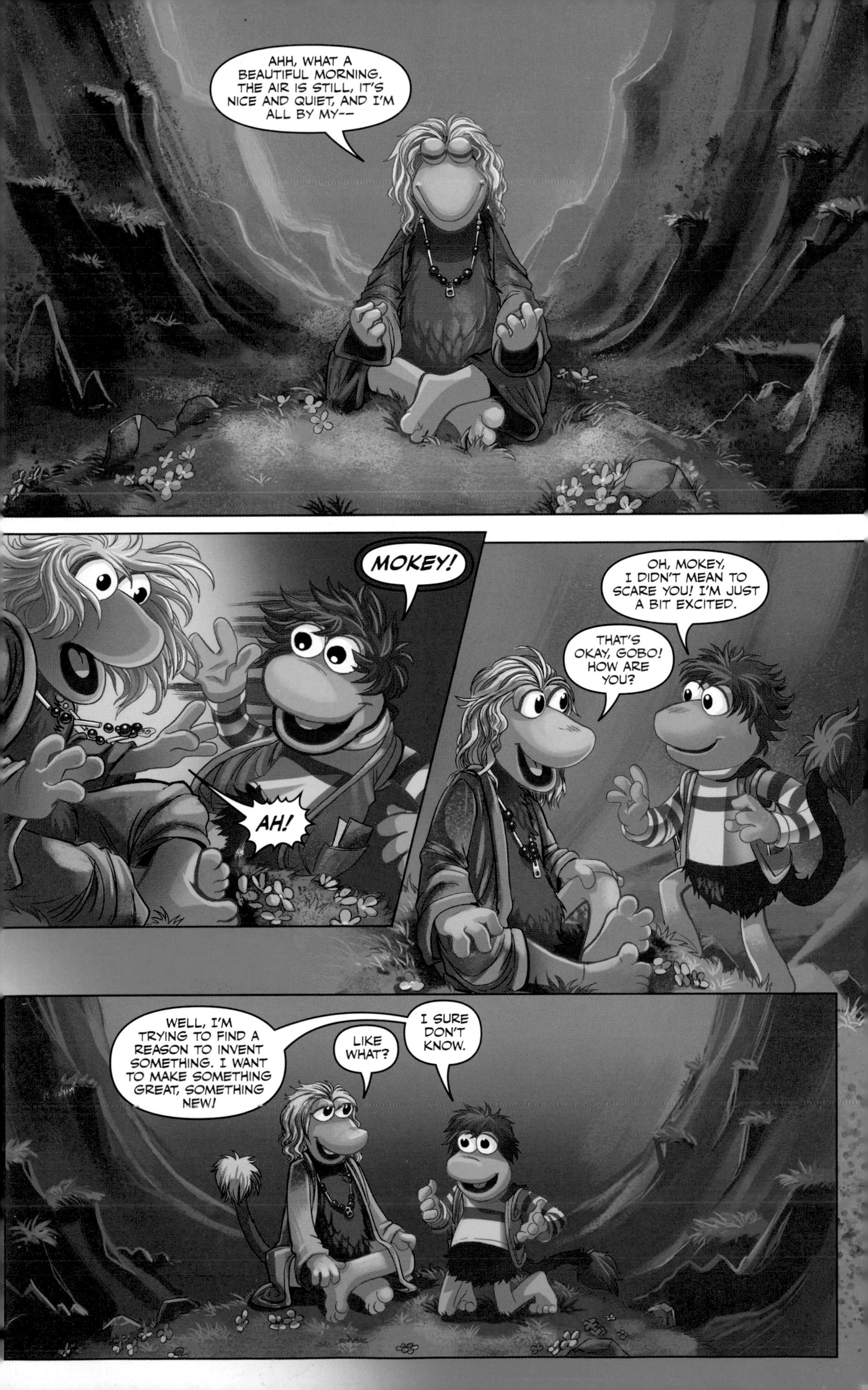
AHH, WHAT A BEAUTIFUL MORNING. THE AIR IS STILL, IT'S NICE AND QUIET, AND I'M ALL BY MY--
MOKEY!
AH!
OH, MOKEY, I DIDN'T MEAN TO SCARE YOU! I'M JUST A BIT EXCITED.
THAT'S OKAY, GOBO! HOW ARE YOU?
WELL, I'M TRYING TO FIND A REASON TO INVENT SOMETHING. I WANT TO MAKE SOMETHING GREAT, SOMETHING NEW!
LIKE WHAT?
I SURE DON'T KNOW.

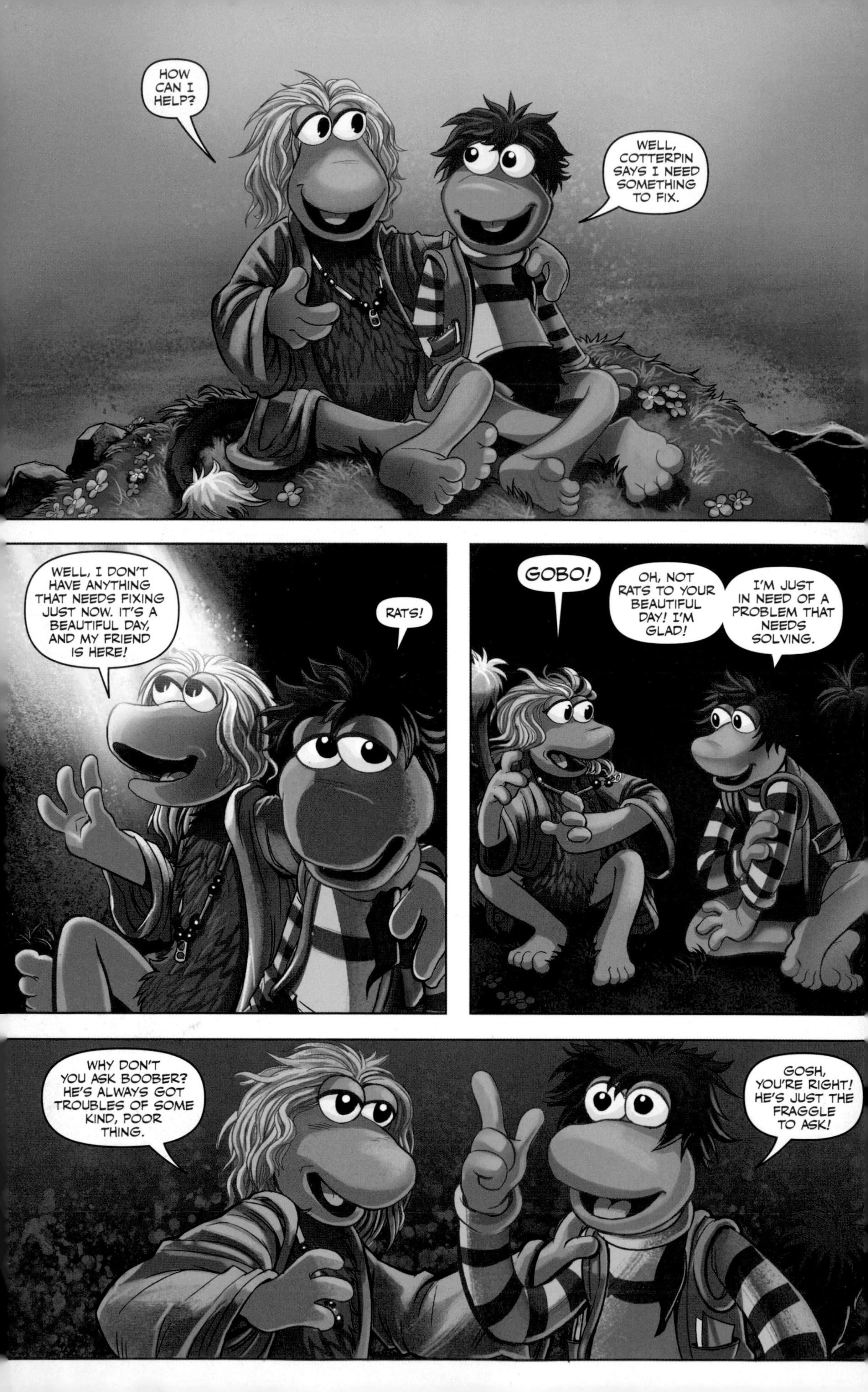
HOW CAN I HELP?
WELL, COTTERPIN SAYS I NEED SOMETHING TO FIX.
WELL, I DON'T HAVE ANYTHING THAT NEEDS FIXING JUST NOW. IT'S A BEAUTIFUL DAY, AND MY FRIEND IS HERE!
RATS!
GOBO!
OH, NOT RATS TO YOUR BEAUTIFUL DAY! I'M GLAD!
I'M JUST IN NEED OF A PROBLEM THAT NEEDS SOLVING.
WHY DON'T YOU ASK BOOBER? HE'S ALWAYS GOT TROUBLES OF SOME KIND, POOR THING.
GOSH, YOU'RE RIGHT! HE'S JUST THE FRAGGLE TO ASK!

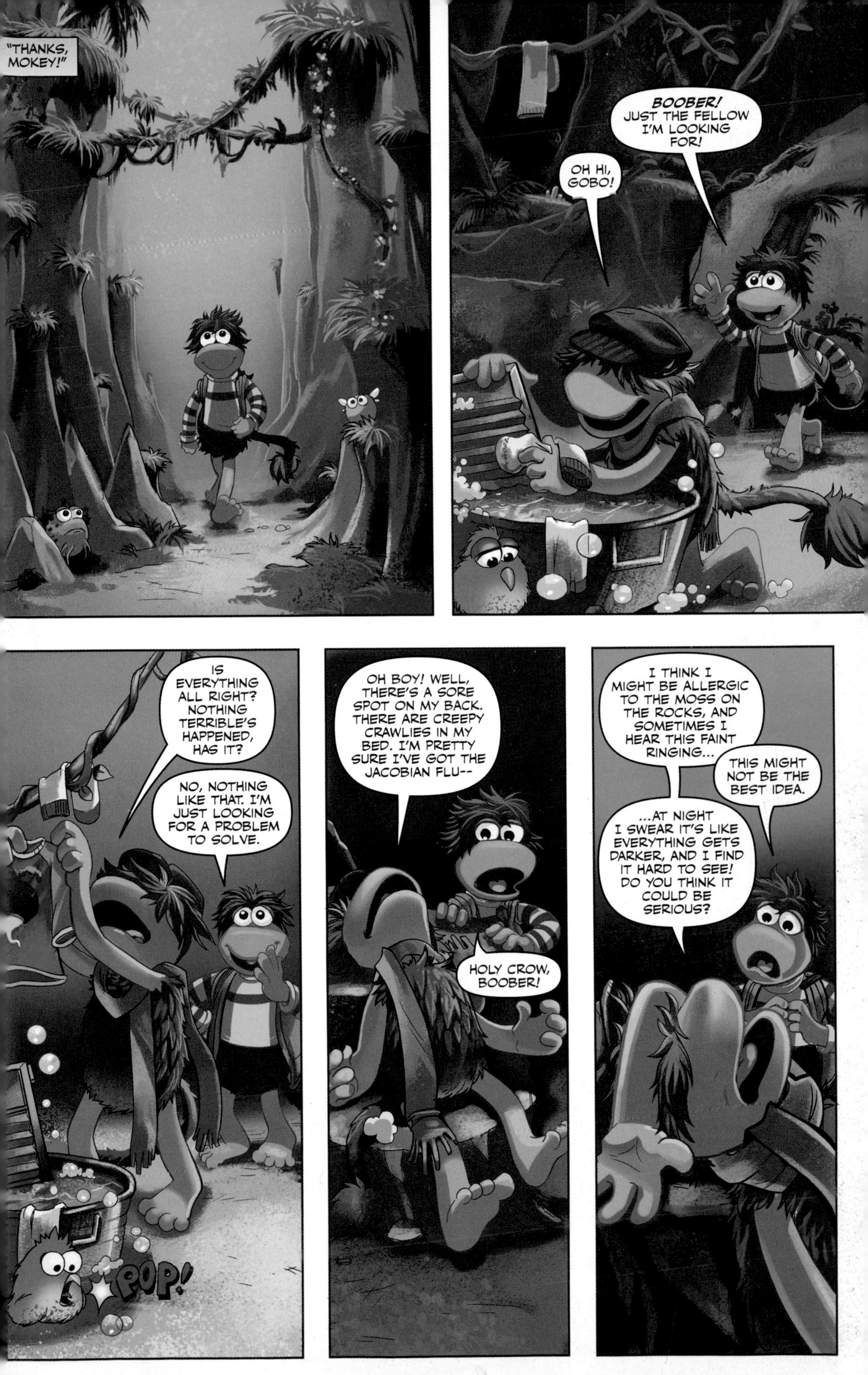
"THANKS, MOKEY!"
BOOBER! JUST THE FELLOW I'M LOOKING FOR!
OH HI, GOBO!
IS EVERYTHING ALL RIGHT? NOTHING TERRIBLE'S HAPPENED, HAS IT?
NO, NOTHING LIKE THAT. I'M JUST LOOKING FOR A PROBLEM TO SOLVE.
POP!
OH BOY! WELL, THERE'S A SORE SPOT ON MY BACK. THERE ARE CREEPY CRAWLIES IN MY BED. I'M PRETTY SURE I'VE GOT THE JACOBIAN FLU--
HOLY CROW, BOOBER!
I THINK I MIGHT BE ALLERGIC TO THE MOSS ON THE ROCKS, AND SOMETIMES I HEAR THIS FAINT RINGING...
...AT NIGHT I SWEAR IT'S LIKE EVERYTHING GETS DARKER, AND I FIND IT HARD TO SEE! DO YOU THINK IT COULD BE SERIOUS?
THIS MIGHT NOT BE THE BEST IDEA.

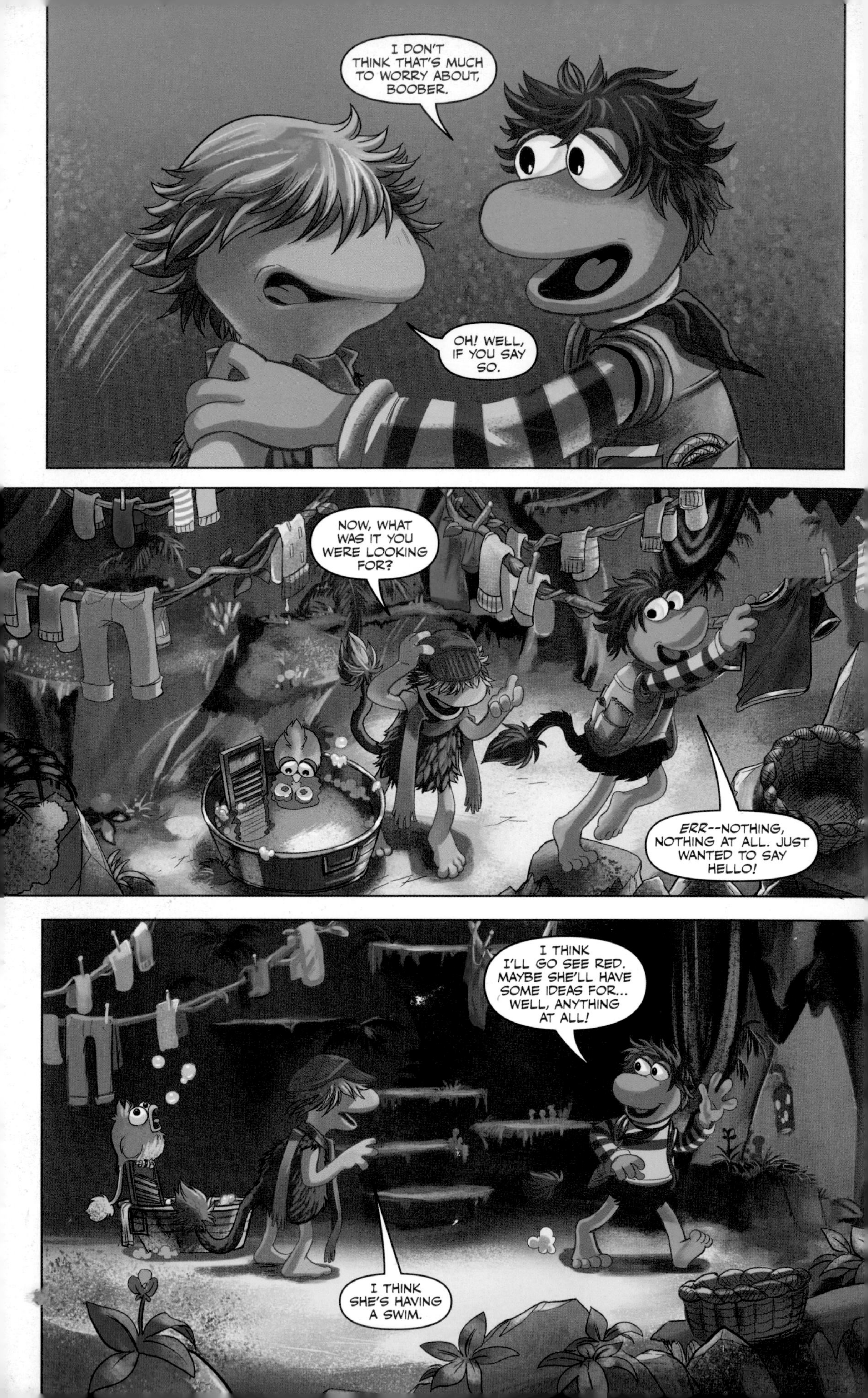
I DON'T THINK THAT'S MUCH TO WORRY ABOUT, BOOBER.
OH! WELL, IF YOU SAY SO.
NOW, WHAT WAS IT YOU WERE LOOKING FOR?
ERR--NOTHING, NOTHING AT ALL. JUST WANTED TO SAY HELLO!
I THINK I'LL GO SEE RED. MAYBE SHE'LL HAVE SOME IDEAS FOR... WELL, ANYTHING AT ALL!
I THINK SHE'S HAVING A SWIM.

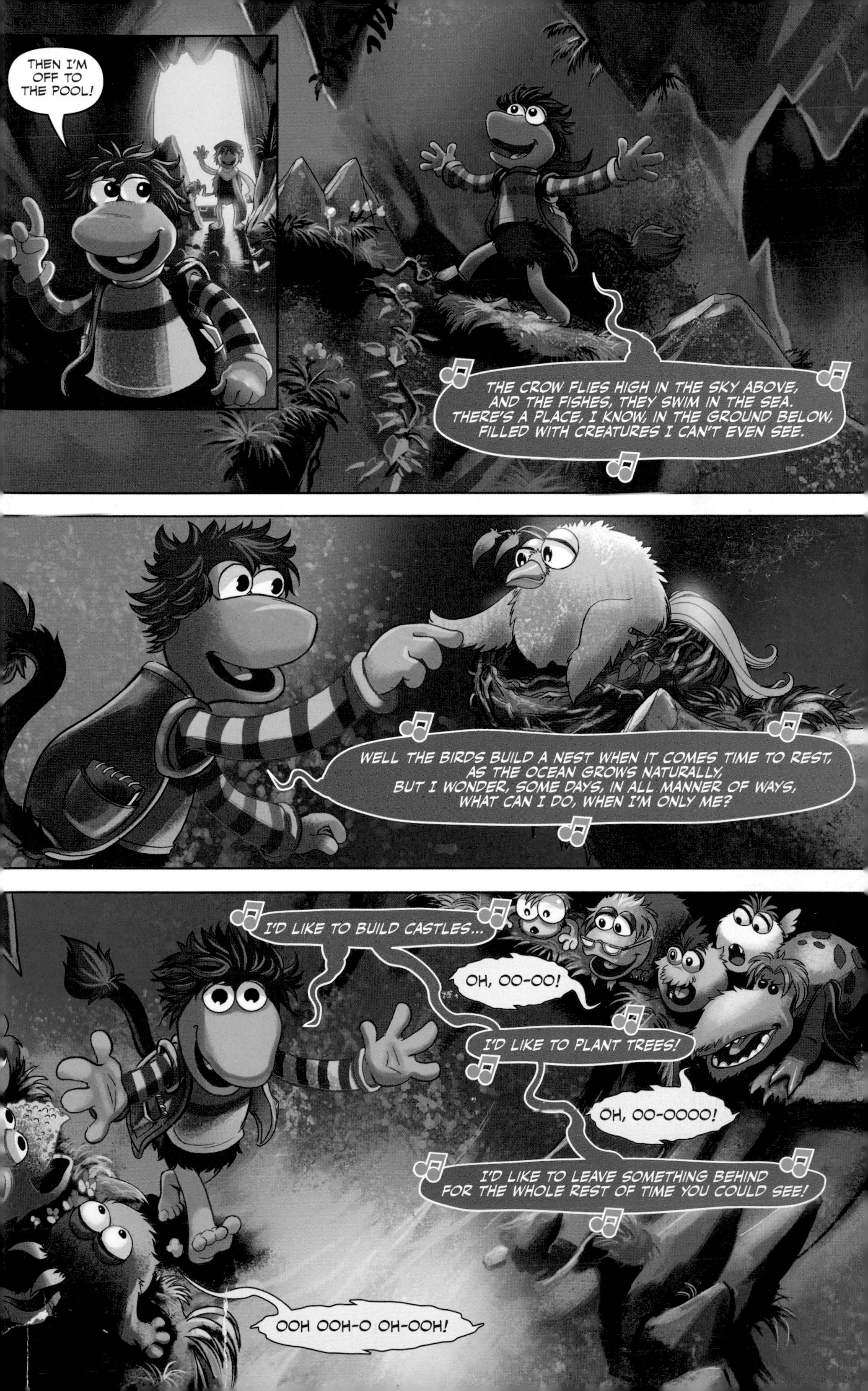
THEN I'M OFF TO THE POOL!
THE CROW FLIES HIGH IN THE SKY ABOVE, AND THE FISHES, THEY SWIM IN THE SEA. THERE'S A PLACE, I KNOW, IN THE GROUND BELOW, FILLED WITH CREATURES I CAN'T EVEN SEE.
WELL THE BIRDS BUILD A NEST WHEN IT COMES TIME TO REST, AS THE OCEAN GROWS NATURALLY, BUT I WONDER, SOME DAYS, IN ALL MANNER OF WAYS, WHAT CAN I DO, WHEN I'M ONLY ME?
I'D LIKE TO BUILD CASTLES...
OH, OO-OO!
I'D LIKE TO PLANT TREES!
OH, OO-OOOO!
I'D LIKE TO LEAVE SOMETHING BEHIND FOR THE WHOLE REST OF TIME YOU COULD SEE!
OOH OOH-O OH-OOH!

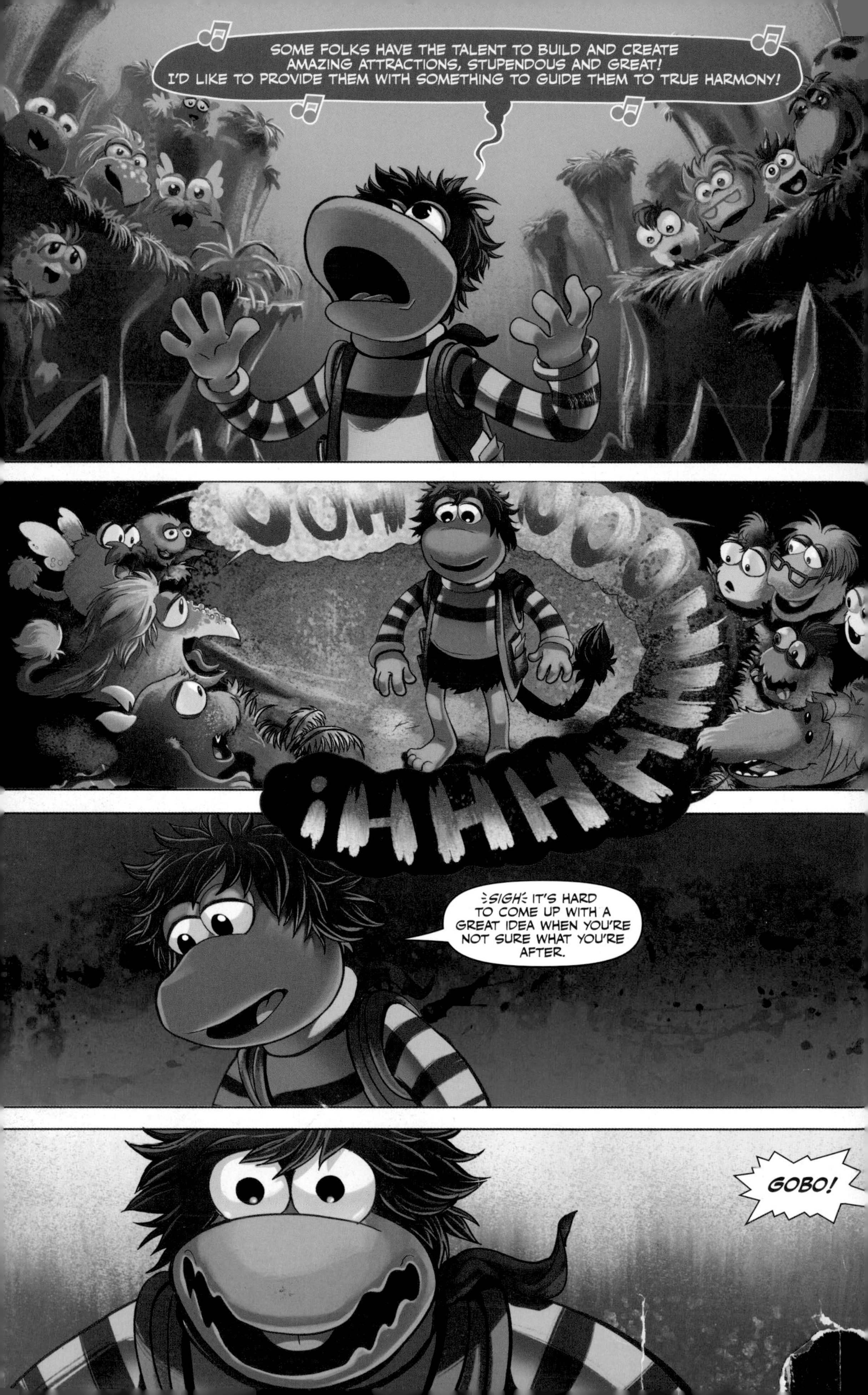
SOME FOLKS HAVE THE TALENT TO BUILD AND CREATE AMAZING ATTRACTIONS, STUPENDOUS AND GREAT! I'D LIKE TO PROVIDE THEM WITH SOMETHING TO GUIDE THEM TO TRUE HARMONY!
OOHHHOOOOHHHHHH!
SIGH IT'S HARD TO COME UP WITH A GREAT IDEA WHEN YOU'RE NOT SURE WHAT YOU'RE AFTER.
GOBO!

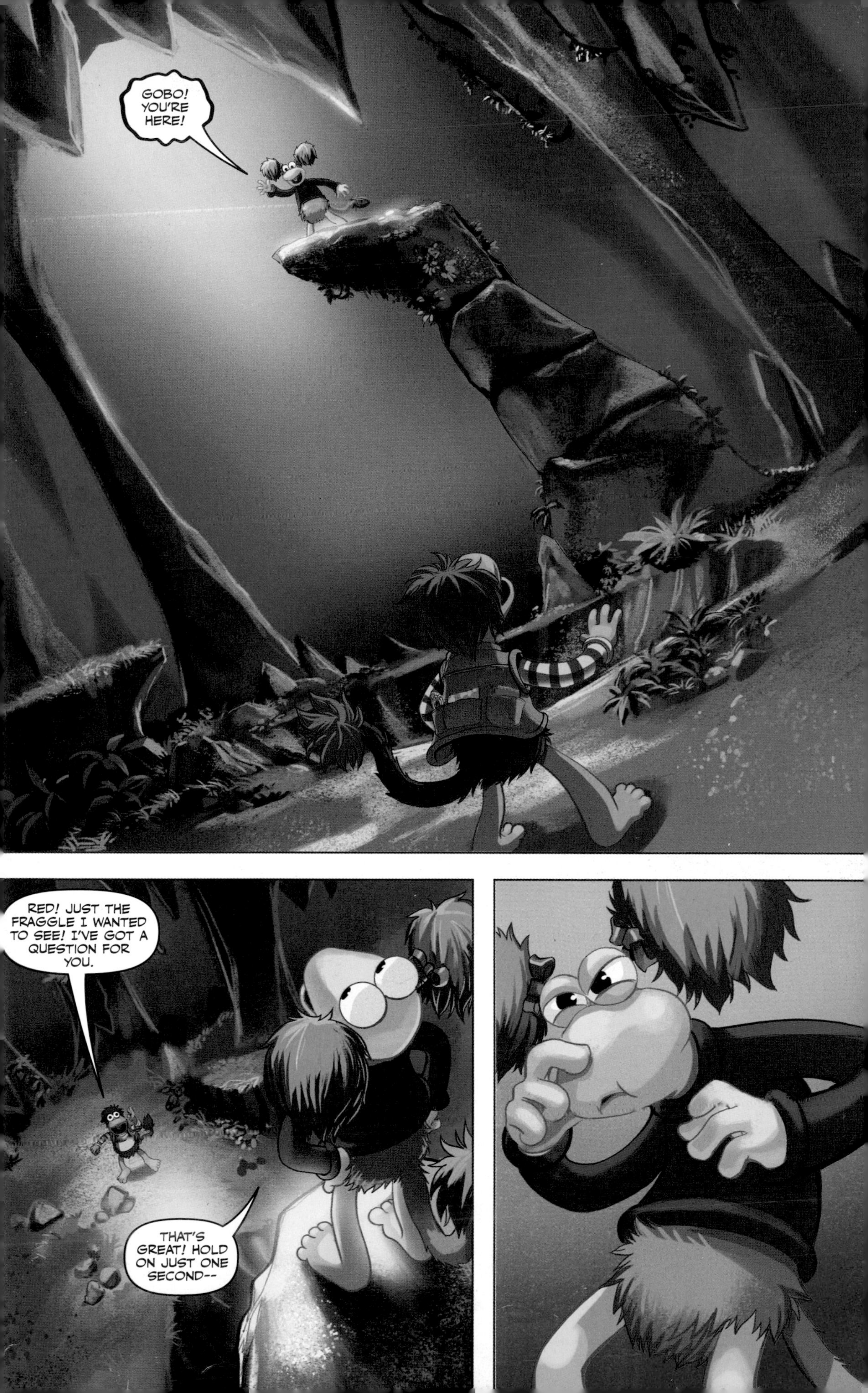
GOBO! YOU'RE HERE!
RED! JUST THE FRAGGLE I WANTED TO SEE! I'VE GOT A QUESTION FOR YOU.
THAT'S GREAT! HOLD ON JUST ONE SECOND--

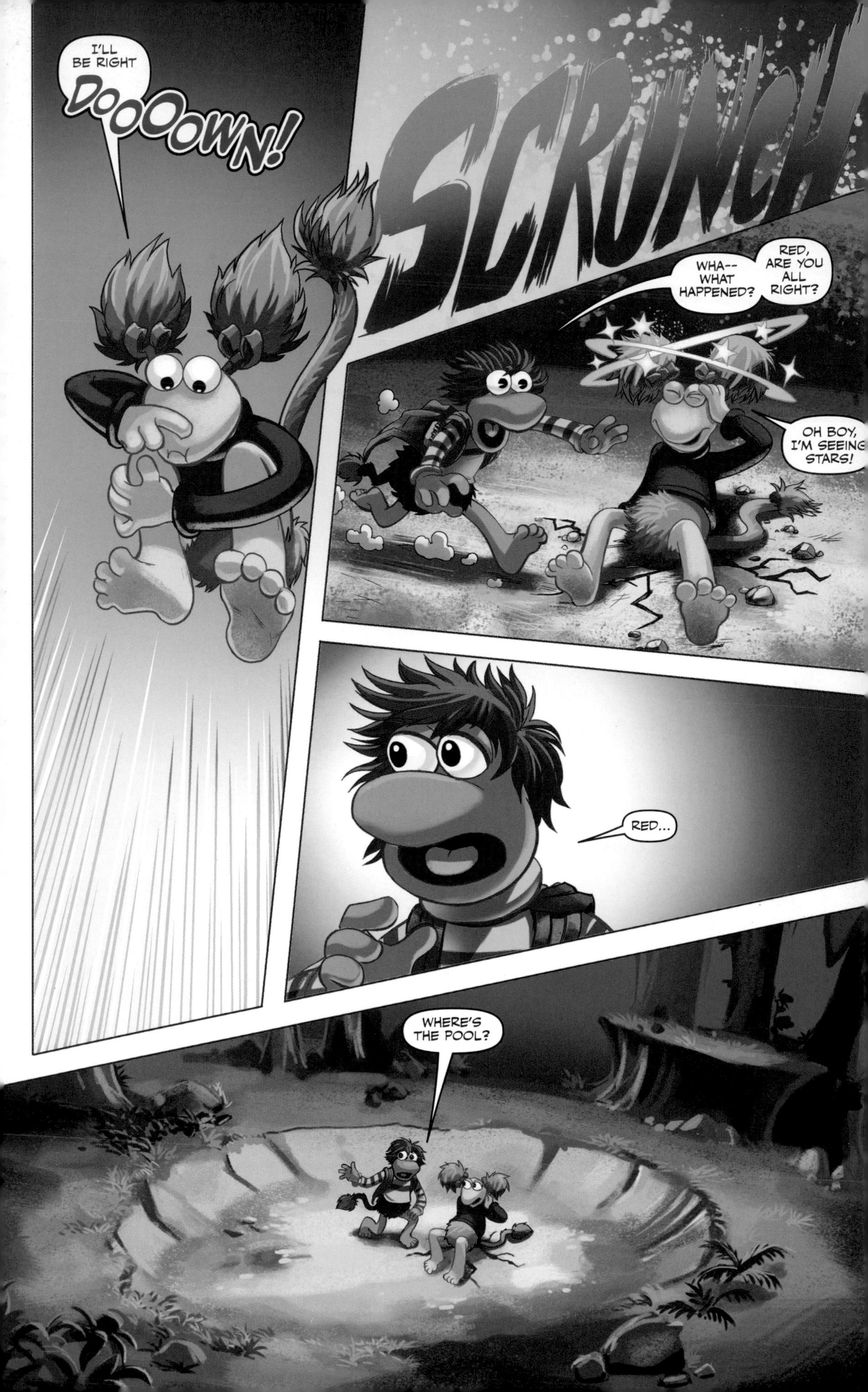
I'LL BE RIGHT DOOOOWN!
SCRUNCH
WHA-- WHAT HAPPENED?
RED, ARE YOU ALL RIGHT?
OH BOY, I'M SEEING STARS!
RED...
WHERE'S THE POOL?

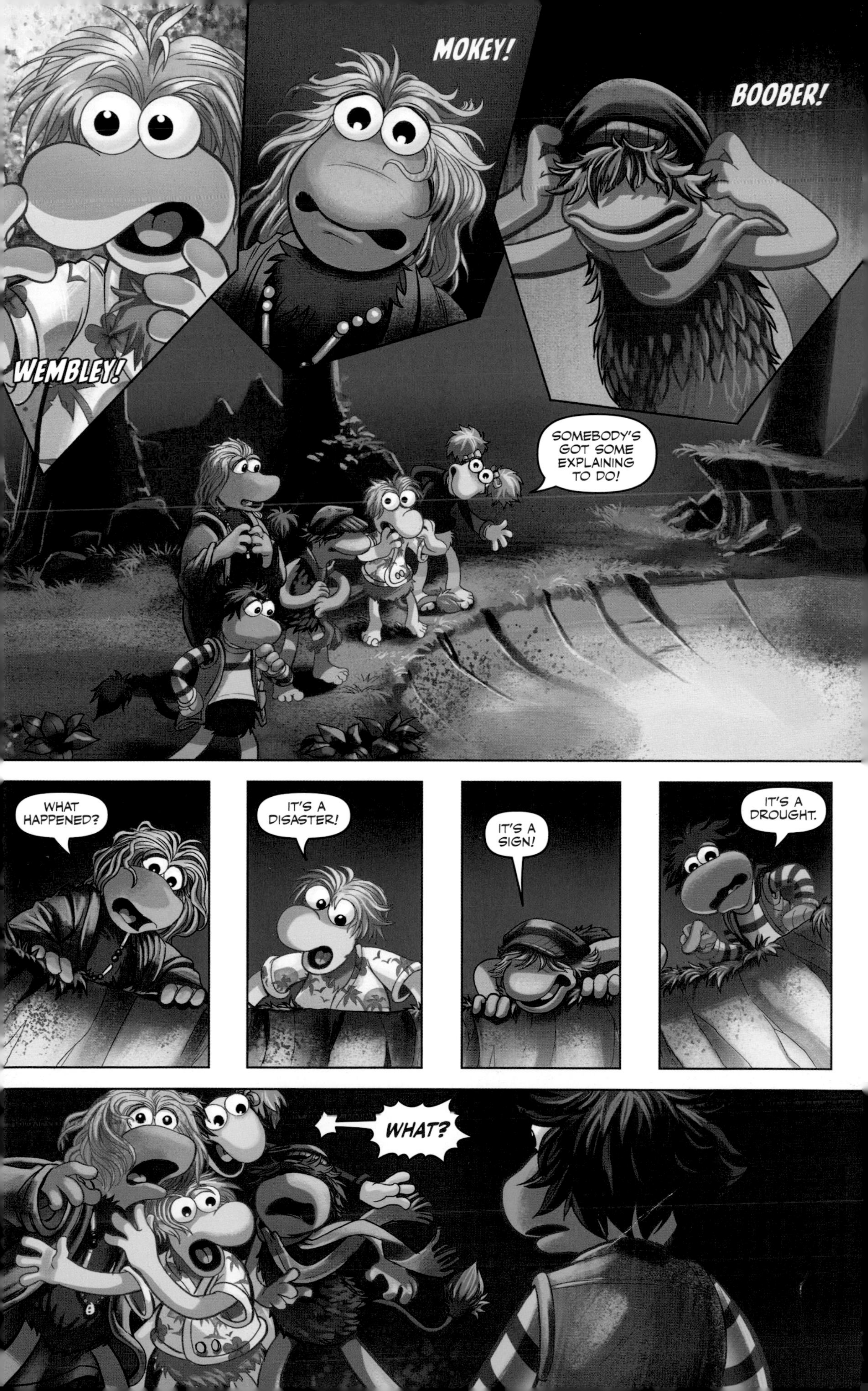
WEMBLEY!
MOKEY!
BOOBER!
SOMEBODY'S GOT SOME EXPLAINING TO DO!
WHAT HAPPENED?
IT'S A DISASTER!
IT'S A SIGN!
IT'S A DROUGHT.
WHAT?

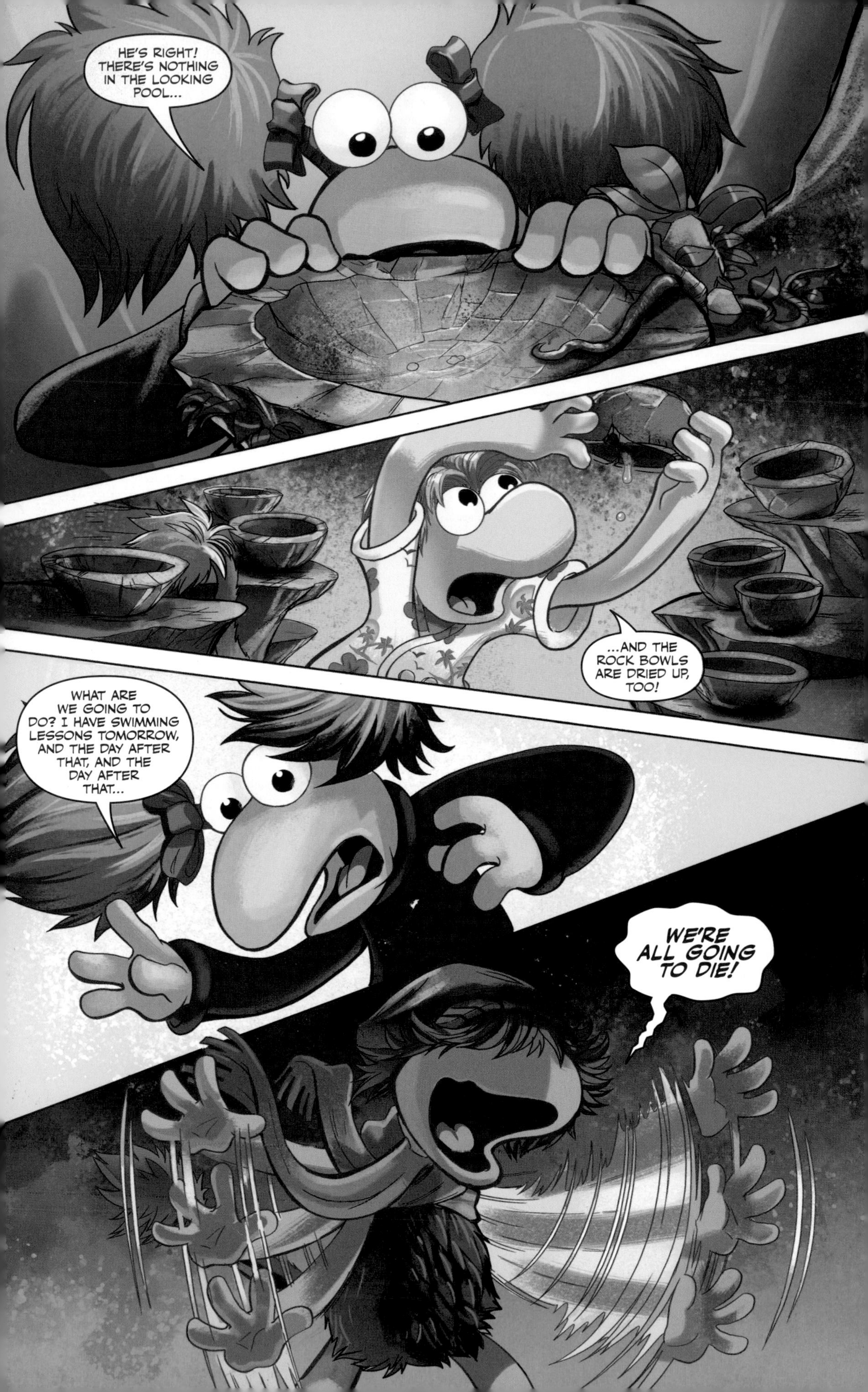
HE'S RIGHT! THERE'S NOTHING IN THE LOOKING POOL...
...AND THE ROCK BOWLS ARE DRIED UP, TOO!
WHAT ARE WE GOING TO DO? I HAVE SWIMMING LESSONS TOMORROW, AND THE DAY AFTER THAT, AND THE DAY AFTER THAT...
WE'RE ALL GOING TO DIE!

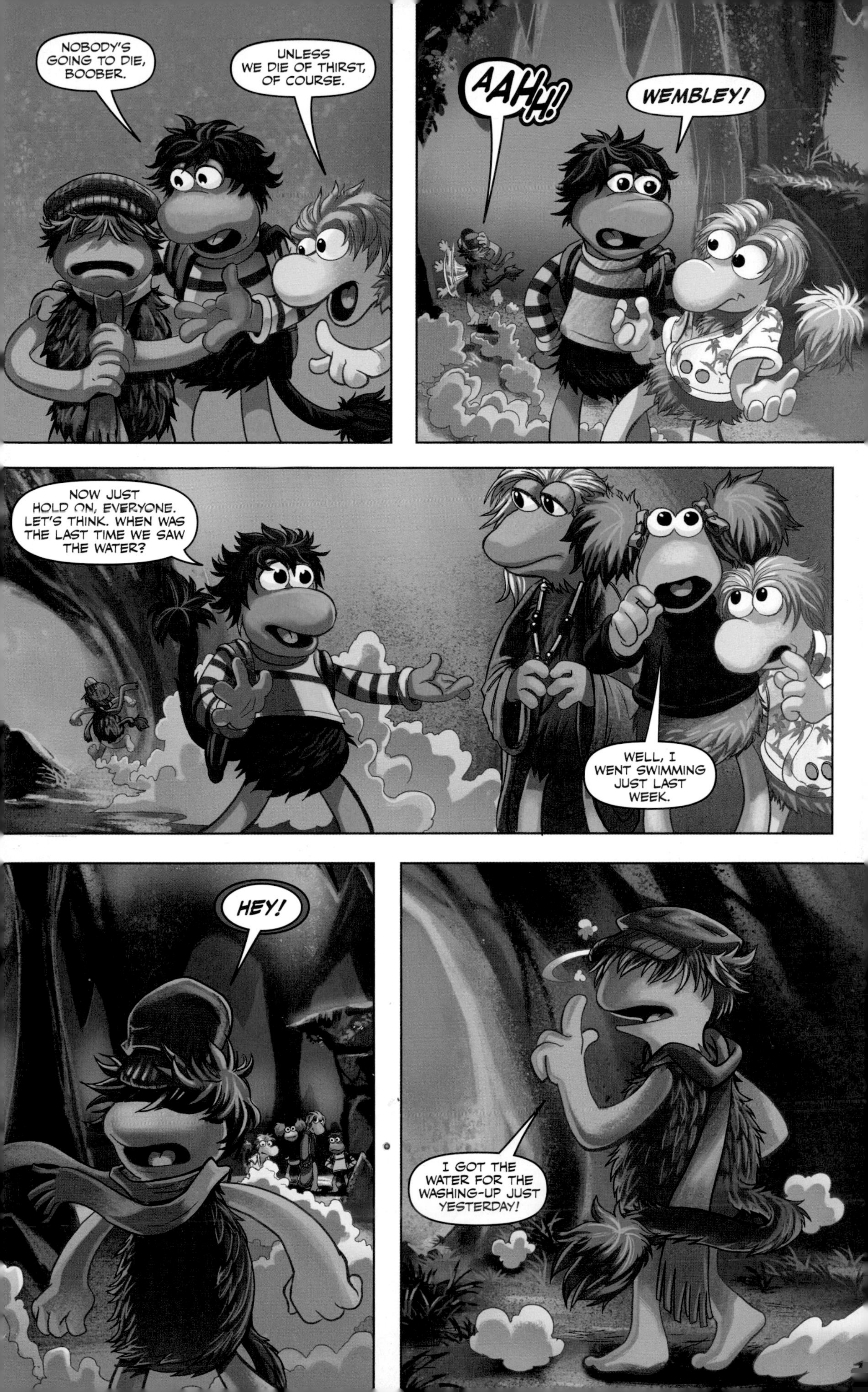
NOBODY'S GOING TO DIE, BOOBER.
UNLESS WE DIE OF THIRST, OF COURSE.
AAHH!
WEMBLEY!
NOW JUST HOLD ON, EVERYONE. LET'S THINK. WHEN WAS THE LAST TIME WE SAW THE WATER?
WELL, I WENT SWIMMING JUST LAST WEEK.
HEY!
I GOT THE WATER FOR THE WASHING-UP JUST YESTERDAY!

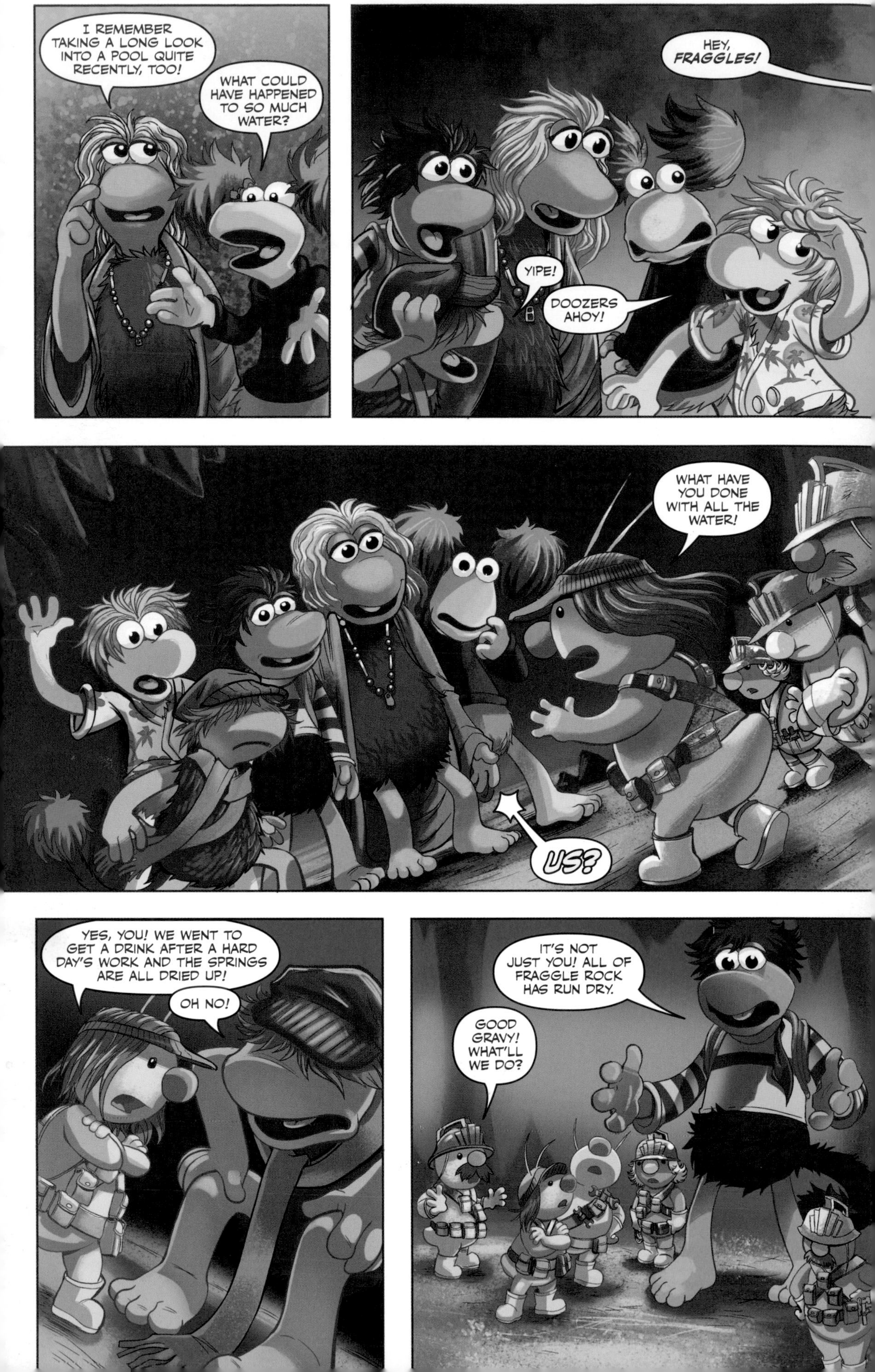

I REMEMBER TAKING A LONG LOOK INTO A POOL QUITE RECENTLY, TOO!
WHAT COULD HAVE HAPPENED TO SO MUCH WATER?
HEY, FRAGGLES!
YIPE!
DOOZERS AHOY!
WHAT HAVE YOU DONE WITH ALL THE WATER!
US?
YES, YOU! WE WENT TO GET A DRINK AFTER A HARD DAY'S WORK AND THE SPRINGS ARE ALL DRIED UP!
OH NO!
IT'S NOT JUST YOU! ALL OF FRAGGLE ROCK HAS RUN DRY.
GOOD GRAVY! WHAT'LL WE DO?

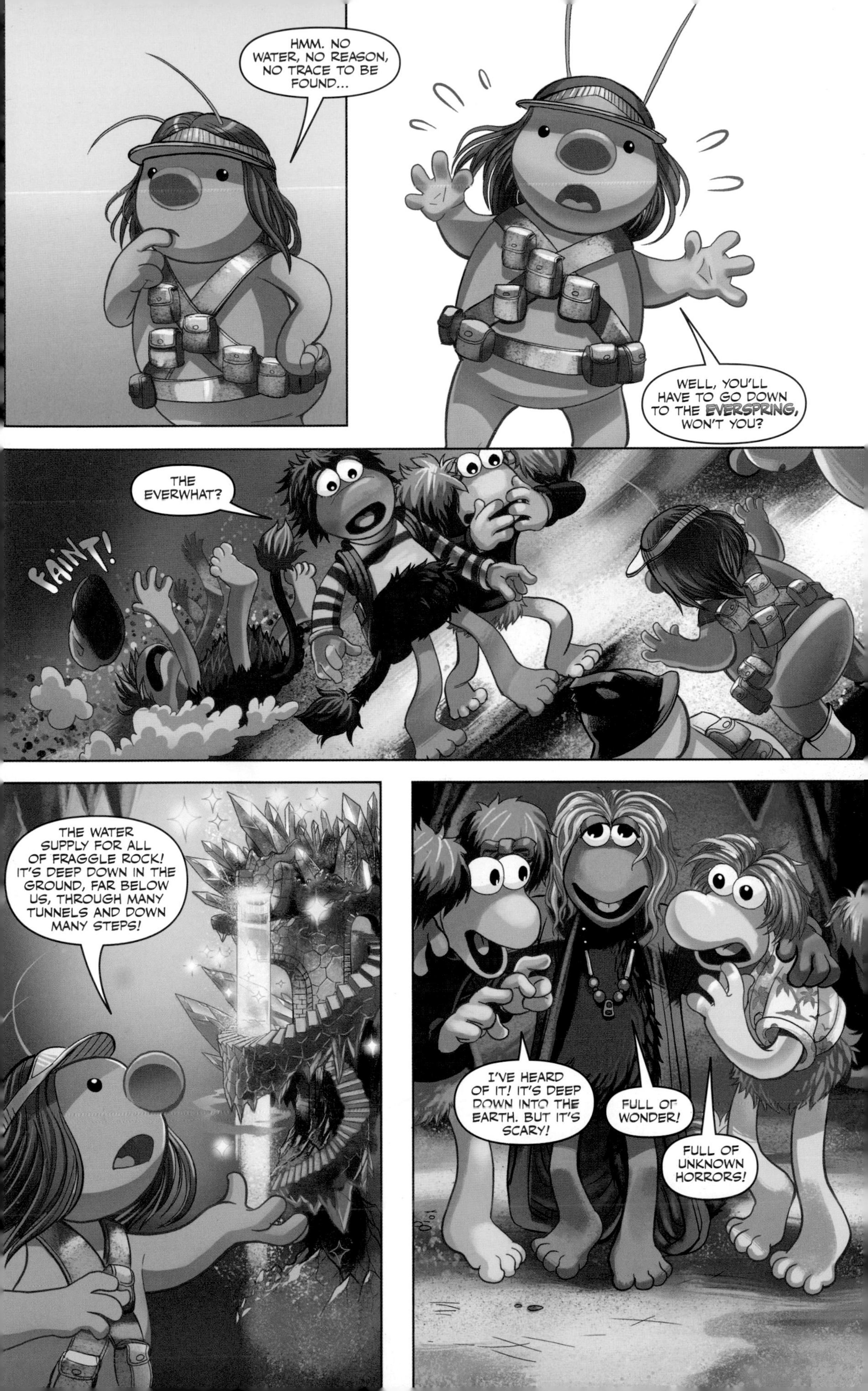
HMM. NO WATER, NO REASON, NO TRACE TO BE FOUND...
WELL, YOU'LL HAVE TO GO DOWN TO THE EVERSPRING, WON'T YOU?
THE EVERWHAT?
FAINT!
THE WATER SUPPLY FOR ALL OF FRAGGLE ROCK! IT'S DEEP DOWN IN THE GROUND, FAR BELOW US, THROUGH MANY TUNNELS AND DOWN MANY STEPS!
I'VE HEARD OF IT! IT'S DEEP DOWN INTO THE EARTH. BUT IT'S SCARY!
FULL OF WONDER!
FULL OF UNKNOWN HORRORS!

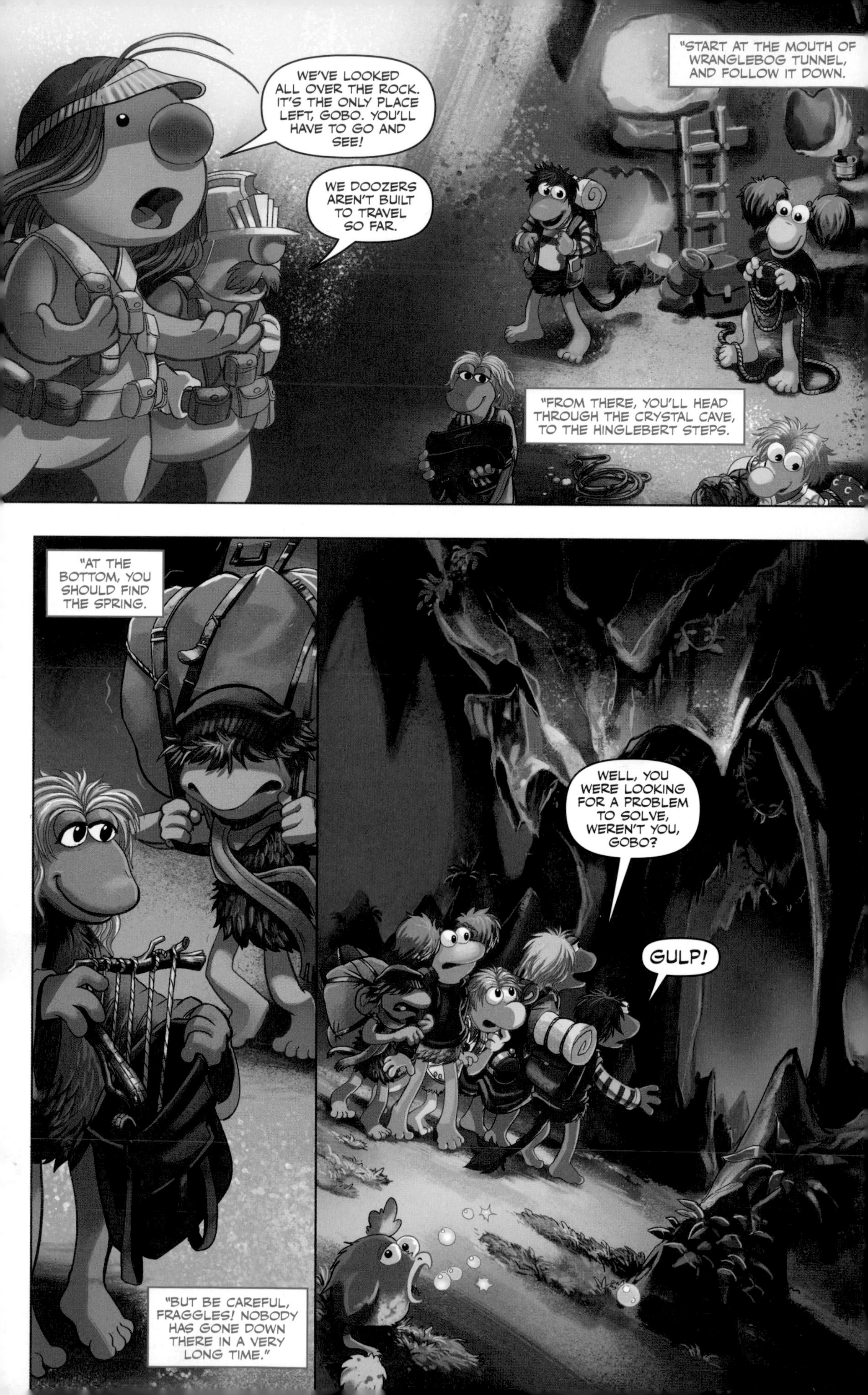

WE'VE LOOKED ALL OVER THE ROCK. IT'S THE ONLY PLACE LEFT, GOBO. YOU'LL HAVE TO GO AND SEE!
WE DOOZERS AREN'T BUILT TO TRAVEL SO FAR.
"START AT THE MOUTH OF WRANGLEBOG TUNNEL, AND FOLLOW IT DOWN.
"FROM THERE, YOU'LL HEAD THROUGH THE CRYSTAL CAVE, TO THE HINGLEBERT STEPS.
"AT THE BOTTOM, YOU SHOULD FIND THE SPRING.
"BUT BE CAREFUL, FRAGGLES! NOBODY HAS GONE DOWN THERE IN A VERY LONG TIME."
WELL, YOU WERE LOOKING FOR A PROBLEM TO SOLVE, WEREN'T YOU, GOBO?
GULP!

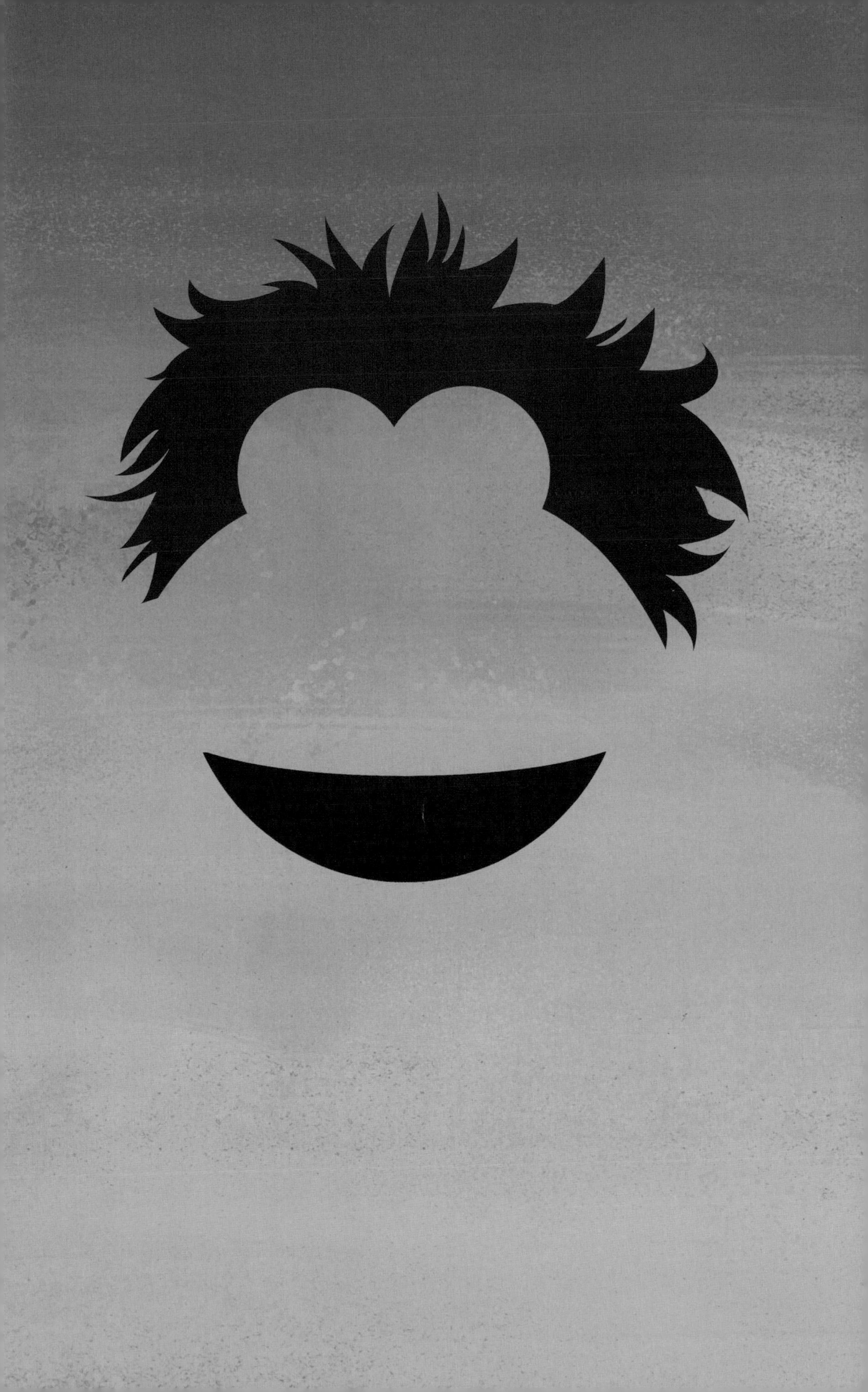

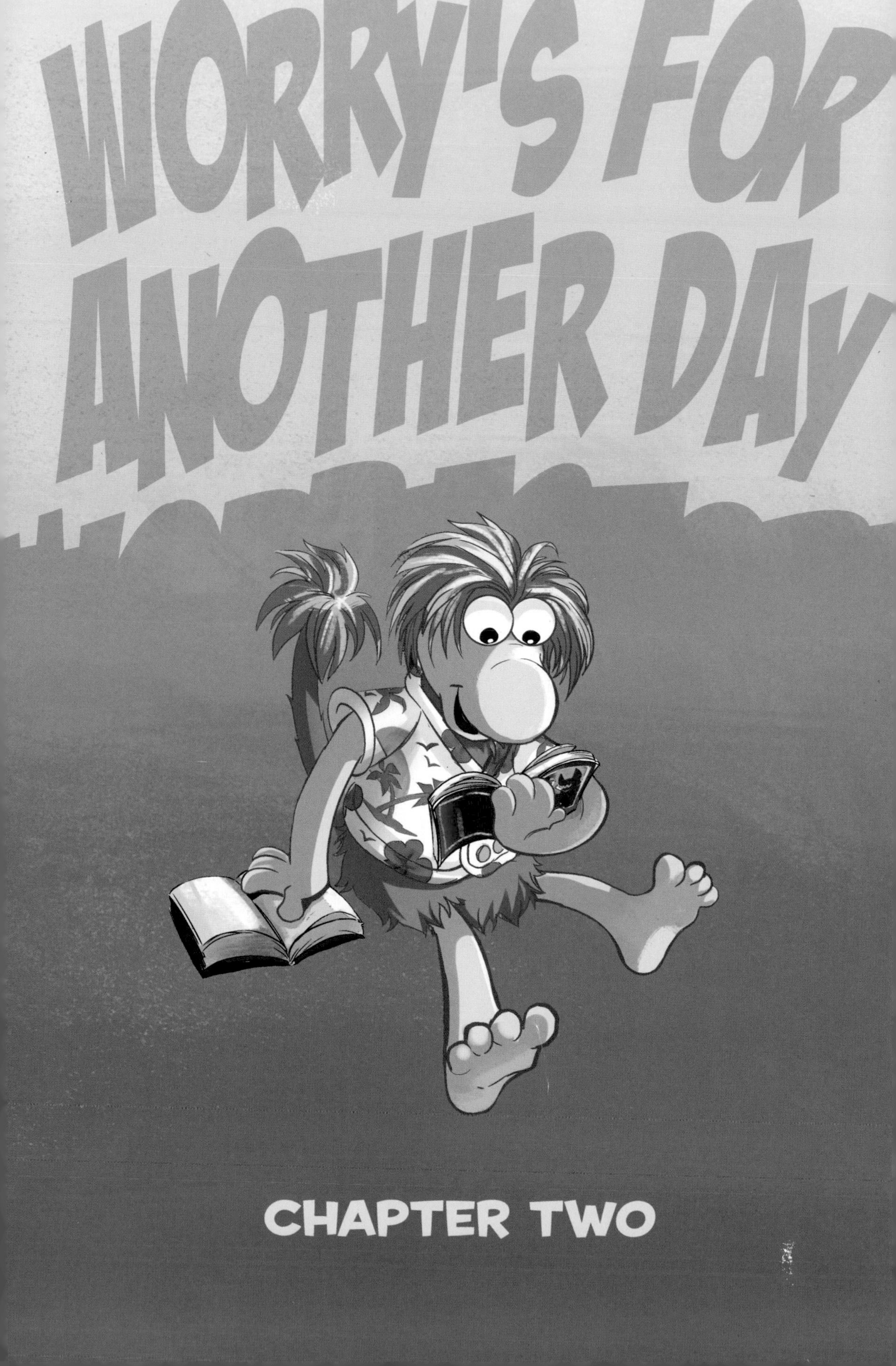
WORRY'S FOR ANOTHER DAY

CHAPTER TWO

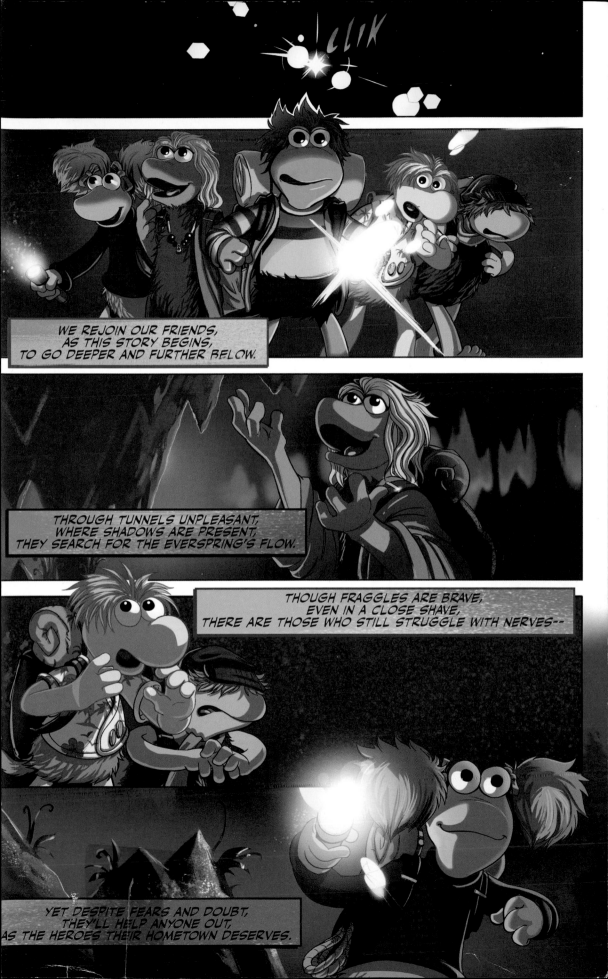

CLIK

WE REJOIN OUR FRIENDS,
AS THIS STORY BEGINS,
TO GO DEEPER AND FURTHER BELOW.

THROUGH TUNNELS UNPLEASANT,
WHERE SHADOWS ARE PRESENT,
THEY SEARCH FOR THE EVERSPRING'S FLOW.

THOUGH FRAGGLES ARE BRAVE,
EVEN IN A CLOSE SHAVE,
THERE ARE THOSE WHO STILL STRUGGLE WITH NERVES--

YET DESPITE FEARS AND DOUBT,
THEY'LL HELP ANYONE OUT,
AS THE HEROES THEIR HOMETOWN DESERVES.

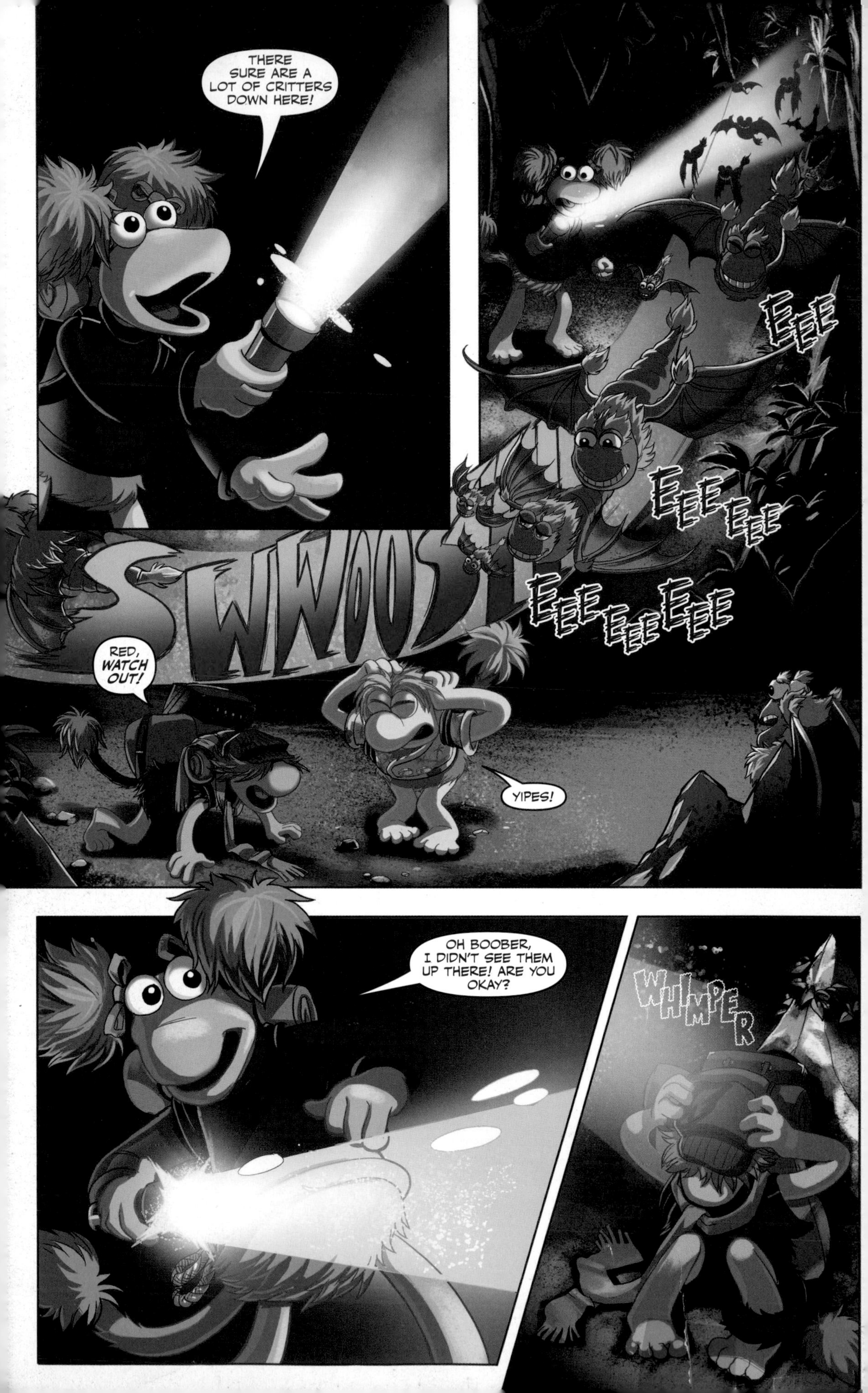
THERE SURE ARE A LOT OF CRITTERS DOWN HERE!
EEE
EEEEEE
SWWOOSH
EEEEEEEEE
RED, WATCH OUT!
YIPES!
OH BOOBER, I DIDN'T SEE THEM UP THERE! ARE YOU OKAY?
WHIMPER

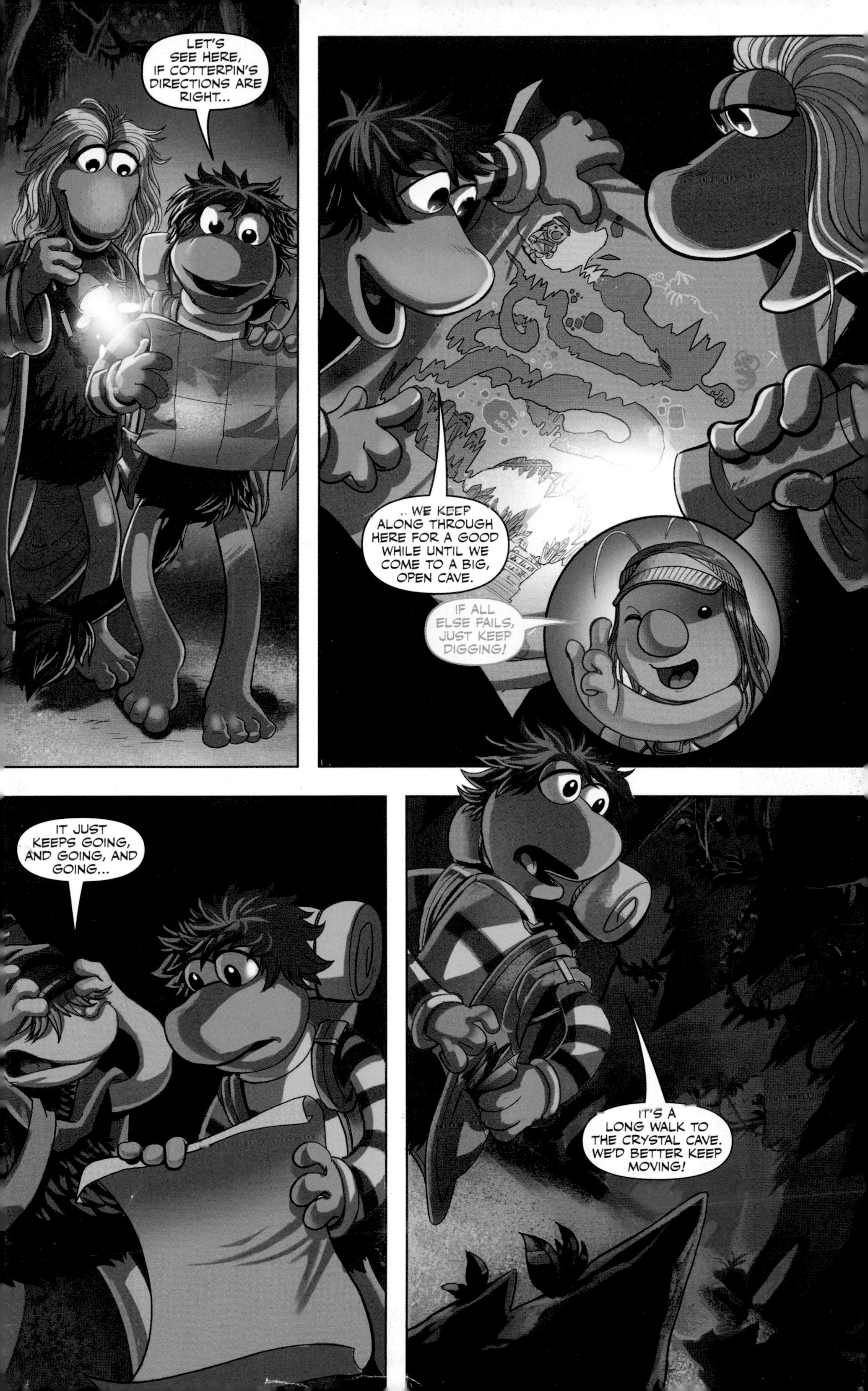
LET'S SEE HERE, IF COTTERPIN'S DIRECTIONS ARE RIGHT...
.. WE KEEP ALONG THROUGH HERE FOR A GOOD WHILE UNTIL WE COME TO A BIG, OPEN CAVE.
IF ALL ELSE FAILS, JUST KEEP DIGGING!
IT JUST KEEPS GOING, AND GOING, AND GOING...
IT'S A LONG WALK TO THE CRYSTAL CAVE. WE'D BETTER KEEP MOVING!

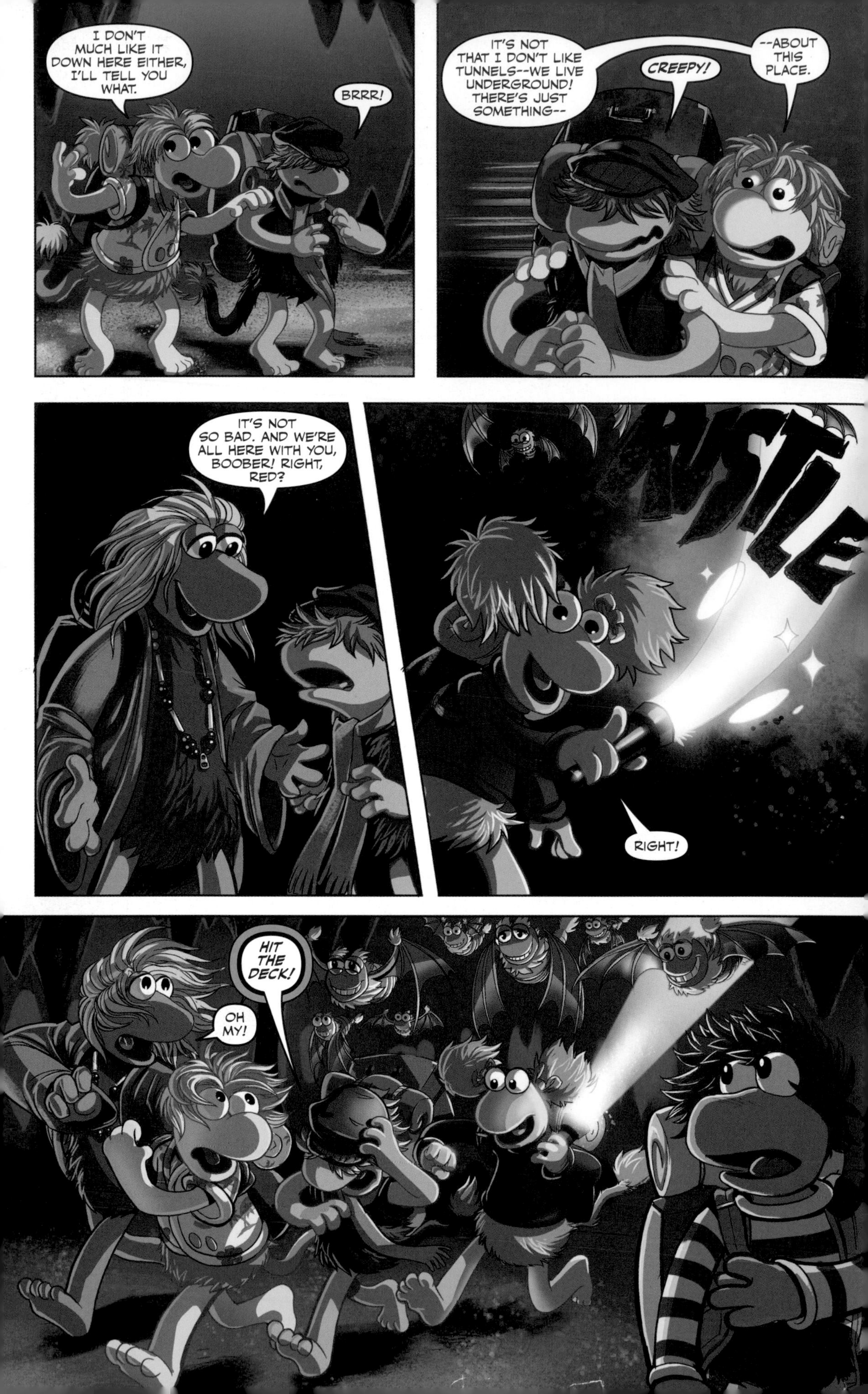
I DON'T MUCH LIKE IT DOWN HERE EITHER, I'LL TELL YOU WHAT.
BRRR!
IT'S NOT THAT I DON'T LIKE TUNNELS--WE LIVE UNDERGROUND! THERE'S JUST SOMETHING--
CREEPY!
--ABOUT THIS PLACE.
IT'S NOT SO BAD. AND WE'RE ALL HERE WITH YOU, BOOBER! RIGHT, RED?
RIGHT!
HIT THE DECK!
OH MY!

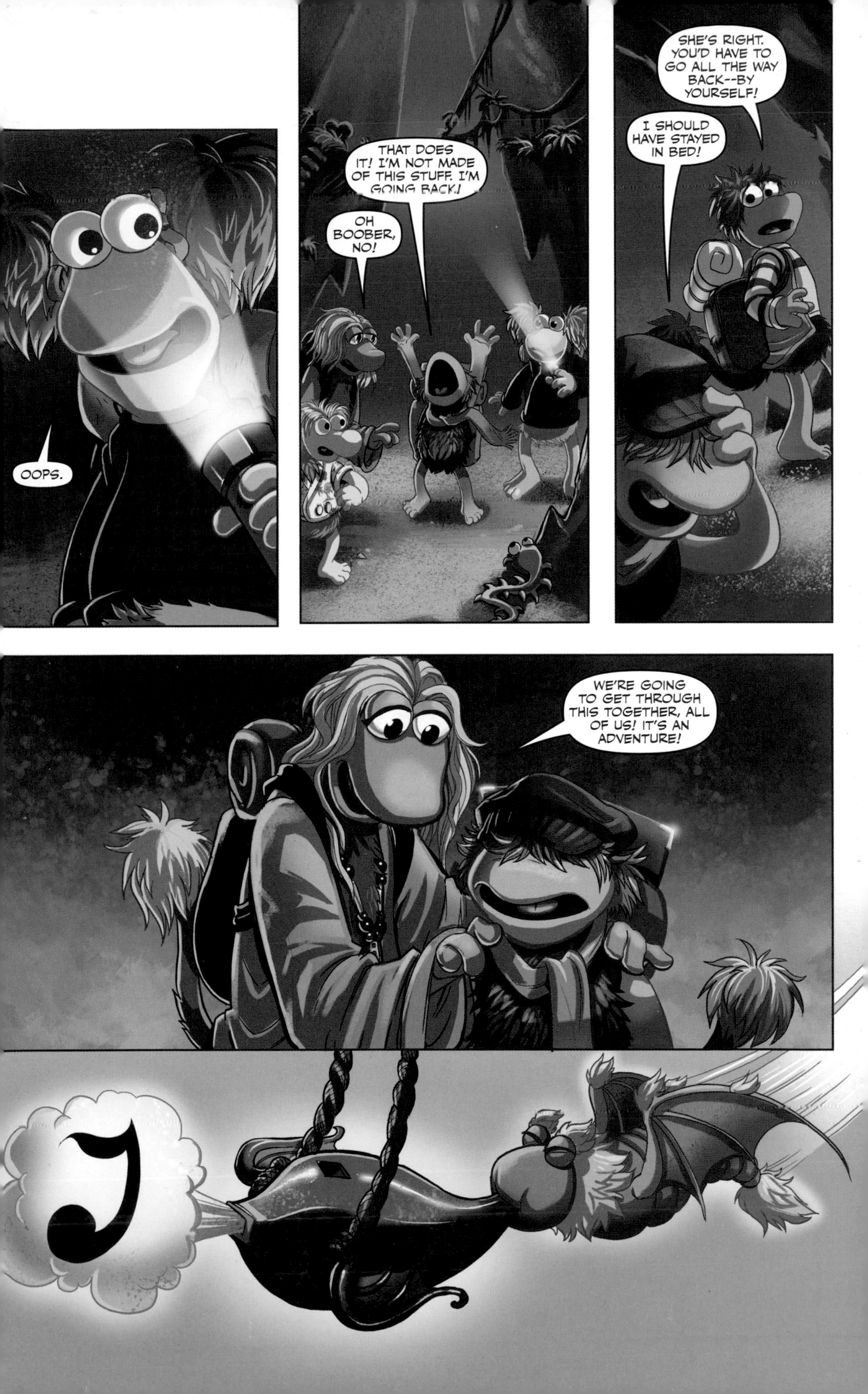
OOPS.
THAT DOES IT! I'M NOT MADE OF THIS STUFF. I'M GOING BACK!
OH BOOBER, NO!
SHE'S RIGHT. YOU'D HAVE TO GO ALL THE WAY BACK--BY YOURSELF!
I SHOULD HAVE STAYED IN BED!
WE'RE GOING TO GET THROUGH THIS TOGETHER, ALL OF US! IT'S AN ADVENTURE!

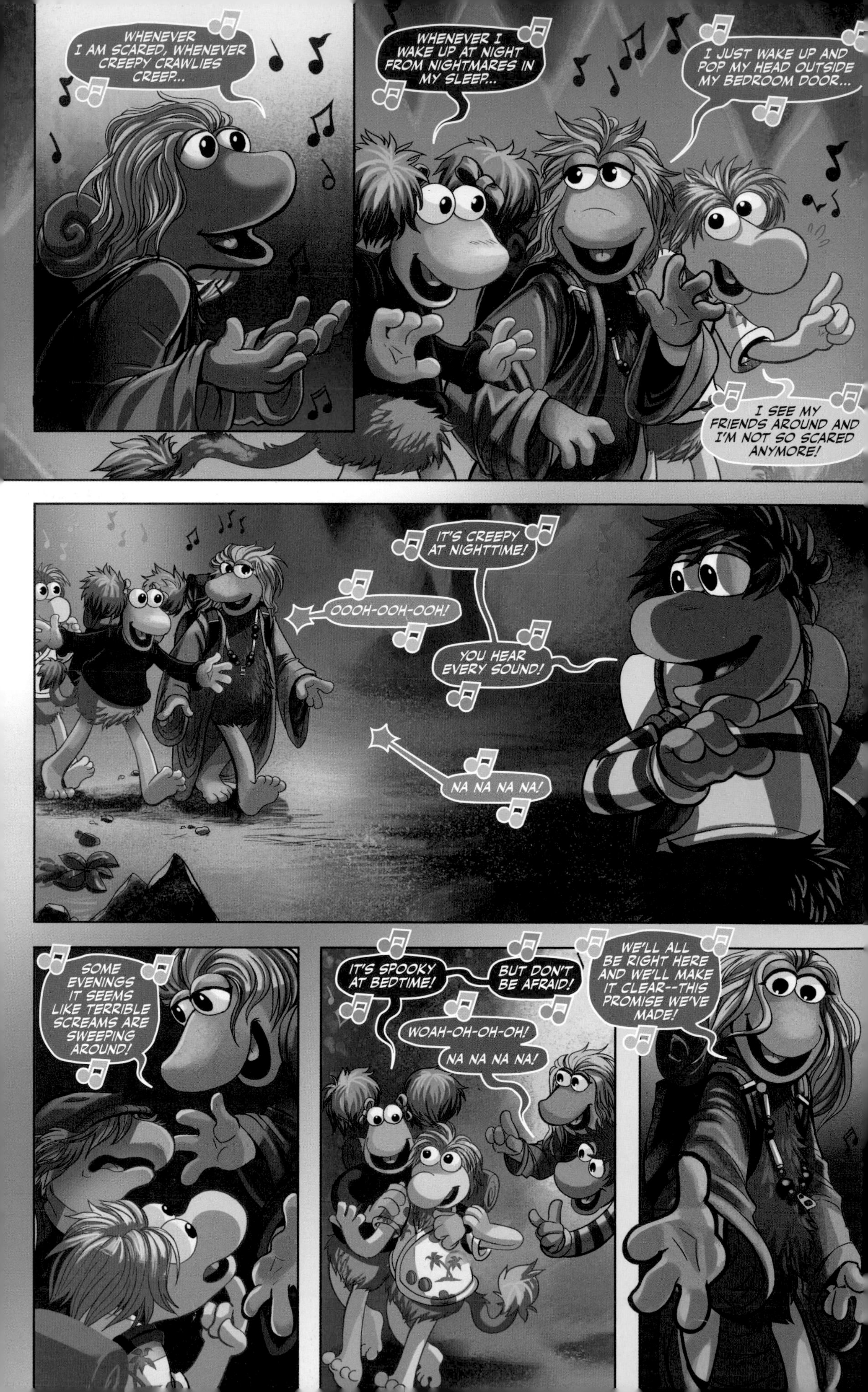
WHENEVER I AM SCARED, WHENEVER CREEPY CRAWLIES CREEP...
WHENEVER I WAKE UP AT NIGHT FROM NIGHTMARES IN MY SLEEP...
I JUST WAKE UP AND POP MY HEAD OUTSIDE MY BEDROOM DOOR...
I SEE MY FRIENDS AROUND AND I'M NOT SO SCARED ANYMORE!
IT'S CREEPY AT NIGHTTIME!
OOOH-OOH-OOH!
YOU HEAR EVERY SOUND!
NA NA NA NA!
SOME EVENINGS IT SEEMS LIKE TERRIBLE SCREAMS ARE SWEEPING AROUND!
IT'S SPOOKY AT BEDTIME!
BUT DON'T BE AFRAID!
WOAH-OH-OH-OH!
NA NA NA NA!
WE'LL ALL BE RIGHT HERE AND WE'LL MAKE IT CLEAR--THIS PROMISE WE'VE MADE!

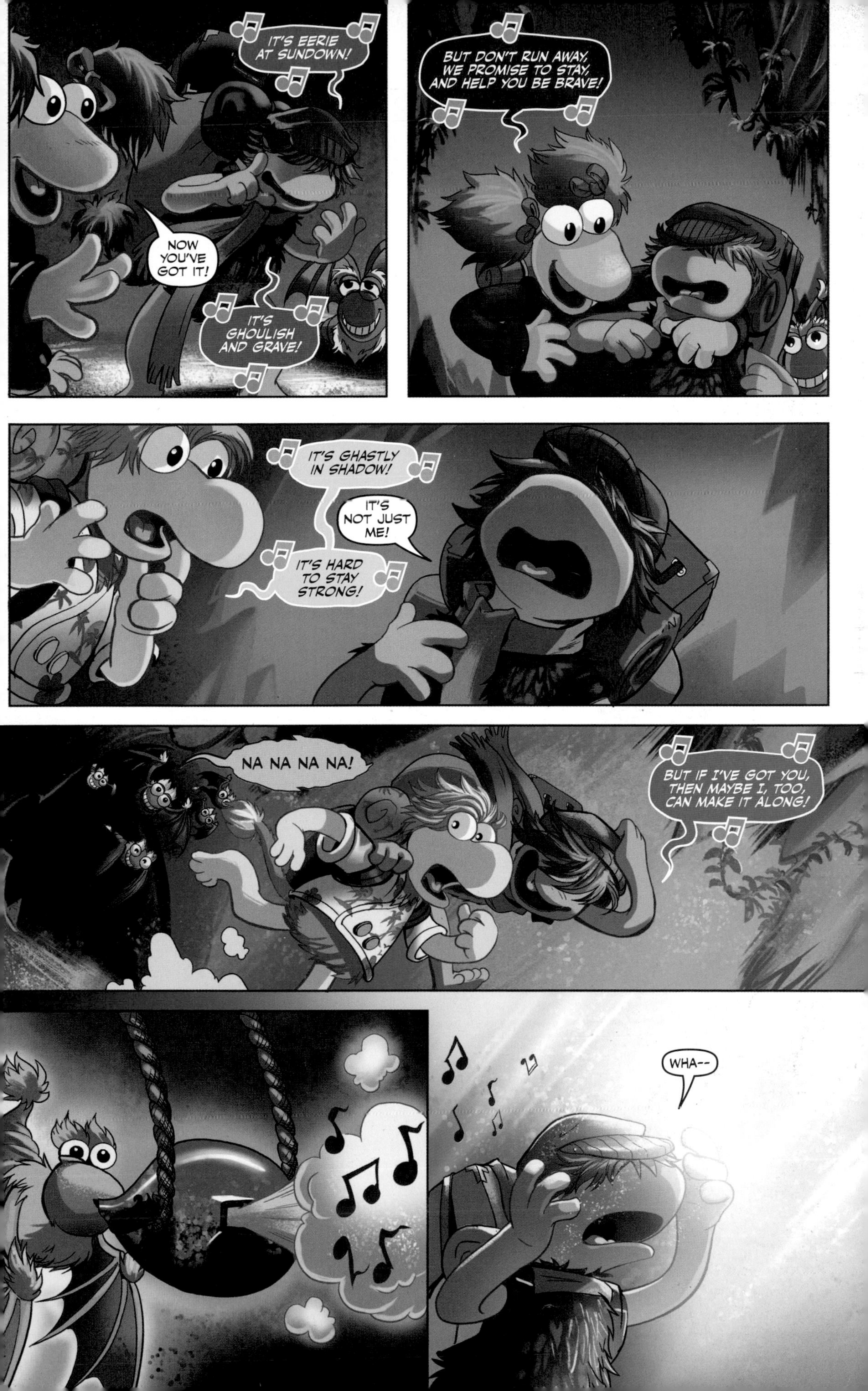
IT'S EERIE AT SUNDOWN!
NOW YOU'VE GOT IT!
IT'S GHOULISH AND GRAVE!
BUT DON'T RUN AWAY, WE PROMISE TO STAY, AND HELP YOU BE BRAVE!
IT'S GHASTLY IN SHADOW!
IT'S NOT JUST ME!
IT'S HARD TO STAY STRONG!
NA NA NA NA!
BUT IF I'VE GOT YOU, THEN MAYBE I, TOO, CAN MAKE IT ALONG!
WHA--

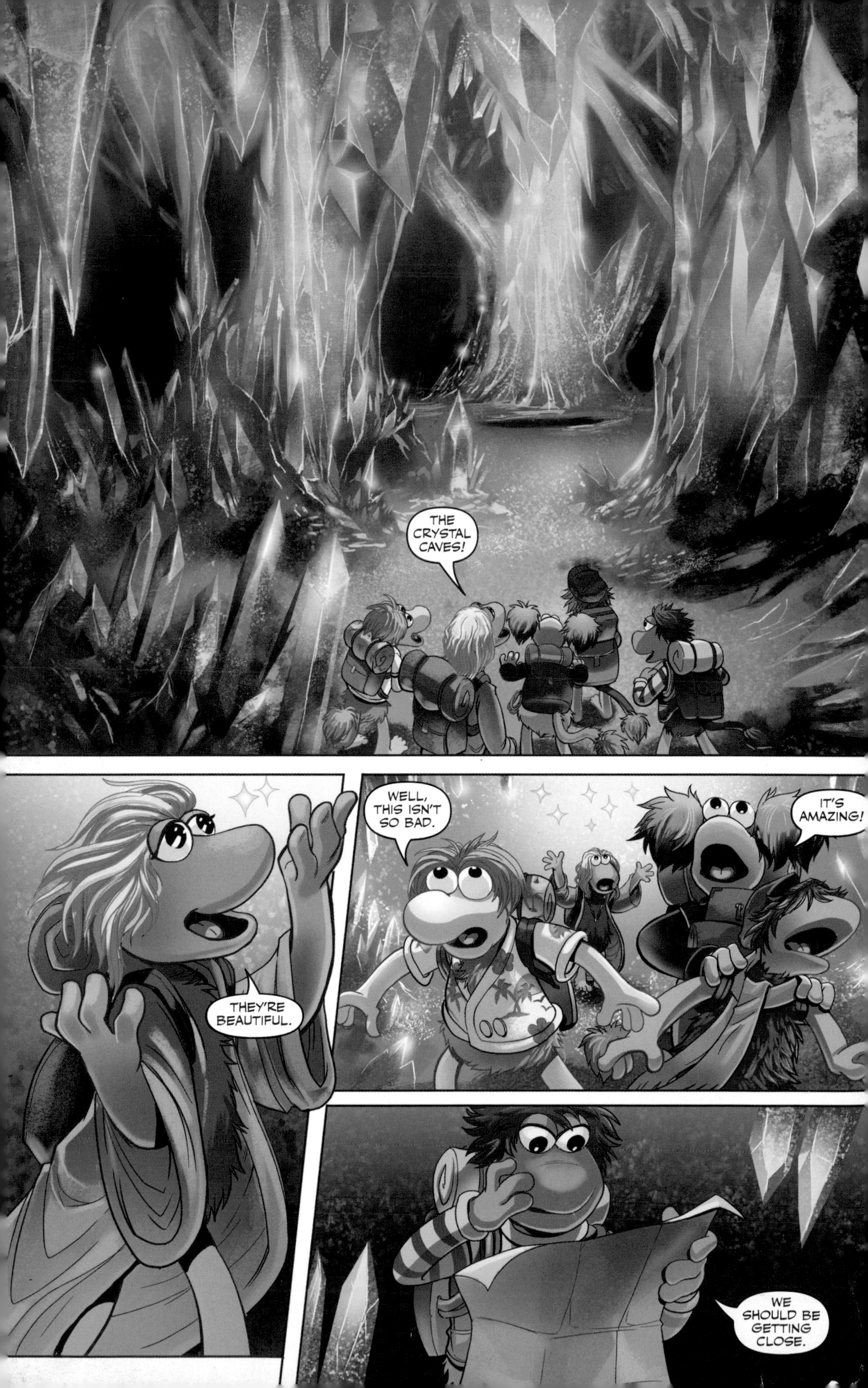
THE CRYSTAL CAVES!
THEY'RE BEAUTIFUL.
WELL, THIS ISN'T SO BAD.
IT'S AMAZING!
WE SHOULD BE GETTING CLOSE.

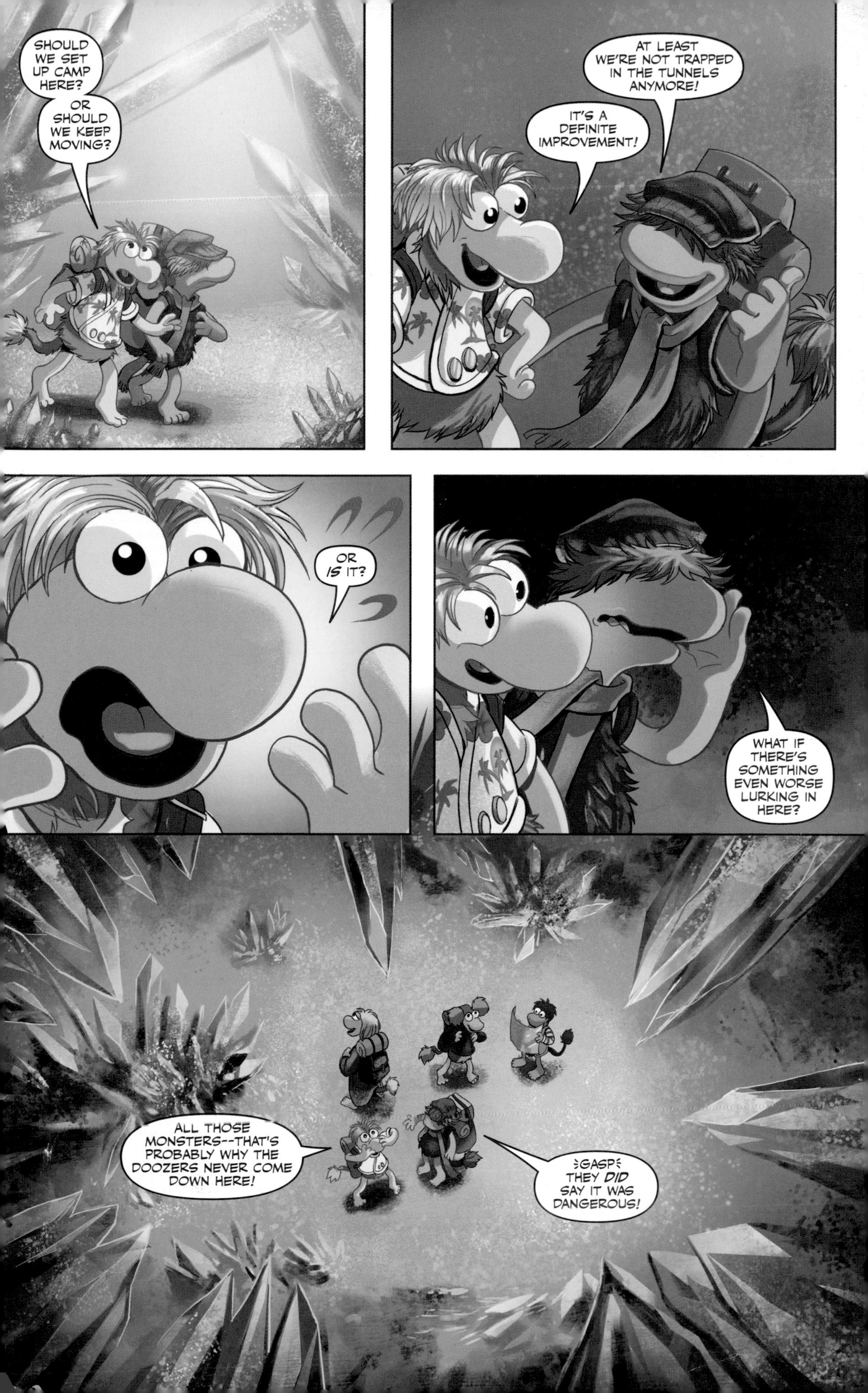
SHOULD WE SET UP CAMP HERE?
OR SHOULD WE KEEP MOVING?
AT LEAST WE'RE NOT TRAPPED IN THE TUNNELS ANYMORE!
IT'S A DEFINITE IMPROVEMENT!
OR *IS* IT?
WHAT IF THERE'S SOMETHING EVEN WORSE LURKING IN HERE?
ALL THOSE MONSTERS--THAT'S PROBABLY WHY THE DOOZERS NEVER COME DOWN HERE!
GASP THEY *DID* SAY IT WAS DANGEROUS!

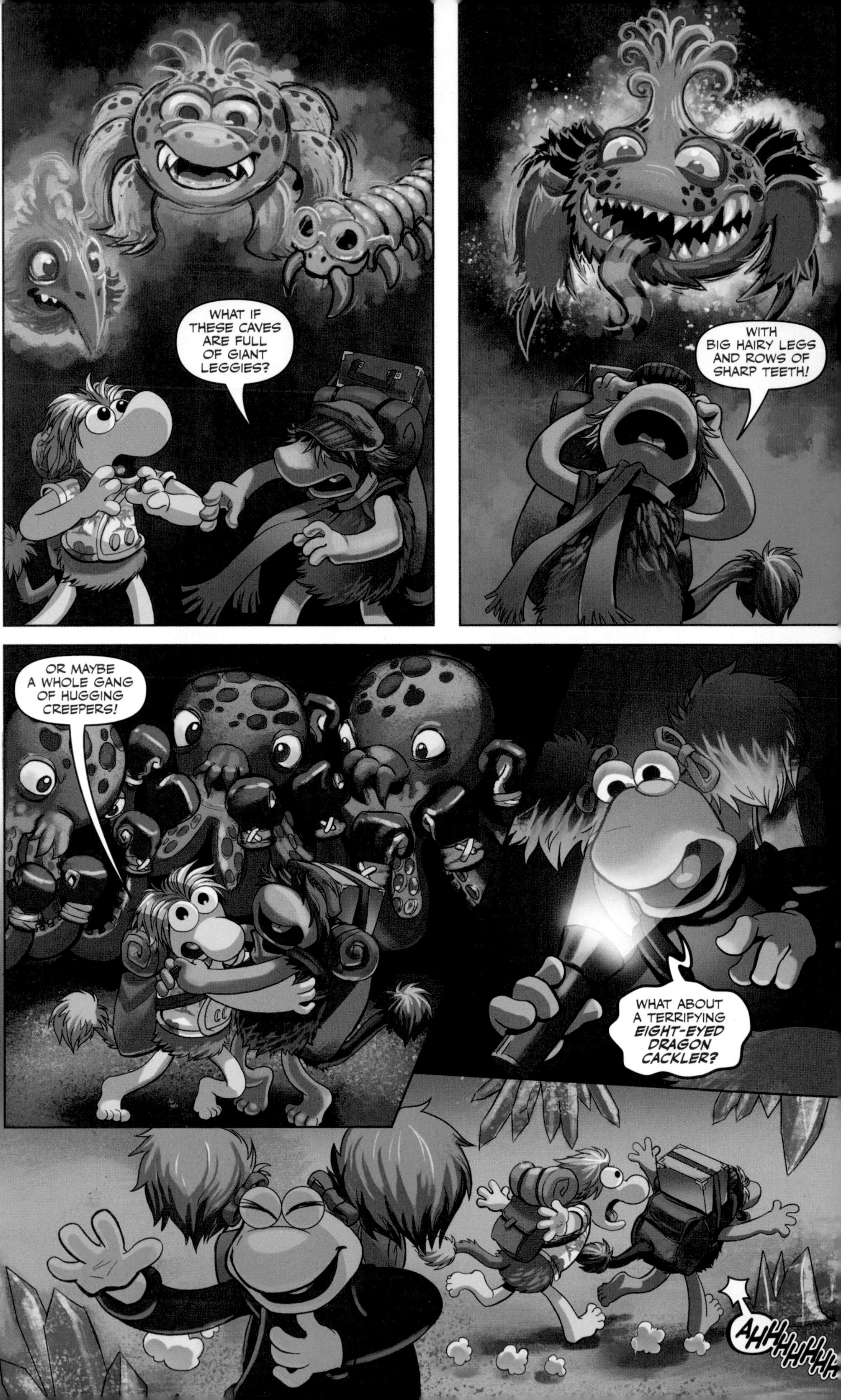
WHAT IF THESE CAVES ARE FULL OF GIANT LEGGIES?
WITH BIG HAIRY LEGS AND ROWS OF SHARP TEETH!
OR MAYBE A WHOLE GANG OF HUGGING CREEPERS!
WHAT ABOUT A TERRIFYING *EIGHT-EYED DRAGON CACKLER?*
AHHHHHHH

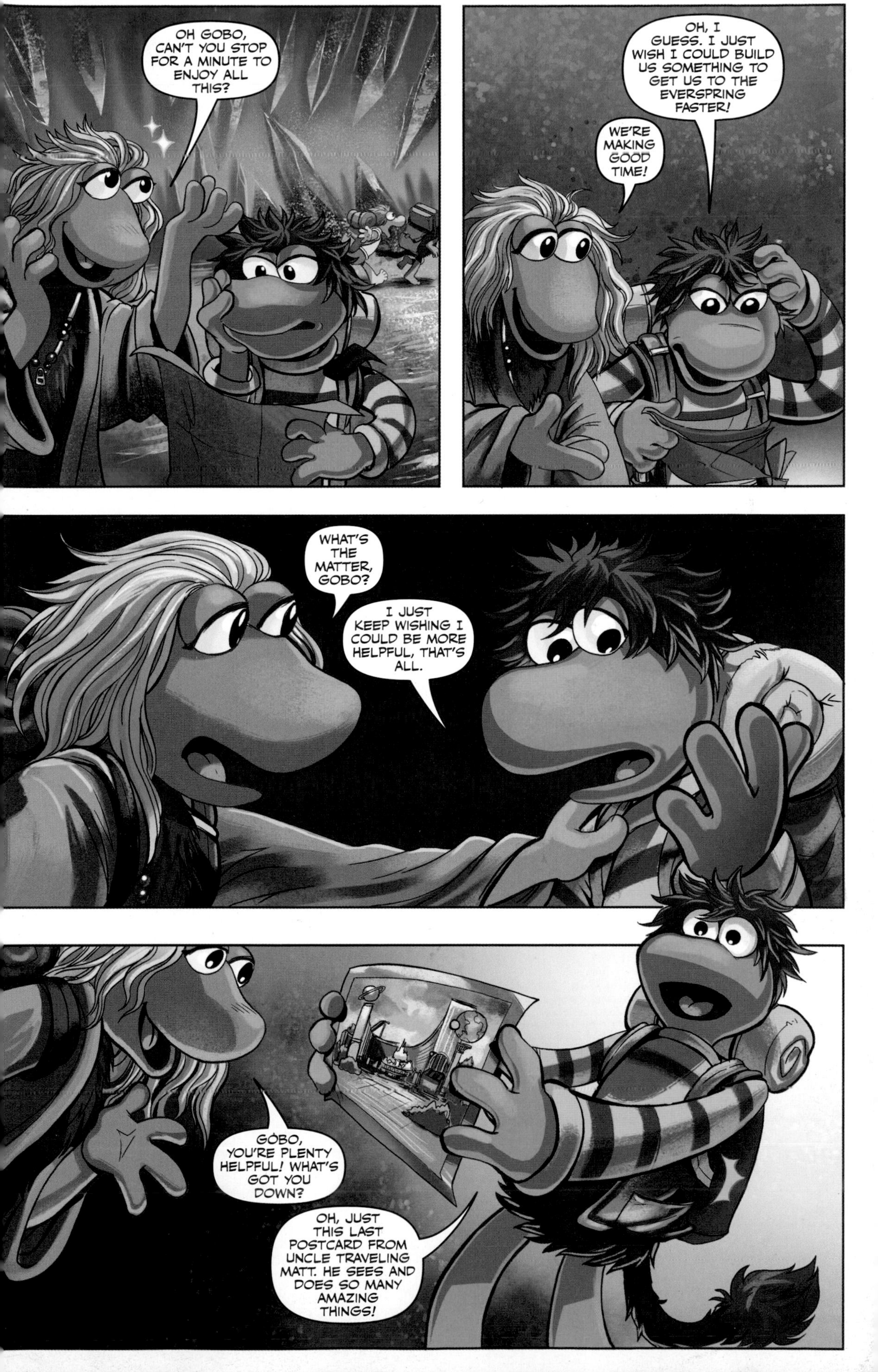
OH GOBO, CAN'T YOU STOP FOR A MINUTE TO ENJOY ALL THIS?
WE'RE MAKING GOOD TIME!
OH, I GUESS. I JUST WISH I COULD BUILD US SOMETHING TO GET US TO THE EVERSPRING FASTER!
WHAT'S THE MATTER, GOBO?
I JUST KEEP WISHING I COULD BE MORE HELPFUL, THAT'S ALL.
GOBO, YOU'RE PLENTY HELPFUL! WHAT'S GOT YOU DOWN?
OH, JUST THIS LAST POSTCARD FROM UNCLE TRAVELING MATT. HE SEES AND DOES SO MANY AMAZING THINGS!

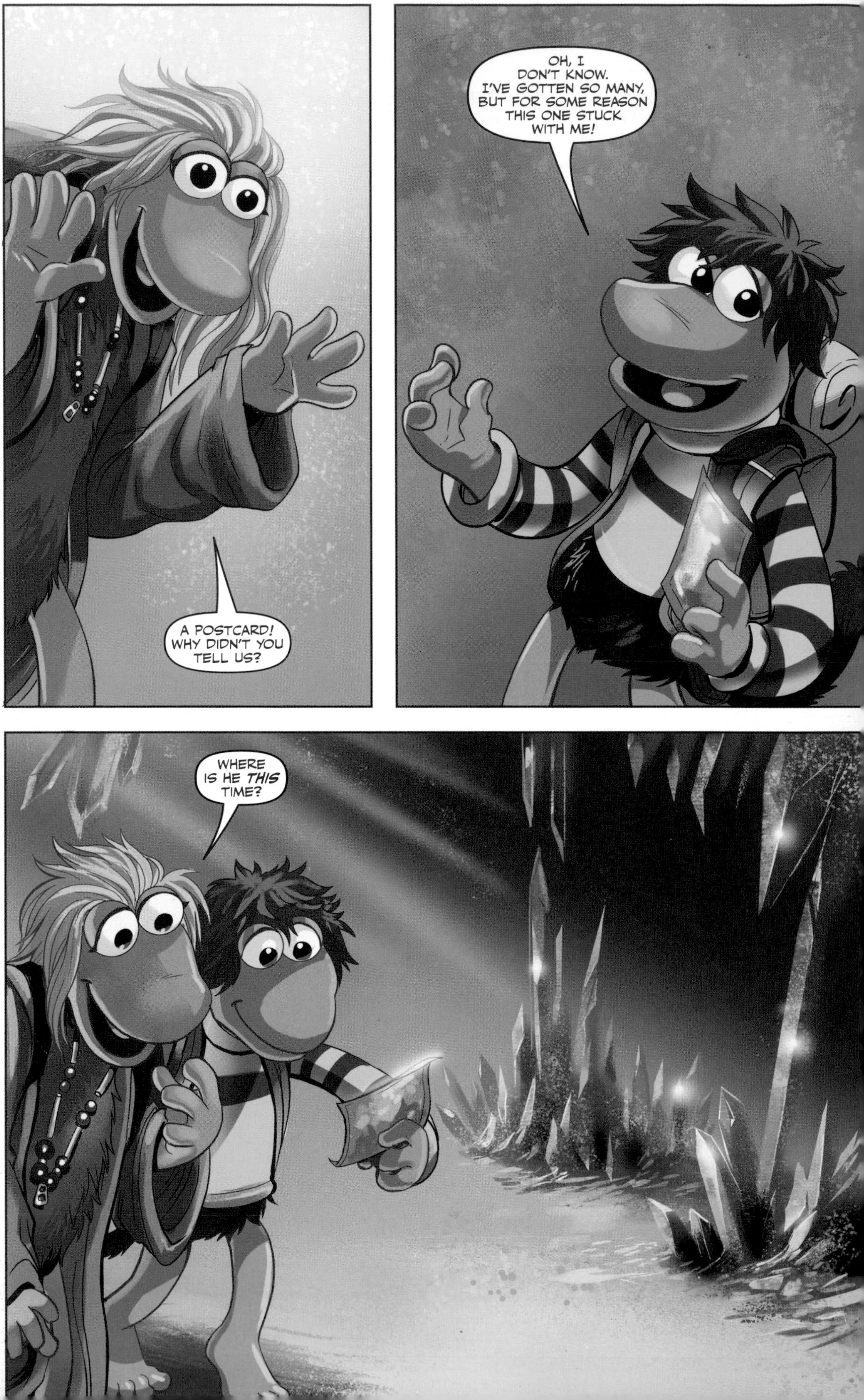
A POSTCARD! WHY DIDN'T YOU TELL US?
OH, I DON'T KNOW. I'VE GOTTEN SO MANY, BUT FOR SOME REASON THIS ONE STUCK WITH ME!
WHERE IS HE *THIS* TIME?

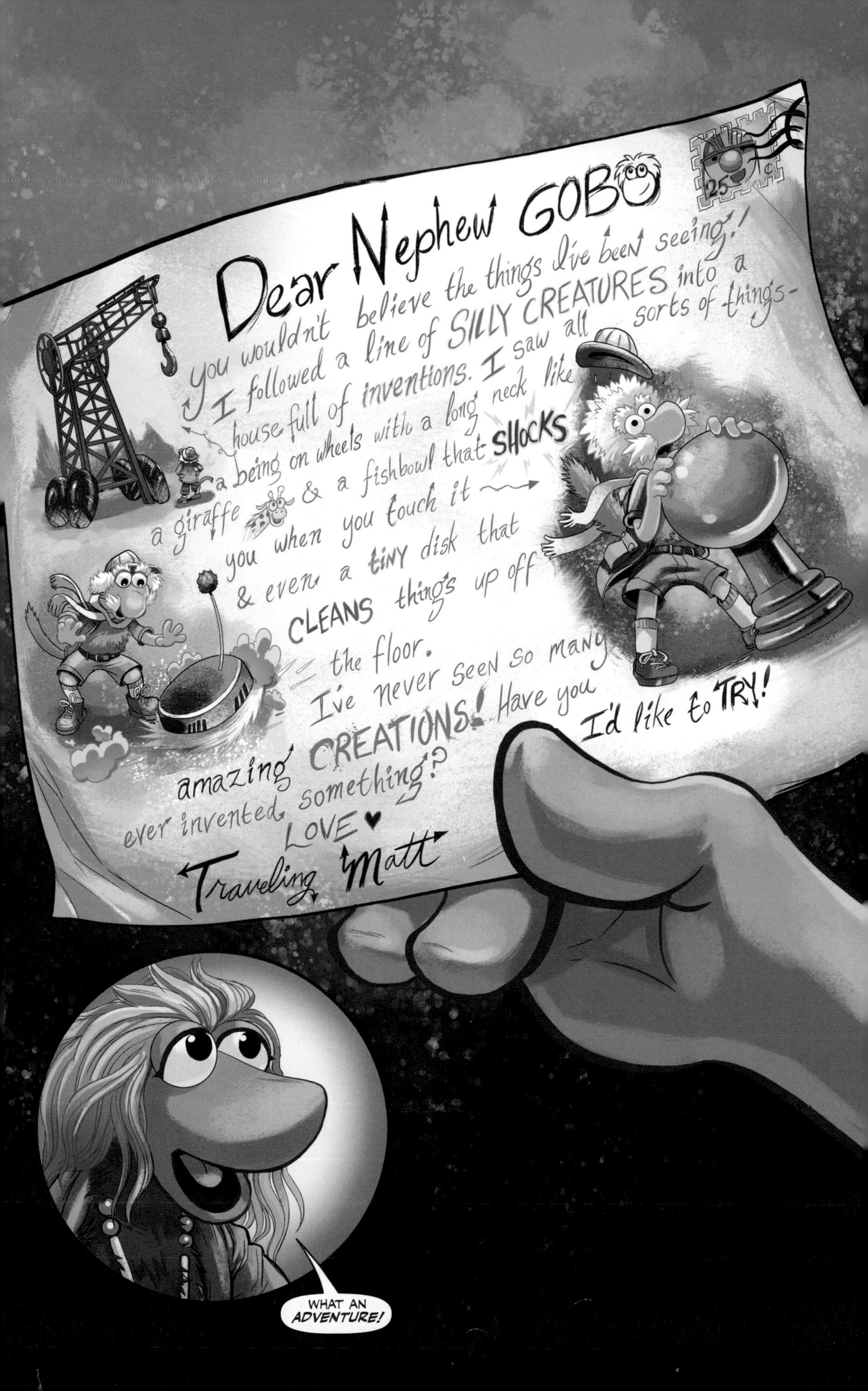

Dear Nephew GOBO
you wouldn't believe the things I've been seeing!
I followed a line of SILLY CREATURES into a
house full of inventions. I saw all sorts of things-
a being on wheels with a long neck like
a giraffe & a fishbowl that SHOCKS
you when you touch it
& even a tiny disk that
CLEANS things up off
the floor.
I've never seen so many
amazing CREATIONS! Have you
ever invented something?
I'd like to TRY!
LOVE
Traveling Matt
WHAT AN ADVENTURE!

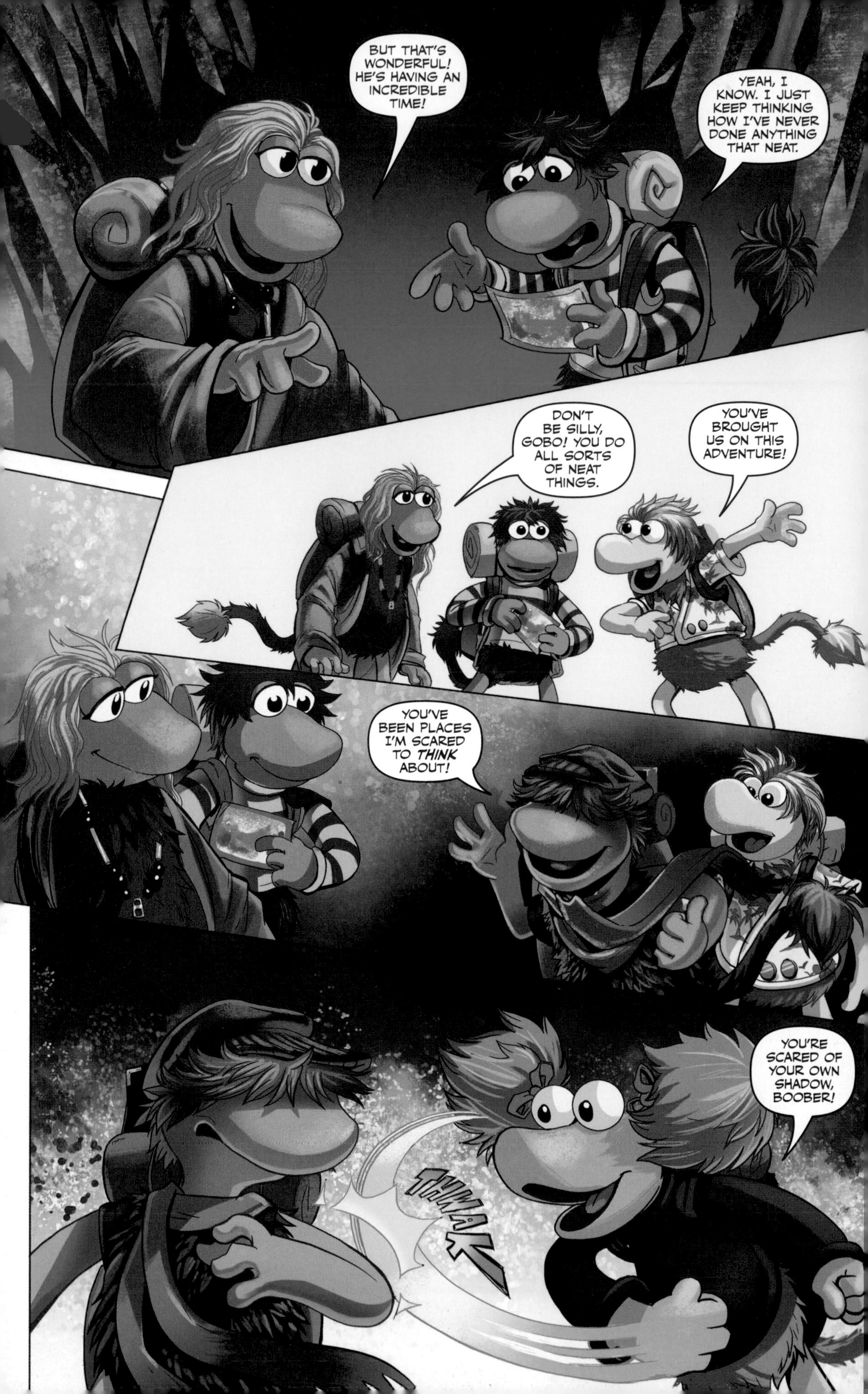
BUT THAT'S WONDERFUL! HE'S HAVING AN INCREDIBLE TIME!
YEAH, I KNOW. I JUST KEEP THINKING HOW I'VE NEVER DONE ANYTHING THAT NEAT.
DON'T BE SILLY, GOBO! YOU DO ALL SORTS OF NEAT THINGS.
YOU'VE BROUGHT US ON THIS ADVENTURE!
YOU'VE BEEN PLACES I'M SCARED TO *THINK* ABOUT!
YOU'RE SCARED OF YOUR OWN SHADOW, BOOBER!
THWAK

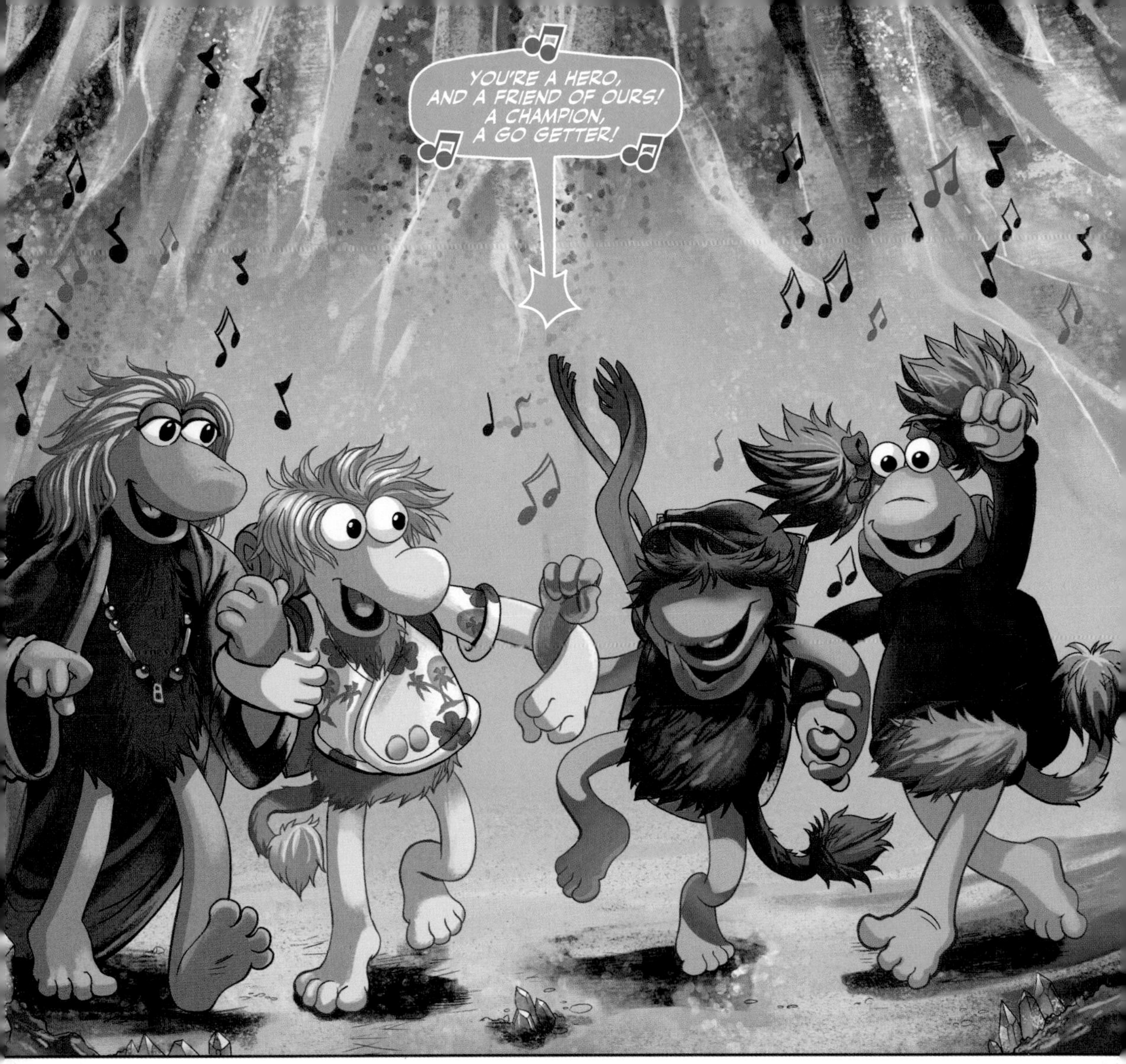
YOU'RE A HERO, AND A FRIEND OF OURS! A CHAMPION, A GO GETTER!

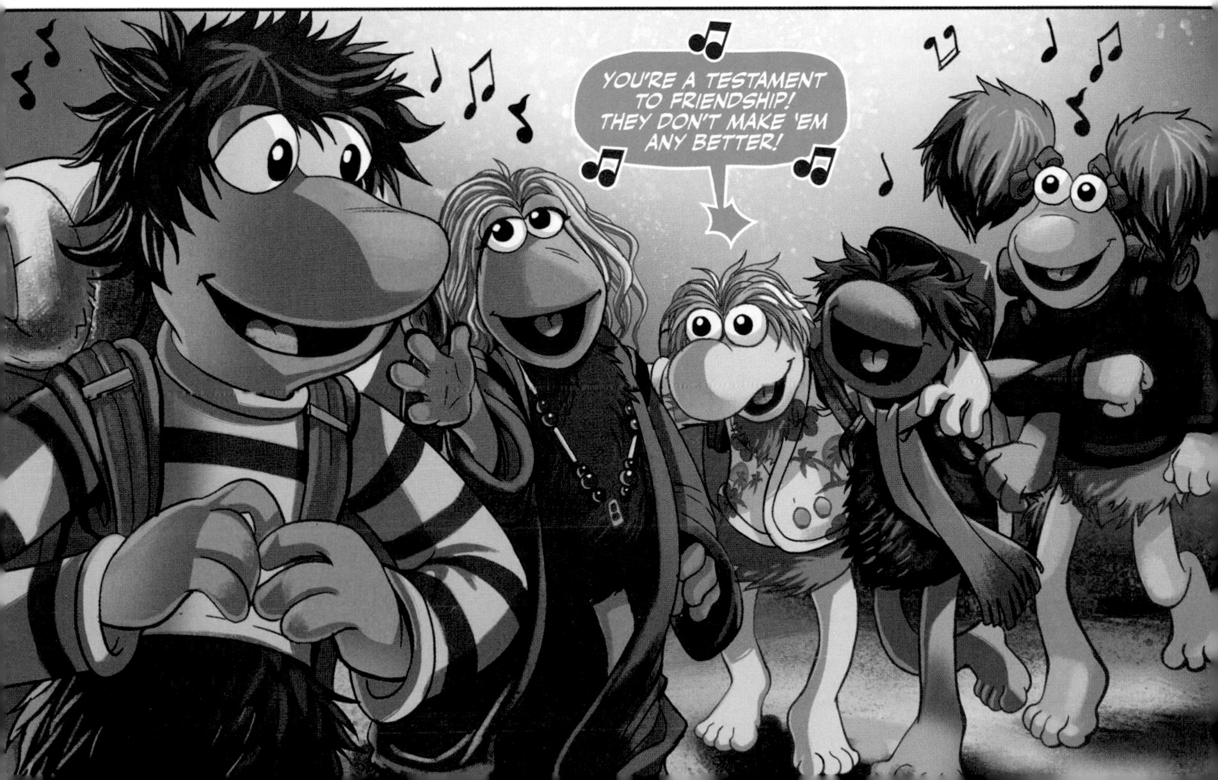
YOU'RE A TESTAMENT TO FRIENDSHIP! THEY DON'T MAKE 'EM ANY BETTER!

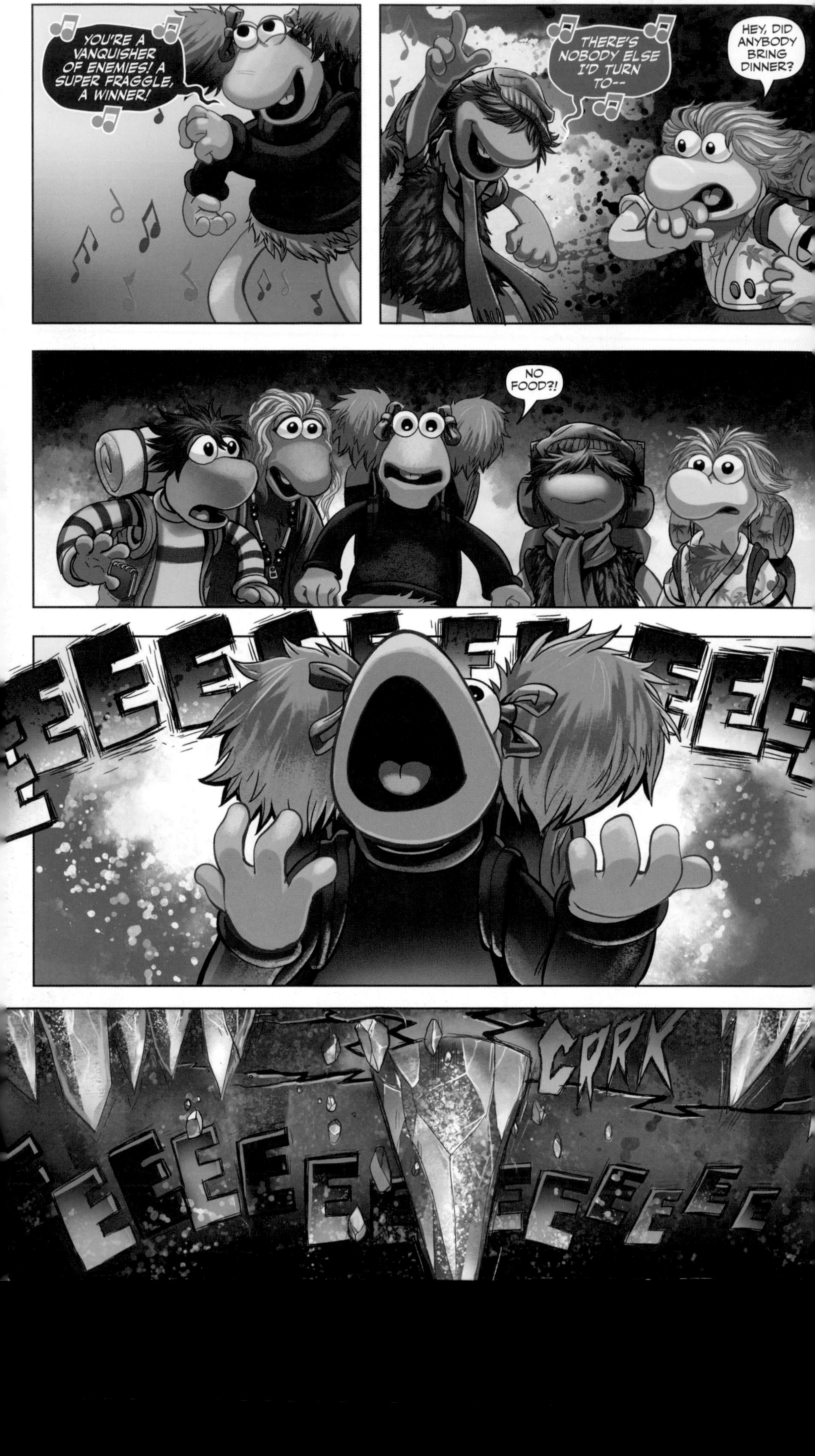
YOU'RE A VANQUISHER OF ENEMIES! A SUPER FRAGGLE, A WINNER!
THERE'S NOBODY ELSE I'D TURN TO--
HEY, DID ANYBODY BRING DINNER?
NO FOOD?!
CRRK

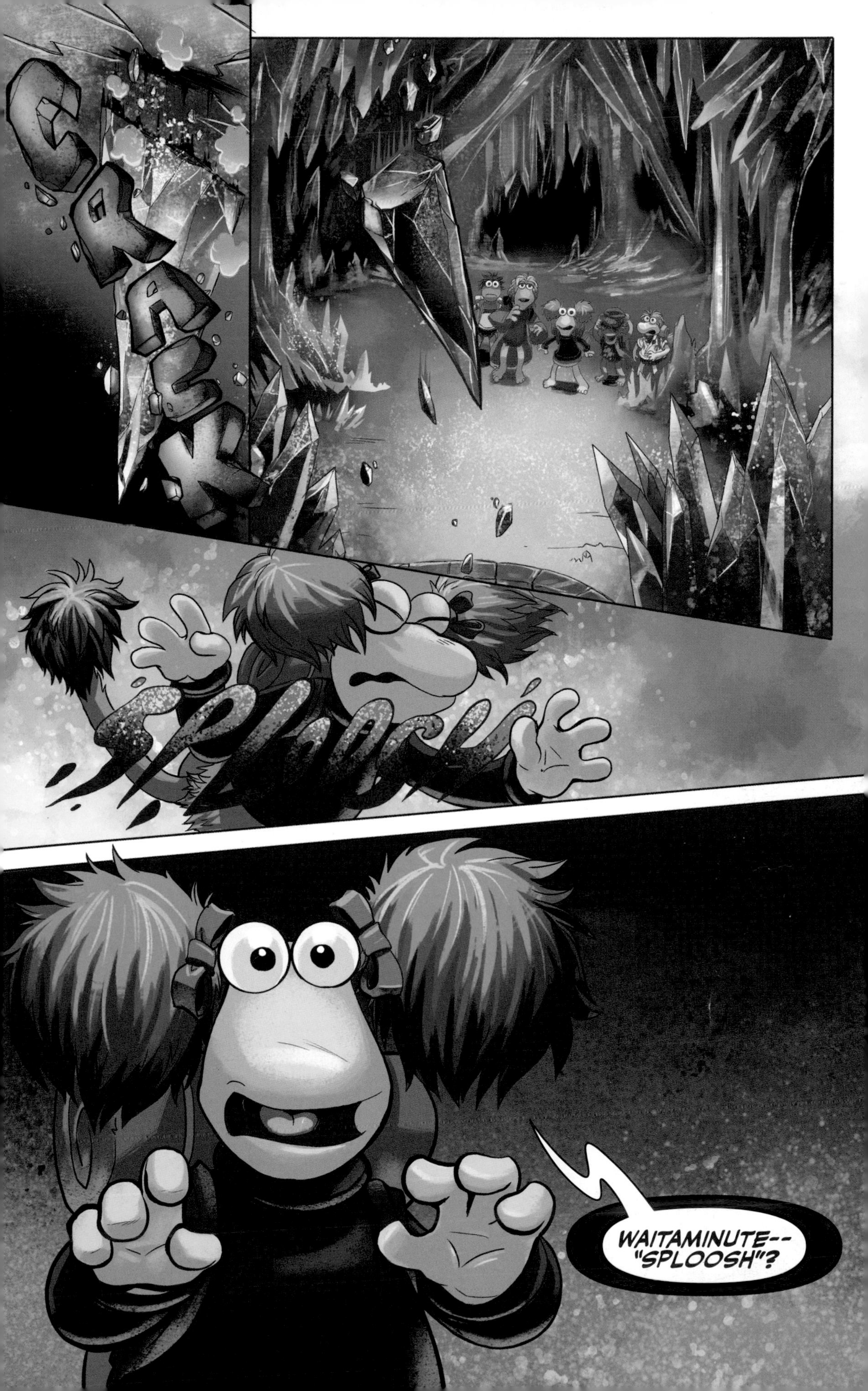
CRACK
WAITAMINUTE-- "SPLOOSH"?

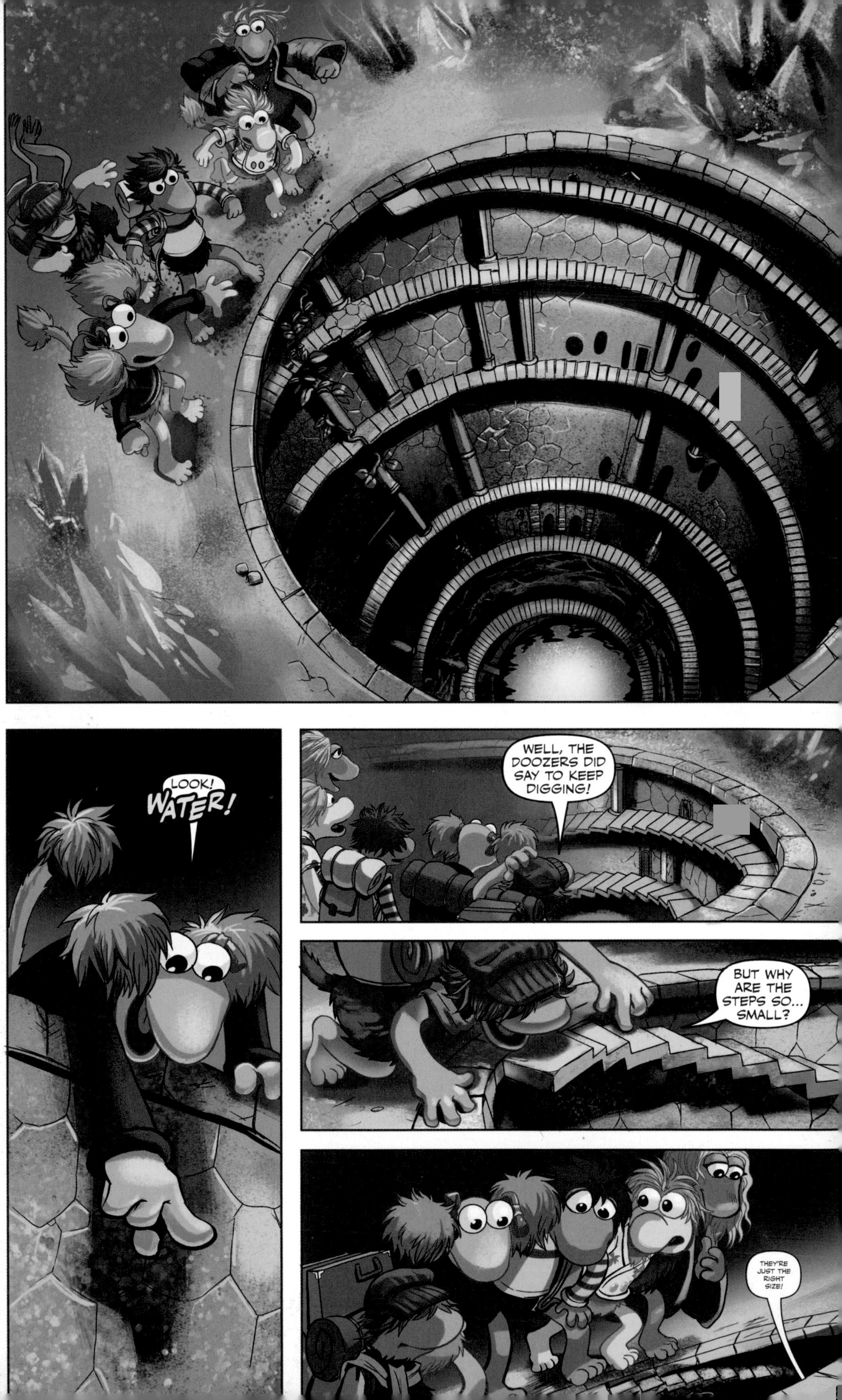
LOOK! WATER!
WELL, THE DOOZERS DID SAY TO KEEP DIGGING!
BUT WHY ARE THE STEPS SO... SMALL?
THEY'RE JUST THE RIGHT SIZE!

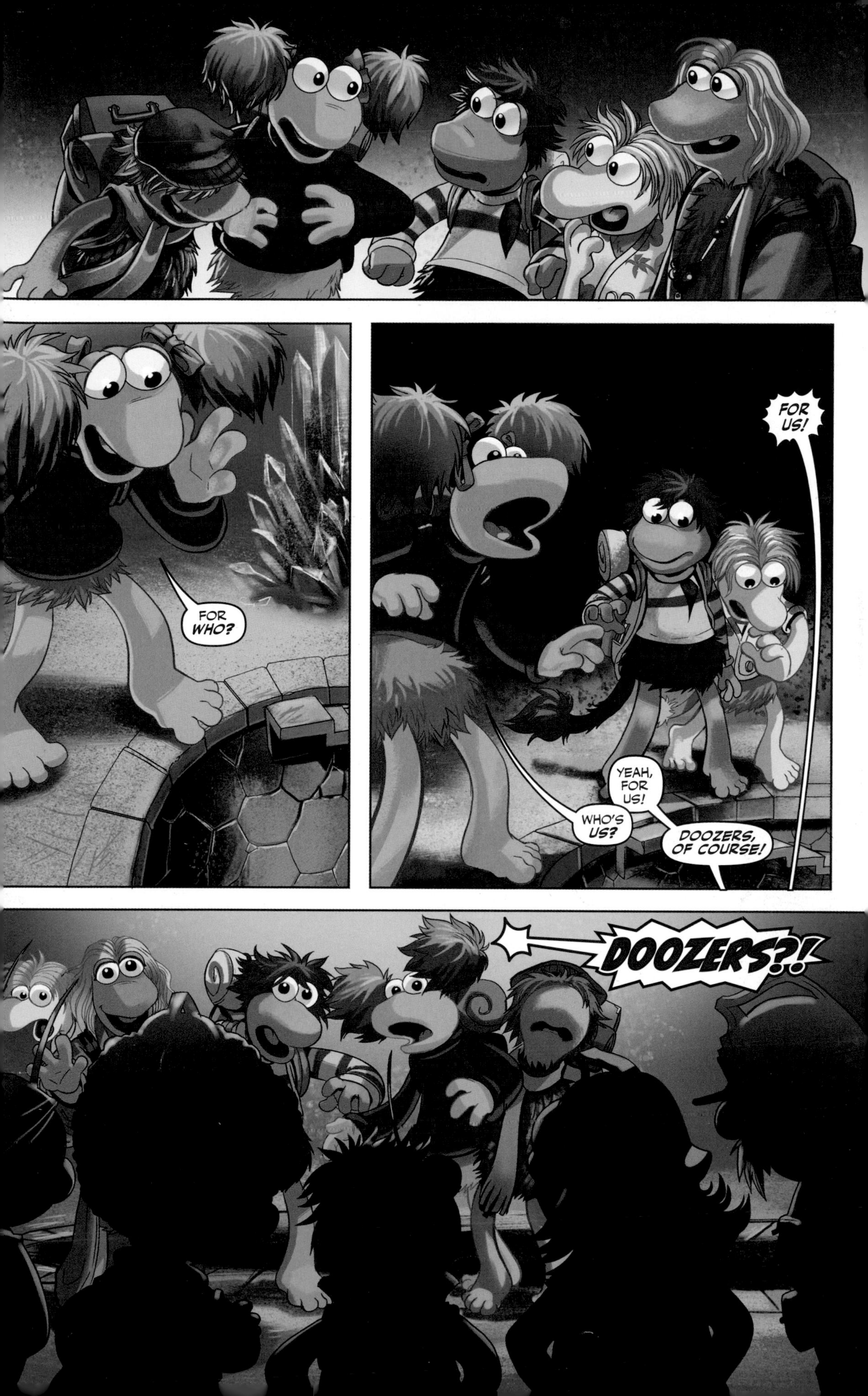
FOR WHO?
FOR US!
WHO'S US?
YEAH, FOR US!
DOOZERS, OF COURSE!
DOOZERS?!

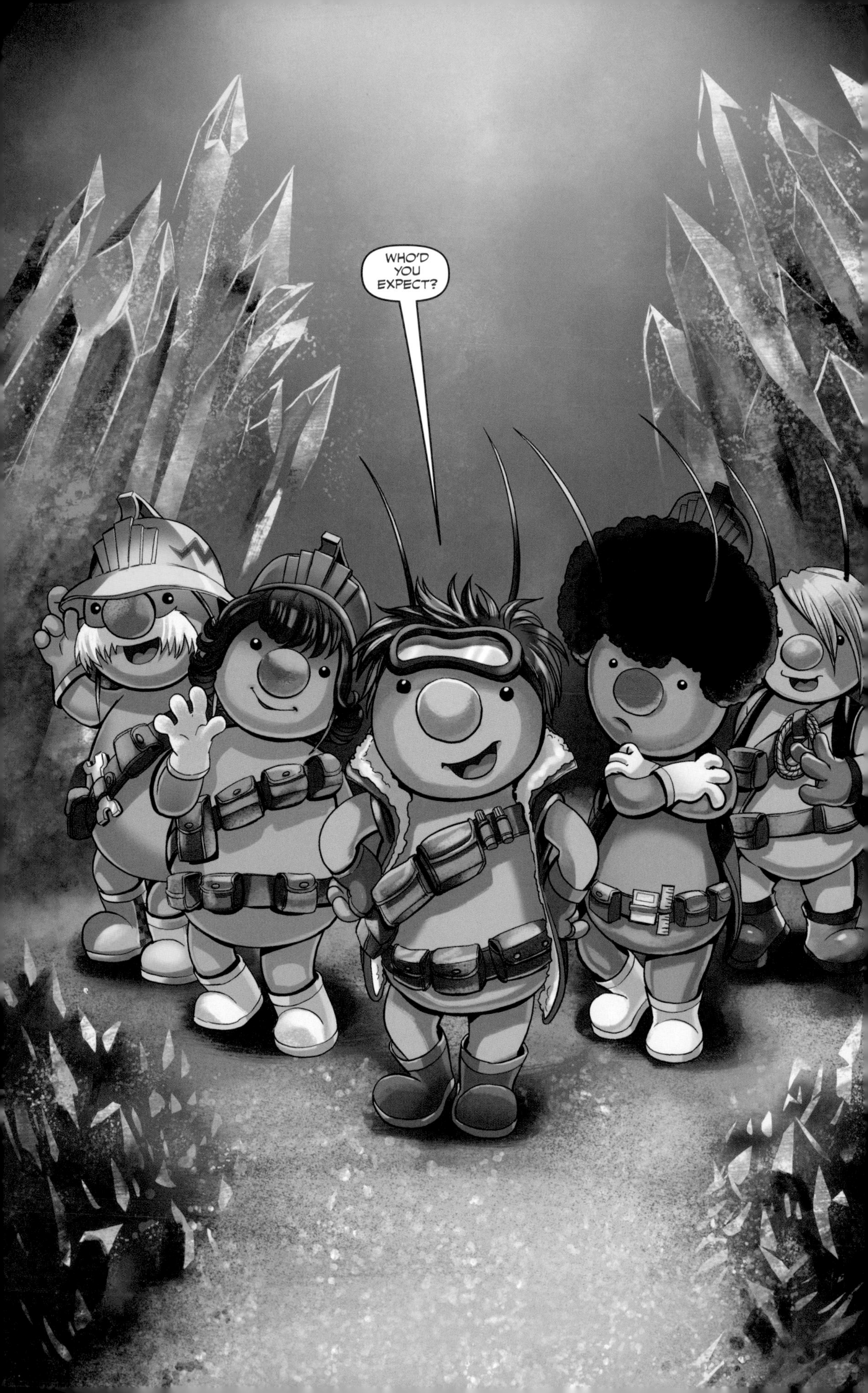
WHO'D YOU EXPECT?

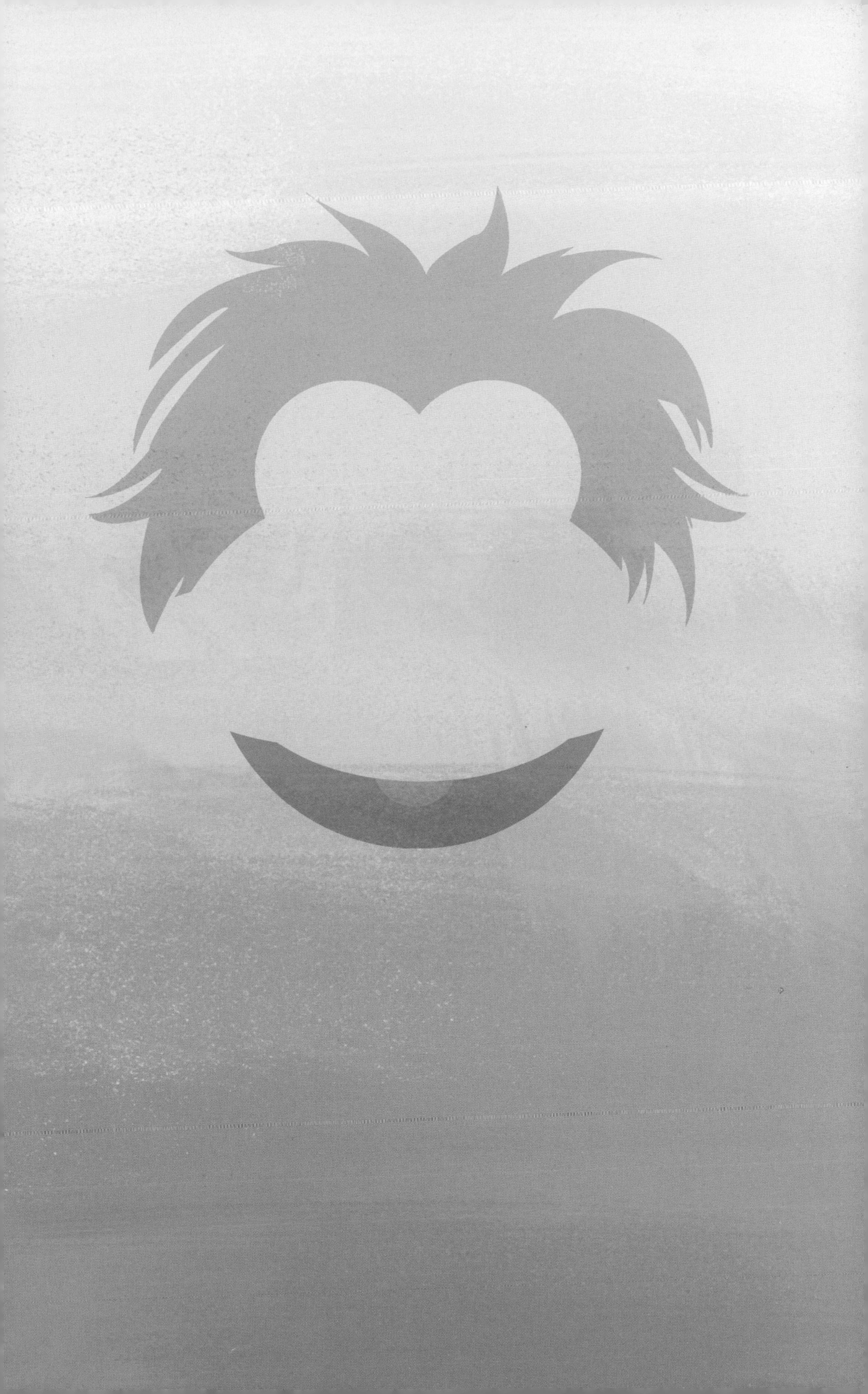

LET THE MUSIC PLAY

CHAPTER THREE

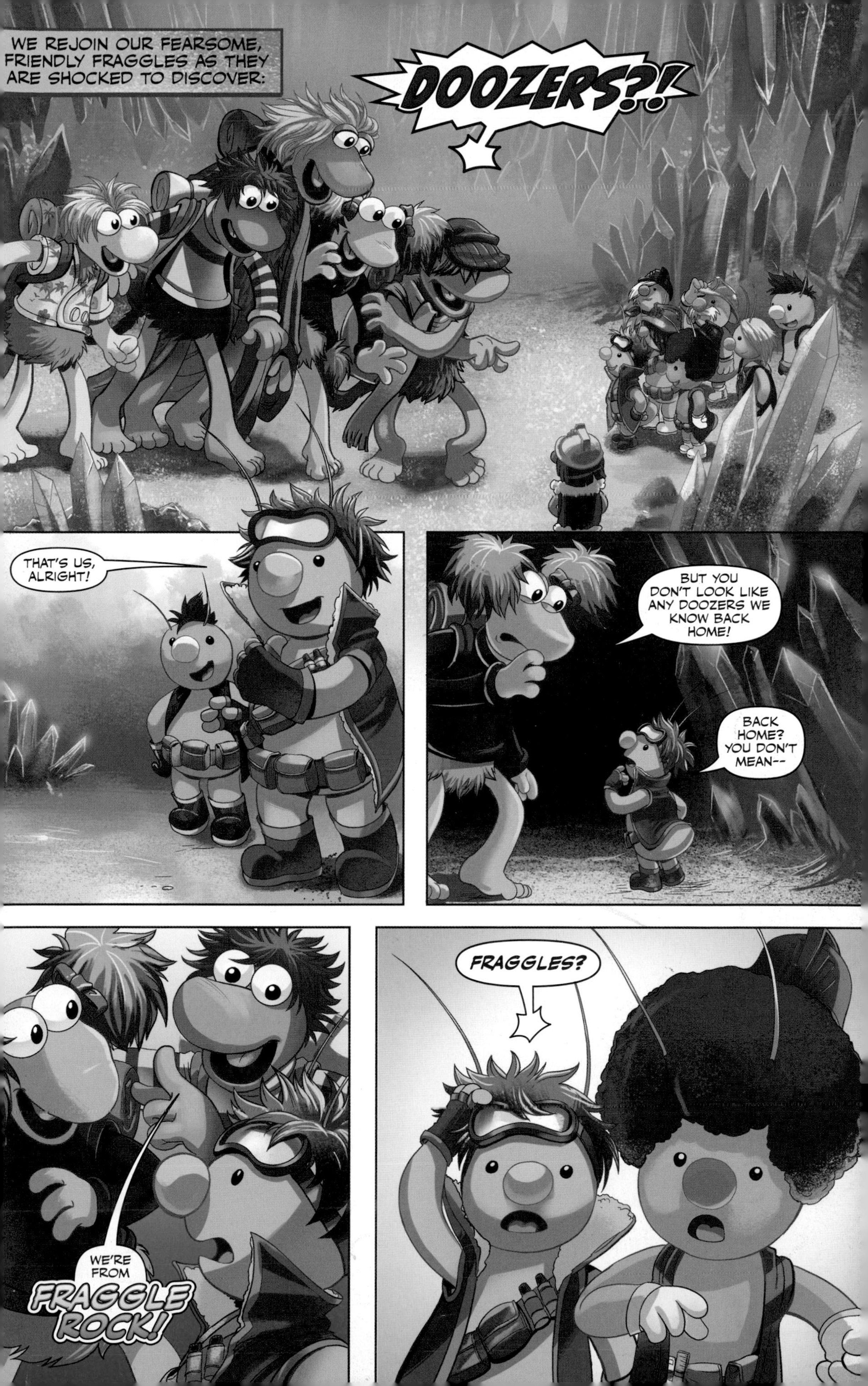
WE REJOIN OUR FEARSOME, FRIENDLY FRAGGLES AS THEY ARE SHOCKED TO DISCOVER:
DOOZERS?!
THAT'S US, ALRIGHT!
BUT YOU DON'T LOOK LIKE ANY DOOZERS WE KNOW BACK HOME!
BACK HOME? YOU DON'T MEAN--
WE'RE FROM
FRAGGLE ROCK!
FRAGGLES?

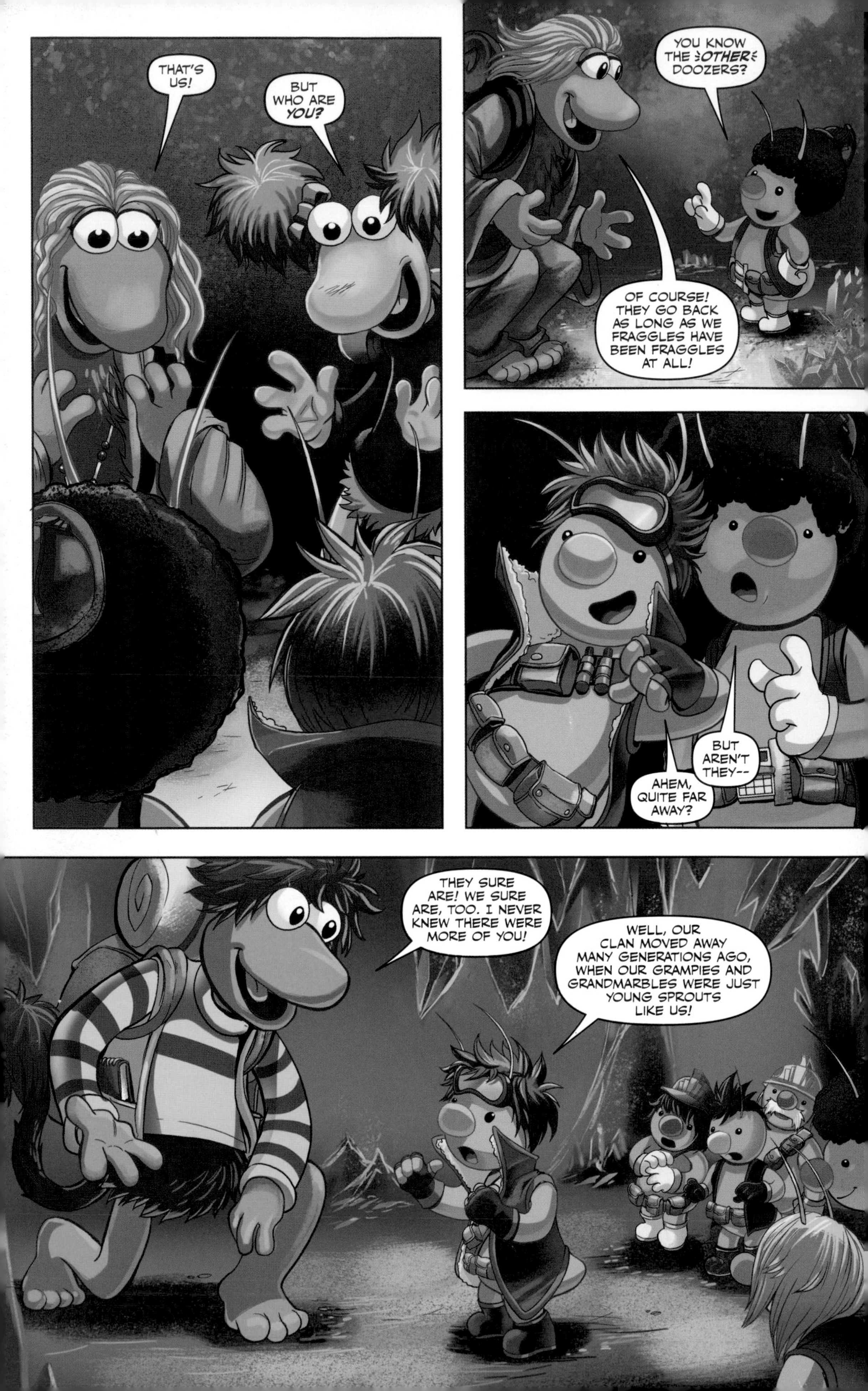
THAT'S US!
BUT WHO ARE YOU?
YOU KNOW THE OTHER DOOZERS?
OF COURSE! THEY GO BACK AS LONG AS WE FRAGGLES HAVE BEEN FRAGGLES AT ALL!
BUT AREN'T THEY--
AHEM, QUITE FAR AWAY?
THEY SURE ARE! WE SURE ARE, TOO. I NEVER KNEW THERE WERE MORE OF YOU!
WELL, OUR CLAN MOVED AWAY MANY GENERATIONS AGO, WHEN OUR GRAMPIES AND GRANDMARBLES WERE JUST YOUNG SPROUTS LIKE US!

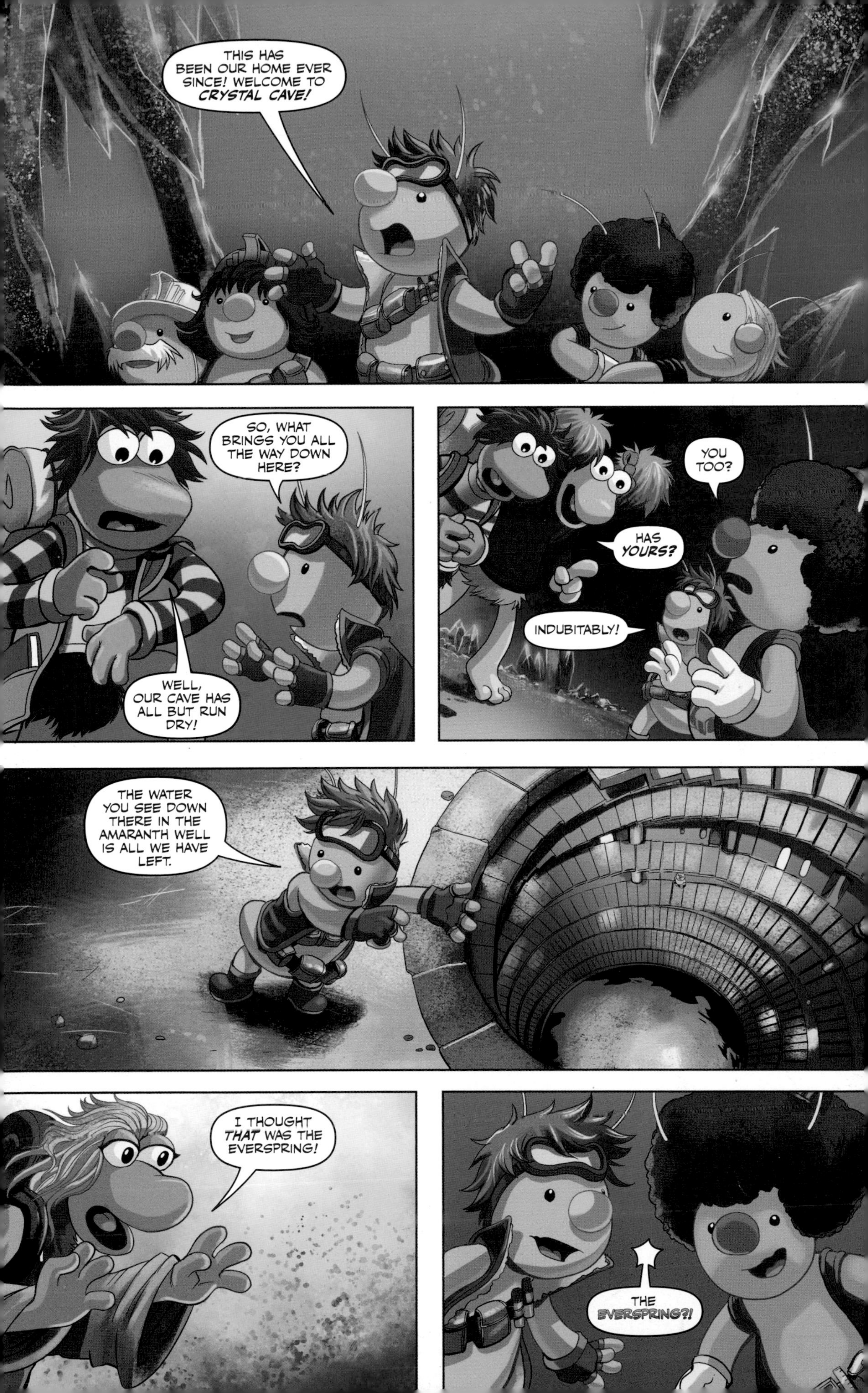
THIS HAS BEEN OUR HOME EVER SINCE! WELCOME TO *CRYSTAL CAVE!*
SO, WHAT BRINGS YOU ALL THE WAY DOWN HERE?
WELL, OUR CAVE HAS ALL BUT RUN DRY!
YOU TOO?
HAS *YOURS?*
INDUBITABLY!
THE WATER YOU SEE DOWN THERE IN THE AMARANTH WELL IS ALL WE HAVE LEFT.
I THOUGHT *THAT* WAS THE EVERSPRING!
THE EVERSPRING?!

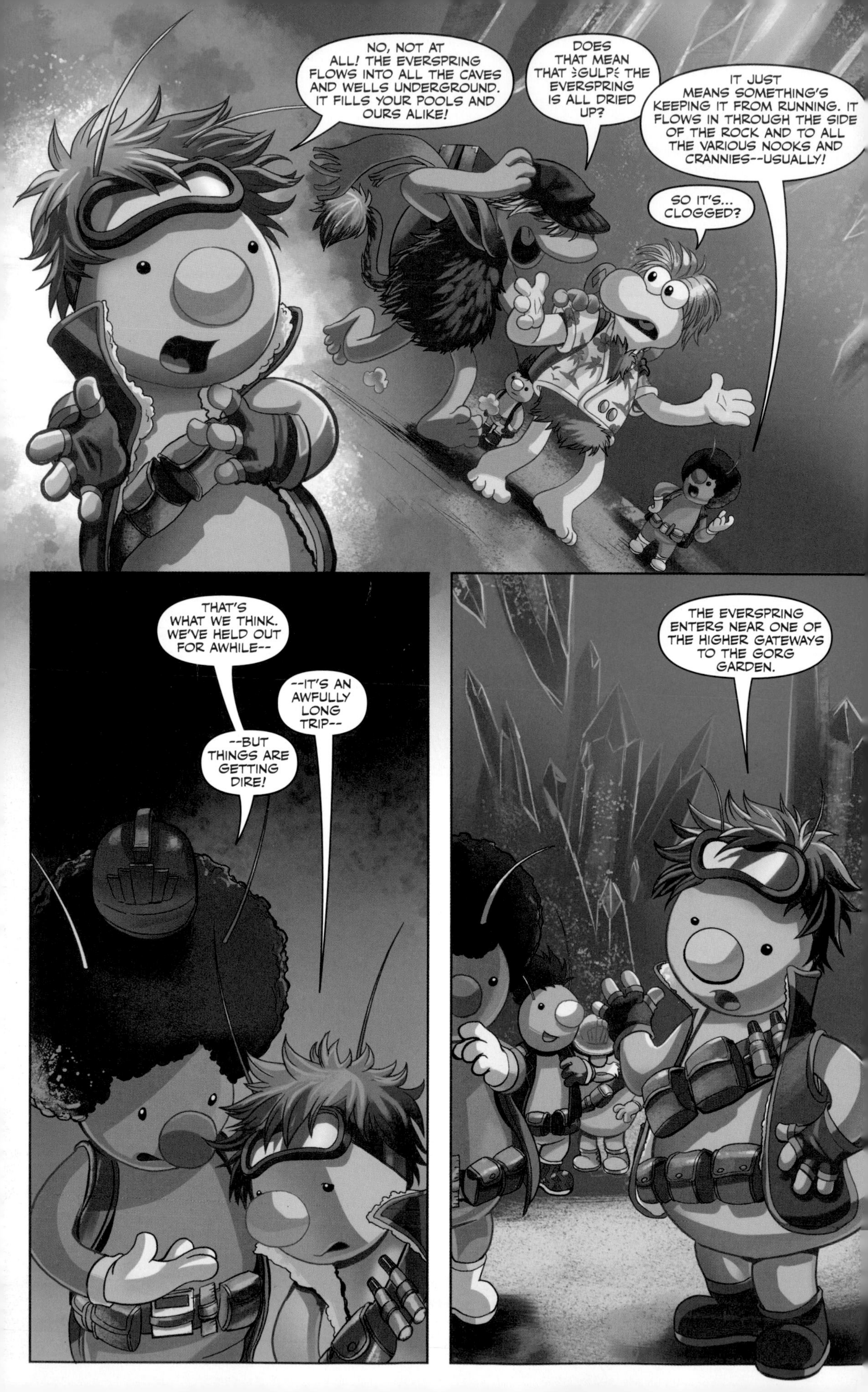
NO, NOT AT ALL! THE EVERSPRING FLOWS INTO ALL THE CAVES AND WELLS UNDERGROUND. IT FILLS YOUR POOLS AND OURS ALIKE!
DOES THAT MEAN THAT ⋟GULP⋞ THE EVERSPRING IS ALL DRIED UP?
IT JUST MEANS SOMETHING'S KEEPING IT FROM RUNNING. IT FLOWS IN THROUGH THE SIDE OF THE ROCK AND TO ALL THE VARIOUS NOOKS AND CRANNIES--USUALLY!
SO IT'S... CLOGGED?
THAT'S WHAT WE THINK. WE'VE HELD OUT FOR AWHILE--
--IT'S AN AWFULLY LONG TRIP--
--BUT THINGS ARE GETTING DIRE!
THE EVERSPRING ENTERS NEAR ONE OF THE HIGHER GATEWAYS TO THE GORG GARDEN.

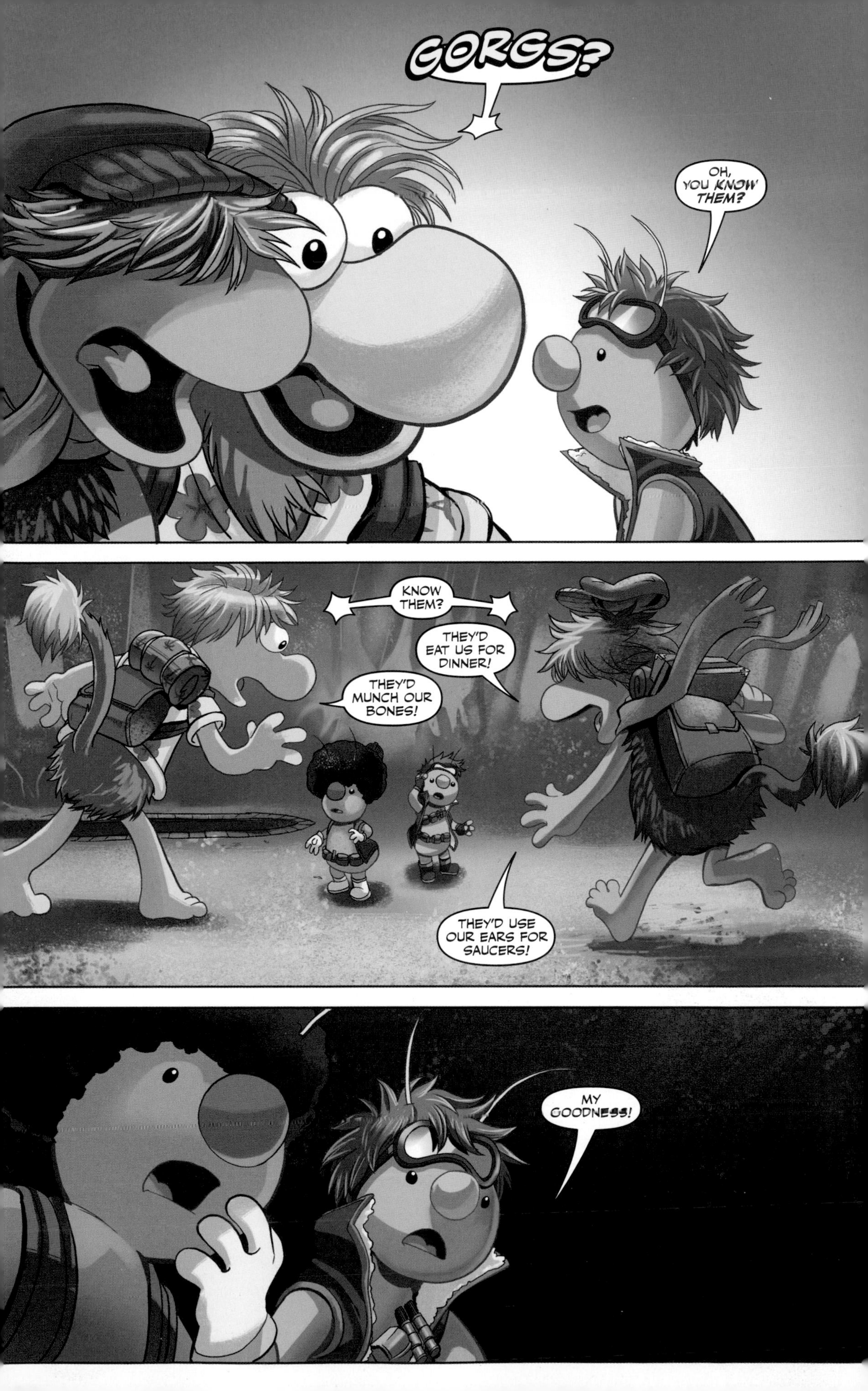
GORGS?
OH, YOU KNOW THEM?
KNOW THEM?
THEY'D EAT US FOR DINNER!
THEY'D MUNCH OUR BONES!
THEY'D USE OUR EARS FOR SAUCERS!
MY GOODNESS!

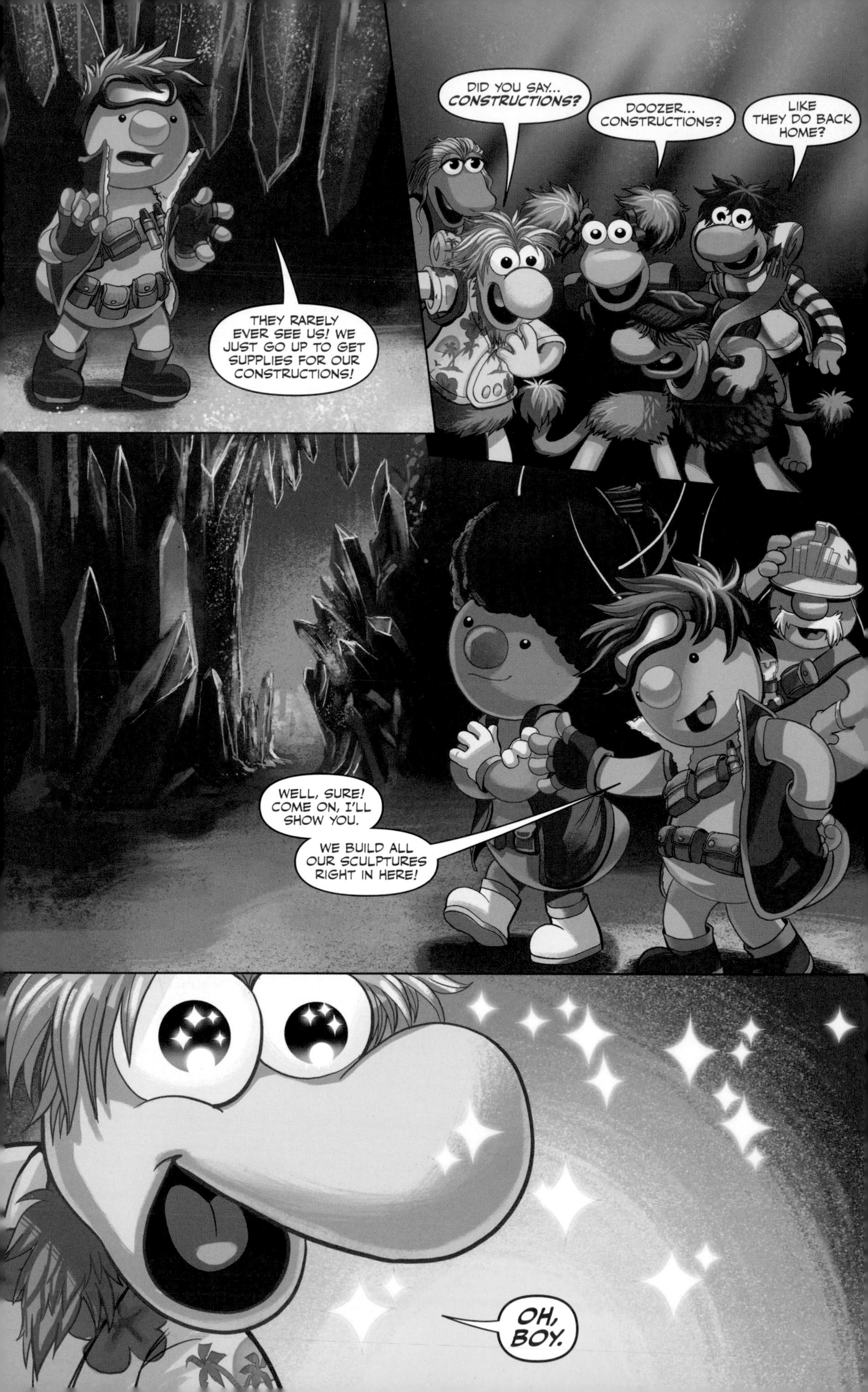
THEY RARELY EVER SEE US! WE JUST GO UP TO GET SUPPLIES FOR OUR CONSTRUCTIONS!
DID YOU SAY... CONSTRUCTIONS?
DOOZER... CONSTRUCTIONS?
LIKE THEY DO BACK HOME?
WELL, SURE! COME ON, I'LL SHOW YOU.
WE BUILD ALL OUR SCULPTURES RIGHT IN HERE!
OH, BOY.

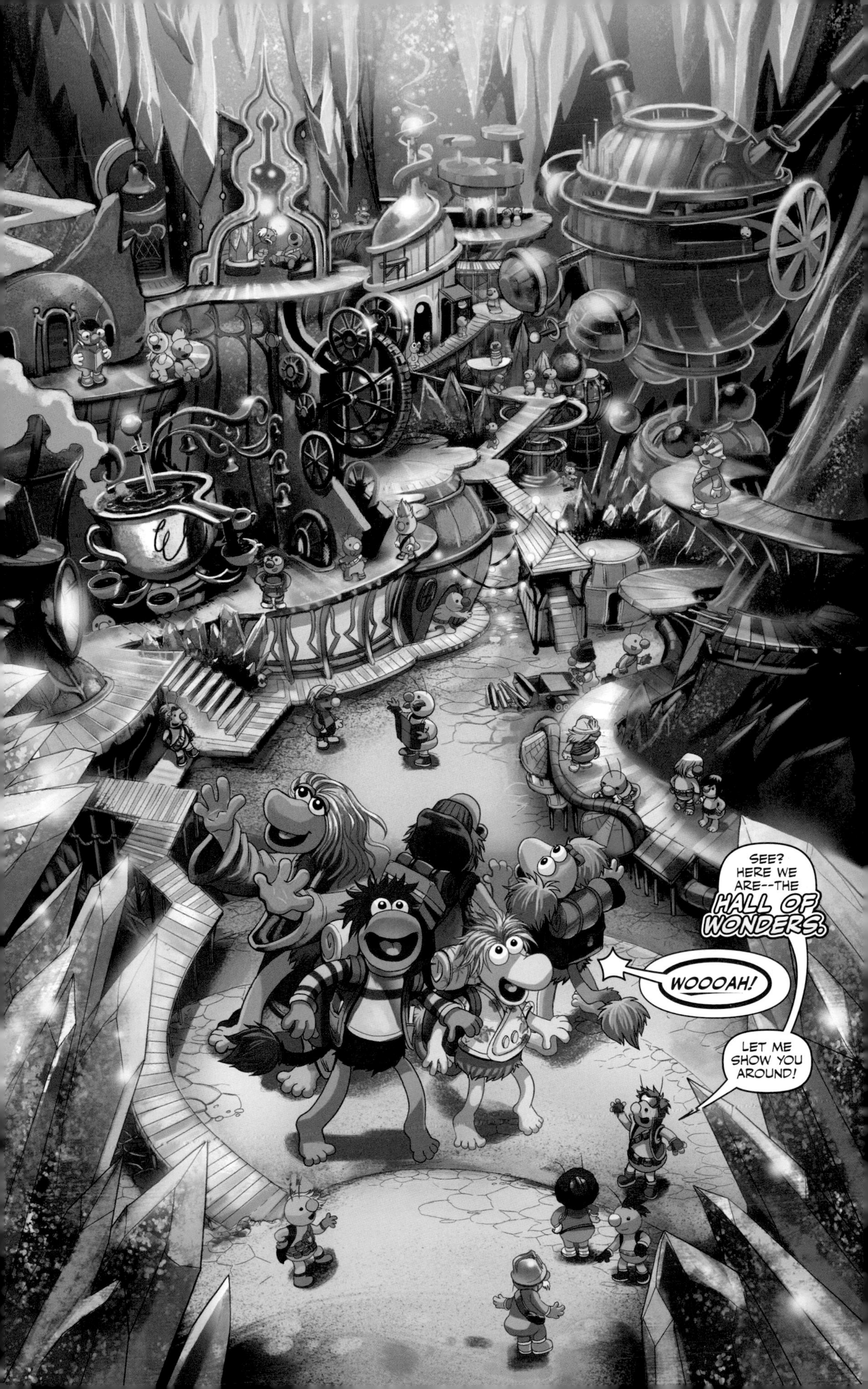
SEE? HERE WE ARE--THE HALL OF WONDERS.
WOOOAH!
LET ME SHOW YOU AROUND!

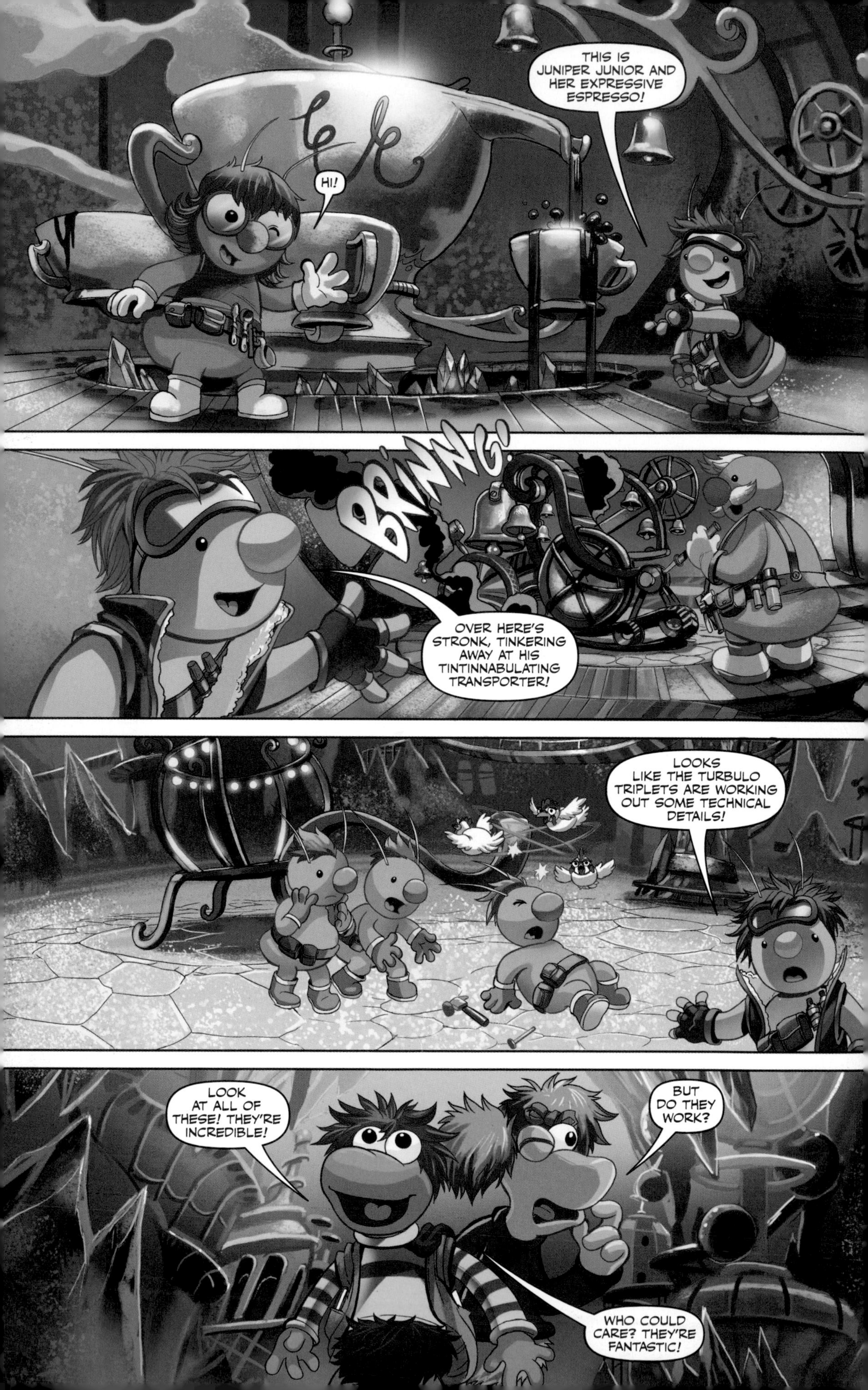
THIS IS JUNIPER JUNIOR AND HER EXPRESSIVE ESPRESSO!
HI!
BRINNG!
OVER HERE'S STRONK, TINKERING AWAY AT HIS TINTINNABULATING TRANSPORTER!
LOOKS LIKE THE TURBULO TRIPLETS ARE WORKING OUT SOME TECHNICAL DETAILS!
LOOK AT ALL OF THESE! THEY'RE INCREDIBLE!
BUT DO THEY WORK?
WHO COULD CARE? THEY'RE FANTASTIC!

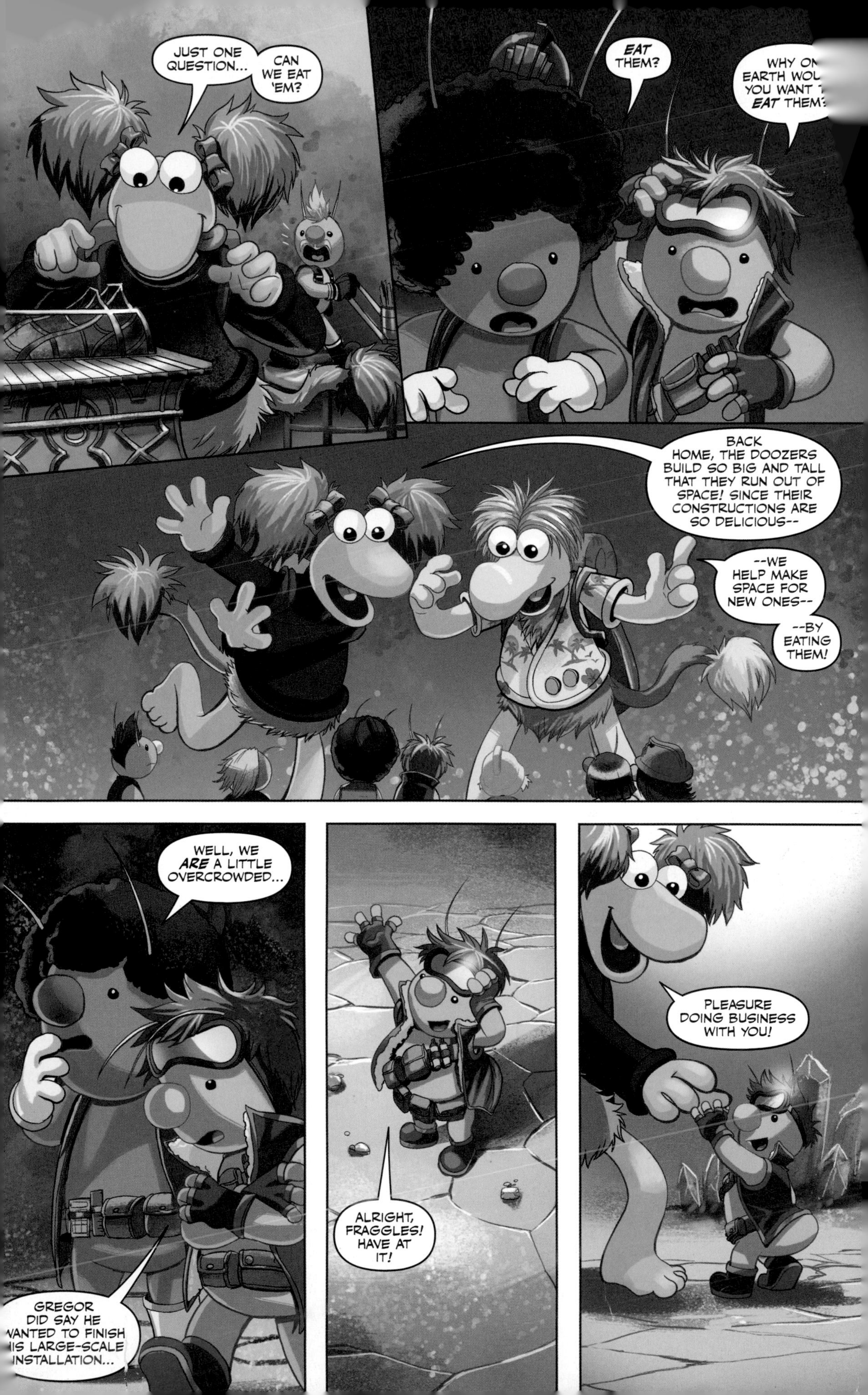
JUST ONE QUESTION...
CAN WE EAT 'EM?
EAT THEM?
WHY ON EARTH WOU YOU WANT T EAT THEM?
BACK HOME, THE DOOZERS BUILD SO BIG AND TALL THAT THEY RUN OUT OF SPACE! SINCE THEIR CONSTRUCTIONS ARE SO DELICIOUS--
--WE HELP MAKE SPACE FOR NEW ONES--
--BY EATING THEM!
WELL, WE ARE A LITTLE OVERCROWDED...
GREGOR DID SAY HE WANTED TO FINISH IS LARGE-SCALE INSTALLATION...
ALRIGHT, FRAGGLES! HAVE AT IT!
PLEASURE DOING BUSINESS WITH YOU!

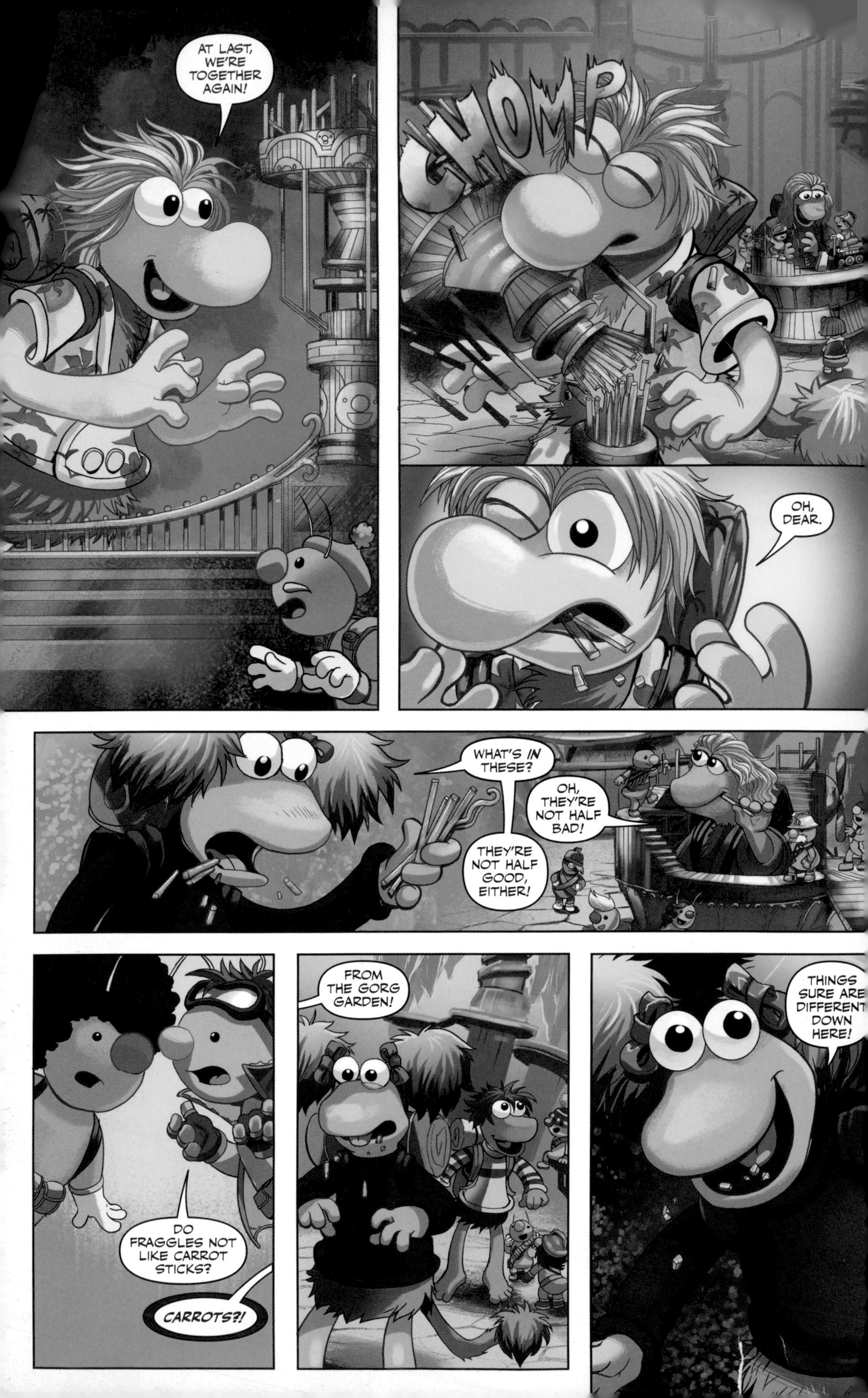
AT LAST, WE'RE TOGETHER AGAIN!
CHOMP
OH, DEAR.
WHAT'S IN THESE?
OH, THEY'RE NOT HALF BAD!
THEY'RE NOT HALF GOOD, EITHER!
DO FRAGGLES NOT LIKE CARROT STICKS?
CARROTS?!
FROM THE GORG GARDEN!
THINGS SURE ARE DIFFERENT DOWN HERE!

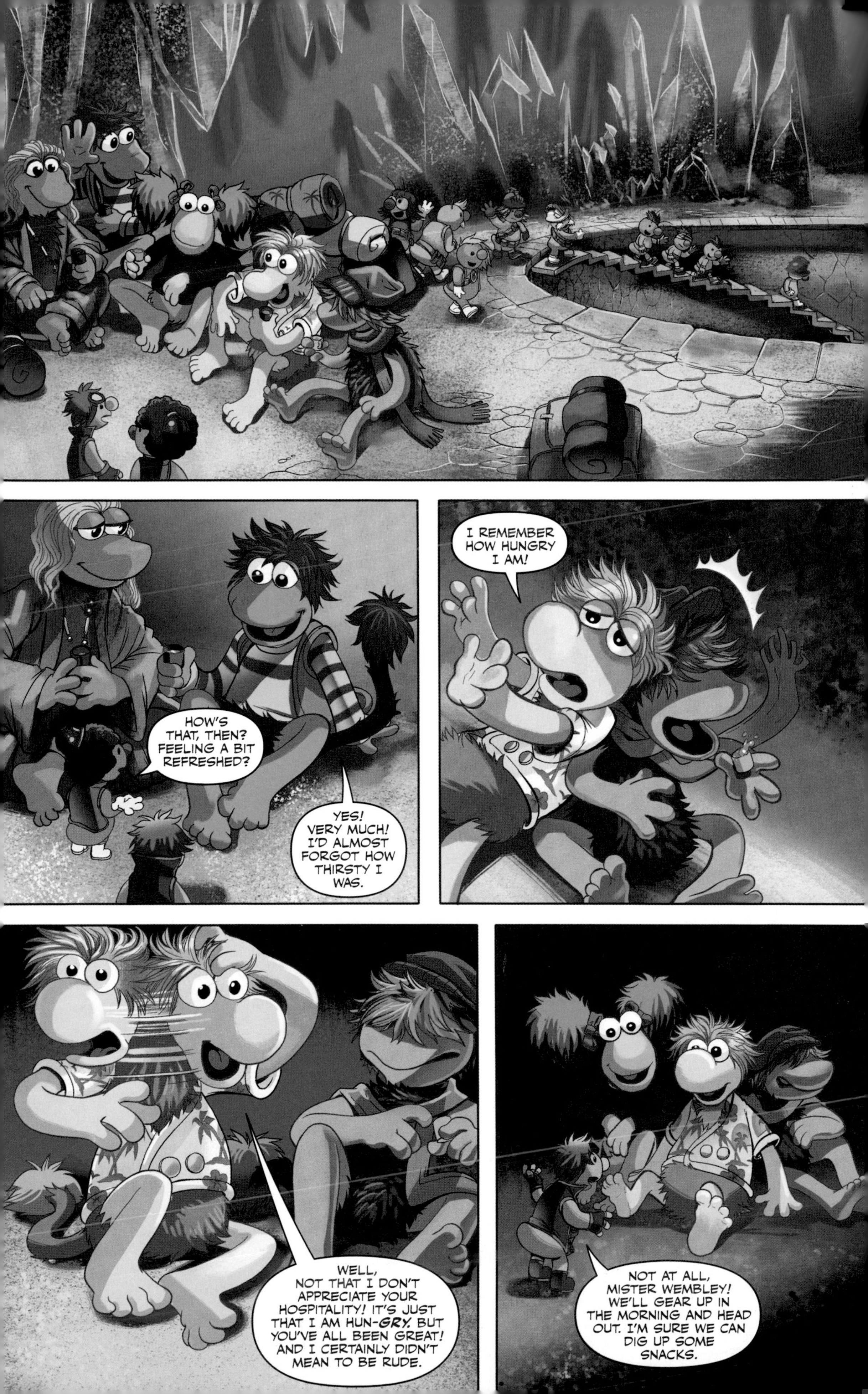
HOW'S THAT, THEN? FEELING A BIT REFRESHED?
YES! VERY MUCH! I'D ALMOST FORGOT HOW THIRSTY I WAS.
I REMEMBER HOW HUNGRY I AM!
WELL, NOT THAT I DON'T APPRECIATE YOUR HOSPITALITY! IT'S JUST THAT I AM HUN-GRY. BUT YOU'VE ALL BEEN GREAT! AND I CERTAINLY DIDN'T MEAN TO BE RUDE.
NOT AT ALL, MISTER WEMBLEY! WE'LL GEAR UP IN THE MORNING AND HEAD OUT. I'M SURE WE CAN DIG UP SOME SNACKS.

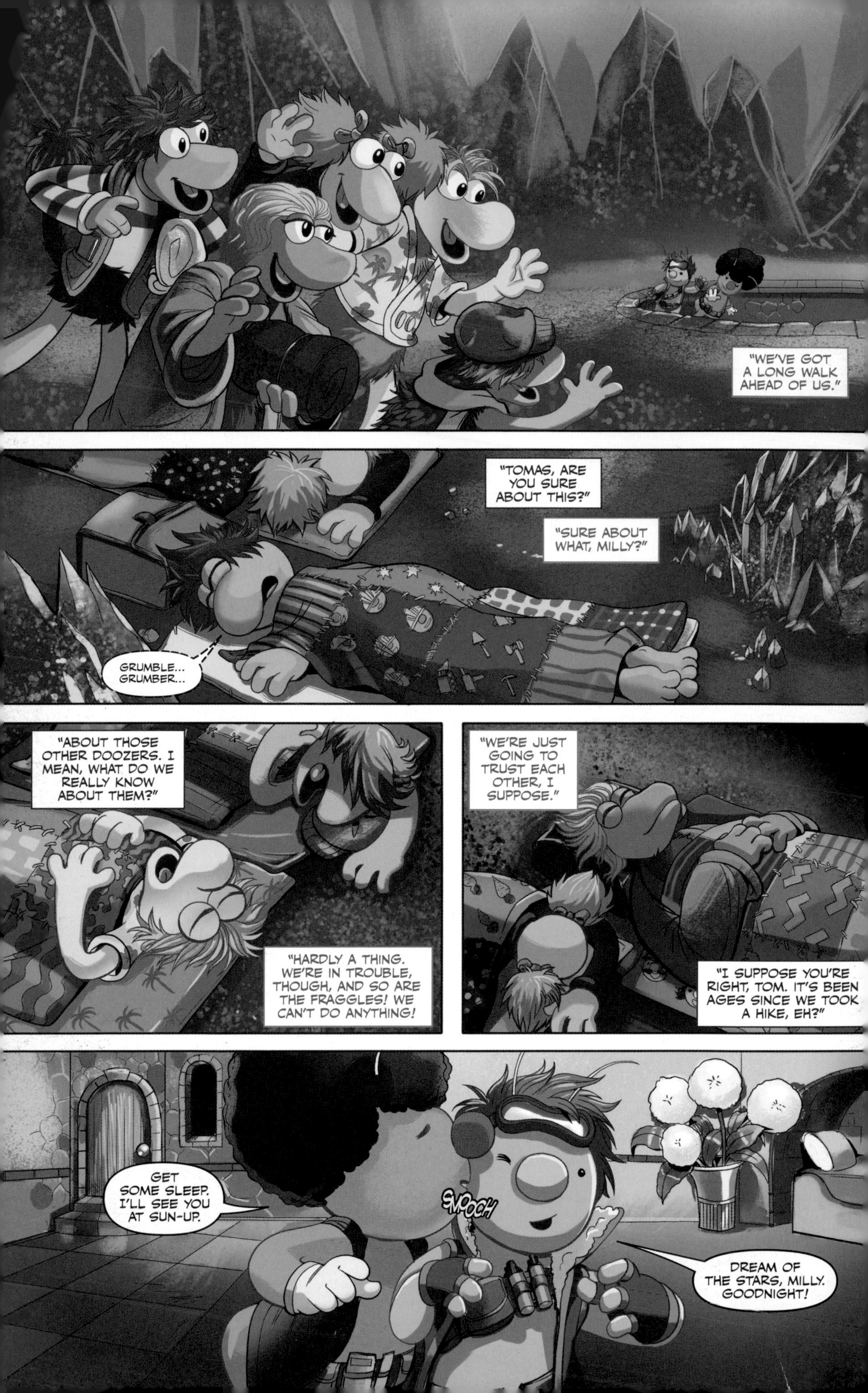
"WE'VE GOT A LONG WALK AHEAD OF US."
"TOMAS, ARE YOU SURE ABOUT THIS?"
"SURE ABOUT WHAT, MILLY?"
GRUMBLE... GRUMBER...
"ABOUT THOSE OTHER DOOZERS. I MEAN, WHAT DO WE REALLY KNOW ABOUT THEM?"
"HARDLY A THING. WE'RE IN TROUBLE, THOUGH, AND SO ARE THE FRAGGLES! WE CAN'T DO ANYTHING!
"WE'RE JUST GOING TO TRUST EACH OTHER, I SUPPOSE."
"I SUPPOSE YOU'RE RIGHT, TOM. IT'S BEEN AGES SINCE WE TOOK A HIKE, EH?"
GET SOME SLEEP. I'LL SEE YOU AT SUN-UP.
SMOOCH
DREAM OF THE STARS, MILLY. GOODNIGHT!

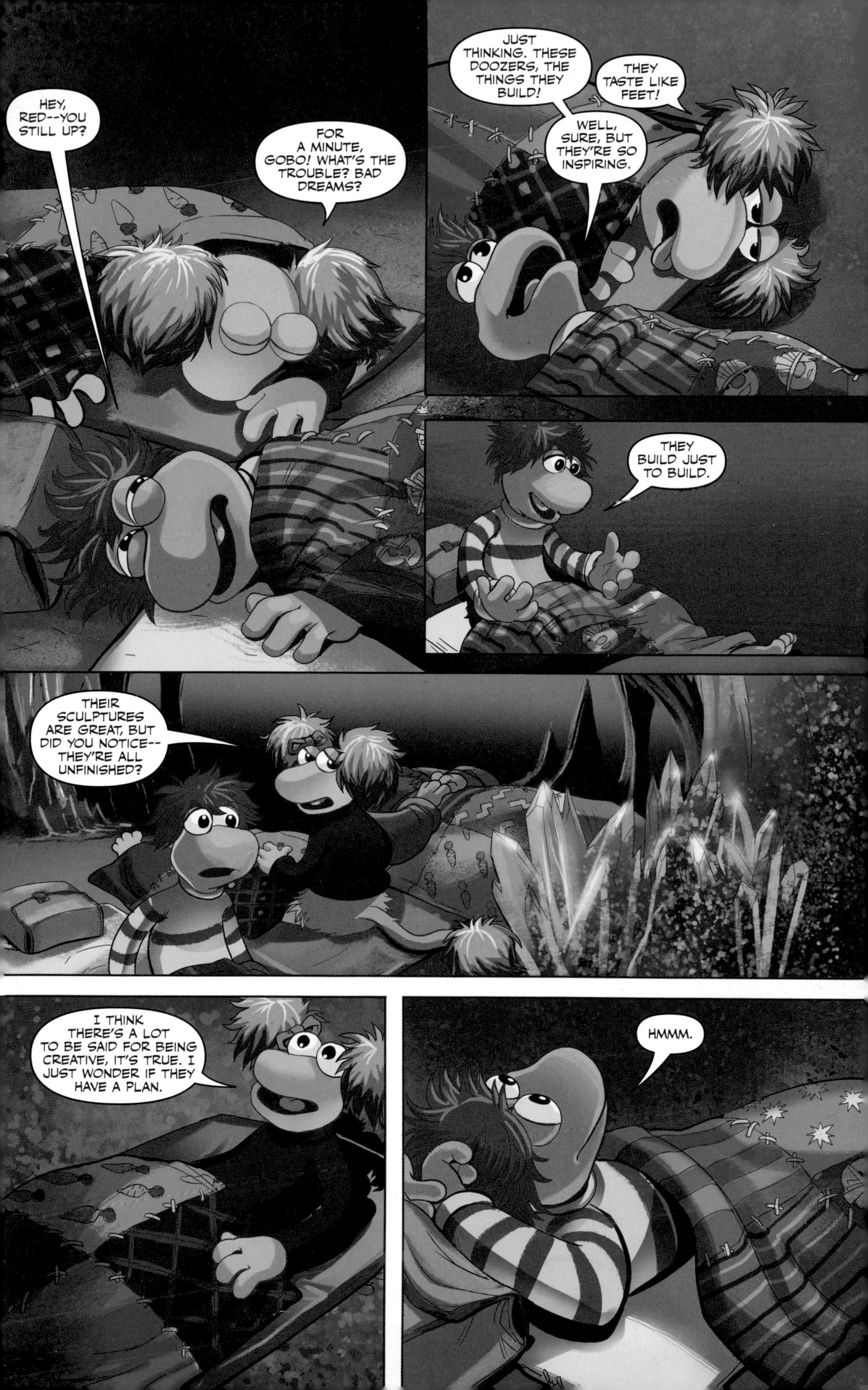
HEY, RED--YOU STILL UP?
FOR A MINUTE, GOBO! WHAT'S THE TROUBLE? BAD DREAMS?
JUST THINKING. THESE DOOZERS, THE THINGS THEY BUILD!
THEY TASTE LIKE FEET!
WELL, SURE, BUT THEY'RE SO INSPIRING.
THEY BUILD JUST TO BUILD.
THEIR SCULPTURES ARE GREAT, BUT DID YOU NOTICE-- THEY'RE ALL UNFINISHED?
I THINK THERE'S A LOT TO BE SAID FOR BEING CREATIVE, IT'S TRUE. I JUST WONDER IF THEY HAVE A PLAN.
HMMM.

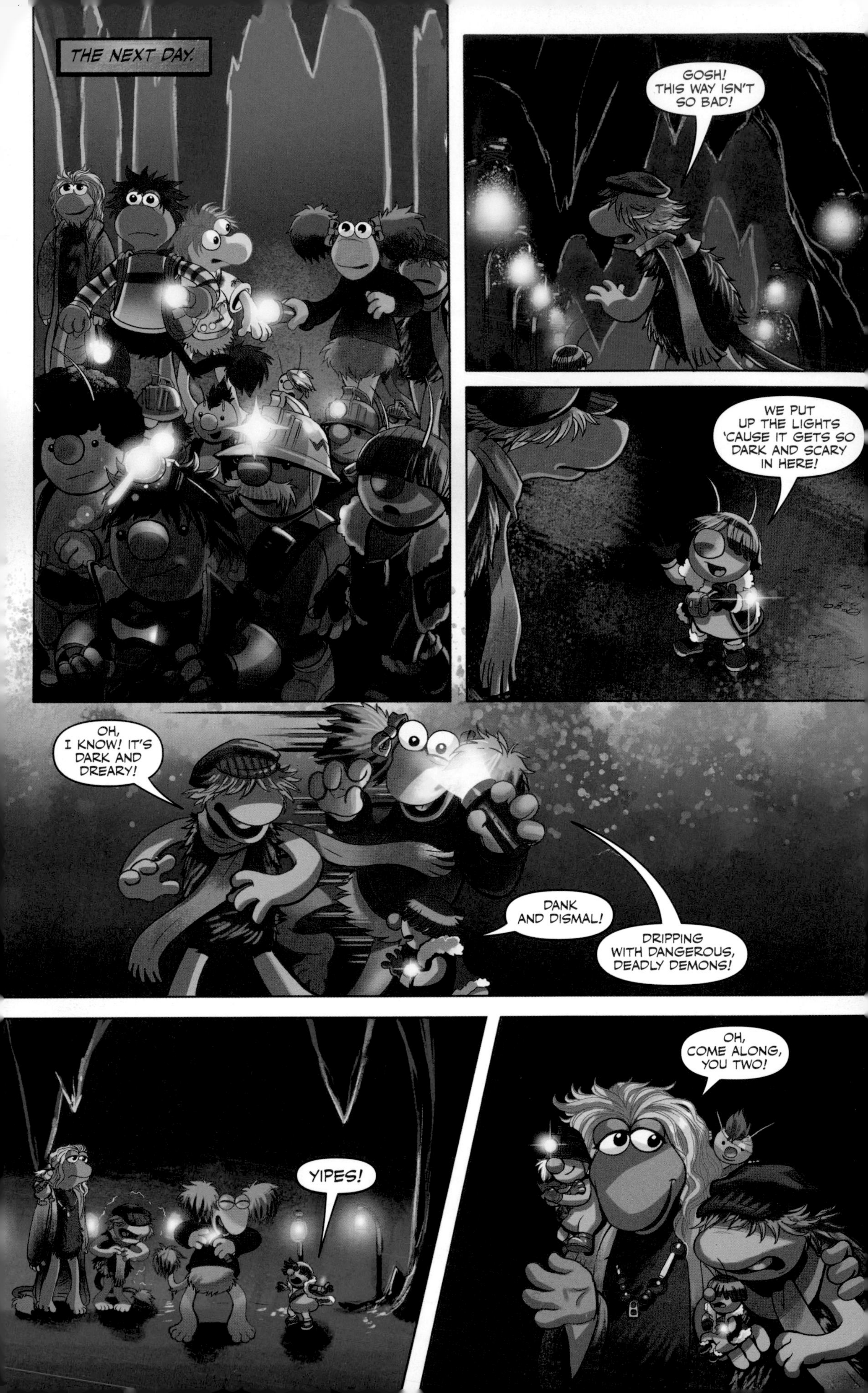
THE NEXT DAY.
GOSH! THIS WAY ISN'T SO BAD!
WE PUT UP THE LIGHTS 'CAUSE IT GETS SO DARK AND SCARY IN HERE!
OH, I KNOW! IT'S DARK AND DREARY!
DANK AND DISMAL!
DRIPPING WITH DANGEROUS, DEADLY DEMONS!
YIPES!
OH, COME ALONG, YOU TWO!

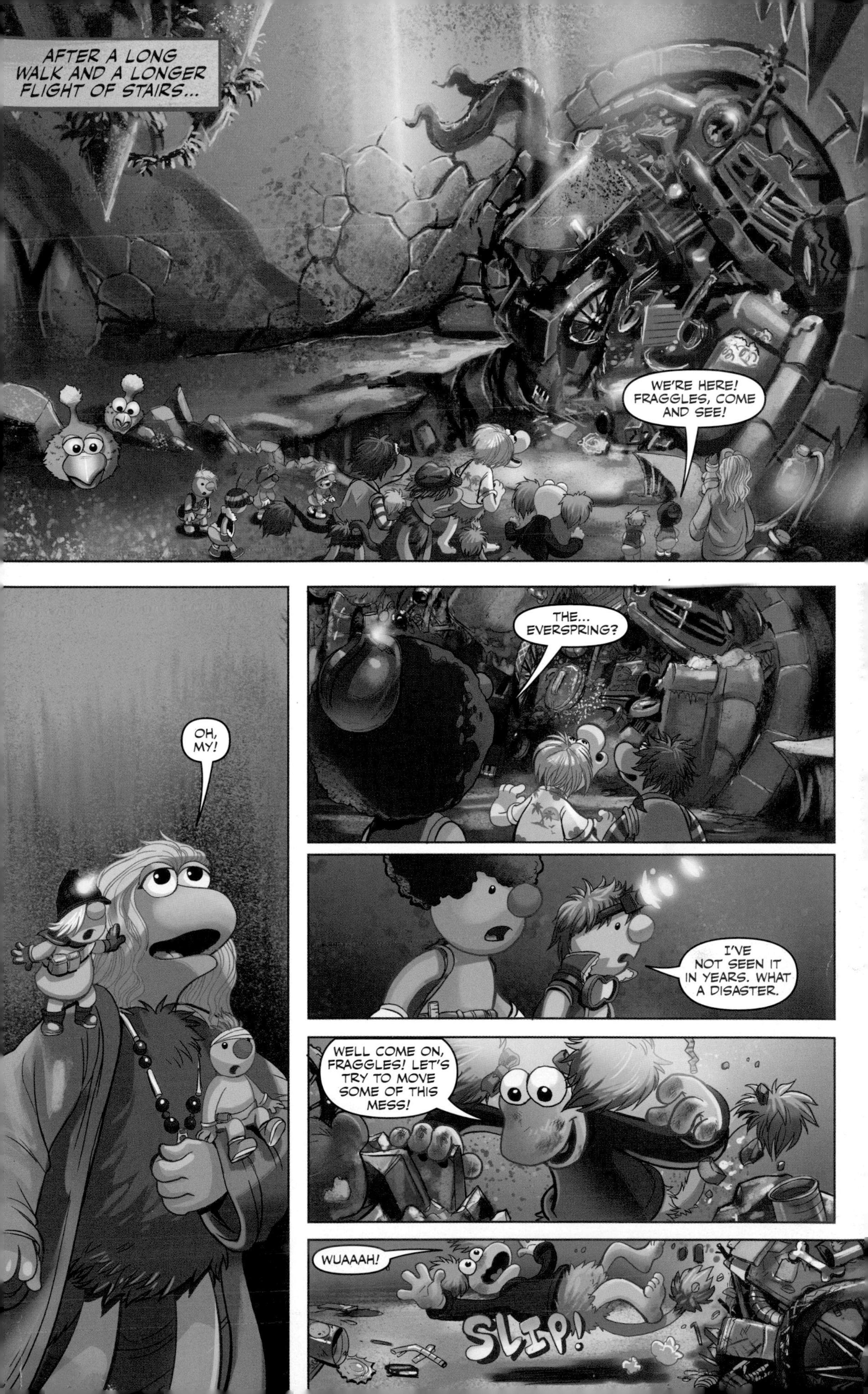
AFTER A LONG WALK AND A LONGER FLIGHT OF STAIRS...
WE'RE HERE! FRAGGLES, COME AND SEE!
OH, MY!
THE... EVERSPRING?
I'VE NOT SEEN IT IN YEARS. WHAT A DISASTER.
WELL COME ON, FRAGGLES! LET'S TRY TO MOVE SOME OF THIS MESS!
WUAAAH!
SLIP!

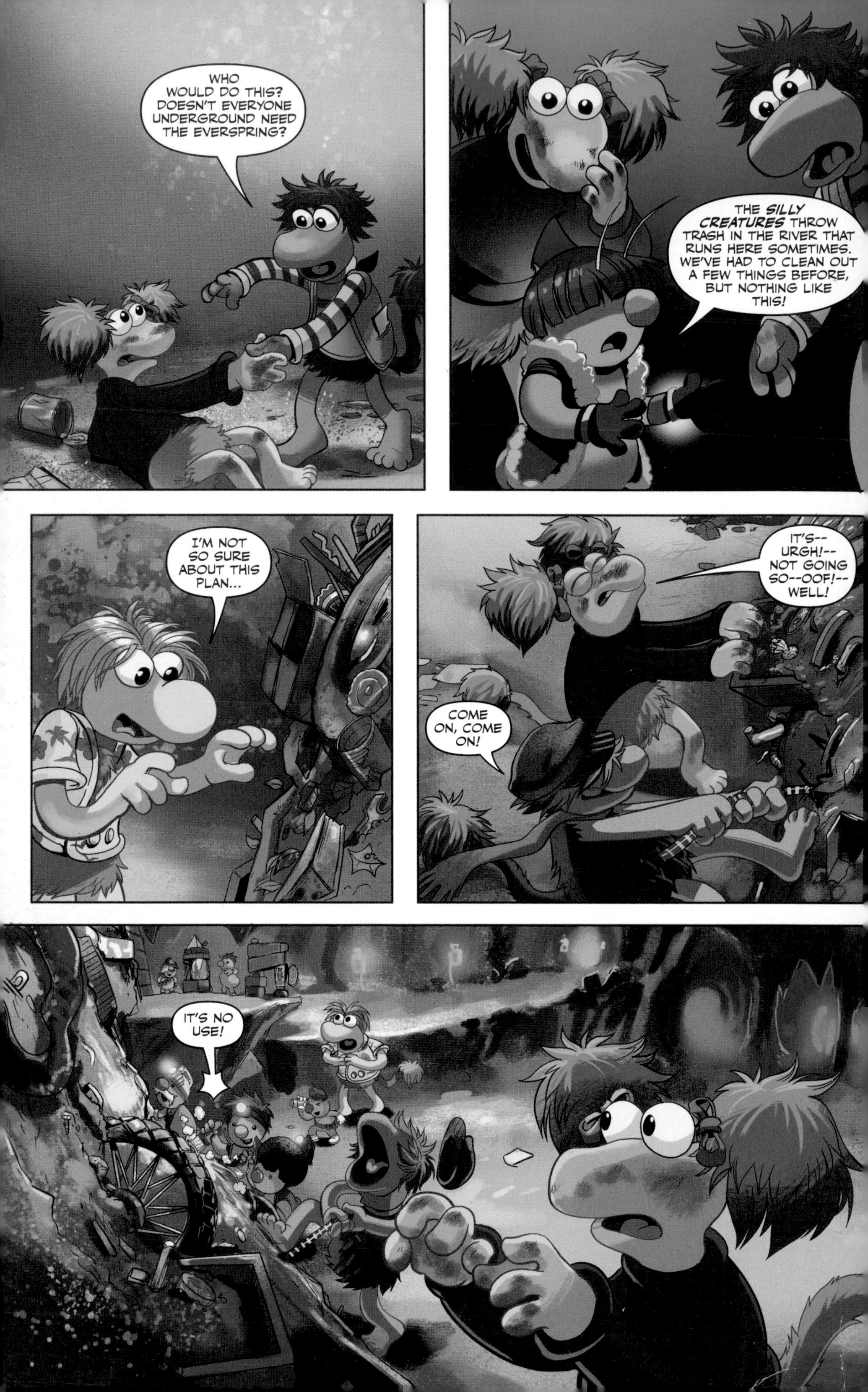
WHO WOULD DO THIS? DOESN'T EVERYONE UNDERGROUND NEED THE EVERSPRING?
THE *SILLY CREATURES* THROW TRASH IN THE RIVER THAT RUNS HERE SOMETIMES. WE'VE HAD TO CLEAN OUT A FEW THINGS BEFORE, BUT NOTHING LIKE THIS!
I'M NOT SO SURE ABOUT THIS PLAN...
IT'S-- URGH!-- NOT GOING SO--OOF!-- WELL!
COME ON, COME ON!
IT'S NO USE!

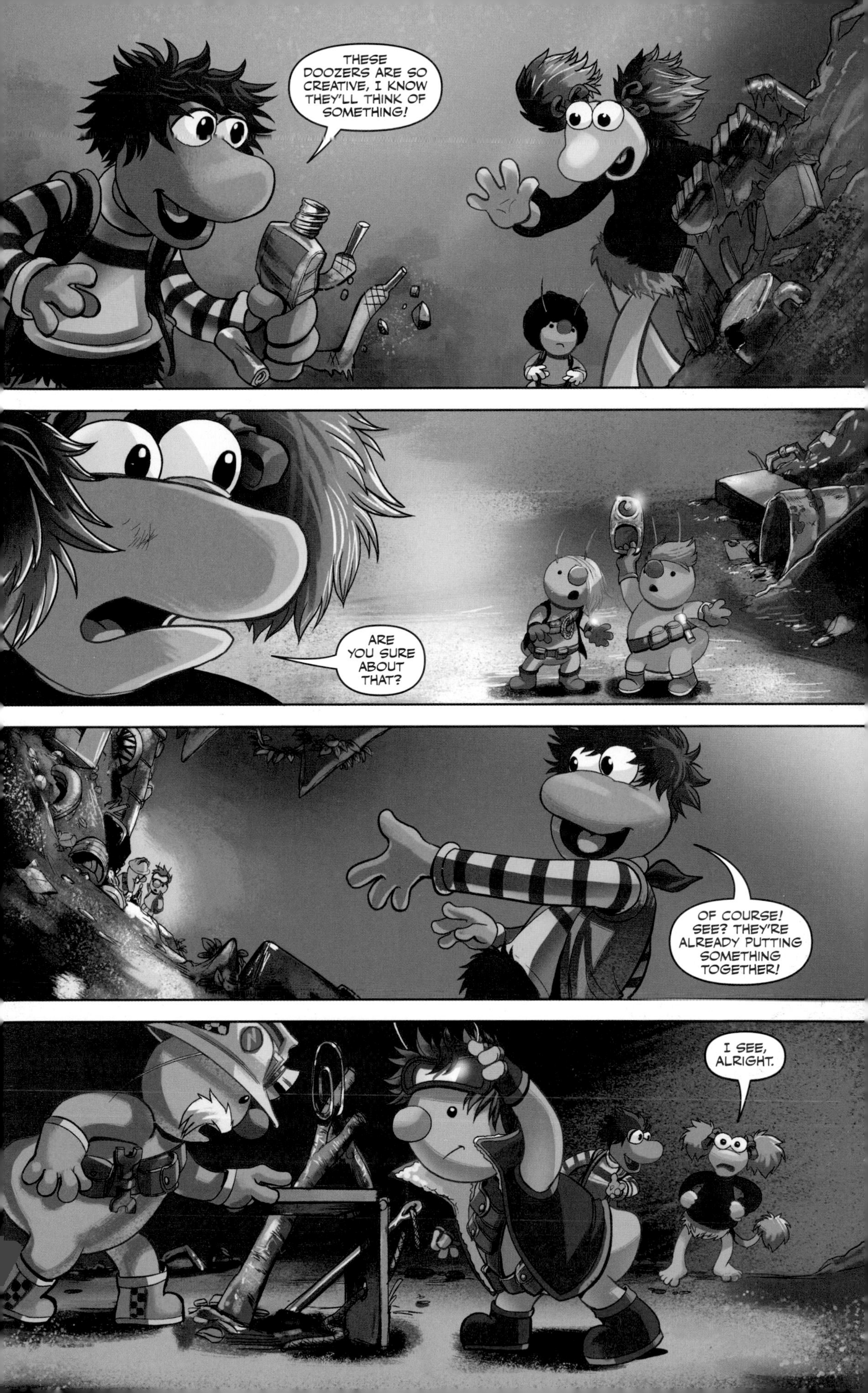
THESE DOOZERS ARE SO CREATIVE, I KNOW THEY'LL THINK OF SOMETHING!
ARE YOU SURE ABOUT THAT?
OF COURSE! SEE? THEY'RE ALREADY PUTTING SOMETHING TOGETHER!
I SEE, ALRIGHT.

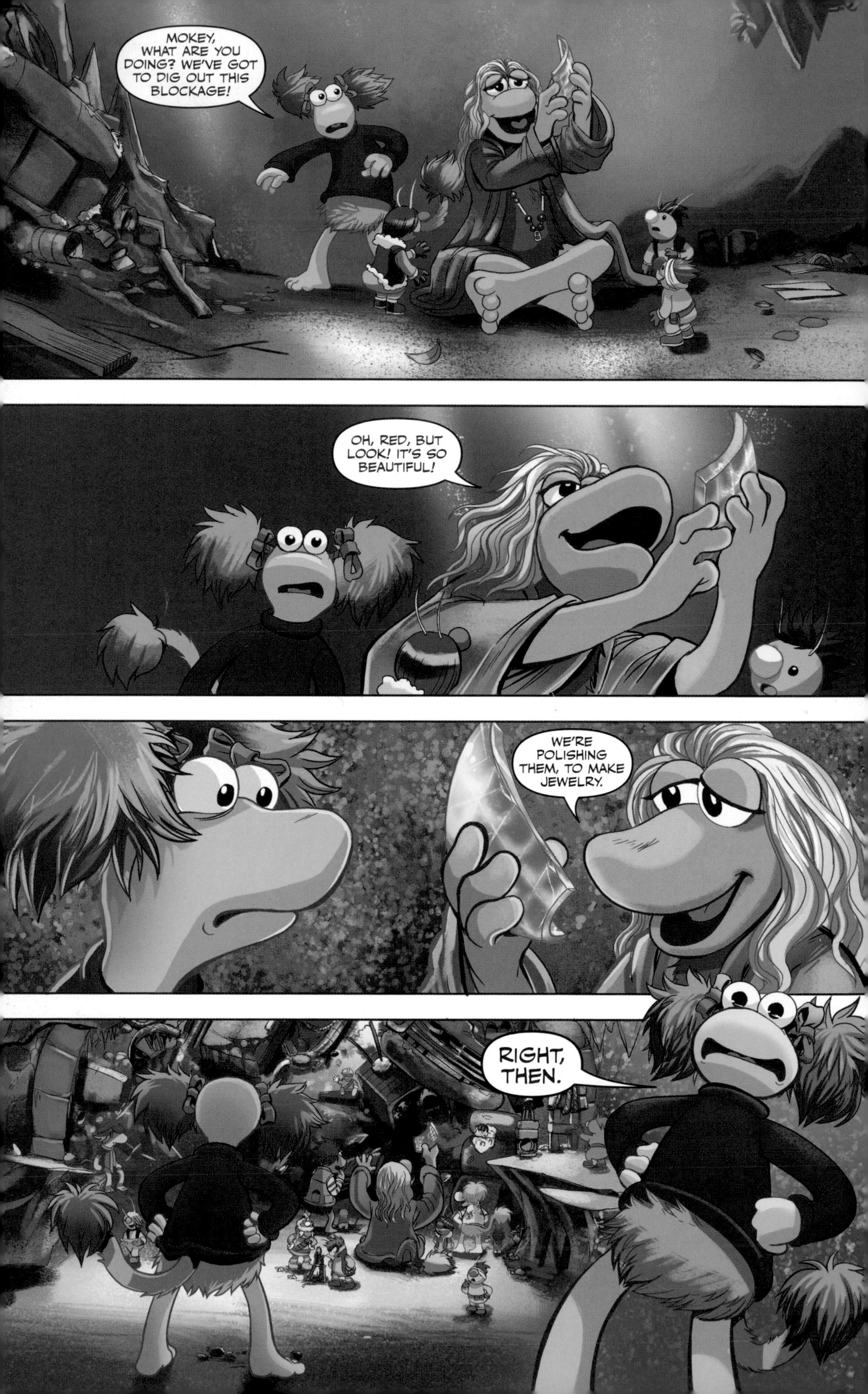
MOKEY, WHAT ARE YOU DOING? WE'VE GOT TO DIG OUT THIS BLOCKAGE!
OH, RED, BUT LOOK! IT'S SO BEAUTIFUL!
WE'RE POLISHING THEM, TO MAKE JEWELRY.
RIGHT, THEN.

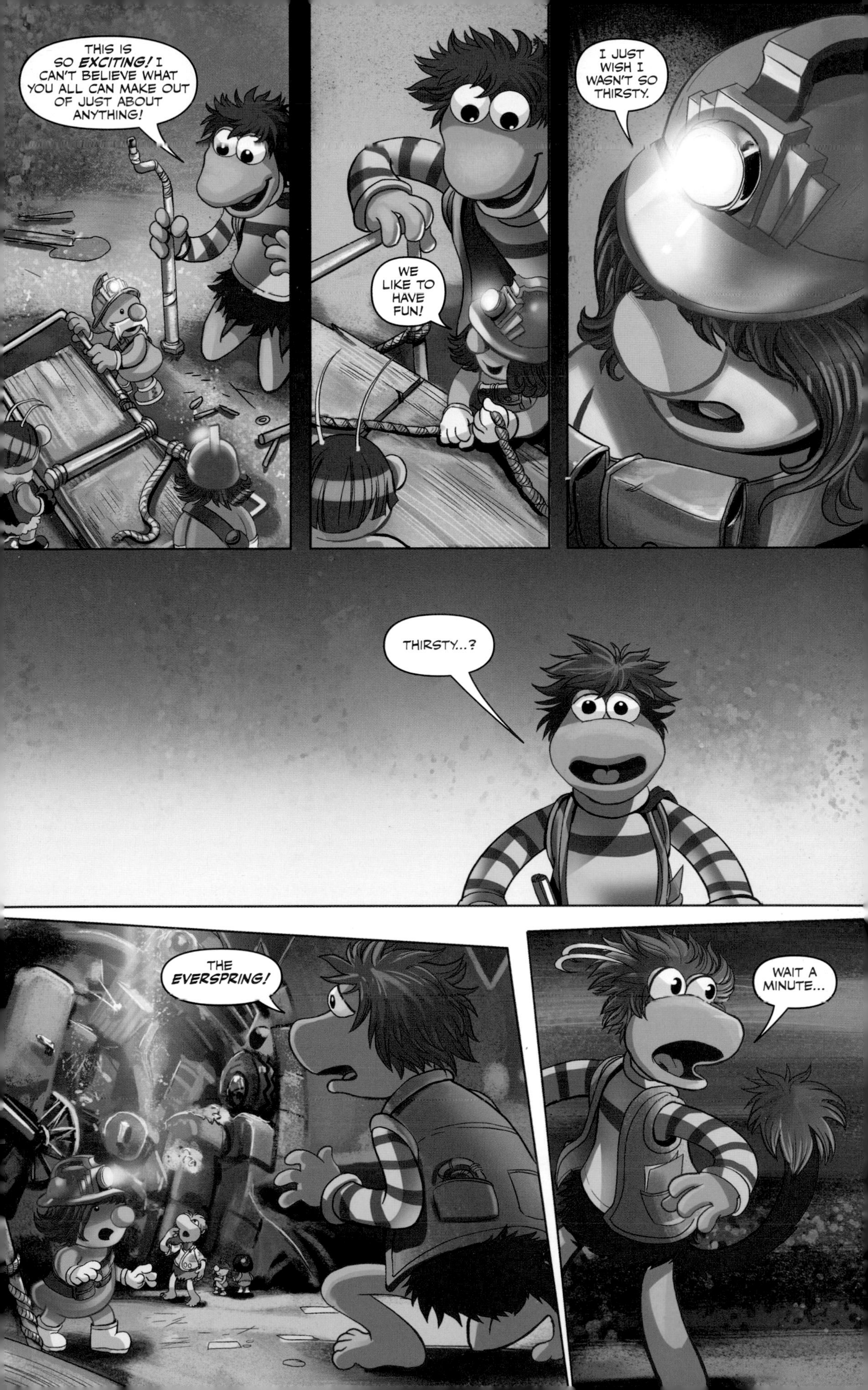
THIS IS SO *EXCITING!* I CAN'T BELIEVE WHAT YOU ALL CAN MAKE OUT OF JUST ABOUT ANYTHING!
WE LIKE TO HAVE FUN!
I JUST WISH I WASN'T SO THIRSTY.
THIRSTY...?
THE *EVERSPRING!*
WAIT A MINUTE...

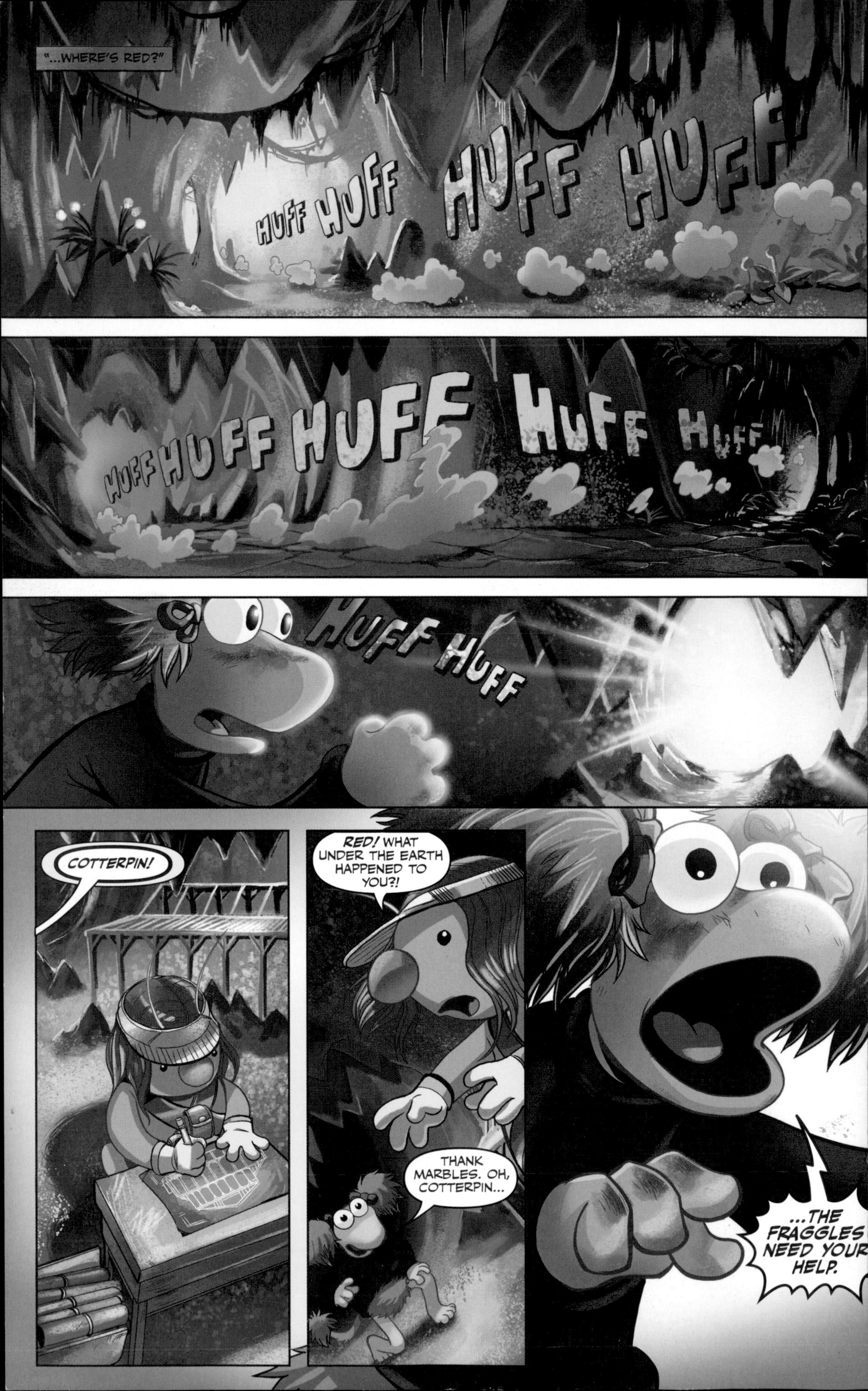
"...WHERE'S RED?"
HUFF HUFF HUFF HUFF
HUFF HUFF HUFF HUFF HUFF
HUFF HUFF
COTTERPIN!
RED! WHAT UNDER THE EARTH HAPPENED TO YOU?!
THANK MARBLES. OH, COTTERPIN...
...THE FRAGGLES NEED YOUR HELP.

DOWN AT FRAGGLE ROCK

CHAPTER FOUR

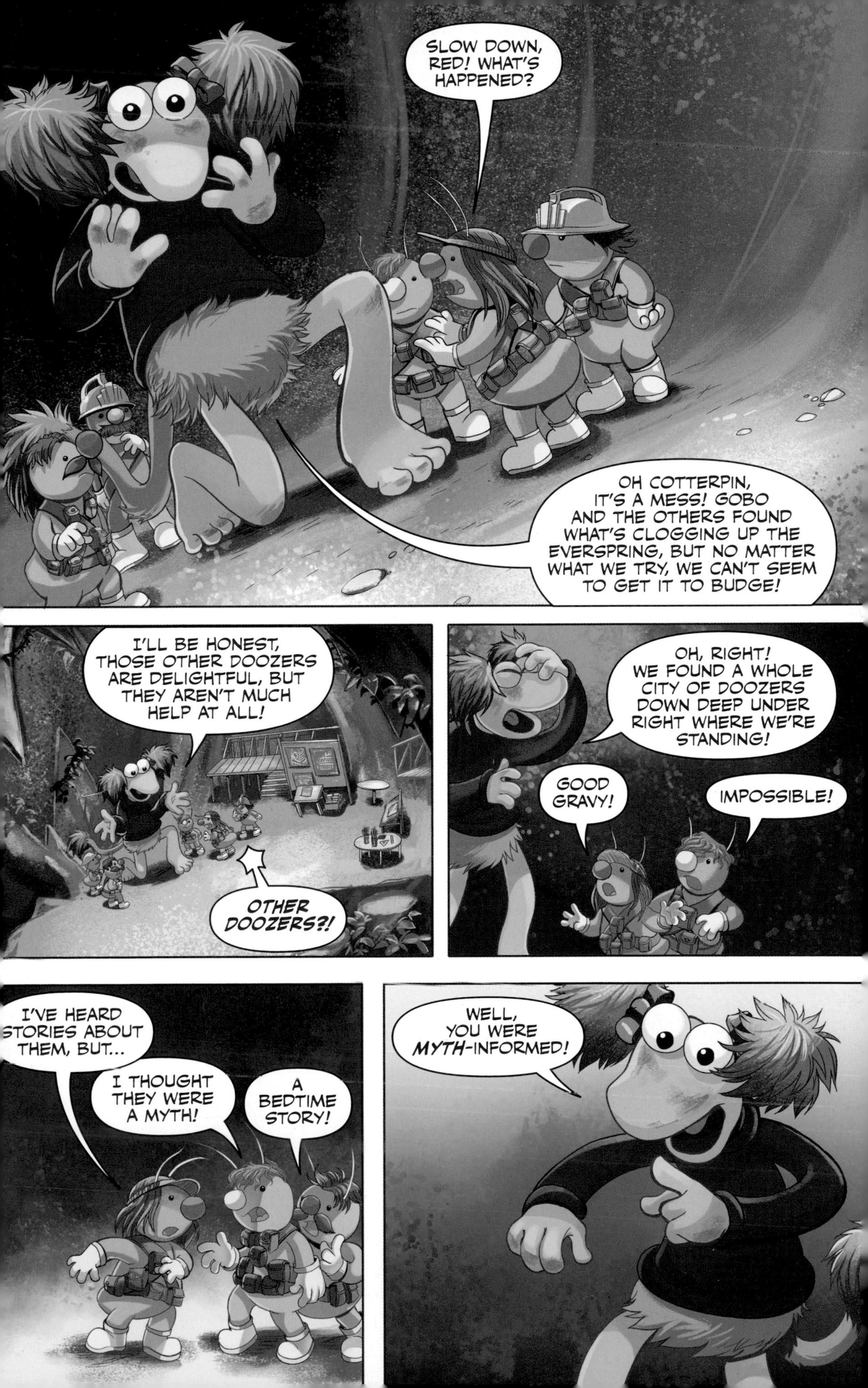
SLOW DOWN, RED! WHAT'S HAPPENED?
OH COTTERPIN, IT'S A MESS! GOBO AND THE OTHERS FOUND WHAT'S CLOGGING UP THE EVERSPRING, BUT NO MATTER WHAT WE TRY, WE CAN'T SEEM TO GET IT TO BUDGE!
I'LL BE HONEST, THOSE OTHER DOOZERS ARE DELIGHTFUL, BUT THEY AREN'T MUCH HELP AT ALL!
OTHER DOOZERS?!
OH, RIGHT! WE FOUND A WHOLE CITY OF DOOZERS DOWN DEEP UNDER RIGHT WHERE WE'RE STANDING!
GOOD GRAVY!
IMPOSSIBLE!
I'VE HEARD STORIES ABOUT THEM, BUT...
I THOUGHT THEY WERE A MYTH!
A BEDTIME STORY!
WELL, YOU WERE *MYTH*-INFORMED!

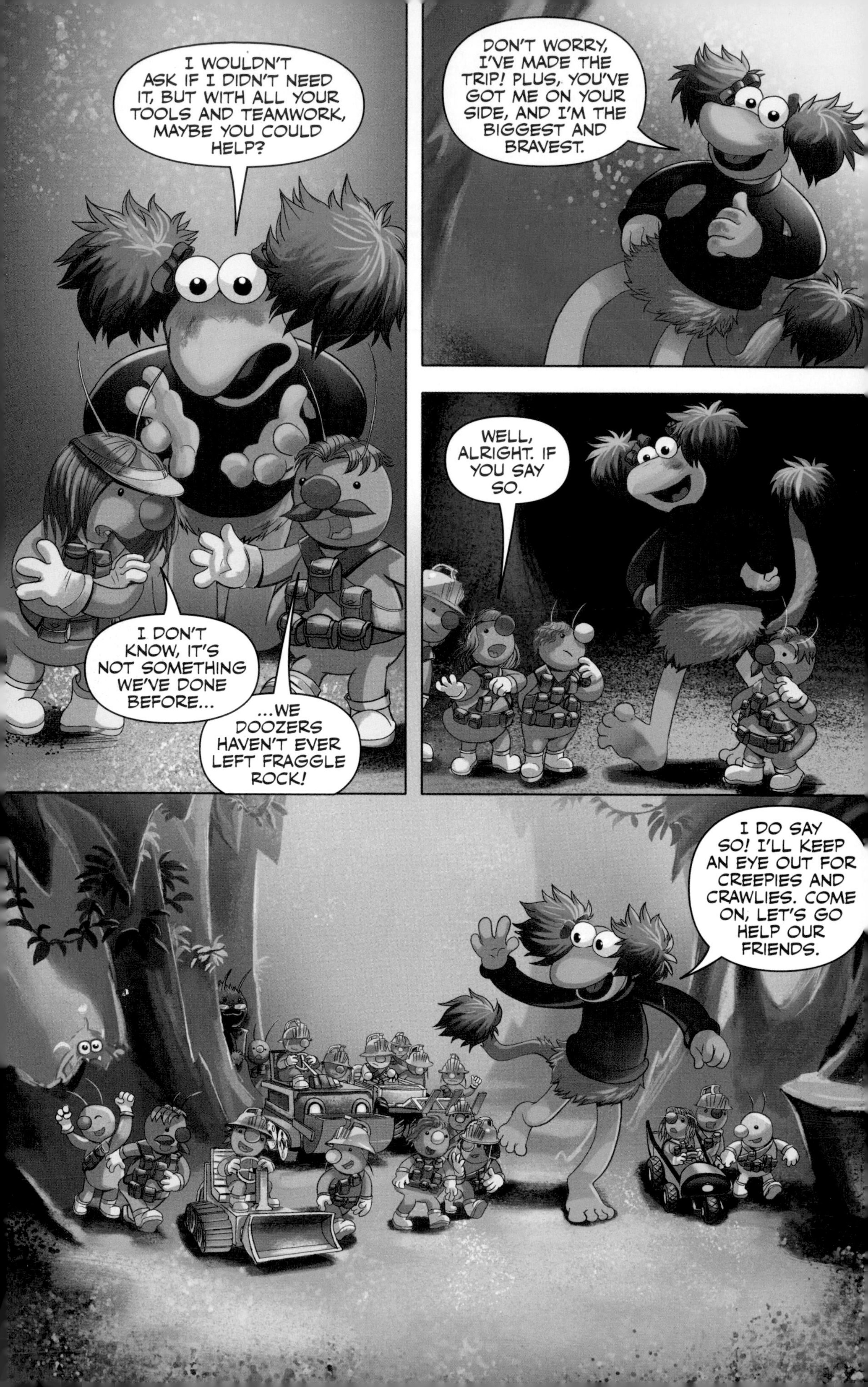
I WOULDN'T ASK IF I DIDN'T NEED IT, BUT WITH ALL YOUR TOOLS AND TEAMWORK, MAYBE YOU COULD HELP?
I DON'T KNOW, IT'S NOT SOMETHING WE'VE DONE BEFORE...
...WE DOOZERS HAVEN'T EVER LEFT FRAGGLE ROCK!
DON'T WORRY, I'VE MADE THE TRIP! PLUS, YOU'VE GOT ME ON YOUR SIDE, AND I'M THE BIGGEST AND BRAVEST.
WELL, ALRIGHT. IF YOU SAY SO.
I DO SAY SO! I'LL KEEP AN EYE OUT FOR CREEPIES AND CRAWLIES. COME ON, LET'S GO HELP OUR FRIENDS.

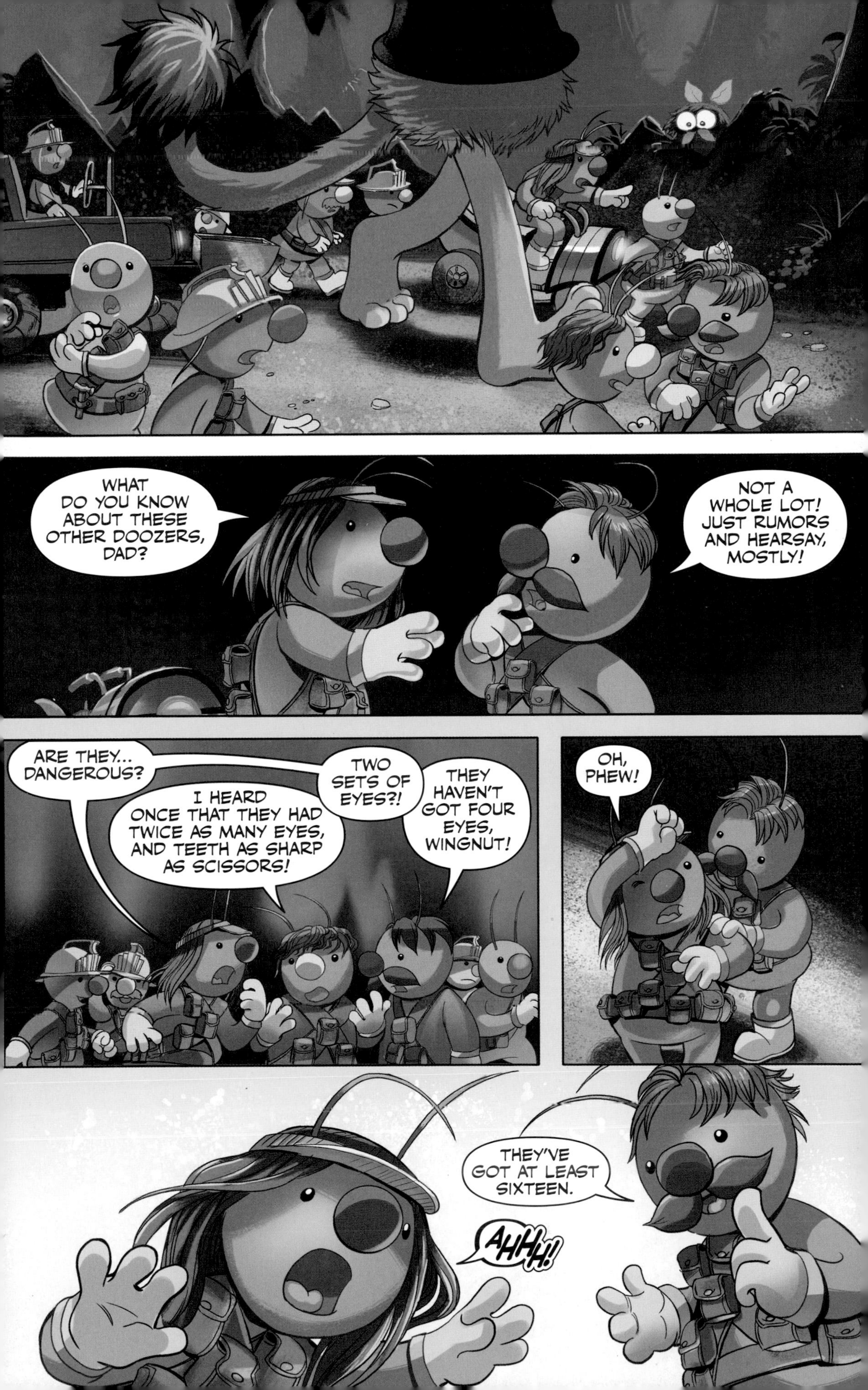
WHAT DO YOU KNOW ABOUT THESE OTHER DOOZERS, DAD?
NOT A WHOLE LOT! JUST RUMORS AND HEARSAY, MOSTLY!
ARE THEY... DANGEROUS?
I HEARD ONCE THAT THEY HAD TWICE AS MANY EYES, AND TEETH AS SHARP AS SCISSORS!
TWO SETS OF EYES?!
THEY HAVEN'T GOT FOUR EYES, WINGNUT!
OH, PHEW!
THEY'VE GOT AT LEAST SIXTEEN.
AHHH!

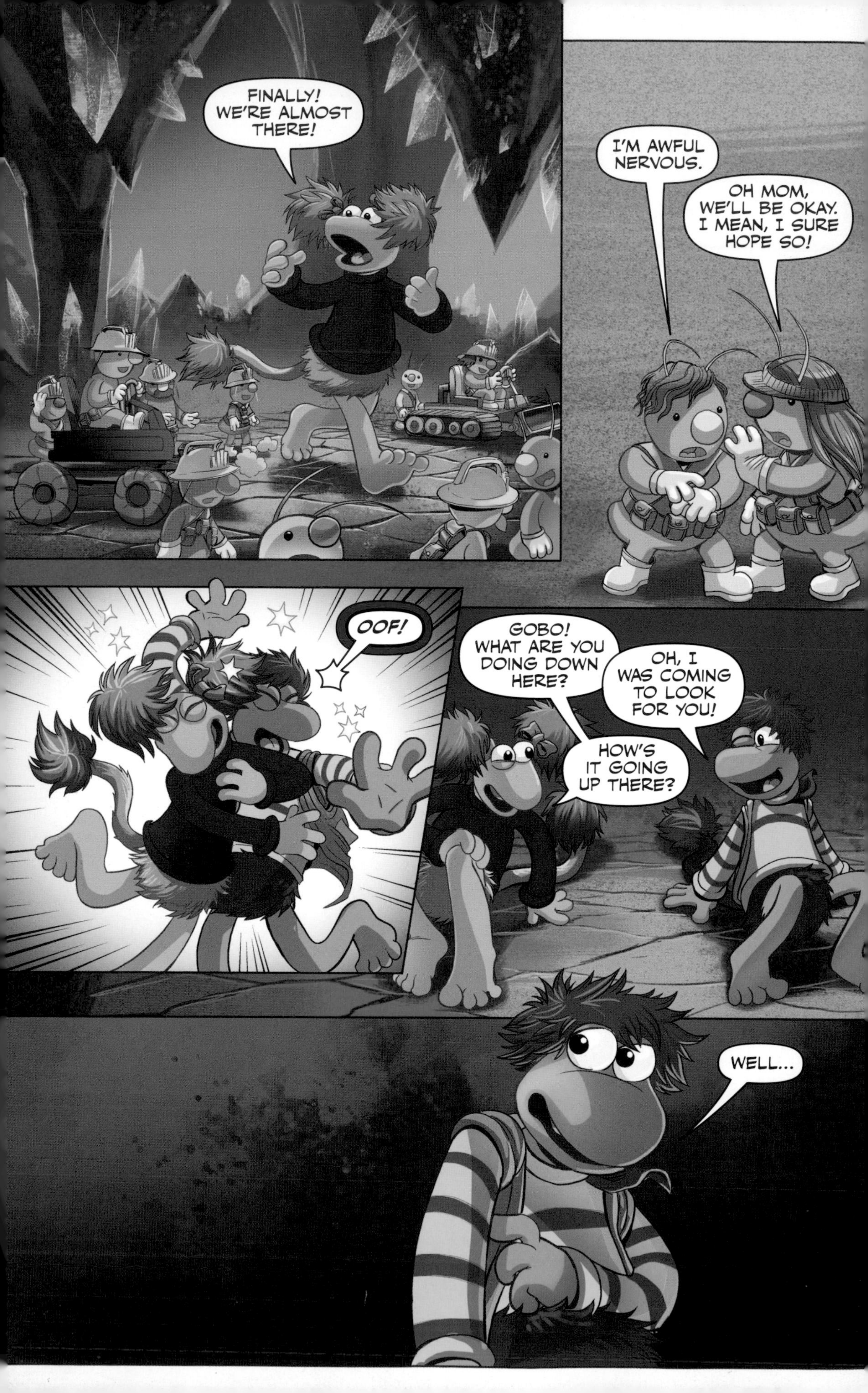
FINALLY! WE'RE ALMOST THERE!
I'M AWFUL NERVOUS.
OH MOM, WE'LL BE OKAY. I MEAN, I SURE HOPE SO!
OOF!
GOBO! WHAT ARE YOU DOING DOWN HERE?
OH, I WAS COMING TO LOOK FOR YOU!
HOW'S IT GOING UP THERE?
WELL...

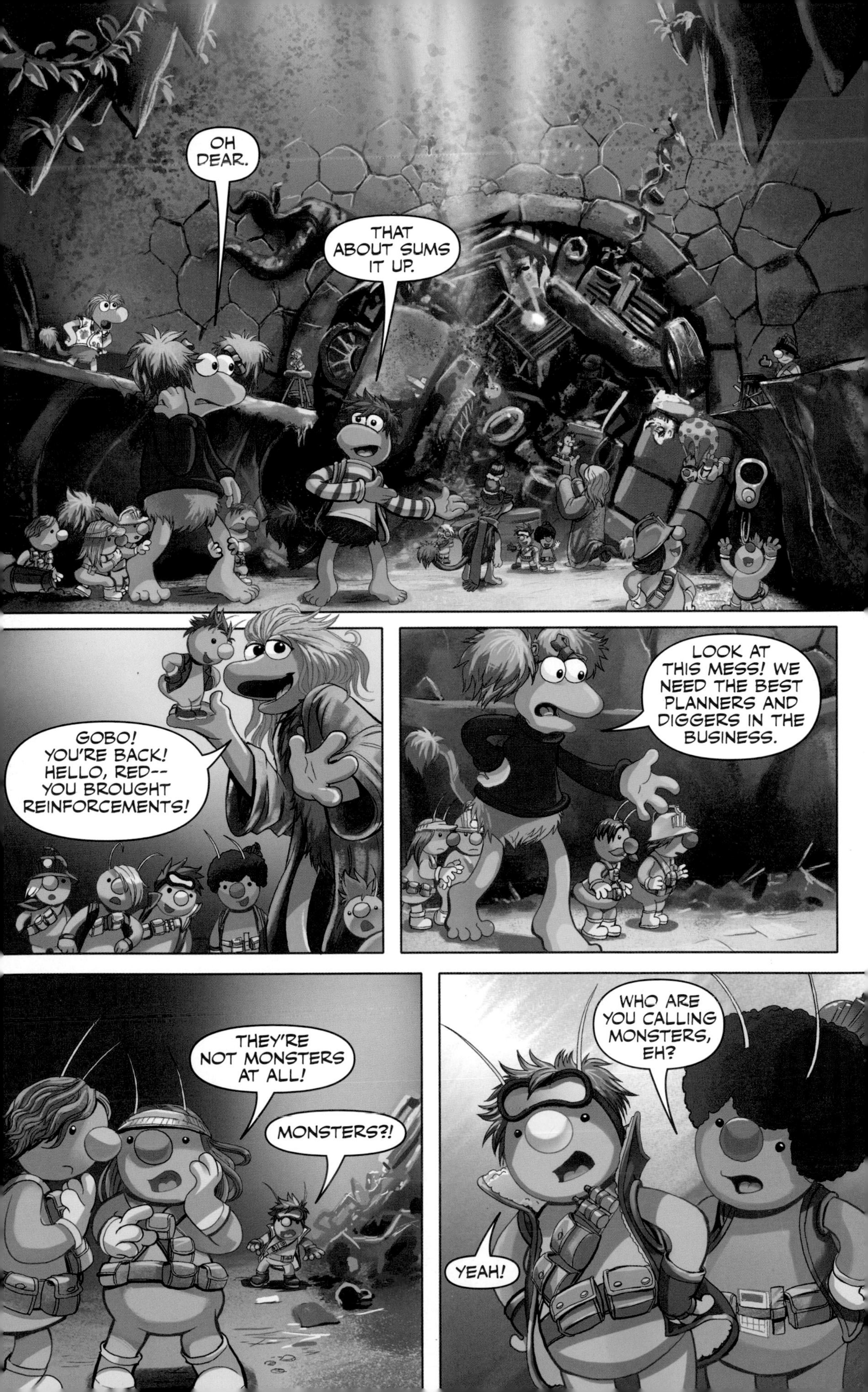
OH DEAR.
THAT ABOUT SUMS IT UP.
GOBO! YOU'RE BACK! HELLO, RED-- YOU BROUGHT REINFORCEMENTS!
LOOK AT THIS MESS! WE NEED THE BEST PLANNERS AND DIGGERS IN THE BUSINESS.
THEY'RE NOT MONSTERS AT ALL!
MONSTERS?!
WHO ARE YOU CALLING MONSTERS, EH?
YEAH!

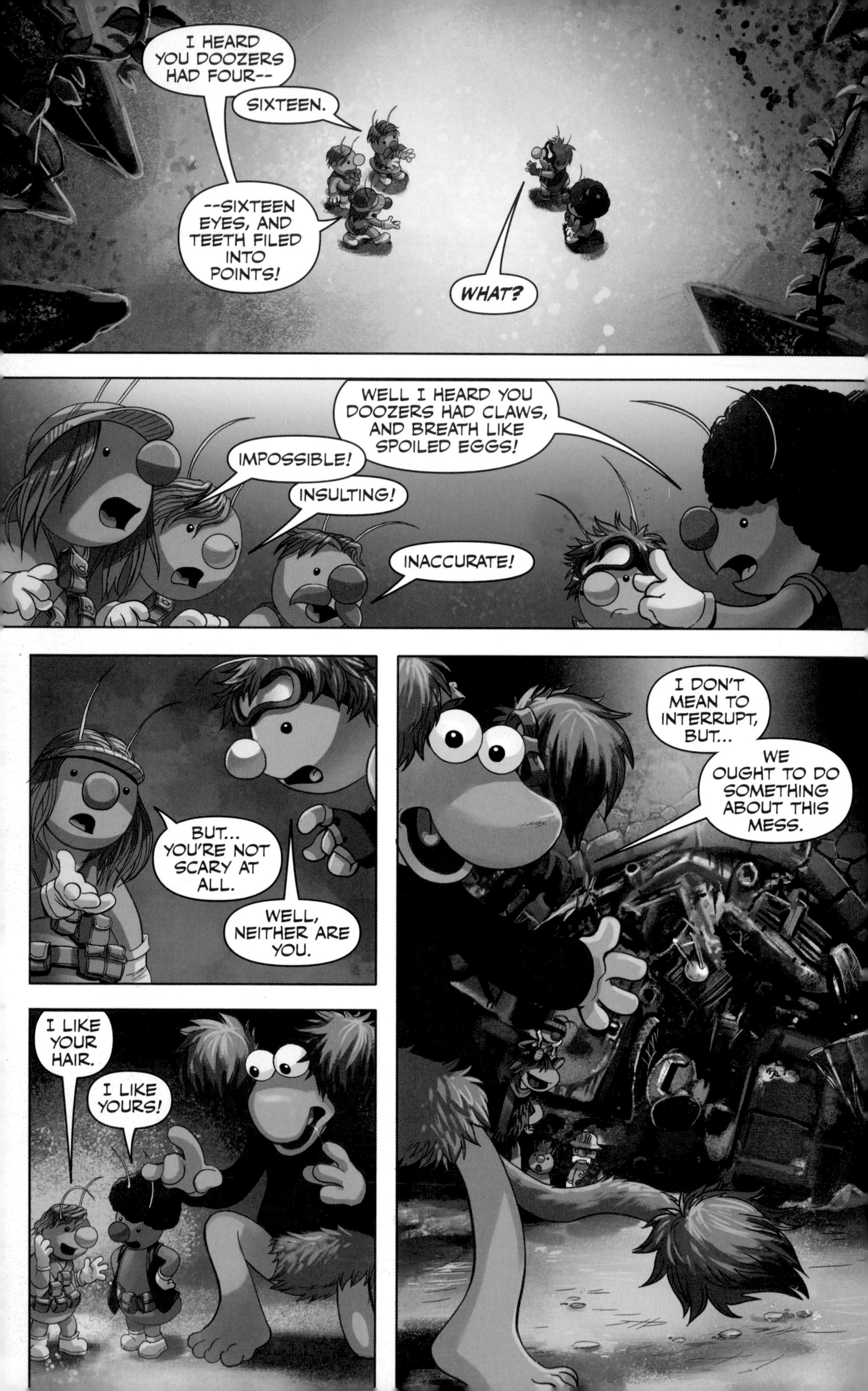
I HEARD YOU DOOZERS HAD FOUR--
SIXTEEN.
--SIXTEEN EYES, AND TEETH FILED INTO POINTS!
WHAT?
WELL I HEARD YOU DOOZERS HAD CLAWS, AND BREATH LIKE SPOILED EGGS!
IMPOSSIBLE!
INSULTING!
INACCURATE!
BUT... YOU'RE NOT SCARY AT ALL.
WELL, NEITHER ARE YOU.
I DON'T MEAN TO INTERRUPT, BUT...
WE OUGHT TO DO SOMETHING ABOUT THIS MESS.
I LIKE YOUR HAIR.
I LIKE YOURS!

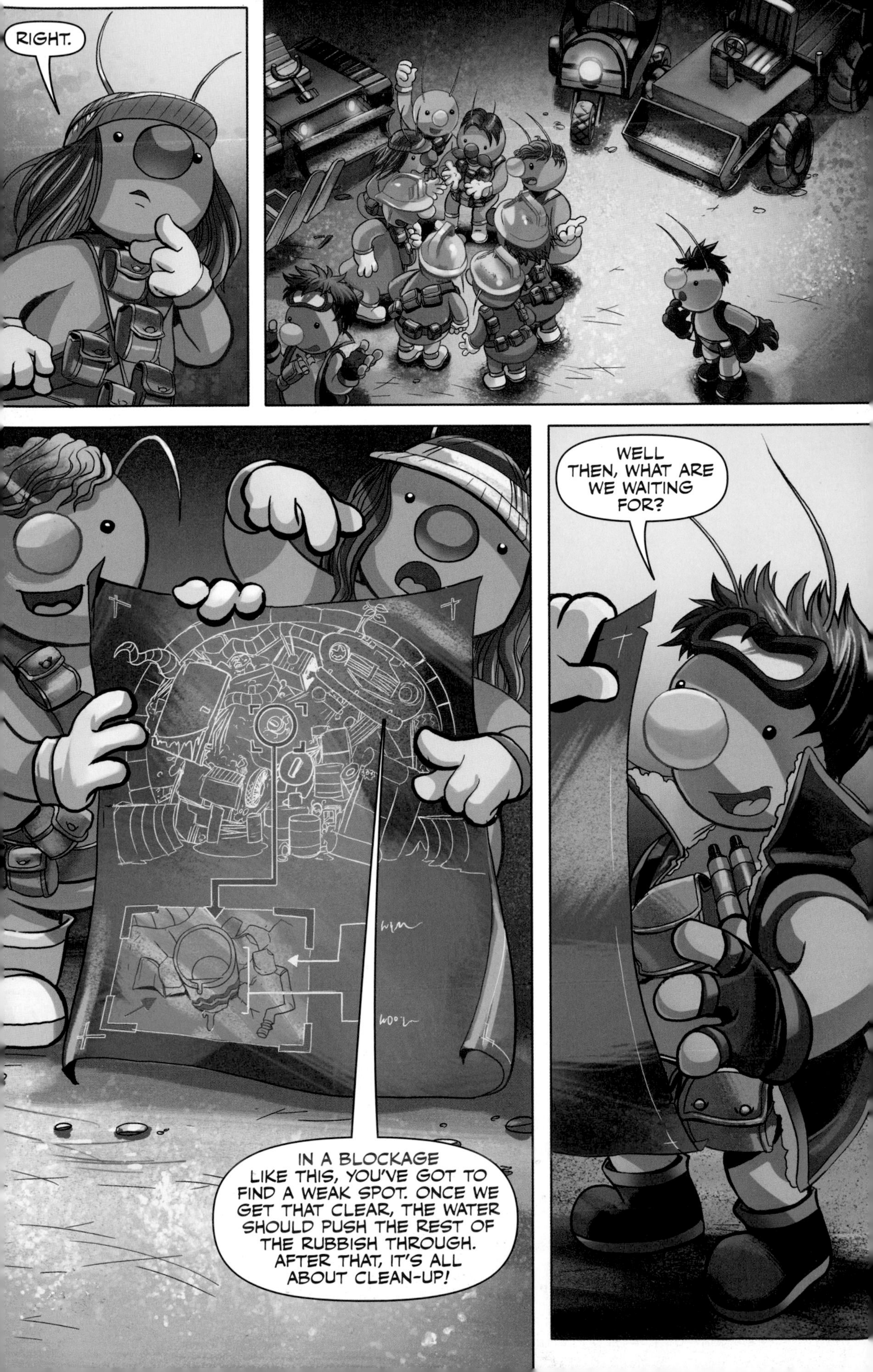
RIGHT.
WELL THEN, WHAT ARE WE WAITING FOR?
IN A BLOCKAGE LIKE THIS, YOU'VE GOT TO FIND A WEAK SPOT. ONCE WE GET THAT CLEAR, THE WATER SHOULD PUSH THE REST OF THE RUBBISH THROUGH. AFTER THAT, IT'S ALL ABOUT CLEAN-UP!

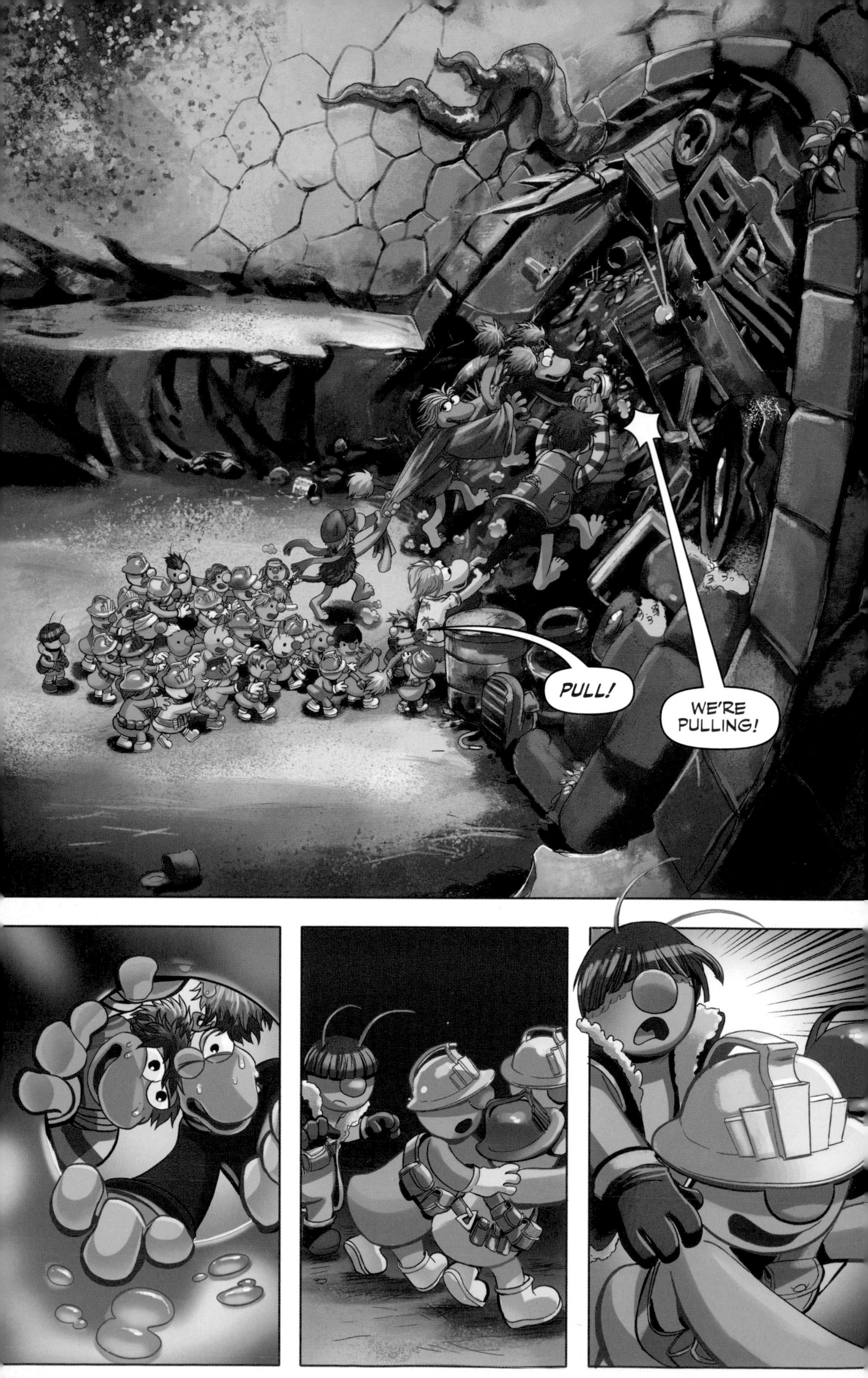
PULL!
WE'RE PULLING!

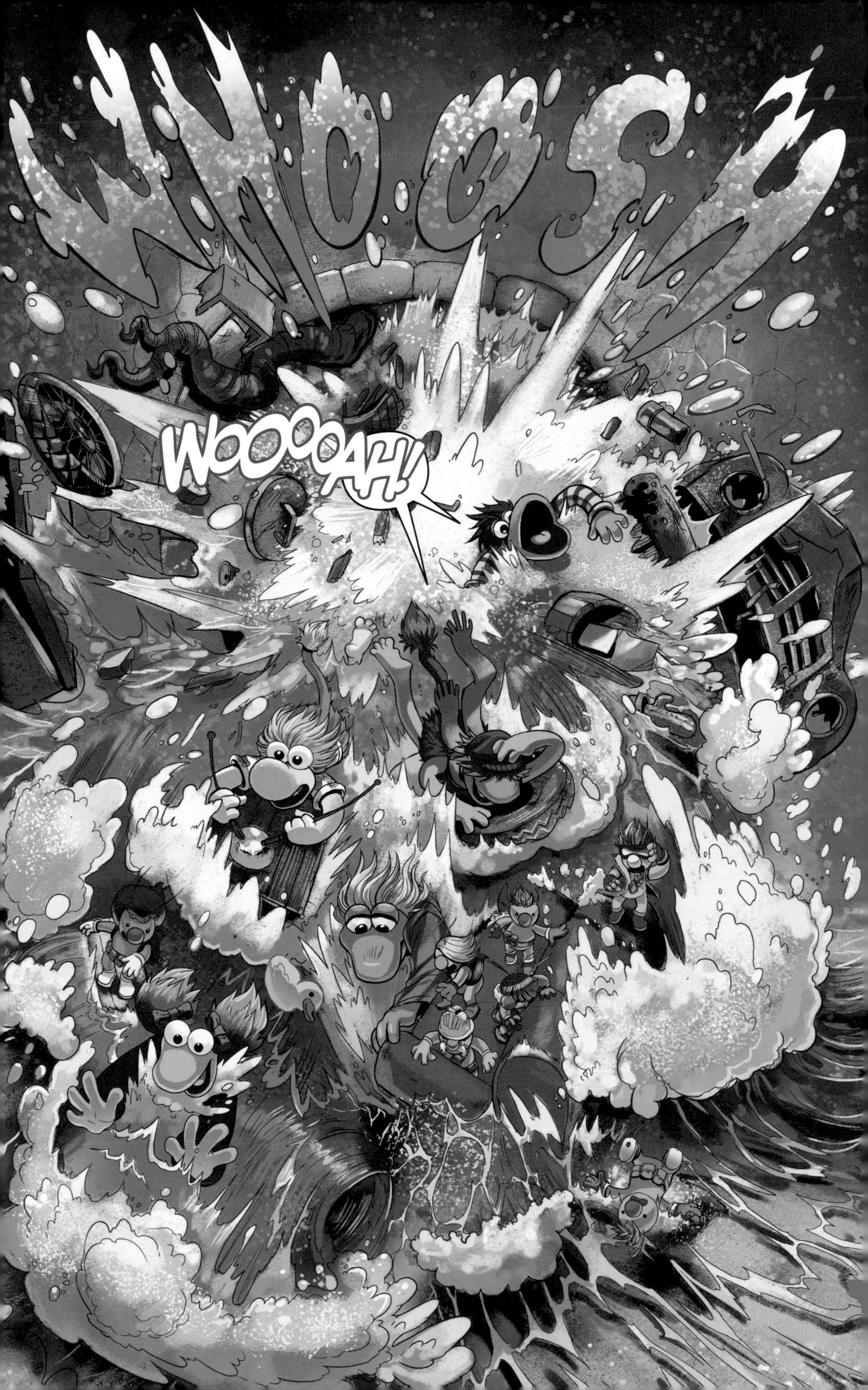
WHOOSH
WOOOOAH!!

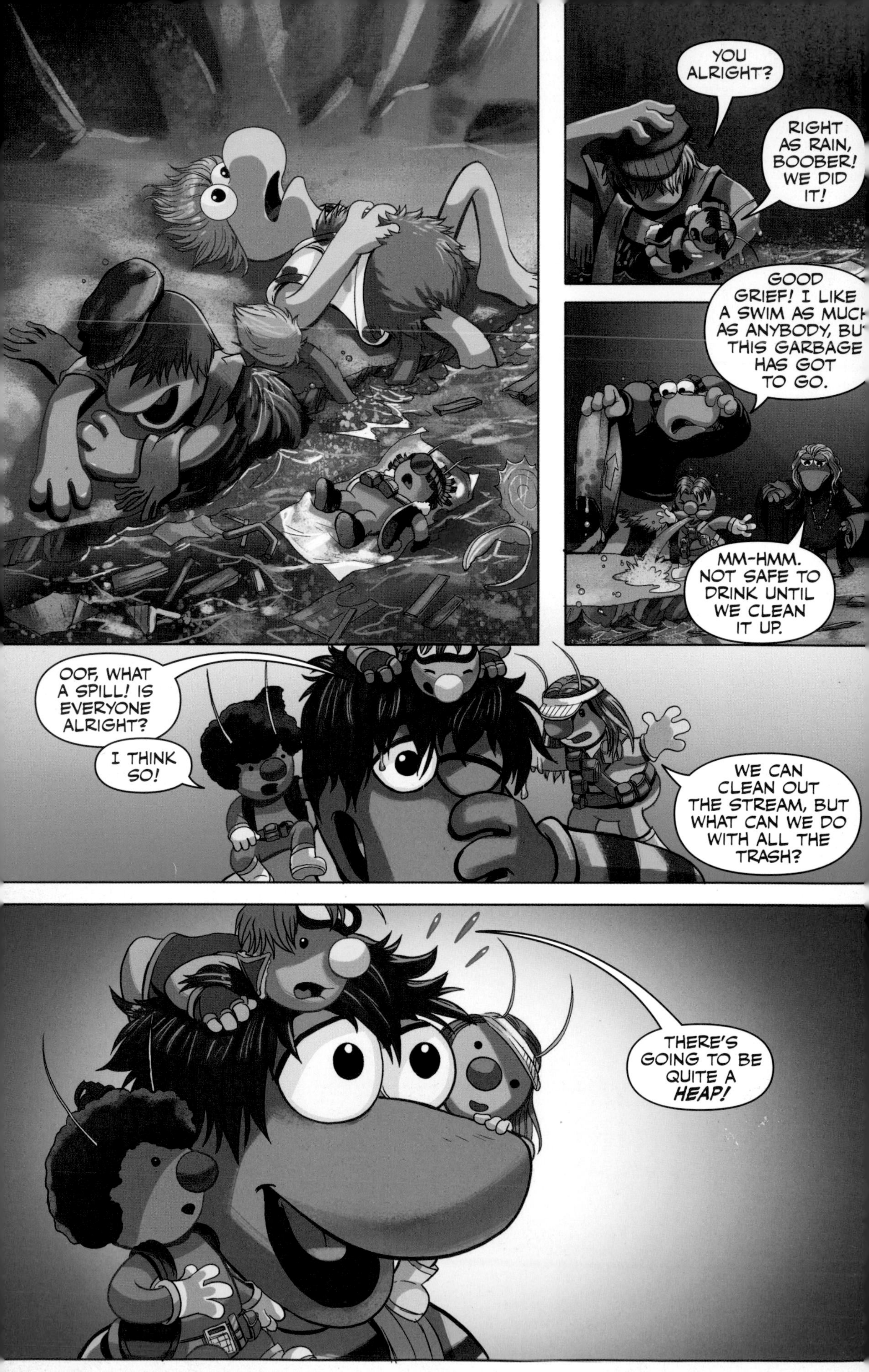
YOU ALRIGHT?
RIGHT AS RAIN, BOOBER! WE DID IT!
GOOD GRIEF! I LIKE A SWIM AS MUCH AS ANYBODY, BUT THIS GARBAGE HAS GOT TO GO.
MM-HMM. NOT SAFE TO DRINK UNTIL WE CLEAN IT UP.
OOF, WHAT A SPILL! IS EVERYONE ALRIGHT?
I THINK SO!
WE CAN CLEAN OUT THE STREAM, BUT WHAT CAN WE DO WITH ALL THE TRASH?
THERE'S GOING TO BE QUITE A *HEAP!*

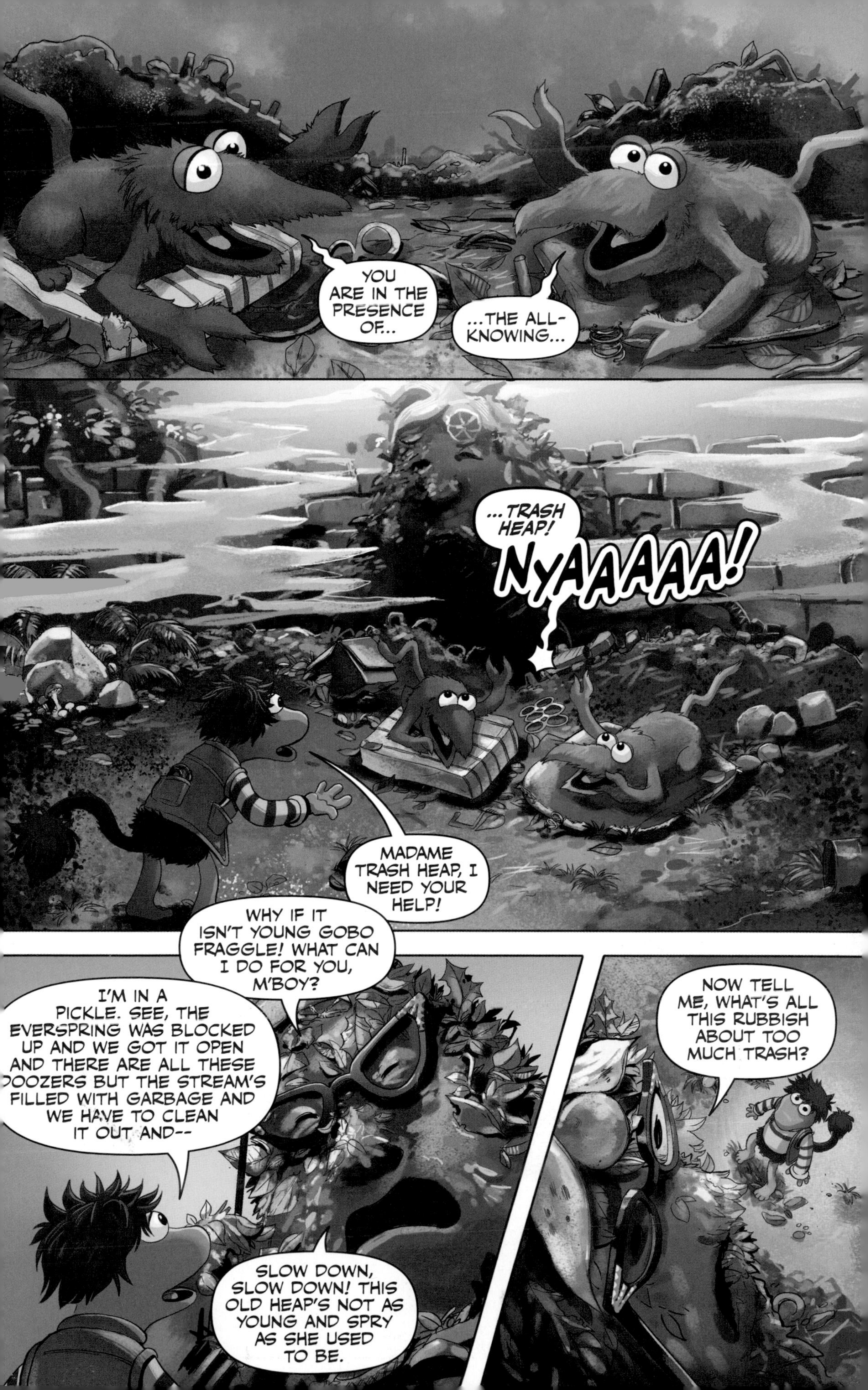
YOU ARE IN THE PRESENCE OF...
...THE ALL-KNOWING...
...TRASH HEAP!
NYAAAAA!
MADAME TRASH HEAP, I NEED YOUR HELP!
WHY IF IT ISN'T YOUNG GOBO FRAGGLE! WHAT CAN I DO FOR YOU, M'BOY?
I'M IN A PICKLE. SEE, THE EVERSPRING WAS BLOCKED UP AND WE GOT IT OPEN AND THERE ARE ALL THESE DOOZERS BUT THE STREAM'S FILLED WITH GARBAGE AND WE HAVE TO CLEAN IT OUT AND--
SLOW DOWN, SLOW DOWN! THIS OLD HEAP'S NOT AS YOUNG AND SPRY AS SHE USED TO BE.
NOW TELL ME, WHAT'S ALL THIS RUBBISH ABOUT TOO MUCH TRASH?

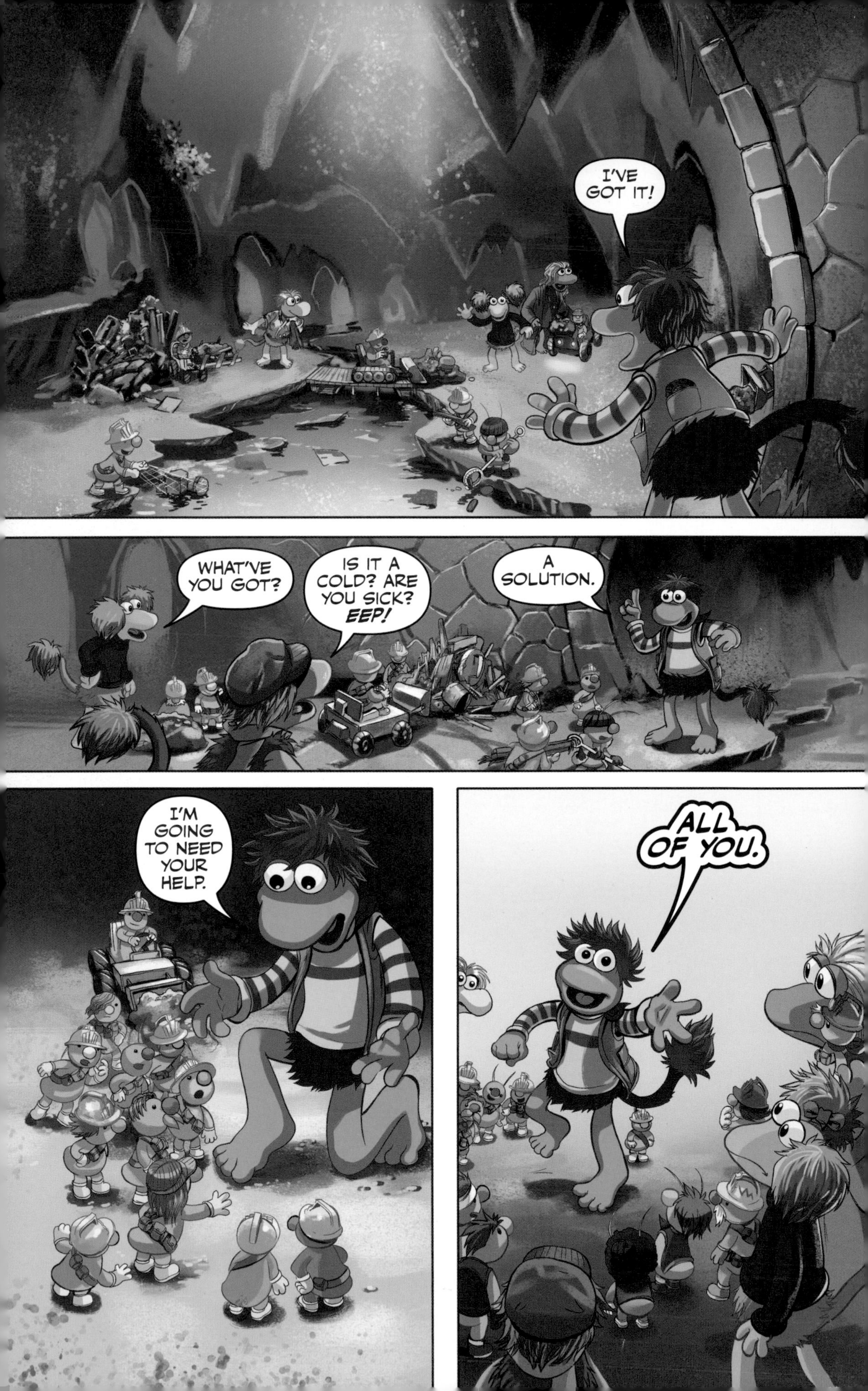
I'VE GOT IT!
WHAT'VE YOU GOT?
IS IT A COLD? ARE YOU SICK? EEP!
A SOLUTION.
I'M GOING TO NEED YOUR HELP.
ALL OF YOU.

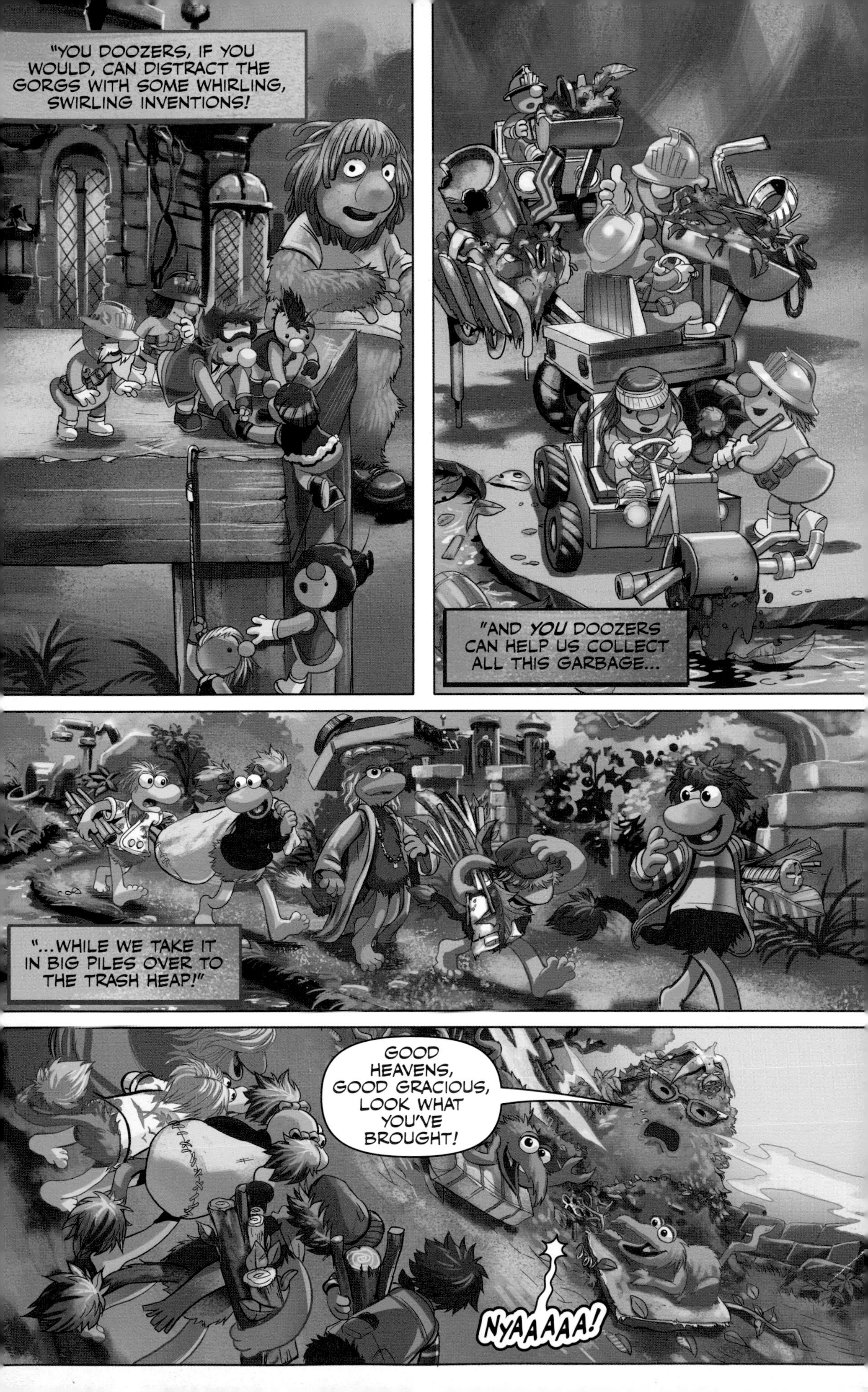
"YOU DOOZERS, IF YOU WOULD, CAN DISTRACT THE GORGS WITH SOME WHIRLING, SWIRLING INVENTIONS!
"AND *YOU* DOOZERS CAN HELP US COLLECT ALL THIS GARBAGE...
"...WHILE WE TAKE IT IN BIG PILES OVER TO THE TRASH HEAP!"
GOOD HEAVENS, GOOD GRACIOUS, LOOK WHAT YOU'VE BROUGHT!
NYAAAAA!

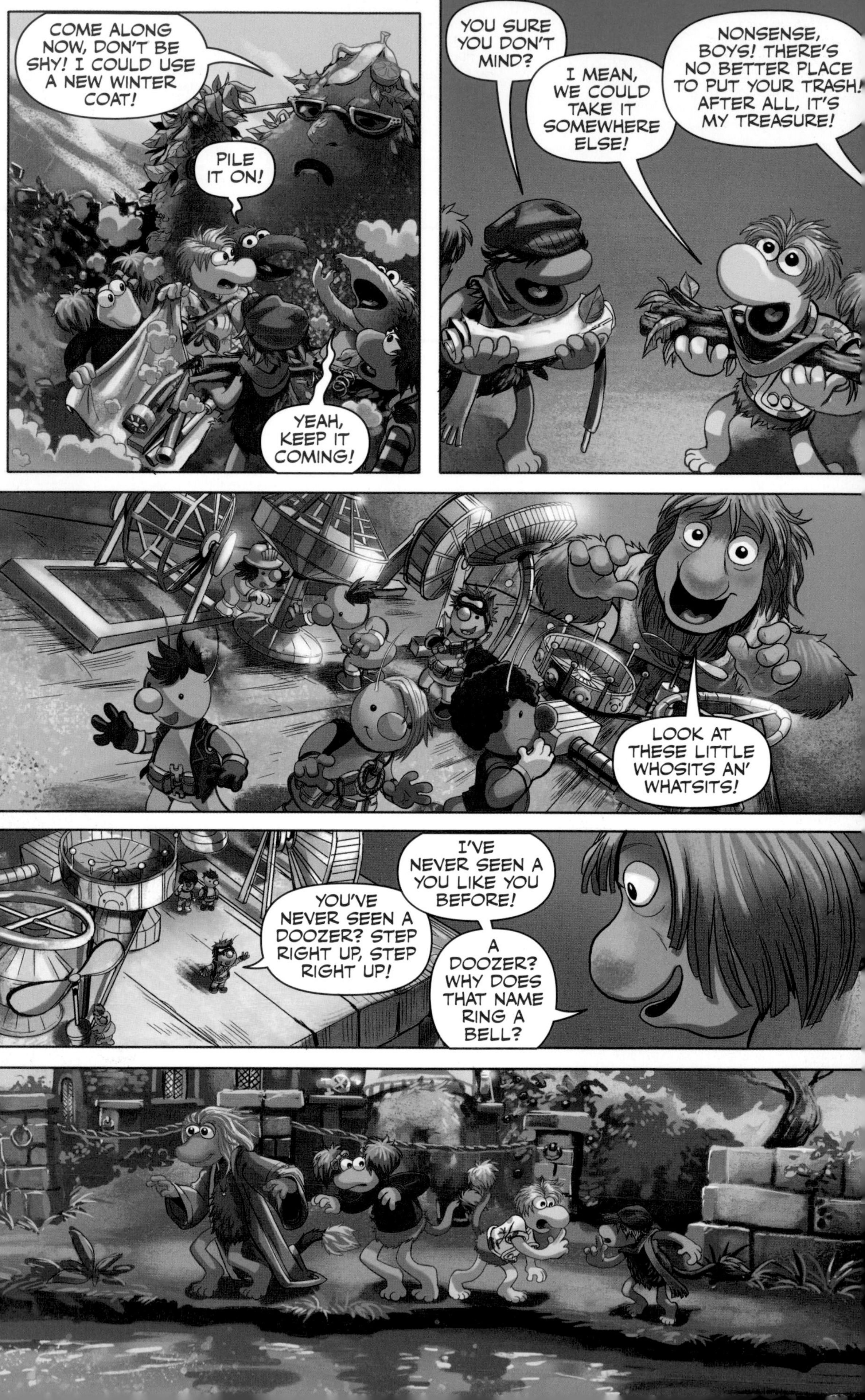
COME ALONG NOW, DON'T BE SHY! I COULD USE A NEW WINTER COAT!
PILE IT ON!
YEAH, KEEP IT COMING!
YOU SURE YOU DON'T MIND?
I MEAN, WE COULD TAKE IT SOMEWHERE ELSE!
NONSENSE, BOYS! THERE'S NO BETTER PLACE TO PUT YOUR TRASH! AFTER ALL, IT'S MY TREASURE!
LOOK AT THESE LITTLE WHOSITS AN' WHATSITS!
I'VE NEVER SEEN A YOU LIKE YOU BEFORE!
YOU'VE NEVER SEEN A DOOZER? STEP RIGHT UP, STEP RIGHT UP!
A DOOZER? WHY DOES THAT NAME RING A BELL?

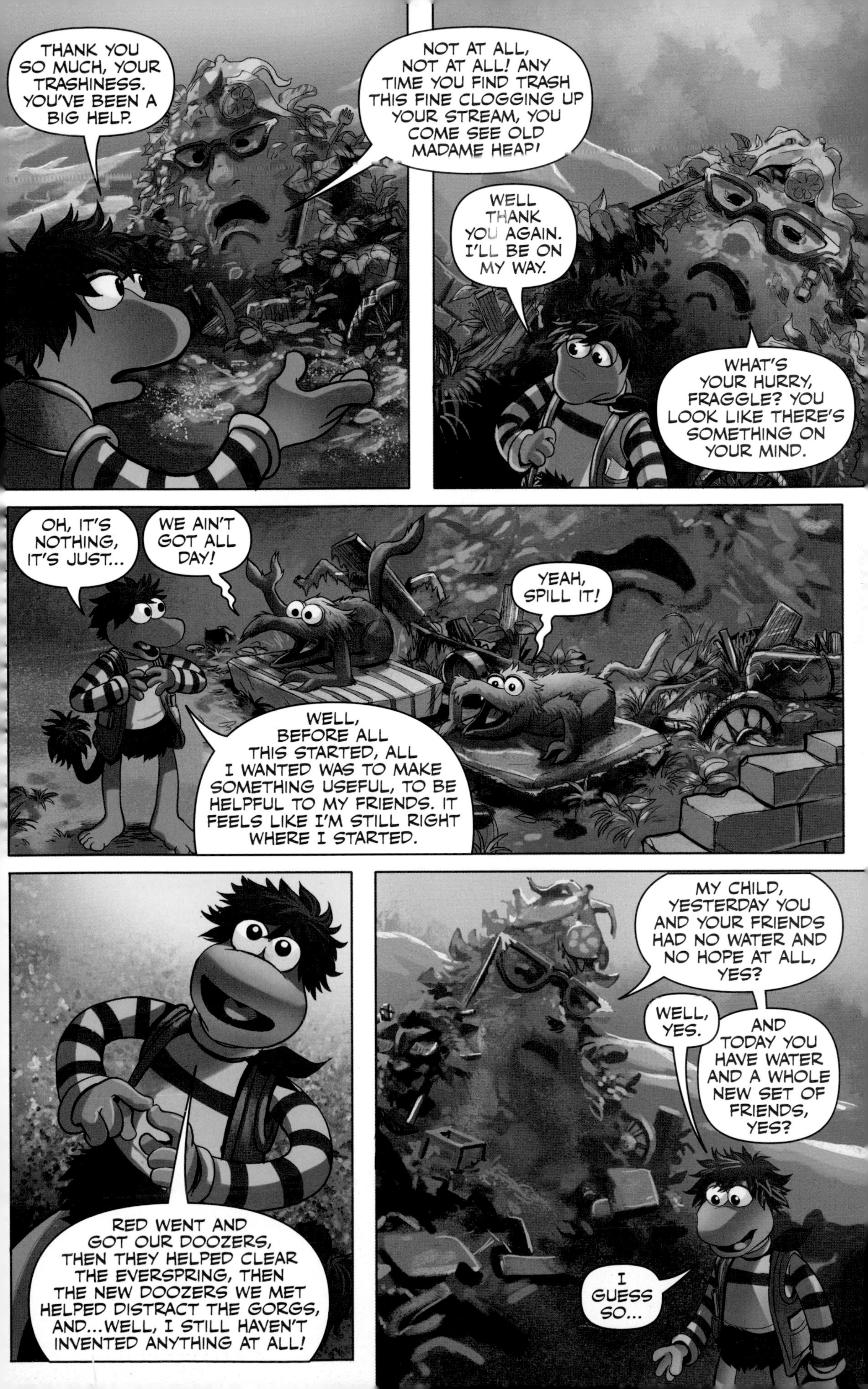

THANK YOU SO MUCH, YOUR TRASHINESS. YOU'VE BEEN A BIG HELP.
NOT AT ALL, NOT AT ALL! ANY TIME YOU FIND TRASH THIS FINE CLOGGING UP YOUR STREAM, YOU COME SEE OLD MADAME HEAP!
WELL THANK YOU AGAIN. I'LL BE ON MY WAY.
WHAT'S YOUR HURRY, FRAGGLE? YOU LOOK LIKE THERE'S SOMETHING ON YOUR MIND.
OH, IT'S NOTHING, IT'S JUST...
WE AIN'T GOT ALL DAY!
YEAH, SPILL IT!
WELL, BEFORE ALL THIS STARTED, ALL I WANTED WAS TO MAKE SOMETHING USEFUL, TO BE HELPFUL TO MY FRIENDS. IT FEELS LIKE I'M STILL RIGHT WHERE I STARTED.
RED WENT AND GOT OUR DOOZERS, THEN THEY HELPED CLEAR THE EVERSPRING, THEN THE NEW DOOZERS WE MET HELPED DISTRACT THE GORGS, AND...WELL, I STILL HAVEN'T INVENTED ANYTHING AT ALL!
MY CHILD, YESTERDAY YOU AND YOUR FRIENDS HAD NO WATER AND NO HOPE AT ALL, YES?
WELL, YES.
AND TODAY YOU HAVE WATER AND A WHOLE NEW SET OF FRIENDS, YES?
I GUESS SO...

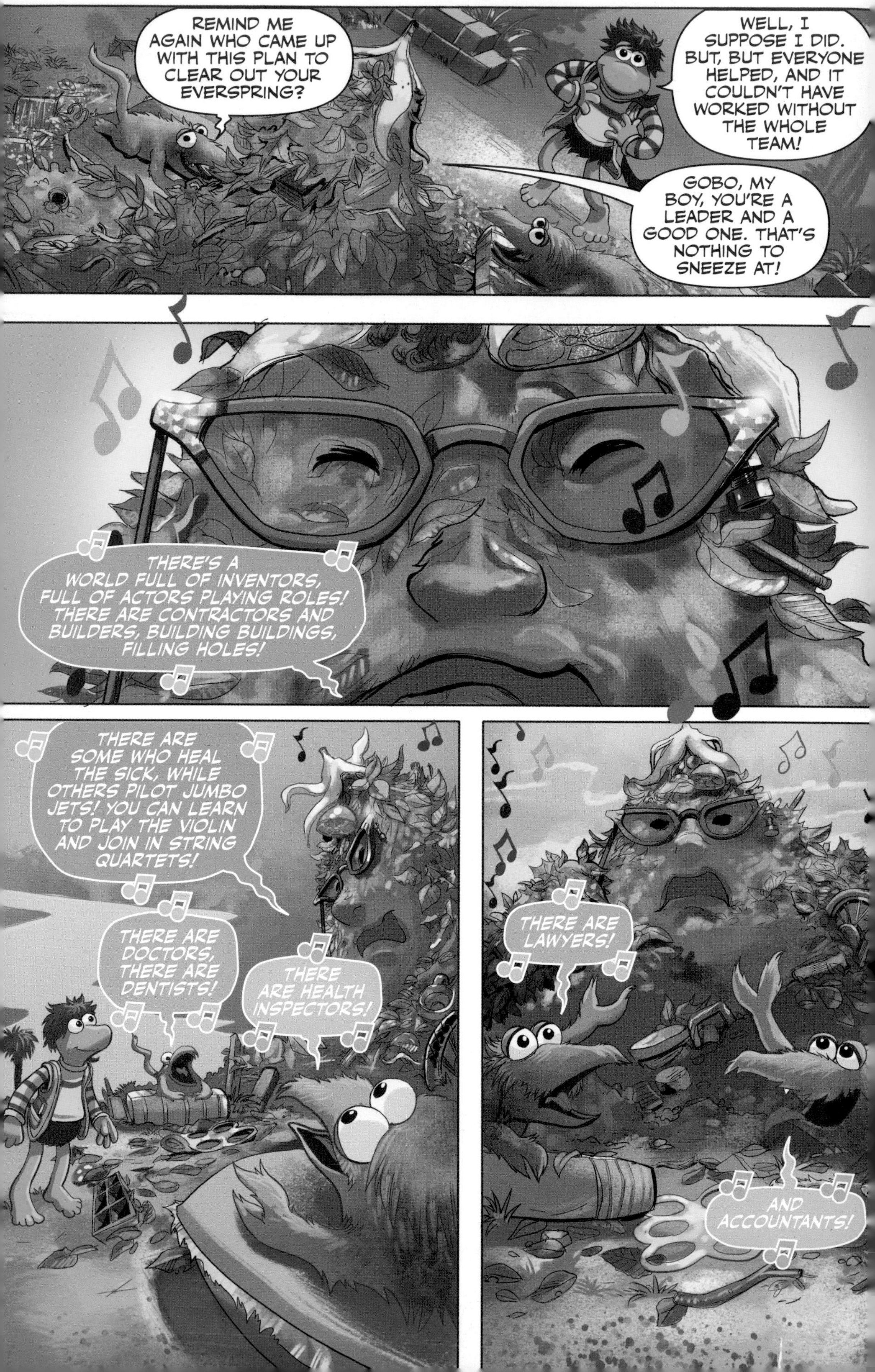
REMIND ME AGAIN WHO CAME UP WITH THIS PLAN TO CLEAR OUT YOUR EVERSPRING?
WELL, I SUPPOSE I DID. BUT, BUT EVERYONE HELPED, AND IT COULDN'T HAVE WORKED WITHOUT THE WHOLE TEAM!
GOBO, MY BOY, YOU'RE A LEADER AND A GOOD ONE. THAT'S NOTHING TO SNEEZE AT!
THERE'S A WORLD FULL OF INVENTORS, FULL OF ACTORS PLAYING ROLES! THERE ARE CONTRACTORS AND BUILDERS, BUILDING BUILDINGS, FILLING HOLES!
THERE ARE SOME WHO HEAL THE SICK, WHILE OTHERS PILOT JUMBO JETS! YOU CAN LEARN TO PLAY THE VIOLIN AND JOIN IN STRING QUARTETS!
THERE ARE DOCTORS, THERE ARE DENTISTS!
THERE ARE HEALTH INSPECTORS!
THERE ARE LAWYERS!
AND ACCOUNTANTS!

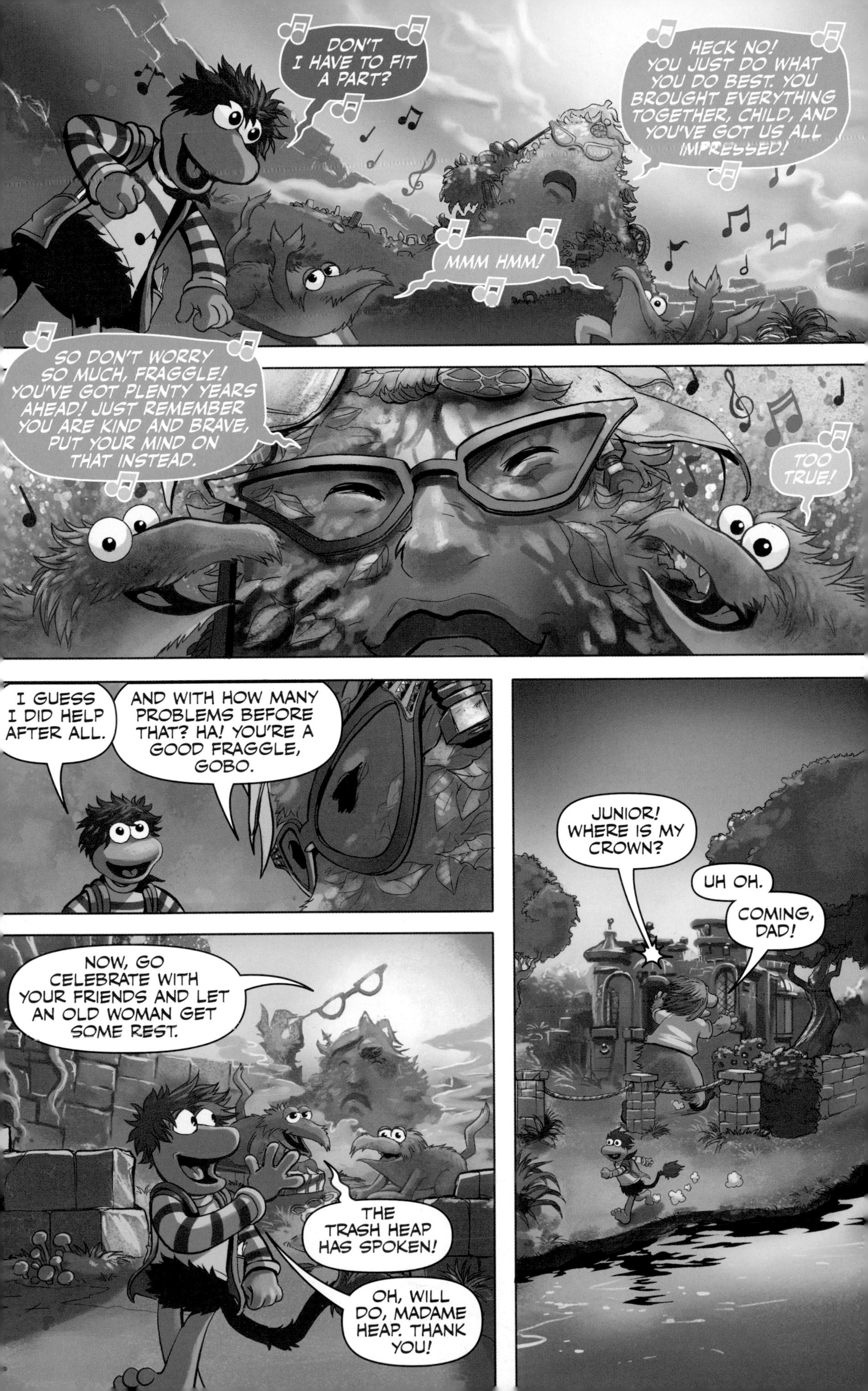
DON'T I HAVE TO FIT A PART?
HECK NO! YOU JUST DO WHAT YOU DO BEST. YOU BROUGHT EVERYTHING TOGETHER, CHILD, AND YOU'VE GOT US ALL IMPRESSED!
MMM HMM!
SO DON'T WORRY SO MUCH, FRAGGLE! YOU'VE GOT PLENTY YEARS AHEAD! JUST REMEMBER YOU ARE KIND AND BRAVE, PUT YOUR MIND ON THAT INSTEAD.
TOO TRUE!
I GUESS I DID HELP AFTER ALL.
AND WITH HOW MANY PROBLEMS BEFORE THAT? HA! YOU'RE A GOOD FRAGGLE, GOBO.
NOW, GO CELEBRATE WITH YOUR FRIENDS AND LET AN OLD WOMAN GET SOME REST.
THE TRASH HEAP HAS SPOKEN!
OH, WILL DO, MADAME HEAP. THANK YOU!
JUNIOR! WHERE IS MY CROWN?
UH OH.
COMING, DAD!

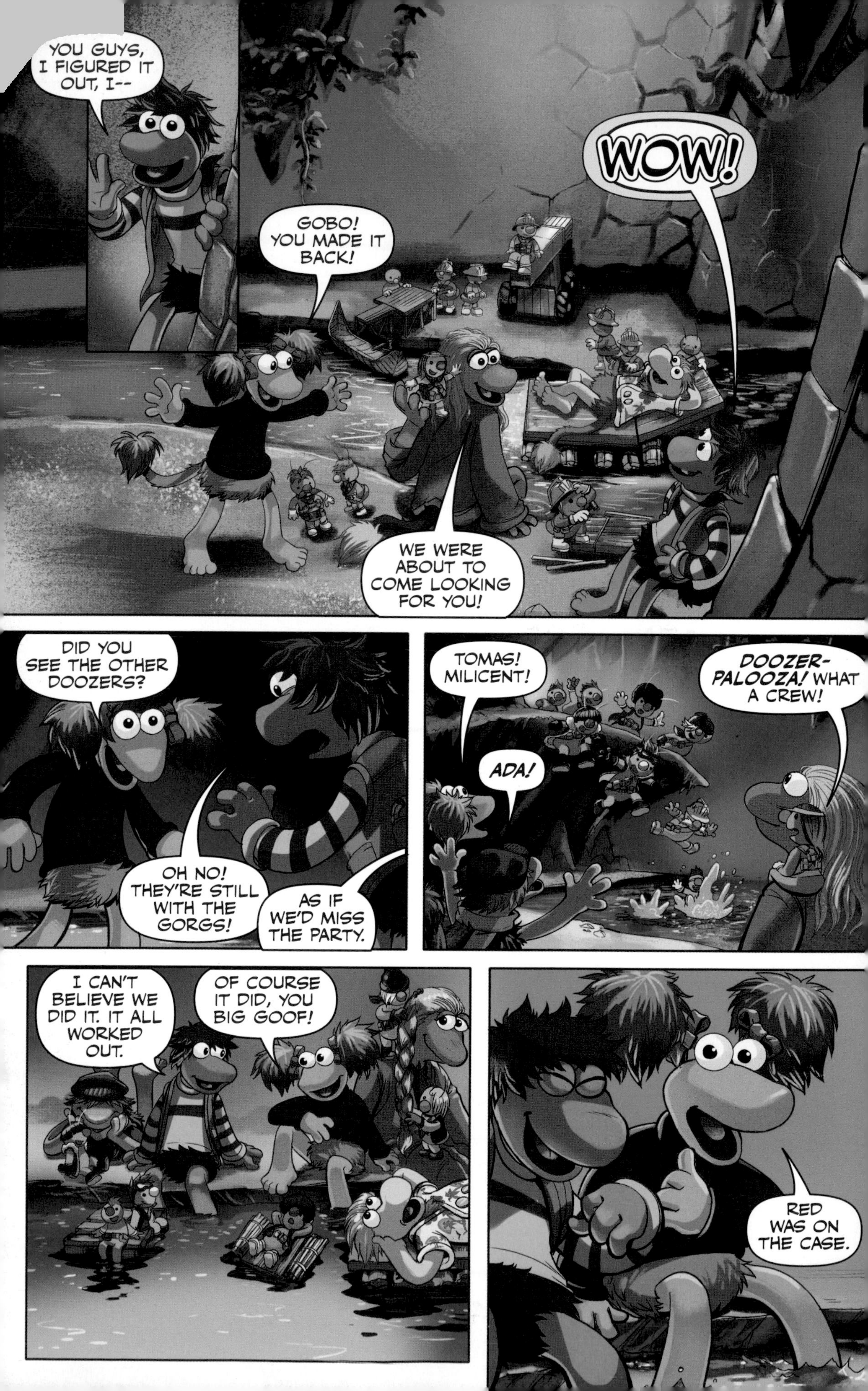
YOU GUYS, I FIGURED IT OUT, I--
GOBO! YOU MADE IT BACK!
WOW!
WE WERE ABOUT TO COME LOOKING FOR YOU!
DID YOU SEE THE OTHER DOOZERS?
OH NO! THEY'RE STILL WITH THE GORGS!
AS IF WE'D MISS THE PARTY.
TOMAS! MILICENT!
ADA!
DOOZER-PALOOZA! WHAT A CREW!
I CAN'T BELIEVE WE DID IT. IT ALL WORKED OUT.
OF COURSE IT DID, YOU BIG GOOF!
RED WAS ON THE CASE.

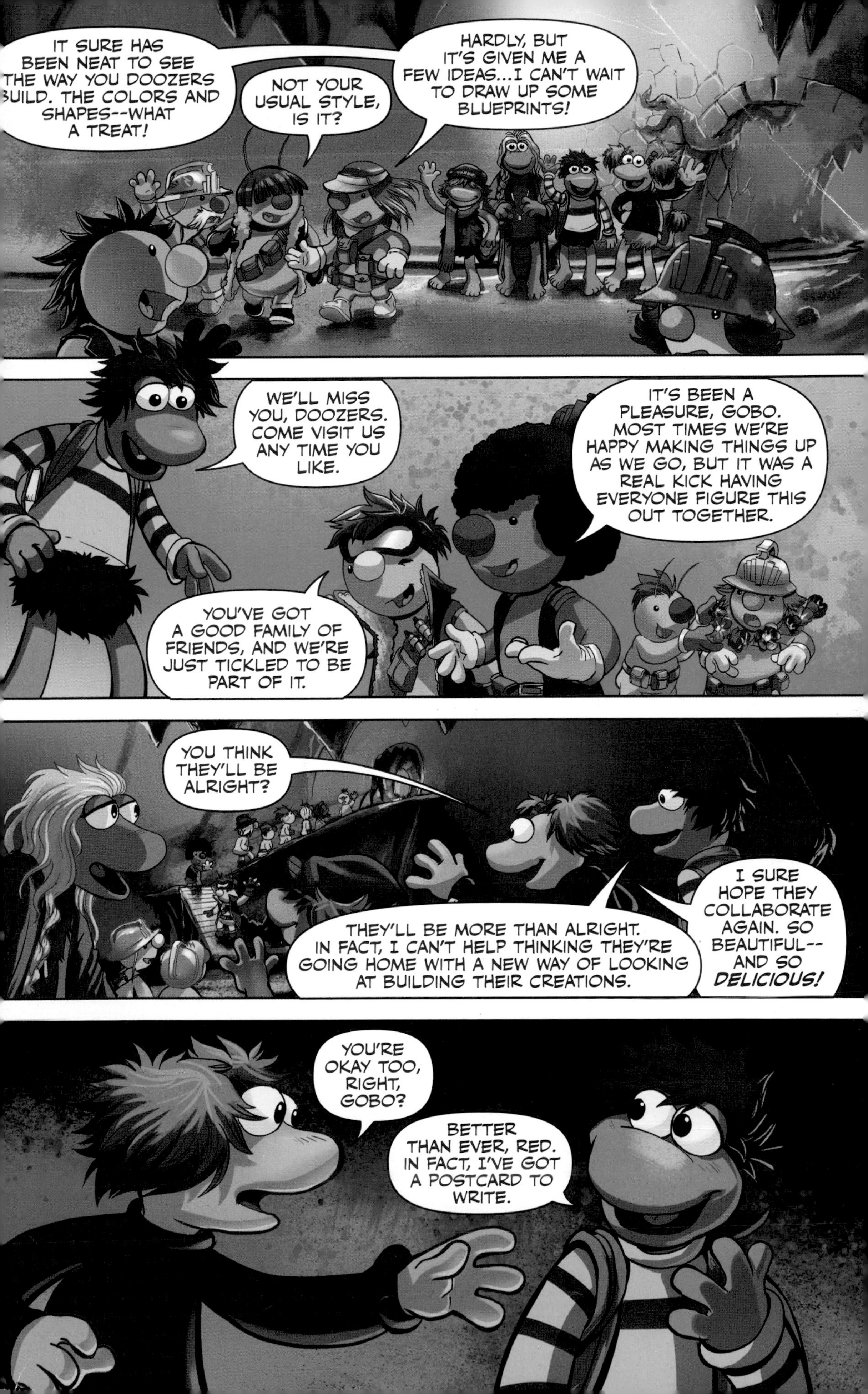
IT SURE HAS BEEN NEAT TO SEE THE WAY YOU DOOZERS BUILD. THE COLORS AND SHAPES--WHAT A TREAT!
NOT YOUR USUAL STYLE, IS IT?
HARDLY, BUT IT'S GIVEN ME A FEW IDEAS...I CAN'T WAIT TO DRAW UP SOME BLUEPRINTS!
WE'LL MISS YOU, DOOZERS. COME VISIT US ANY TIME YOU LIKE.
IT'S BEEN A PLEASURE, GOBO. MOST TIMES WE'RE HAPPY MAKING THINGS UP AS WE GO, BUT IT WAS A REAL KICK HAVING EVERYONE FIGURE THIS OUT TOGETHER.
YOU'VE GOT A GOOD FAMILY OF FRIENDS, AND WE'RE JUST TICKLED TO BE PART OF IT.
YOU THINK THEY'LL BE ALRIGHT?
THEY'LL BE MORE THAN ALRIGHT. IN FACT, I CAN'T HELP THINKING THEY'RE GOING HOME WITH A NEW WAY OF LOOKING AT BUILDING THEIR CREATIONS.
I SURE HOPE THEY COLLABORATE AGAIN. SO BEAUTIFUL--AND SO DELICIOUS!
YOU'RE OKAY TOO, RIGHT, GOBO?
BETTER THAN EVER, RED. IN FACT, I'VE GOT A POSTCARD TO WRITE.

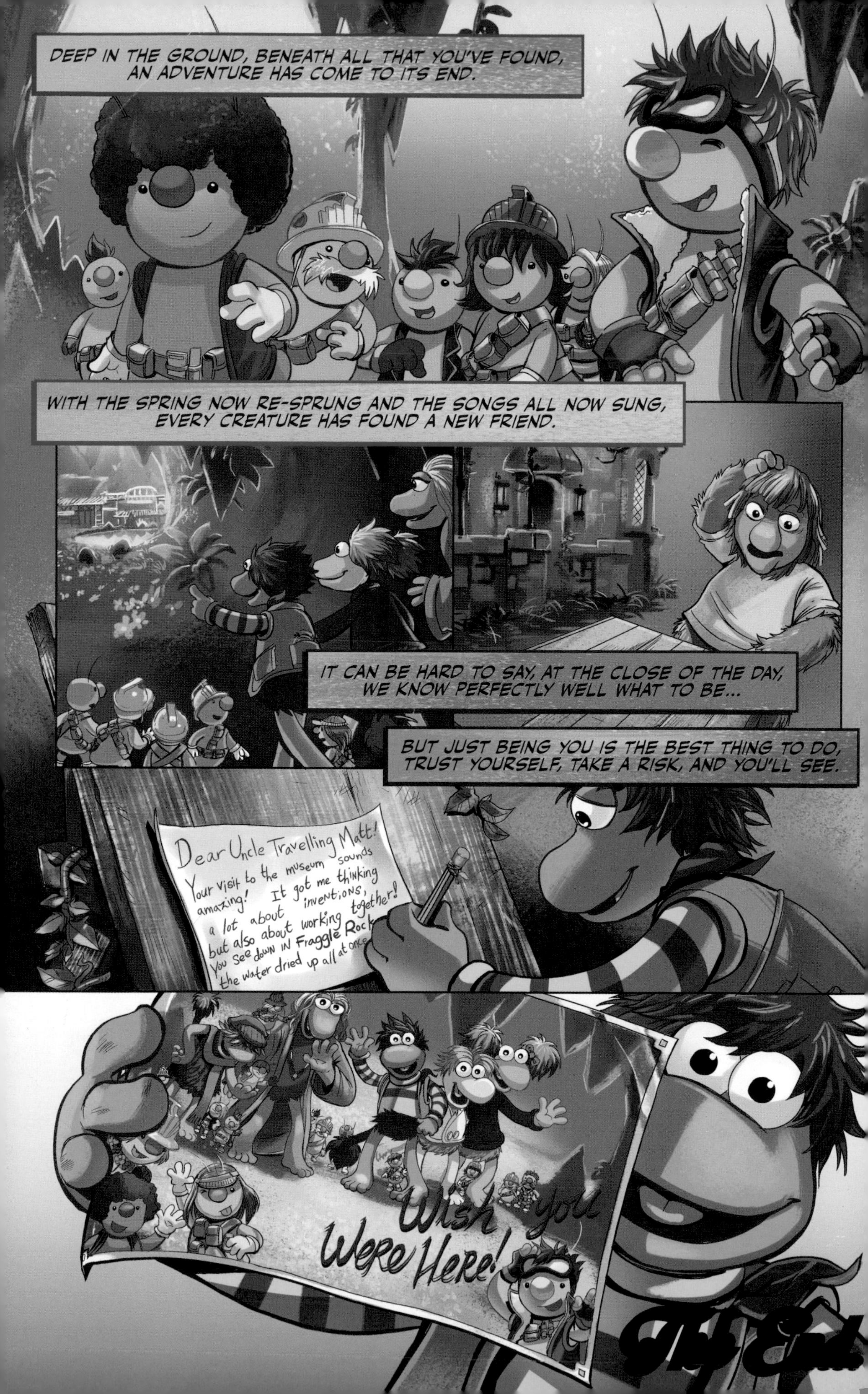
DEEP IN THE GROUND, BENEATH ALL THAT YOU'VE FOUND, AN ADVENTURE HAS COME TO ITS END.
WITH THE SPRING NOW RE-SPRUNG AND THE SONGS ALL NOW SUNG, EVERY CREATURE HAS FOUND A NEW FRIEND.
IT CAN BE HARD TO SAY, AT THE CLOSE OF THE DAY, WE KNOW PERFECTLY WELL WHAT TO BE...
BUT JUST BEING YOU IS THE BEST THING TO DO, TRUST YOURSELF, TAKE A RISK, AND YOU'LL SEE.
Dear Uncle Travelling Matt!
Your visit to the museum sounds amazing! It got me thinking a lot about inventions, but also about working together! You see down in Fraggle Rock the water dried up all at once
Wish you Were Here!
The End

THE RESIDENTS OF

GOBO IS THE NATURAL LEADER OF THE FRAGGLE FIVE. HE IS AN EXPLORER, SPENDING HIS DAYS CHARTING THE UNEXPLORED (AND EXPLORED-BUT-FORGOTTEN) REGIONS OF FRAGGLE ROCK. HE IS HIGHLY RESPECTED BY OTHER FRAGGLES, ALTHOUGH THEY OCCASIONALLY FIND HIM A LITTLE POMPOUS. HE IS ALSO SOMEWHAT EGOCENTRIC, WHICH CAN MAKE IT HARD FOR HIM TO ADMIT MISTAKES. AS A LEADER, GOBO OFTEN PROVIDES HIS FRIENDS WITH DIRECTION, ALTHOUGH, SINCE HE'S A FRAGGLE, IT'S SOMETIMES A FAIRLY SILLY ONE.

MOKEY IS AN ARTIST, POET AND PHILOSOPHER. SHE SEEMS TO BE IN TOUCH WITH SOME SORT OF HIGHER FRAGGLE CONSCIOUSNESS. MOKEY IS FASCINATED BY THE BEAUTY AND INTRICACY OF THE WORLD AROUND HER, AND IS ALWAYS SEEKING NEW WAYS TO SHARE THIS FEELING WITH OTHERS. MOKEY MAY HAVE HER HEAD IN THE CLOUDS, BUT SHE'S ALSO VERY COURAGEOUS AND RESOURCEFUL. HER JOB IS TO BRAVE THE GORG GARDEN TO GATHER THE RADISHES THE FRAGGLES EAT.

WEMBLEY IS INDECISION PERSONIFIED. HE ONLY OWNS TWO SHIRTS, AND BOTH HAVE A BANANA-TREE MOTIF. IF HE HAD ANY OTHER CLOTHES, HE'D NEVER BE ABLE TO GET DRESSED IN THE MORNING! WEMBLEY HAS AN UNCANNY ABILITY TO FIND MERIT ON BOTH SIDES OF ANY ISSUE. HE IS STEADFAST IN HIS ADMIRATION FOR HIS BEST FRIEND AND ROOMMATE, GOBO. IT WAS GOBO WHO ENCOURAGED WEMBLEY TO APPLY FOR HIS JOB WITH THE FRAGGLE ROCK VOLUNTEER FIRE DEPARTMENT. WEMBLEY IS THE SIREN.

FRAGGLE ROCK

ACCORDING TO **BOOBER** FRAGGLE, THERE ARE ONLY TWO THINGS CERTAIN IN THIS WORLD: DEATH AND LAUNDRY. BOOBER IS TERRIFIED BY THE FORMER AND FASCINATED BY THE LATTER. HE IS ALSO PARANOID AND SUPERSTITIOUS. ACCORDING TO BOOBER, ANYTHING THAT CAN GO WRONG SURELY WILL, AND WHEN IT DOES, IT WILL INEVITABLY HAPPEN TO HIM. BUT BOOBER'S NEGATIVE ATTITUDE HAS A BIG PLUS--HE CAN SEE REAL TROUBLE COMING A MILE AWAY, A USEFUL ATTRIBUTE IN A LAND OF ETERNAL OPTIMISTS!

RED IS A NONSTOP WHIRLIGIG OF ACTIVITY. TO HER FELLOW FRAGGLES, RED IS OFTEN SEEN AS A FLASH OF CRIMSON RACING TO HER NEXT ATHLETIC PURSUIT. SHE IS FRAGGLE ROCK CHAMPION IN TUG-OF-WAR, DIVING WHILE SINGING BACKWARDS, THE BLINDFOLDED ONE-LEGGED RADISH RELAY, AND A NUMBER OF OTHER TRADITIONAL FRAGGLE SPORTS. SHE IS OUTGOING, ENTHUSIASTIC, AND ATHLETIC, BUT TAKE NOTE--HER IMPETUOSITY CAN GET HER INTO REAL TROUBLE.

COTTERPIN DOOZER GETS TO SHINE. THE BEST OF THE BUNCH AT DRAWING MAPS, PLANS, AND DREAMING UP NEW CONSTRUCTIONS, COTTERPIN IS THE CLOSEST FRIEND TO THE FRAGGLES--SHE EVEN TRIED TO JOIN THEM, ONCE! OFTEN THE GO-BETWEEN FOR THE TWO GROUPS, COTTERPIN IS AN EXPERT AT MAKING THINGS WORK!

THE RESIDENTS OF

MILLY IS A FUN-LOVING, QUIRKY DOOZER WITH A SOFT SPOT FOR PASTELS AND PAINTS. MILLY LOVES TO INVENT, BUT HER FAVORITE THING TO DO IS COLOR AND DECORATE THE INVENTIONS! SHE'S GOT A KEEN EYE FOR BOTH DESIGN AND A BIT OF MISCHIEF. SHE SPENDS A FAIR BIT OF TIME REMINDING TOMAS OF HIS RESPONSIBILITIES, ALWAYS ENCOURAGING THE IDEAS OF HER FRIENDS.

TOMAS, ALONG WITH MILLY, TAKES A LEADERSHIP ROLE WITH THE DOOZERS OF CRYSTAL CAVE. HE CAN GET A BIT DISTRACTED BY ALL HIS IDEAS, SWEPT UP IN THE FUN, BUT MOSTLY HE JUST CAN'T WAIT TO GET STARTED ON WHATEVER PROJECT IS NEXT.

CRYSTAL CAVE

ADA IS A LITTLE DOOZER WITH BIG DREAMS AND BIG NERVES! HAVING RARELY TRAVELED OUTSIDE THE COMFORTS OF HOME, THIS ADVENTURE REALLY PUT HER BRAVERY TO THE TEST. ADA LOVES WORKING WITH COGS AND KEYS, A REAL CLOCKWORK FANATIC. SHE GETS SPOOKED SOMETIMES, SO SHE AND BOOBER MAKE QUITE THE TEAM ON THIS ADVENTURE!

WHAT AREN'T **THE TURBULO TRIPLETS** UP TO? THIS INDUSTRIOUS TRIO OF TINKERERS ARE ALWAYS COOKING UP SOMETHING. THEY NEVER SEEM TO STOP BUILDING, EVEN WHEN IT SEEMS THEIR INVENTION MIGHT NEVER WORK! THEY LOVE TO SING AND PLAY IN THE CAVES, BRAVER THAN MOST.

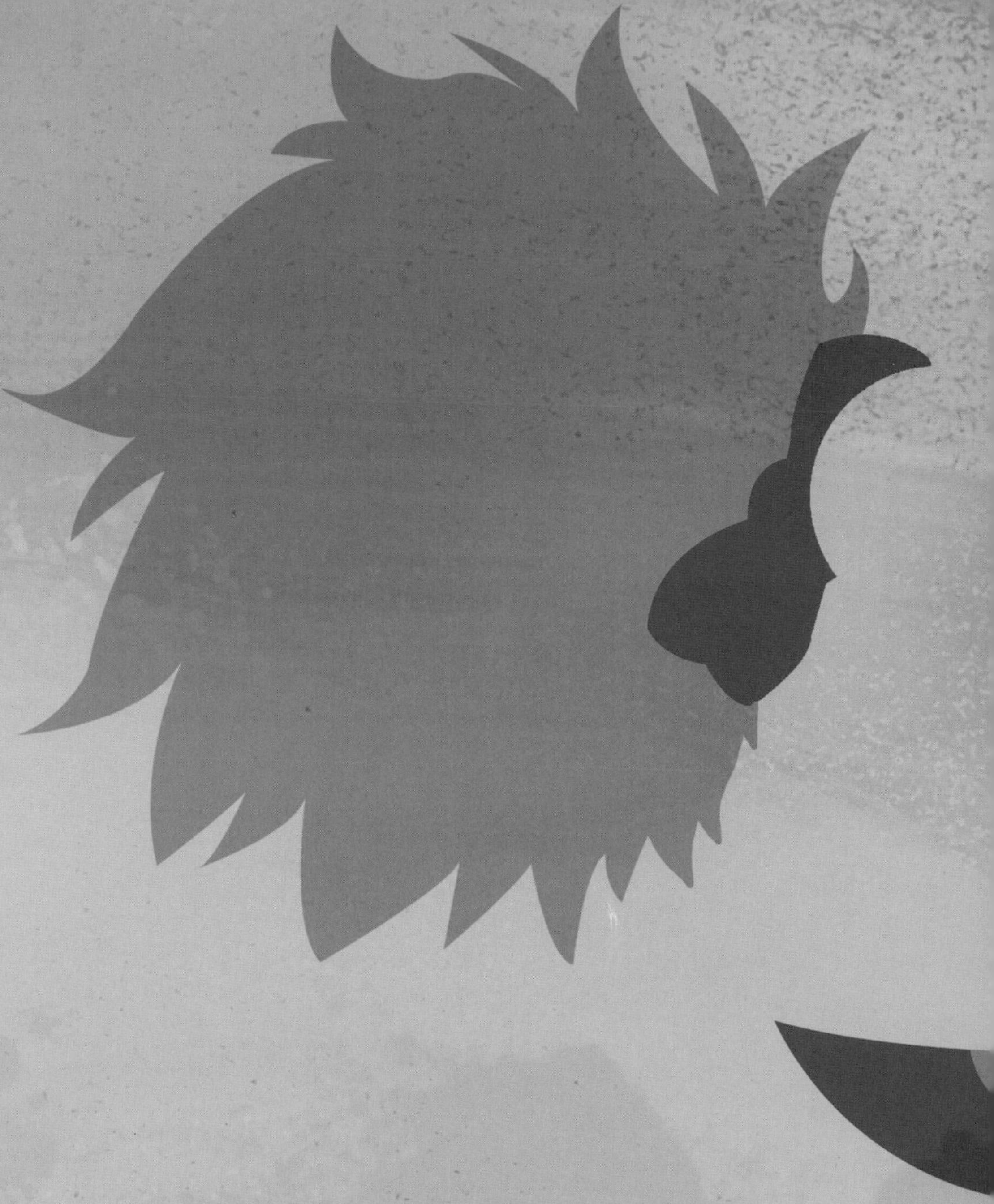

FUN AND GAMES

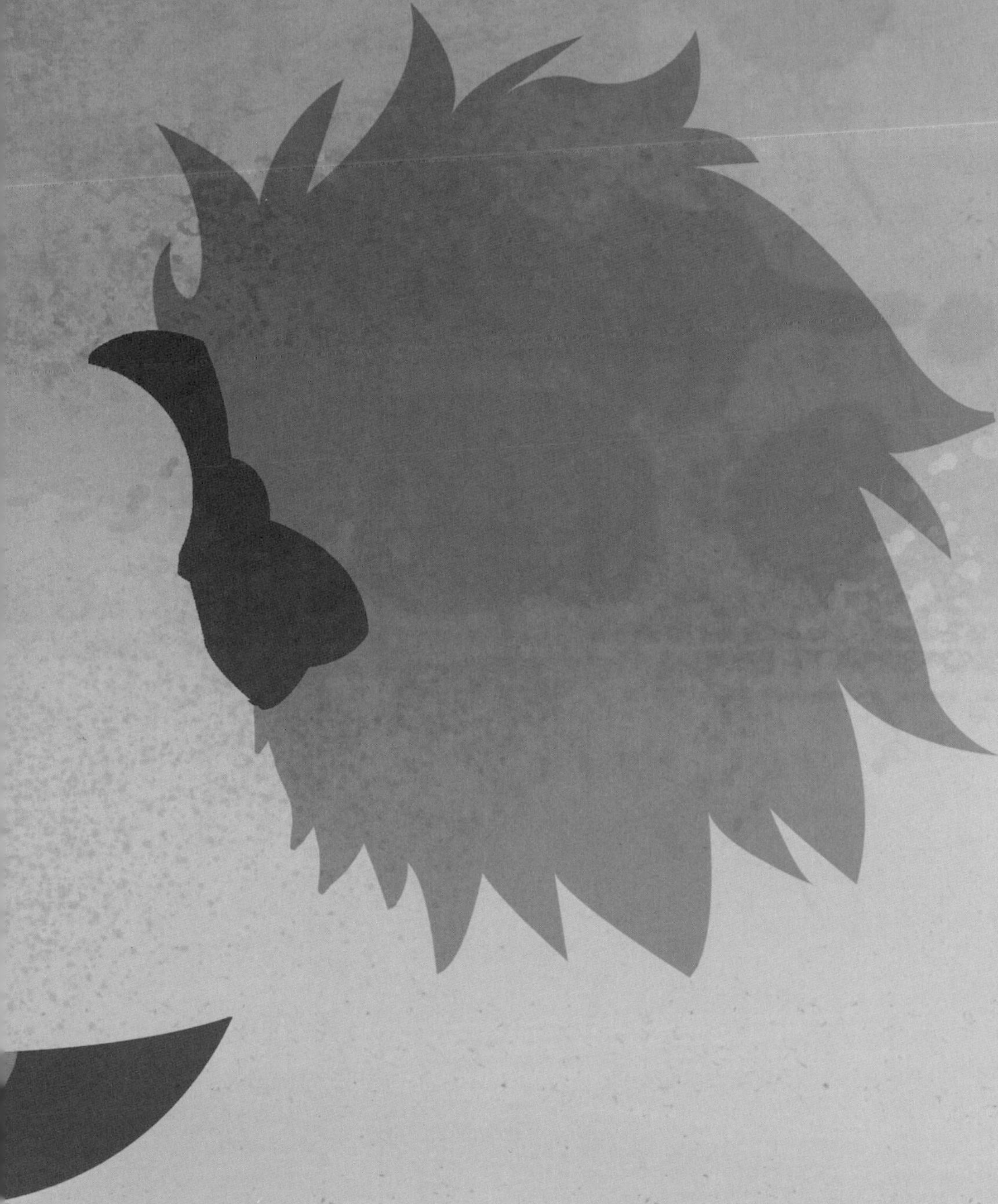

DOWN IN FRAGGLE ROCK!!

JOURNEY CHECKPOINT!

IF THE FRAGGLES ARE GOING TO MAKE IT TO THE EVERSPRING, THEY'LL NEED SUPPLIES FOR THEIR JOURNEY. HELP GOBO AND RED FIND THE WORDS ON THEIR CHECKLIST SO THEY HAVE EVERYTHING THEY NEED.

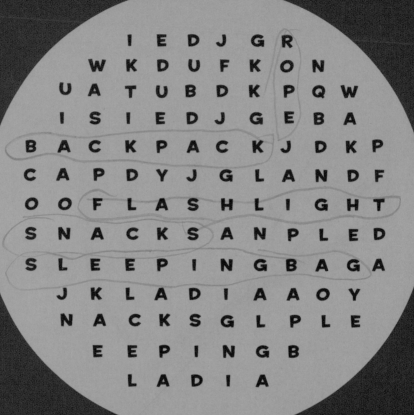

I E D J G R
W K D U F K O N
U A T U B D K P Q W
I S I E D J G E B A
B A C K P A C K J D K P
C A P D Y J G L A N D F
O O F L A S H L I G H T
S N A C K S A N P L E D
S L E E P I N G B A G A
J K L A D I A A O Y
N A C K S G L P L E
E E P I N G B
L A D I A

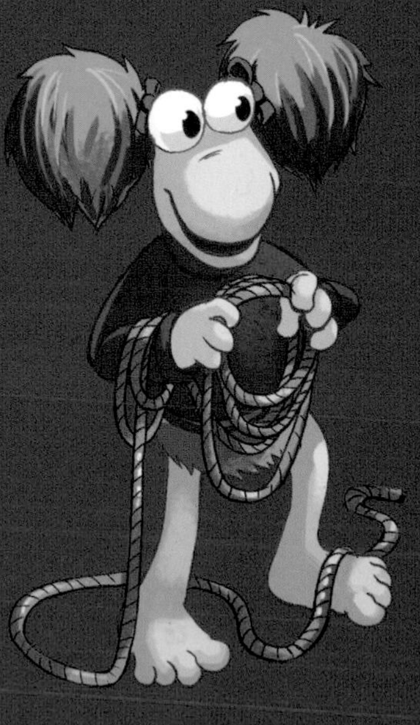

ROPE
FLASHLIGHT
SNACKS
BACKPACK
SLEEPINGBAG

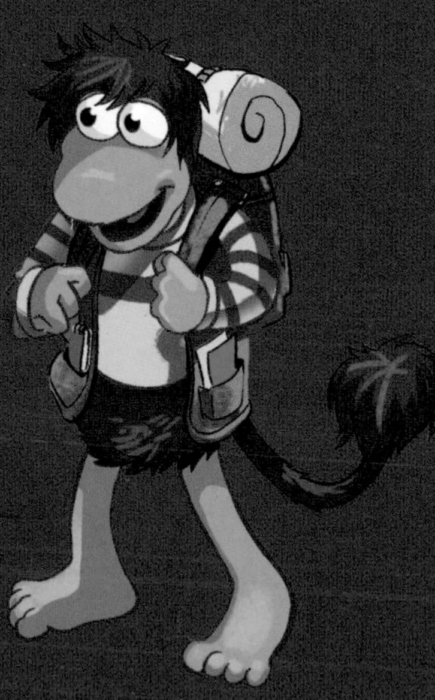

SNAKE DICE GAME

HELP MOKEY AND WEMBLEY MAKE IT THROUGH THE CRYSTAL CAVE, BUT WATCH OUT FOR CREEPY CRITTERS ALONG THE WAY!

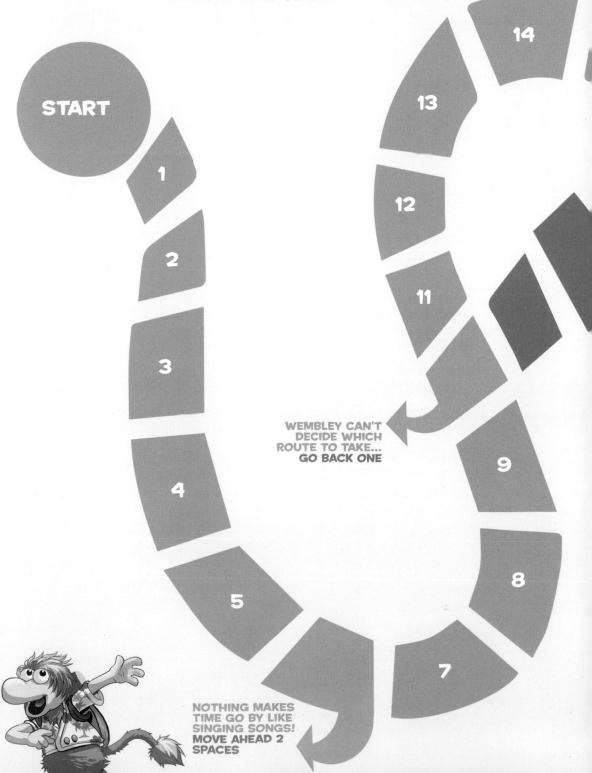

START

1
2
3
4
5
7
8
9
11
12
13
14

WEMBLEY CAN'T DECIDE WHICH ROUTE TO TAKE... **GO BACK ONE**

NOTHING MAKES TIME GO BY LIKE SINGING SONGS! **MOVE AHEAD 2 SPACES**

DRAW A BLUEPRINT

FOR A DOOZER INVENTION OF YOUR OWN!

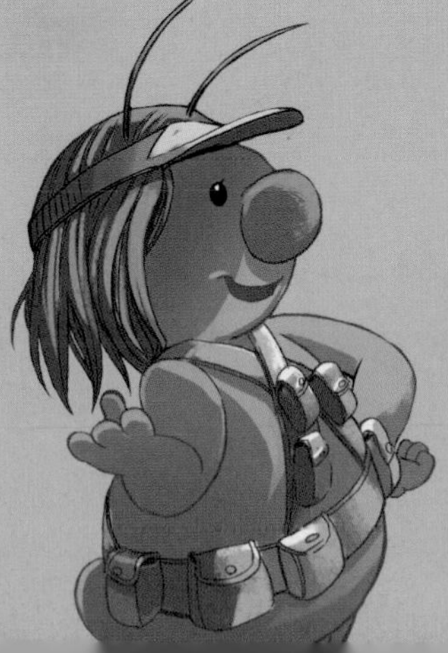

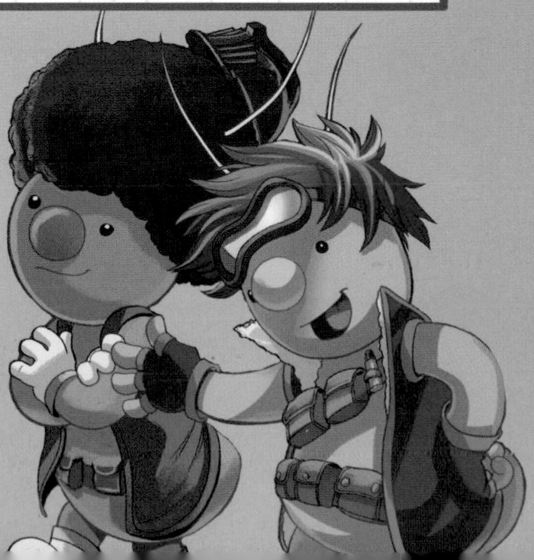

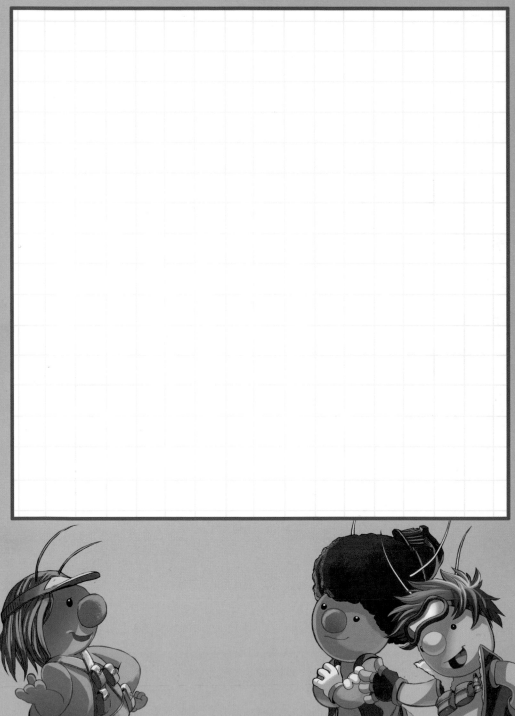

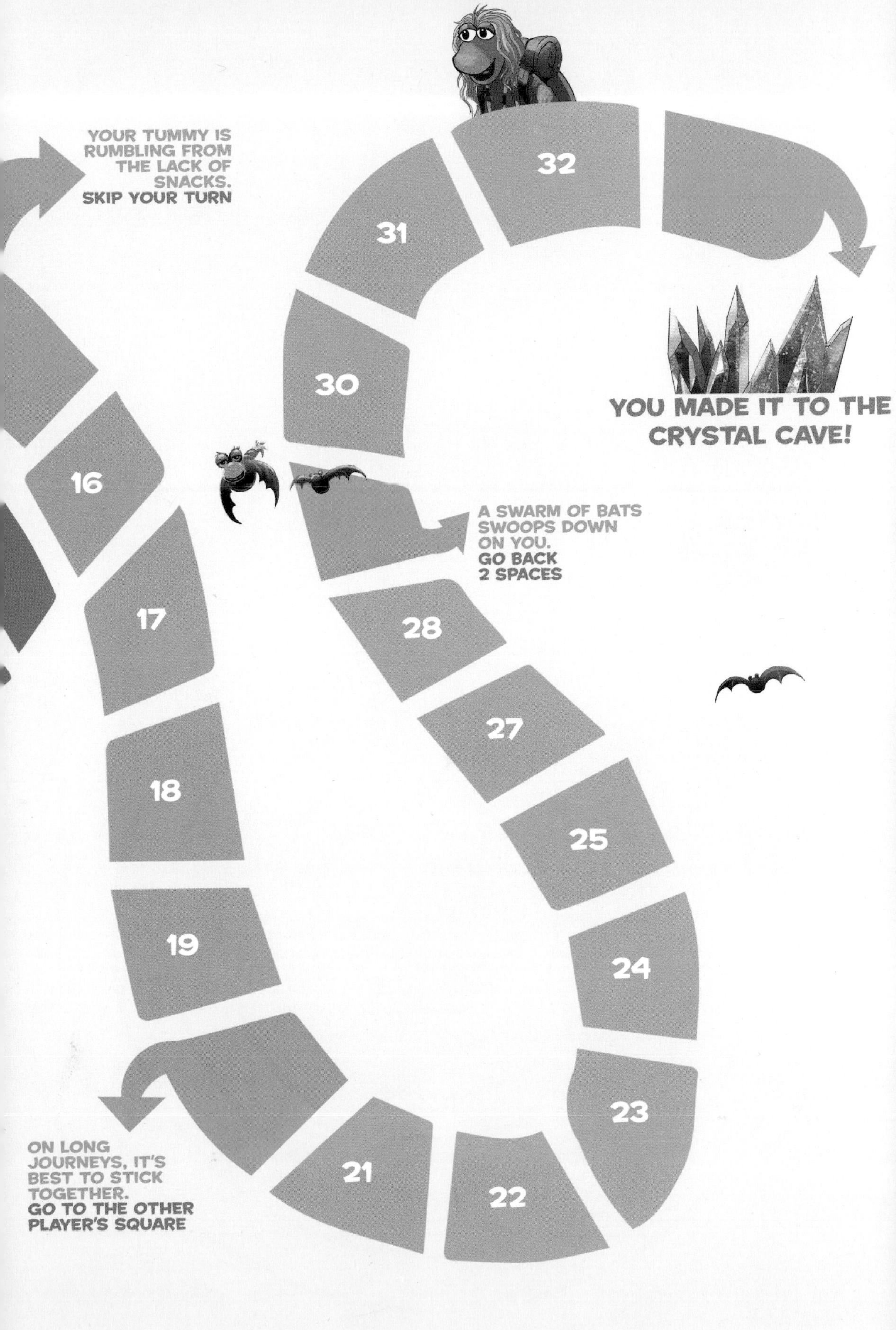
YOUR TUMMY IS RUMBLING FROM THE LACK OF SNACKS.
SKIP YOUR TURN
32
31
30
YOU MADE IT TO THE CRYSTAL CAVE!
16
A SWARM OF BATS SWOOPS DOWN ON YOU.
GO BACK 2 SPACES
17
28
27
18
25
19
24
23
ON LONG JOURNEYS, IT'S BEST TO STICK TOGETHER.
GO TO THE OTHER PLAYER'S SQUARE
21
22

TAKING OUT THE TRASH

HELP BOOBER TAKE THE GARBAGE FROM THE EVERSPRING TO MARJORY THE TRASH HEAP, BUT DON'T GET LOST ALONG THE WAY!

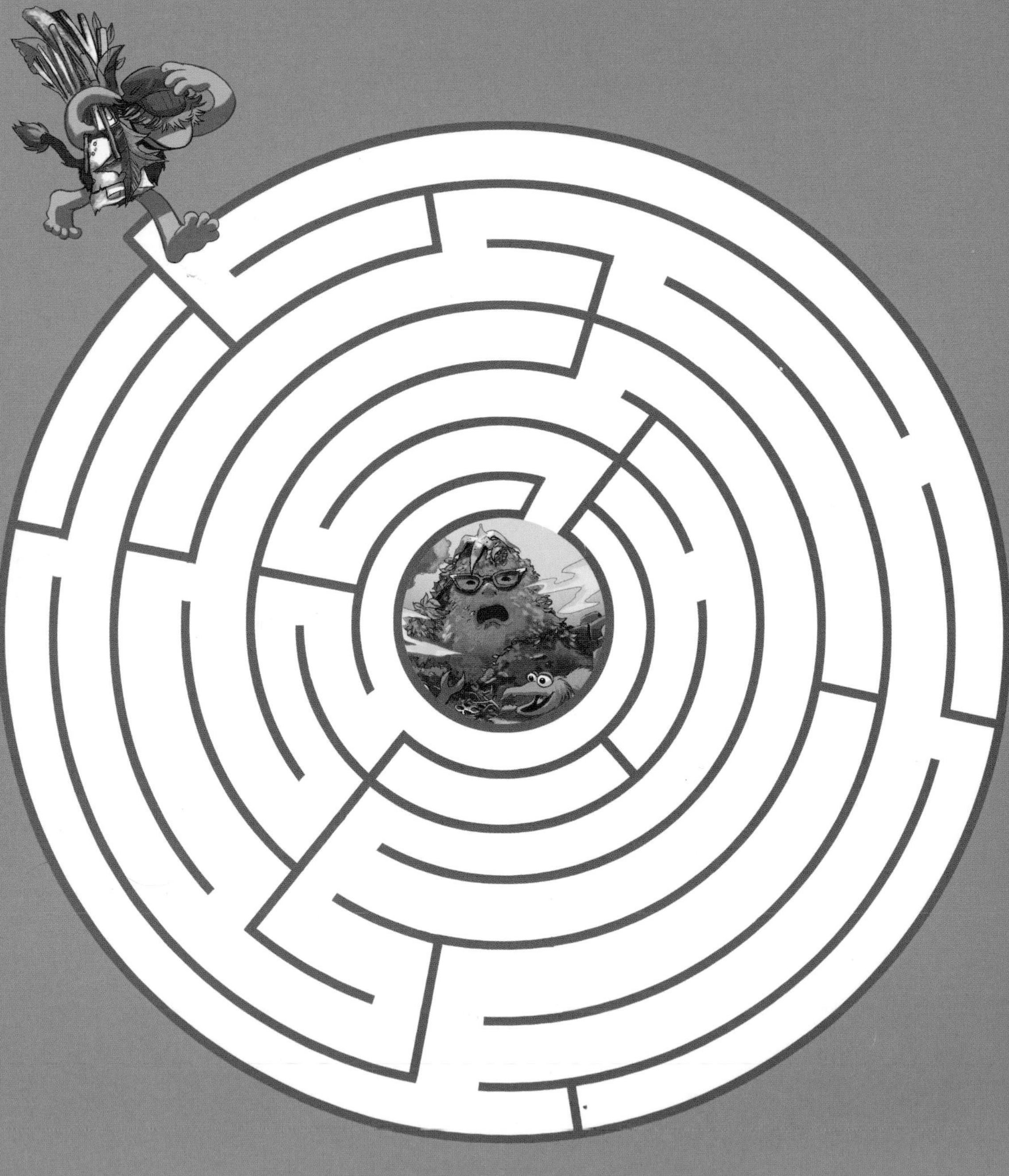

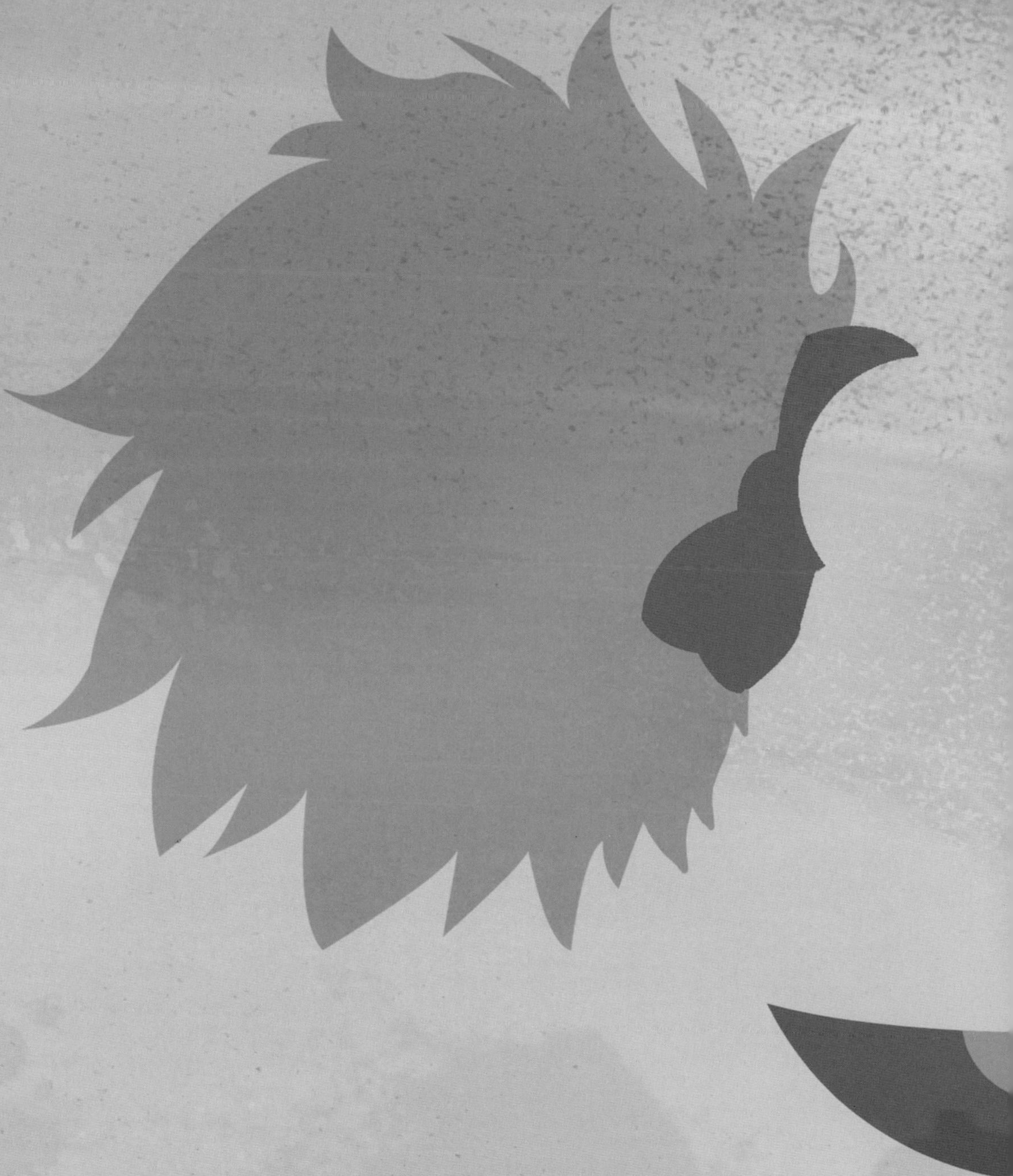

A JOURNEY IN THE MAKING:

A LOOK BEHIND THE SCENES OF THE FRAGGLE'S BIGGEST ADVENTURE YET.

ISSUE 1 PAGE 9:

JAKE: I ABSOLUTELY LOVED HOW KATE DECIDED TO INTRODUCE EACH FRAGGLE ONE AT A TIME BECAUSE I COULD REALLY SHOW THEIR PERSONALITY. DRAWING COMICS IS A LOT ABOUT ACTING IN A WAY, AND IN THIS CASE I COULD SHOWCASE BOOBER'S PARANOID AND DISTRAUGHT ATTITUDE!

YOU'LL ALSO NOTICE THE LITTLE BIRDLIKE CREATURE IN A LOT OF THE PANELS STARTING ON THIS PAGE. I WANTED TO MAKE SURE THAT THE FRAGGLE ROCK BOOK HAD A LOT OF LITTLE DETAILS THAT YOU MIGHT NOT NOTICE UNLESS YOU WERE LOOKING REALLY CAREFULLY. EVEN THOUGH IT WASN'T IN THE SCRIPT, THIS PARTICULAR LITTLE CREATURE SEEMED TO ME LIKE IT SHOULD HAVE A WHOLE LITTLE STORY OF ITS OWN! MAKE SURE TO SPOT ITS REAPPEARANCE ON THE FINAL PAGE OF THE FIRST ISSUE!

KATE: INTRODUCING THE FRAGGLES WAS THE MOST FUN! I LOVED COMING UP WITH LITTLE INSTANCES THAT WOULD BEST SHOW THEM FOR WHO THEY ARE, AND GIVE EVEN READERS WHO MIGHT NOT KNOW THE CHARACTERS A LITTLE TASTE OF WHAT THEY'RE ABOUT. HERE WE SEE BOOBER DOING HIS USUAL WASHING UP, AS WELL AS HIS USUAL MELODRAMATIC ATTITUDE! I LOVE WRITING HIM, HE'S SUCH A SWEET GUY, BUT SO SENSITIVE!

WHAT I LOVE ABOUT THIS COMIC, AND WORKING WITH JAKE, IS LITTLE THINGS LIKE THAT REAPPEARING CREATURE. WHEN YOU'RE REALLY HAVING FUN WITH AN ARTIST, YOU KNOW YOU CAN TRUST THEM TO PUNCH UP YOUR STORIES WITH LITTLE DETAILS TO MAKE THEM SO MUCH BETTER. I'M LOOKING FOR THAT LITTLE GUY RIGHT NOW!

ISSUE 1 PAGE 13:

JAKE: WHAT AN ENTRANCE FOR RED, THE MOST DAREDEVIL AND ENERGETIC OF THE BUNCH! KATE WROTE UP A FITTING SCENARIO WHERE RED IS DOING ANOTHER ONE OF HER TRADEMARK HIGH DIVES! STANDING ATOP THE ROCK, I WANTED IT TO LOOK LIKE IT MIGHT BE A LITTLE DANGEROUS FOR RED TO BE UP THERE. SO IN ORDER TO MAKE IT LOOK PERILOUS, I HAD TO MAKE THE SURROUNDINGS LOOK REALLY BIG! UNLIKE A LOT OF THE CAVES AND TUNNELS IN FRAGGLE ROCK, IN THIS ROOM THERE'S A LOT OF SPACE WITH WALLS FAR OFF IN THE DISTANCE, AND STALACTITES AND STALAGMITES LOOKING BLUE AND HAZY. HOPEFULLY WITH THOSE EFFECTS, AS WELL AS SOME SOFT LIGHT COMING DOWN FROM ABOVE, IT LOOKS LIKE IT COULD BE GARGANTUAN IN THERE!

KATE: RED'S INTRODUCTION WAS PROBABLY MY FAVOURITE... BUT I'M DEFINITELY A BIG FAN OF RED IN GENERAL! SHE ALWAYS STUCK OUT TO ME AS THE BRASH, RULE BENDING, CRAZY BUT FIERCELY LOYAL MEMBER OF THE GROUP, AND I LOVE HER. I WANTED HER TO ENTER INTO THE COMIC WITH A BANG - AND HOW! POOR RED! THINGS GET BETTER FOR HER FROM HERE, OF COURSE, BUT IT CERTAINLY WAS A FUN WAY TO START

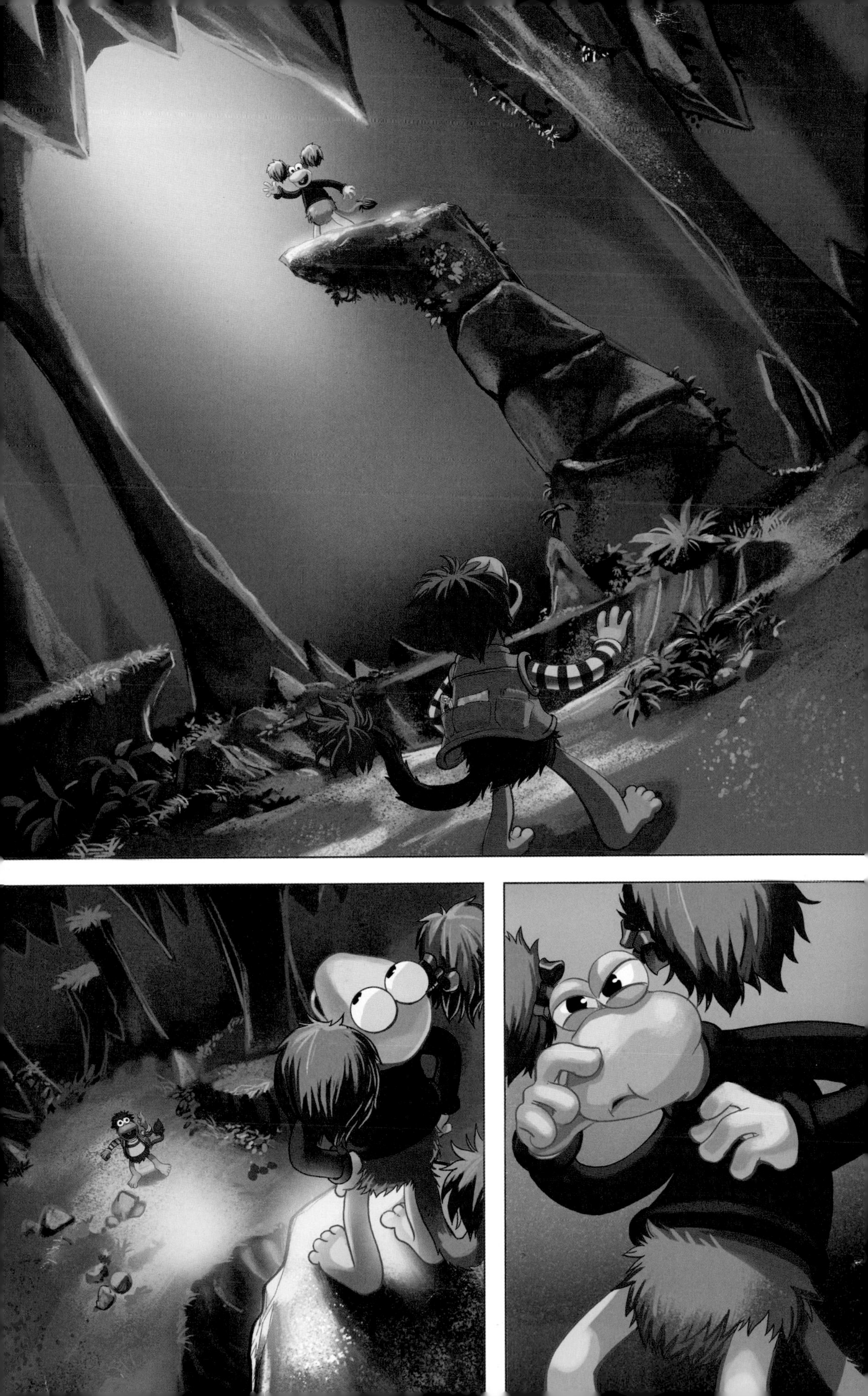

ISSUE 3 PAGE 7:

JAKE: DRAWING ALL THE CRAZY DOO-DADS AND THING-A-MAJIGS THAT THE DOOZERS BUILT WAS SO FUN! IT WAS ALSO REALLY A CHALLENGE TO DRAW THE WHOLE ROOM AND ALL THE LITTLE DOOZERS IN THE BACKGROUND GOING ABOUT THEIR DAY-TO-DAY BUSYWORK. THIS ORIGINALLY WAS A SMALLER PANEL IN THE COMIC, BUT WE DECIDED AT THE LAST MINUTE TO MAKE IT A FULL PAGE!

I ALSO WANTED TO GIVE THESE DOOZER CONSTRUCTIONS MORE COLOR THAN THE TRADITIONAL DOOZER STICKS. SO I REALLY TRIED TO PUSH THE GOLD AND PURPLE COLORS ALONG WITH KEEPING SOME OF THE BLUE COLORS FROM THE CRYSTALS IN THE CAVE. IT TOOK SOME EXTRA TIME TO GET THE BALANCE BETWEEN THOSE COLORS JUST RIGHT BUT IT WAS WORTH THE EXTRA EFFORT!

KATE: THIS PAGE IS SUCH A DREAM TO LOOK AT! WHEN YOU'RE WRITING A STORY LIKE THIS, YOU HAVE AN IDEA HOW IT MIGHT APPEAR ON THE PAGE, BUT YOU NEVER REALLY KNOW UNTIL YOU SEE IT. JAKE BLEW ME AWAY WITH THIS. I WANTED TO SHOW JUST HOW DIFFERENT THEY WERE FROM THE TRADITIONAL DOOZERS WE KNOW AND LOVE, AND JAKE TOOK MY IDEAS AND PAINTED THEM INTO WHAT YOU SEE HERE. COMICS ARE A BIT LIKE MAGIC, THAT WAY. MY FAVOURITE BITS OF THIS WHOLE PAGE ARE THE COLOURFUL STEPS!

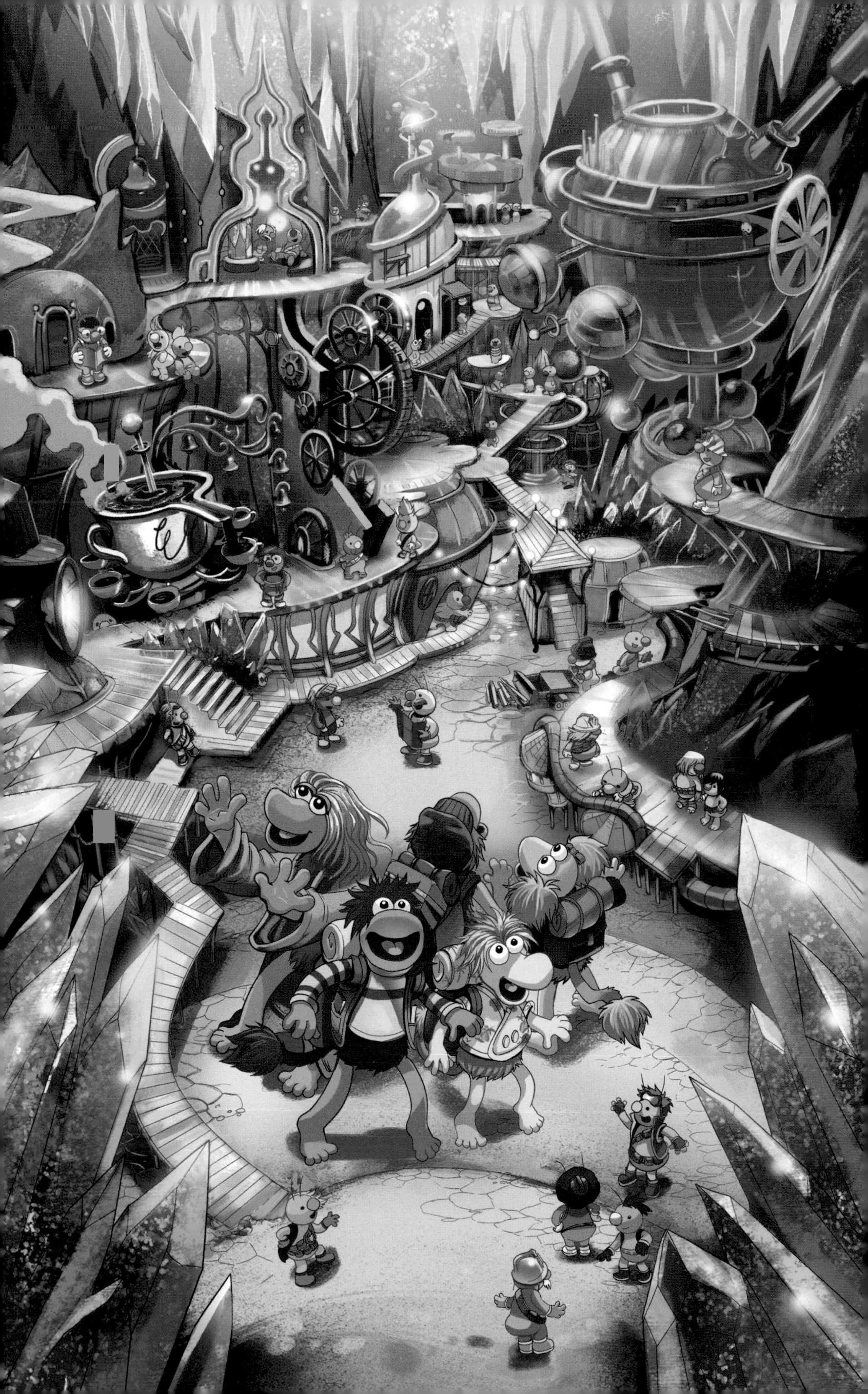

ISSUE 3 PAGE 8:

JAKE: IT WAS COOL TO HAVE TOMAS BE THE GUIDE AND INTRODUCE ALL THE DIFFERENT DOOZERS! I LIKED THE TURBULO TRIPLETS SO MUCH THAT FROM THEN ON YOU'LL SEE THEM IN THE BACKGROUND THROUGHOUT THE STORY.

FOR THESE PANELS I WANTED TO SHOW THE DIFFERENT CONTRAPTIONS THAT THE NEW DOOZERS CREATE, AND MAKE THEM LOOK COOL AND INTRICATE, BUT ALSO AS YOU'LL NOTICE, NONE OF THEIR INVENTIONS ARE WORKING QUITE PROPERLY! THAT WAS AN IMPORTANT POINT TO THE WHOLE STORY: THESE DOOZERS MAKE THINGS THAT LOOK COOL, BUT PERHAPS DON'T ACTUALLY WORK PROPERLY OR DO ANYTHING! THE FIRST TIME I DREW THIS SCENE THOUGH, ALL THE CONTRAPTIONS LOOKED LIKE THEY WERE WORKING TOO WELL! SO WE MADE THE CONTRAPTIONS A LITTLE LESS PERFECT AND YOU'LL SEE THE DIFFERENCES IF YOU COMPARE THE PENCILS TO THE FINAL VERSIONS OF THE PAGE.

KATE: WHEN I THOUGHT OF THE CONSTRUCTIONS THE DOOZERS WOULD BUILD, I ACTUALLY TOOK A LOT OF INSPIRATION FROM AN EPISODE OF THE *MAGIC SCHOOL BUS*, WHERE CARLOS TRIES TO BUILD AN INSTRUMENT AND ENDS UP PUTTING WAY TOO MANY KNICKKNACKS AND THINGAMABOBS ON IT FOR IT TO SOUND ANY GOOD AT ALL! I REALLY WANTED TO SHOW OFF HOW CREATIVE AND FUN-LOVING THESE NEW DOOZERS ARE, WHILE AT THE SAME TIME ILLUSTRATING THAT THEY AREN'T THE BEST PLANNERS IN THE WORLD. I'D DEFINITELY LIKE TO HANG OUT IN THAT CRYSTAL CAVE WITH THEM AND TRY OUT THEIR INVENTIONS, ALL THE SAME!

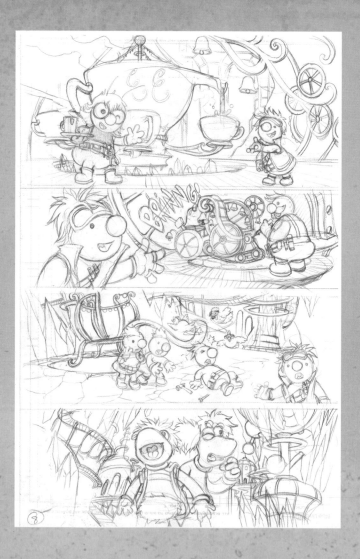

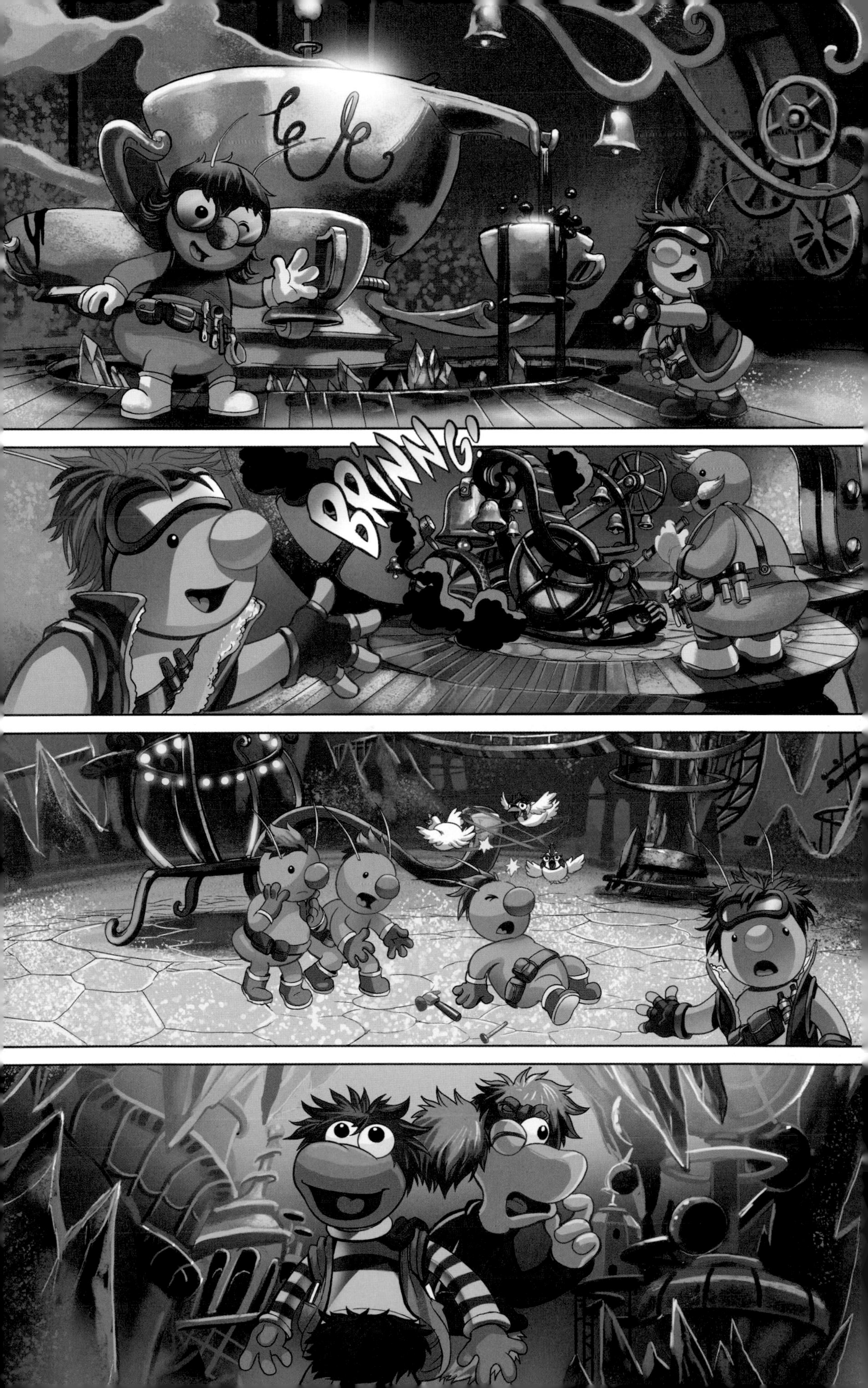
BRINNG!

ISSUE 4 PAGE 8 :

JAKE: SO MANY DOOZERS IN ONE PANEL! ONE THING THAT YOU MIGHT NOTICE IS HOW KIND OF YUCKY THE COLORS ARE IN THIS AREA, ALL DULL BROWNS AND GREENS AND GREYS. I WANTED THIS PAGE SHOWING THE BLOCKAGE OF THE EVERSPRING TO LOOK WAY DIFFERENT FROM THE NEXT PAGE. SO HERE THINGS LOOK REALLY DARK AND DRAB.

KATE: THE CALM BEFORE THE STORM! THIS WAS ONE PAGE THAT TURNED OUT EXACTLY HOW I'D PICTURED IT IN MY HEAD, SO MUCH SO THAT IT SURPRISED ME WHEN I SAW IT! I LOVE ALL THE LITTLE DOOZERS AND HOW THEY'RE INTERACTING. ESPECIALLY THAT DOOZER AT THE BACK... WHAT'RE THEY UP TO? HELP OUT, LITTLE DUDE!

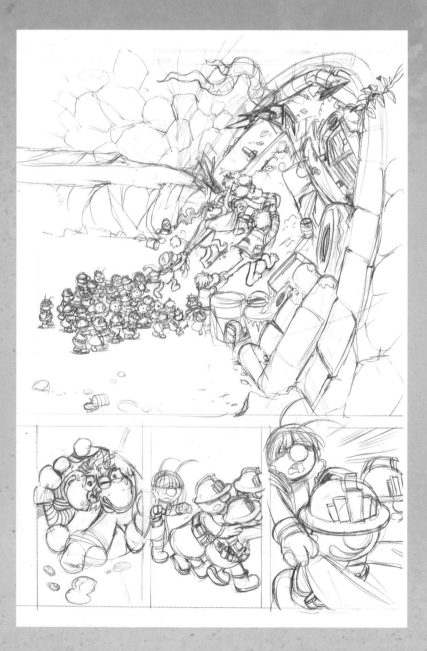

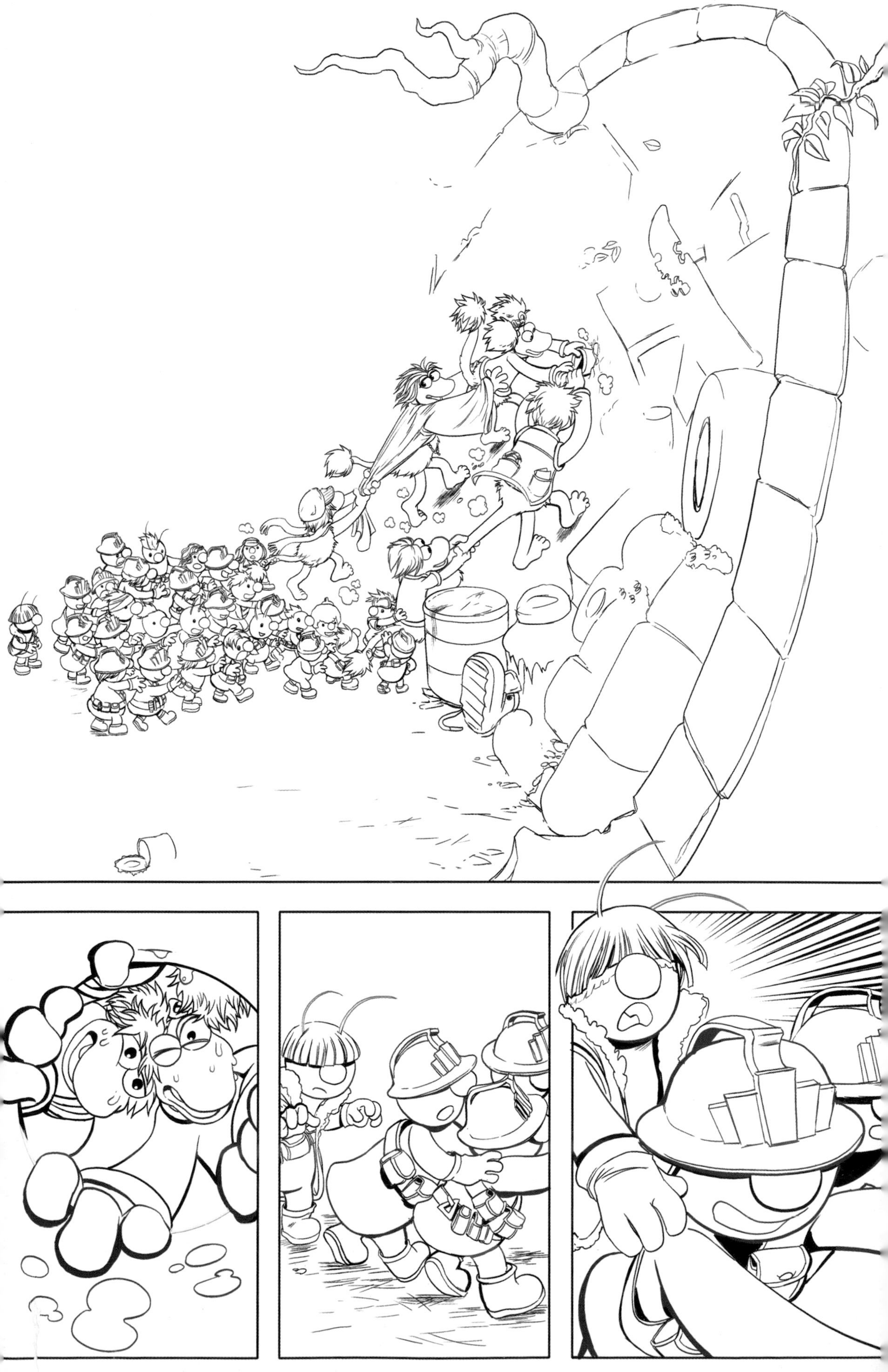

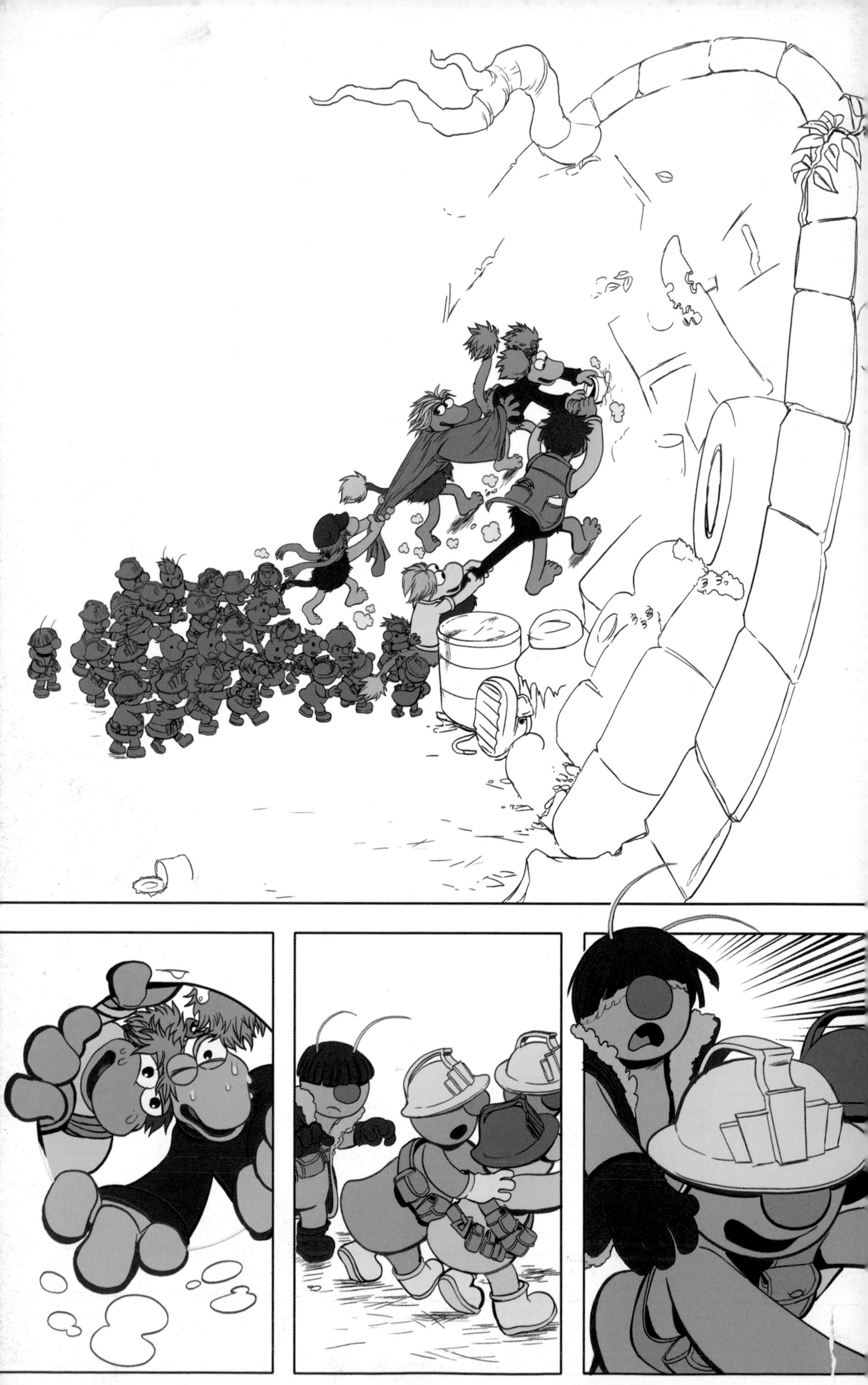

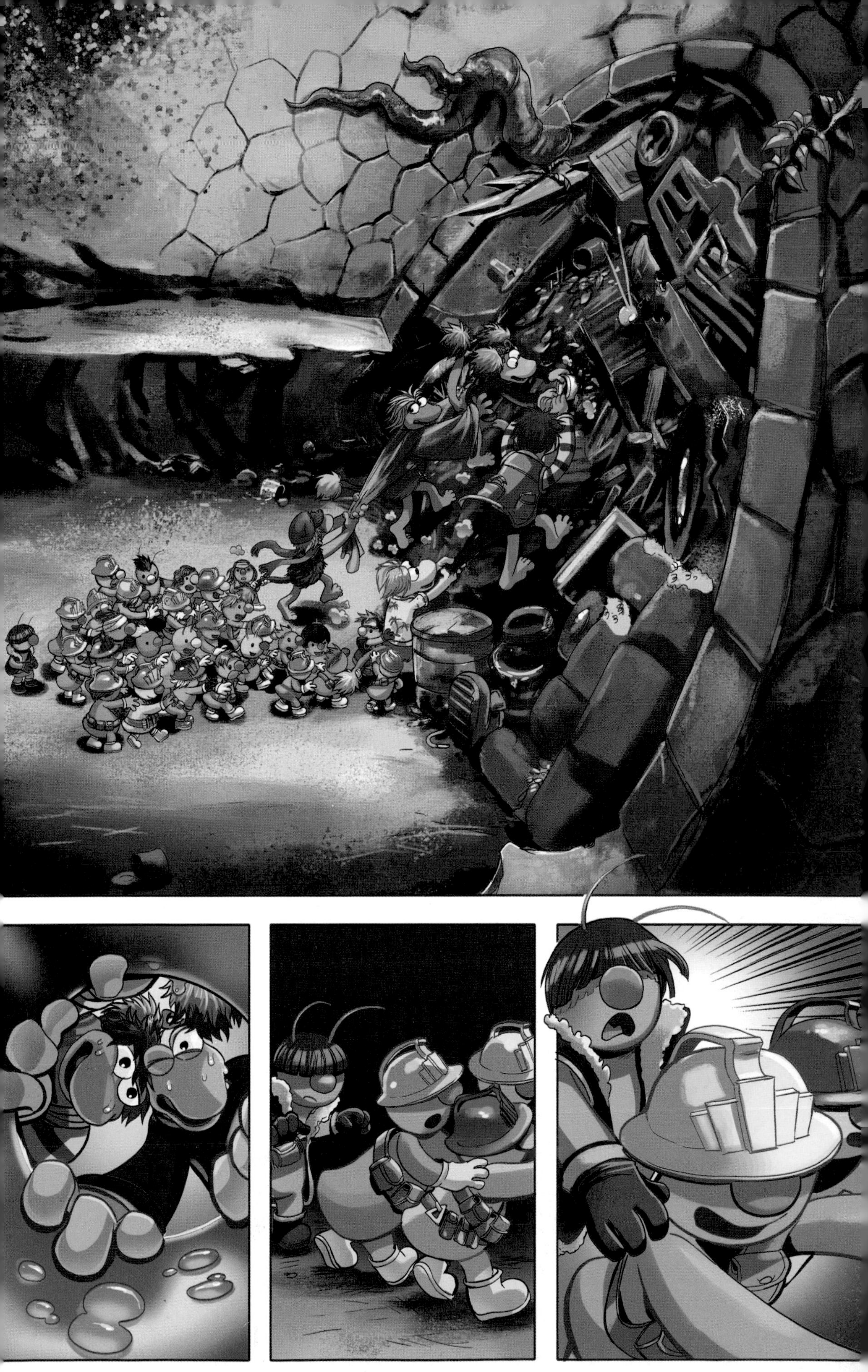

ISSUE 4 PAGE 9:

JAKE: THE WATER IS FINALLY FLOWING! IT'S ALL BLUES AND GREENS AND CONTRASTS NICELY FROM THE PREVIOUS PAGE THAT WAS LITERALLY FULL OF GARBAGE!

I LIKED SHOWING HOW EVERY CHARACTER WAS HANDLING THE GIANT EXPLOSION OF WATER. I WANTED TO MAKE IT LOOK A BIT SCARY BUT ALSO MAYBE LIKE IT WOULD BE A LOT OF FUN TO BE CARRIED ALONG IN THE WAVES OF WATER COMING FROM THE EVERSPRING! IT TURNS OUT THAT MILICENT CAN REALLY SURF!

KATE: I HADN'T NOTICED MILICENT SURFING UNTIL JUST NOW! HAHA! THAT'S SO PERFECT, AND SO RIGHT FOR WHAT SHE'S ALL ABOUT. IN COMICS, WHEN ONE PANEL TAKES UP THE WHOLE PAGE, IT'S CALLED A "SPLASH PAGE," AND THIS IS JUST SUCH A PERFECT EXAMPLE! IT'S A BIG MOMENT, RIGHT AT THE HEIGHT OF OUR ADVENTURE, AND IT COMES ALIVE RIGHT OFF THE PAGE.

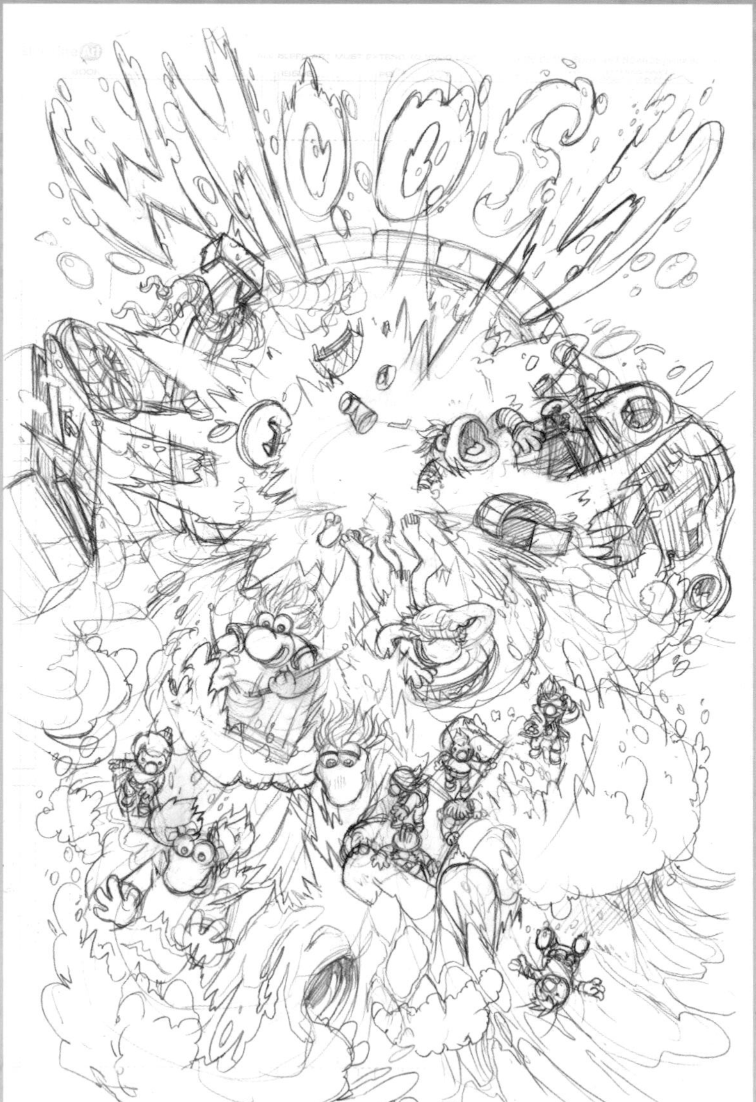
WHOOSH

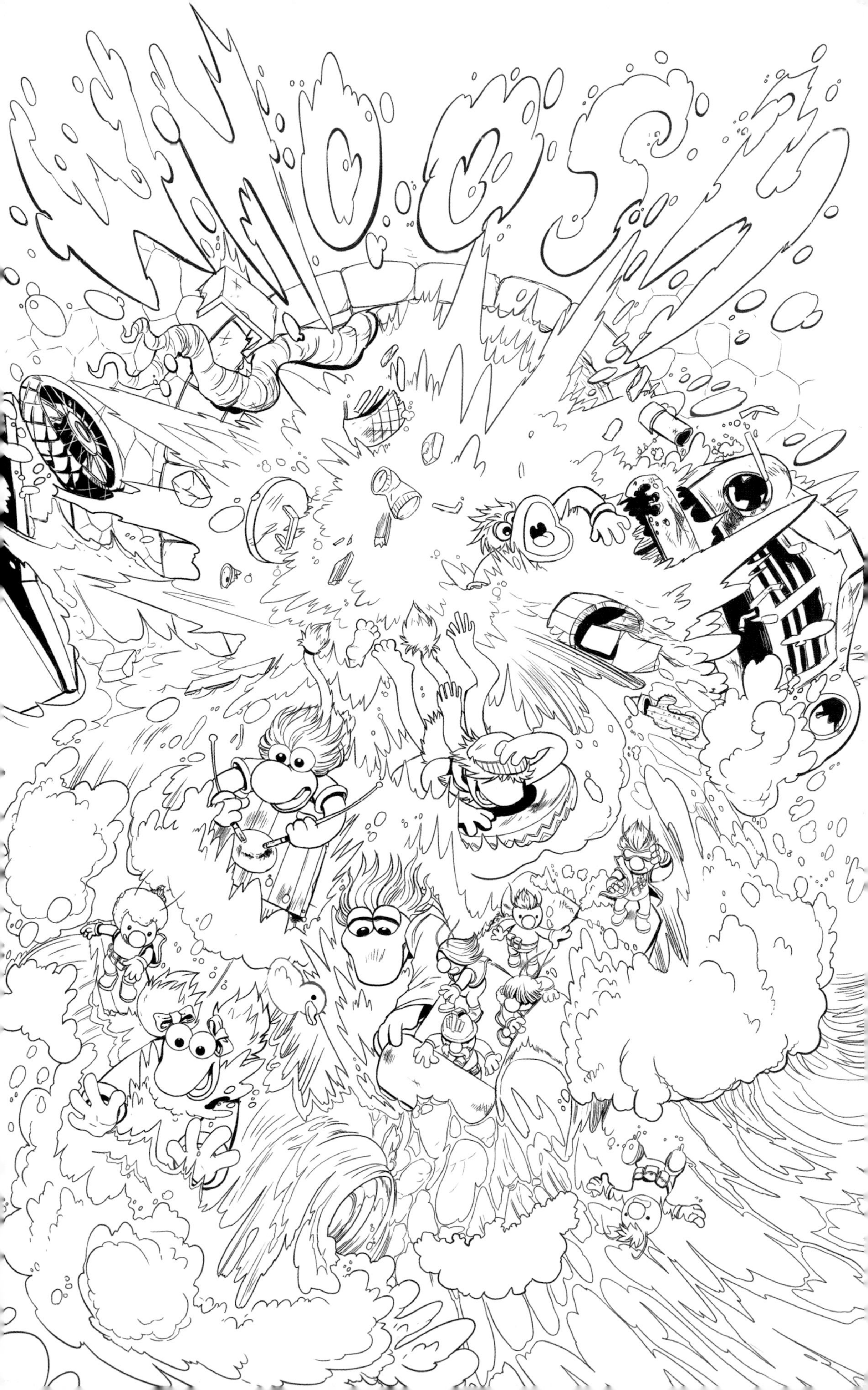
WHOOSH

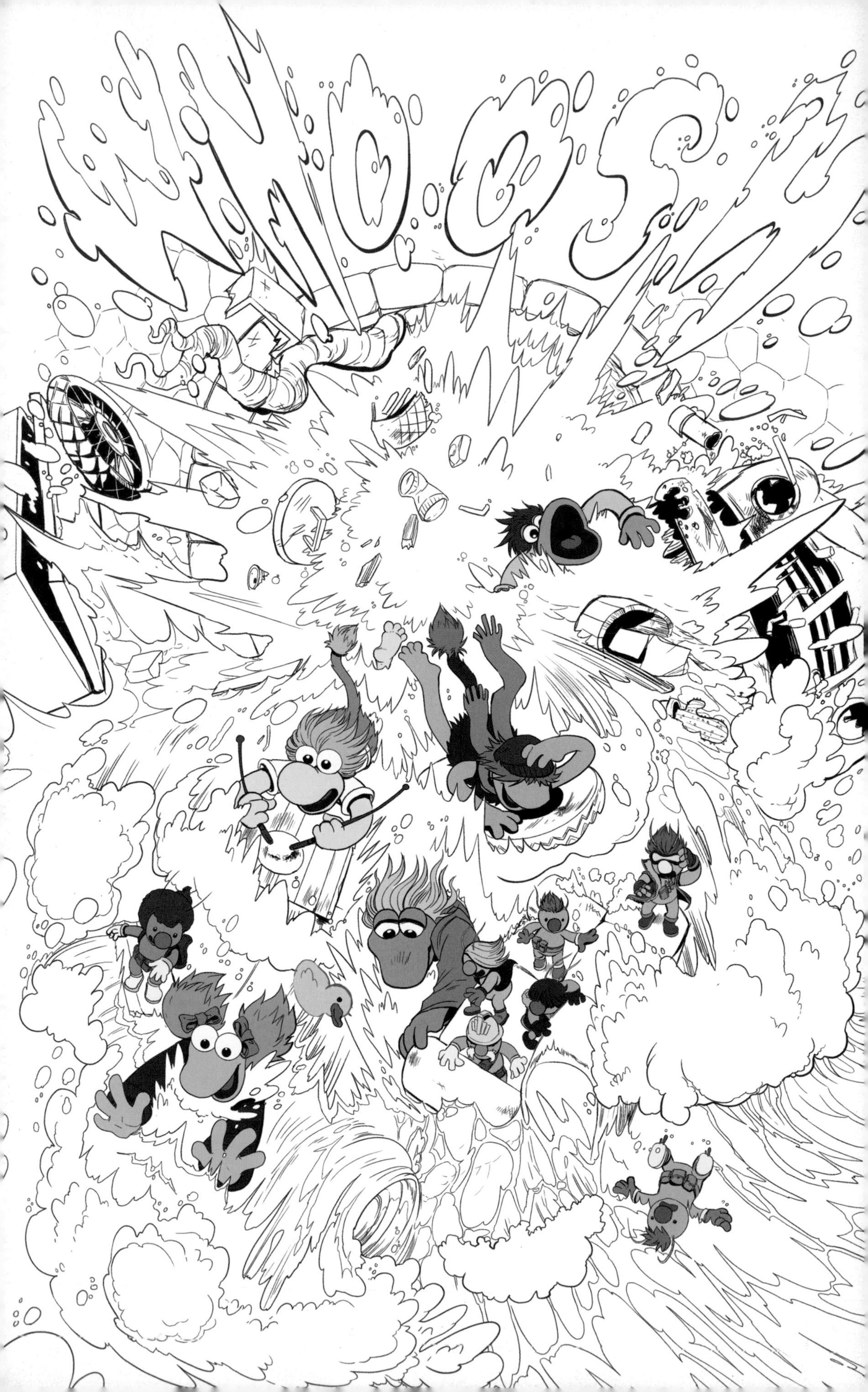
WHOOSH!

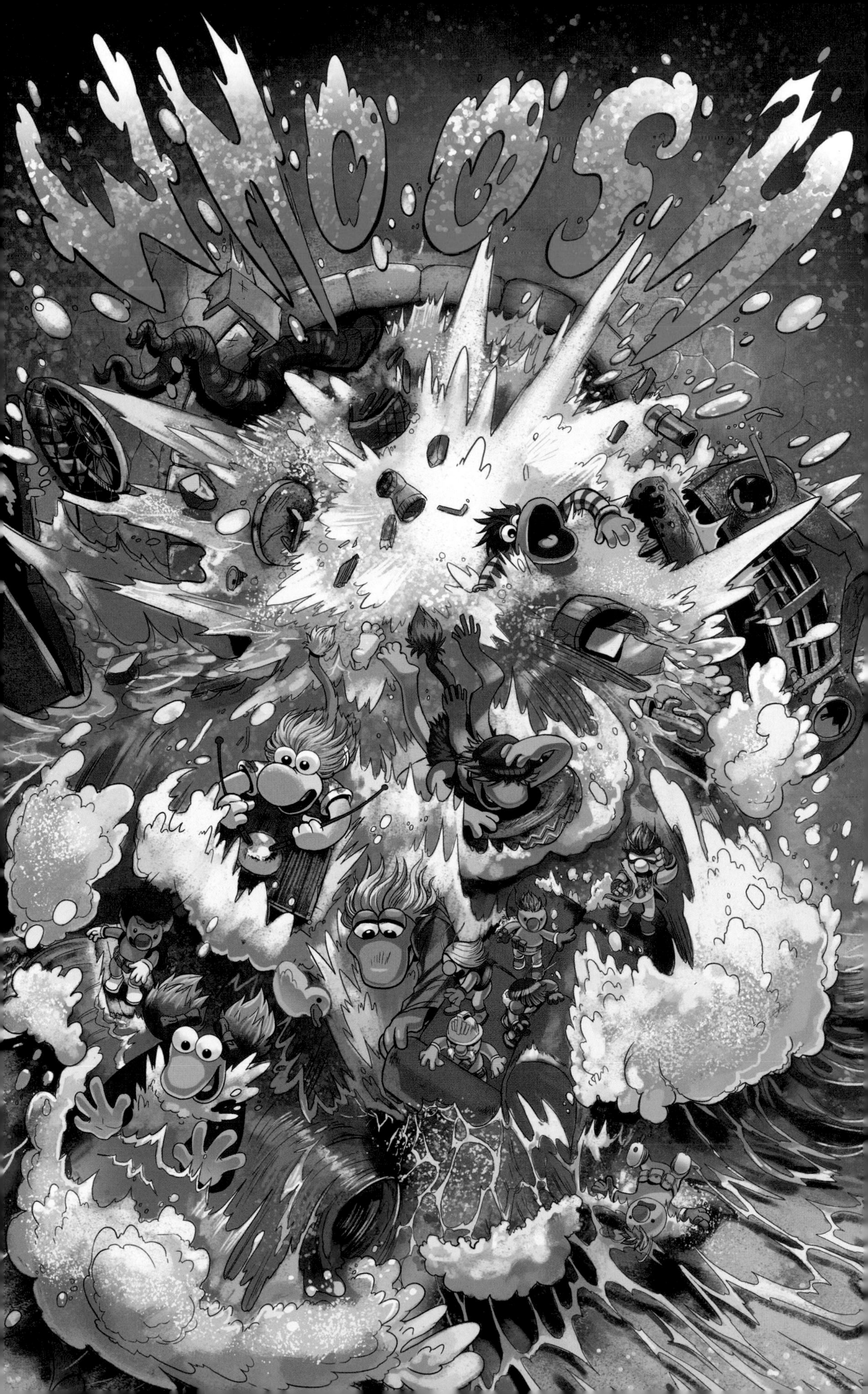
WHOOSH

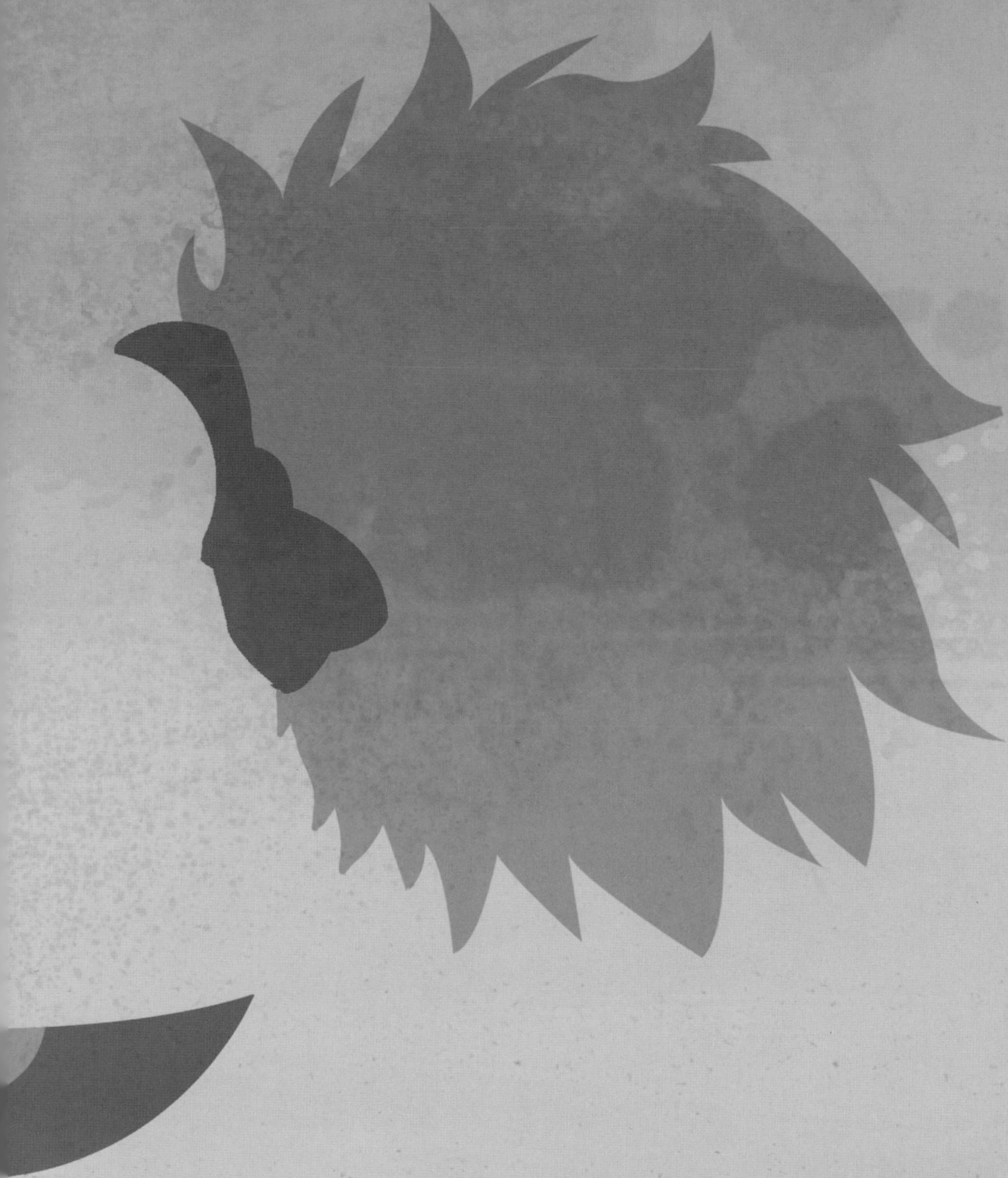

COVER GALLERY

ISSUE 1 COVER BY JAKE MYLER

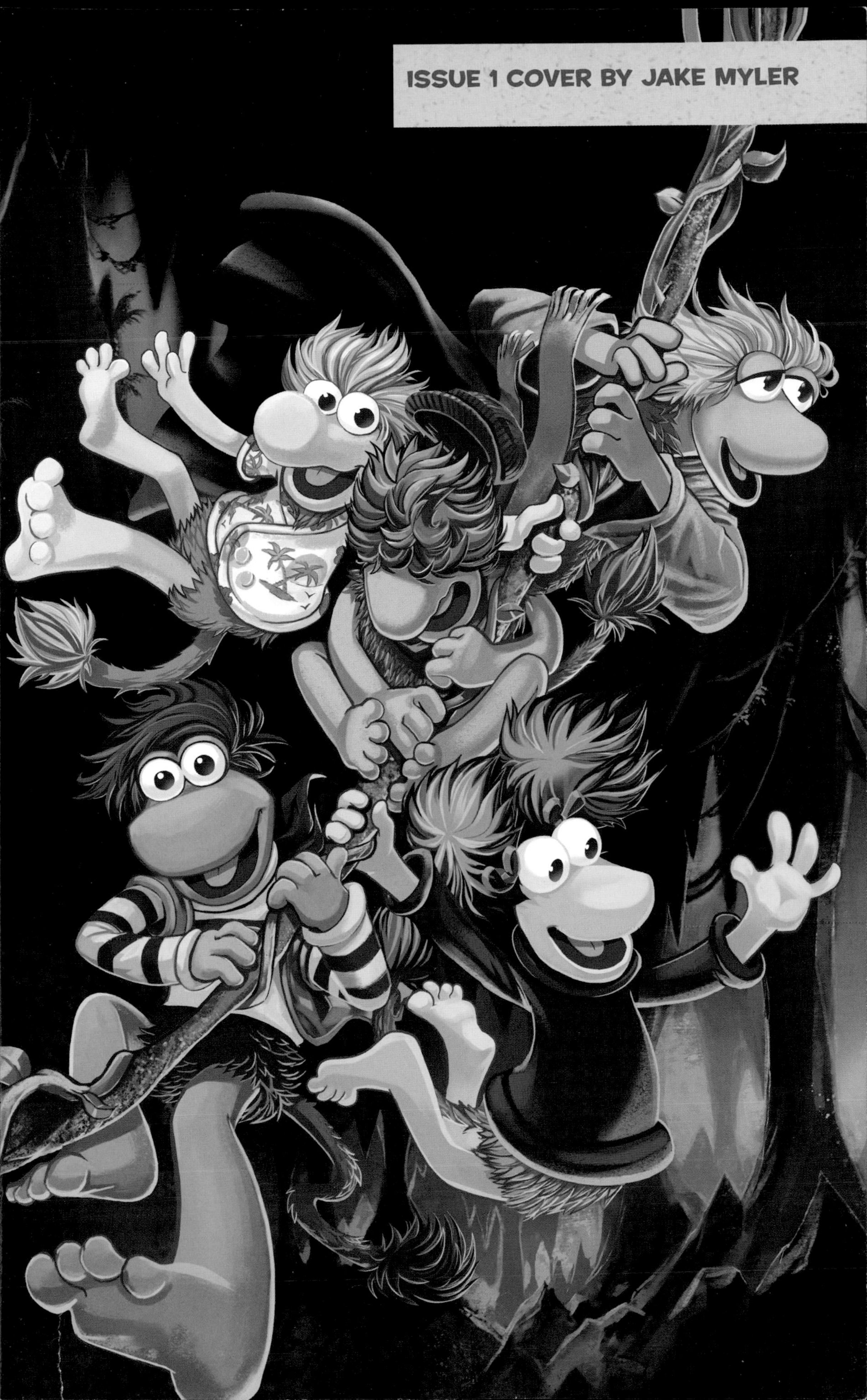

VARIANT COVER BY JAKE MYLER WITH A PHOTO FROM THE JIM HENSON COMPANY ARCHIVES

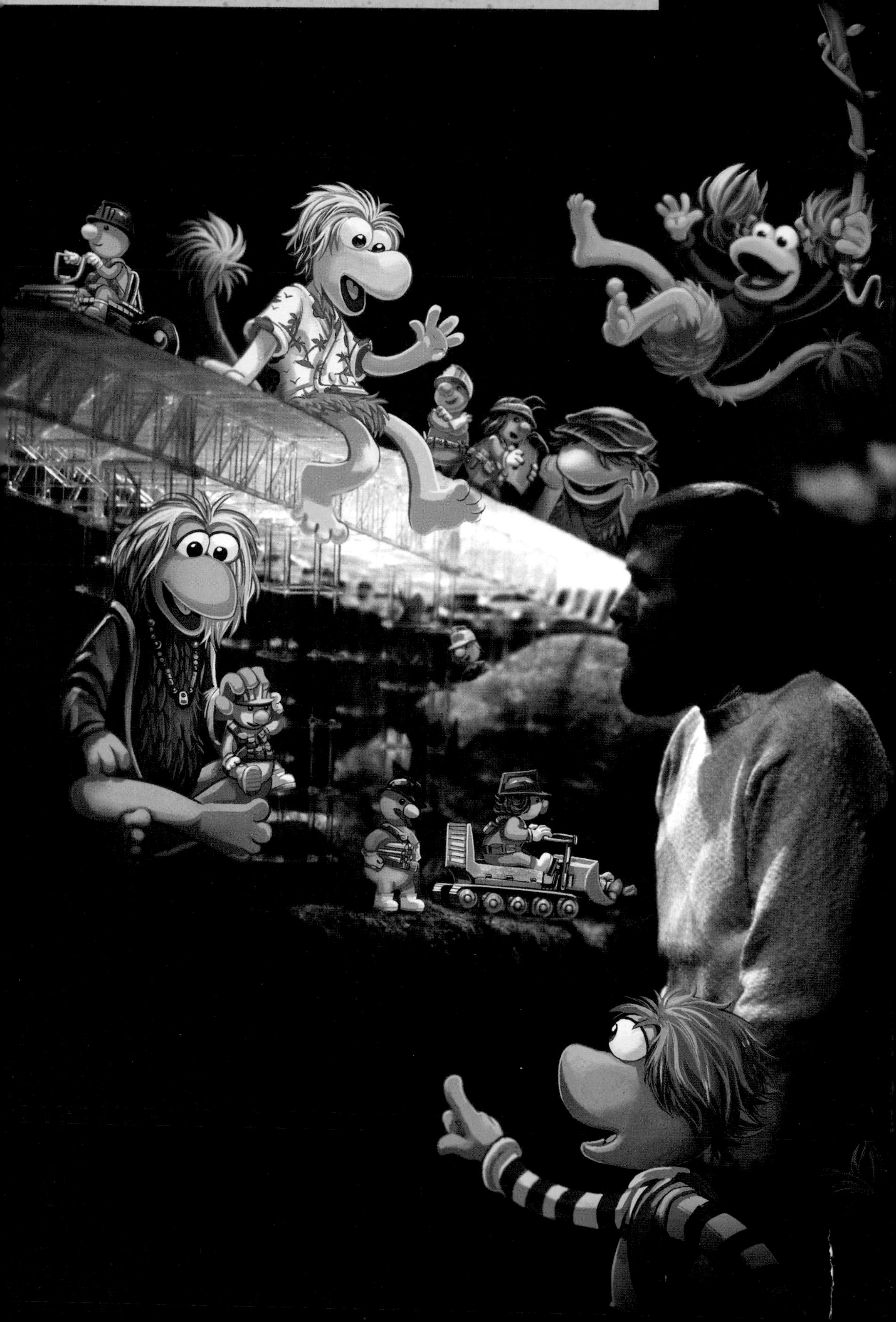

BOOM! EXCLUSIVE COVER BY IAN MCGINTY
WITH COLORS BY FRED STRESING

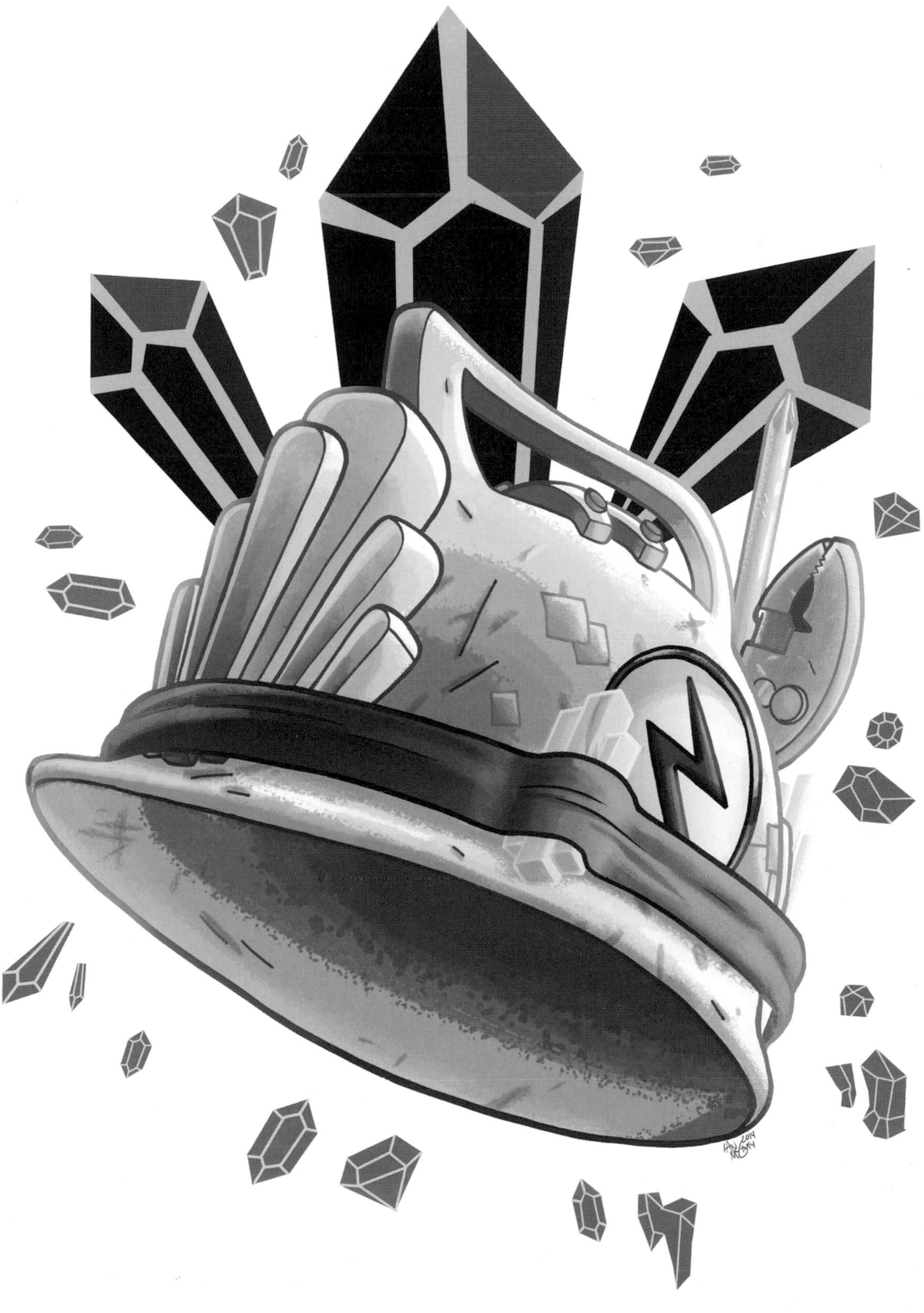

NEW YORK COMIC CON EXCLUSIVE
COVER BY SEAN RUBIN

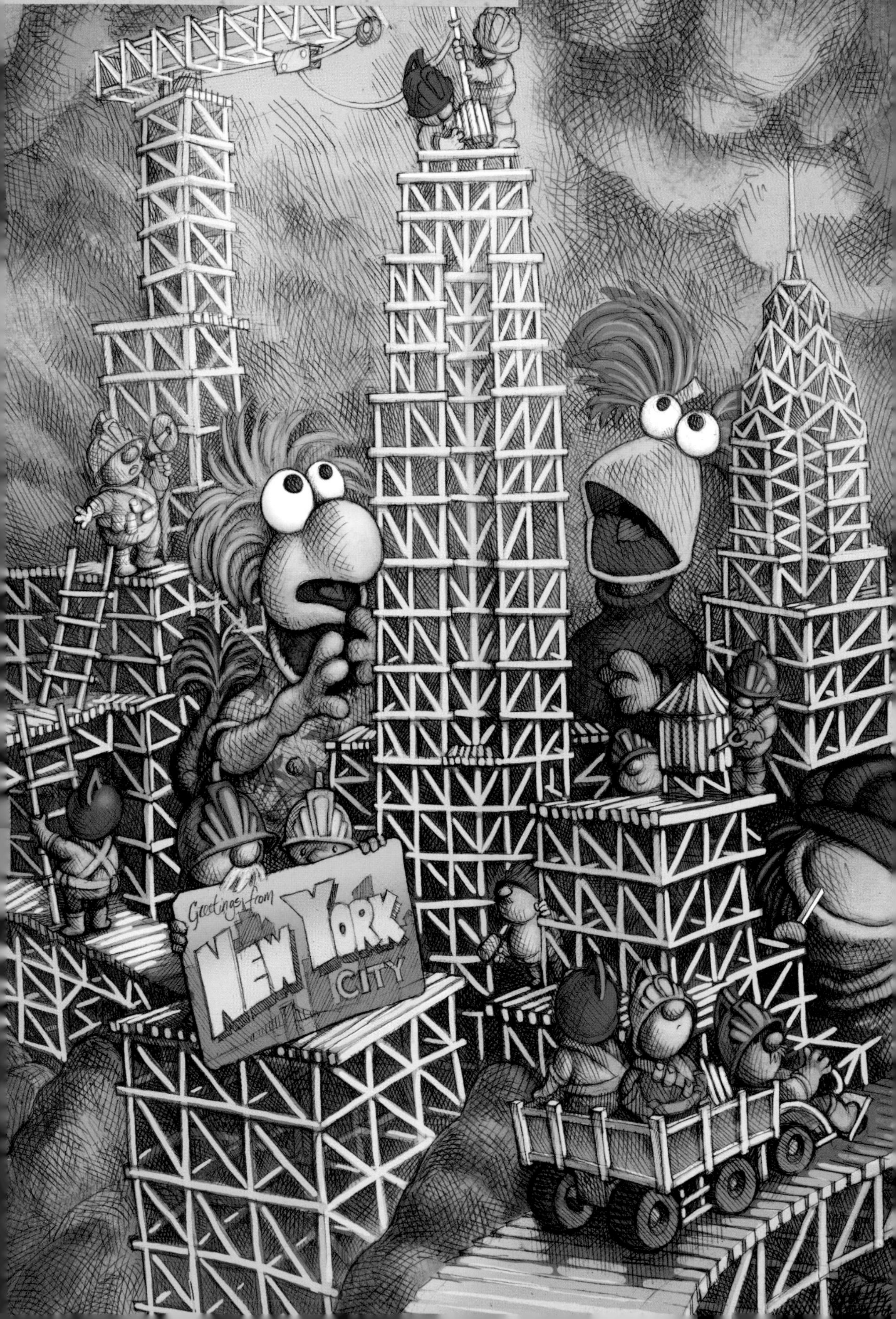
Greetings from
NEW YORK
CITY

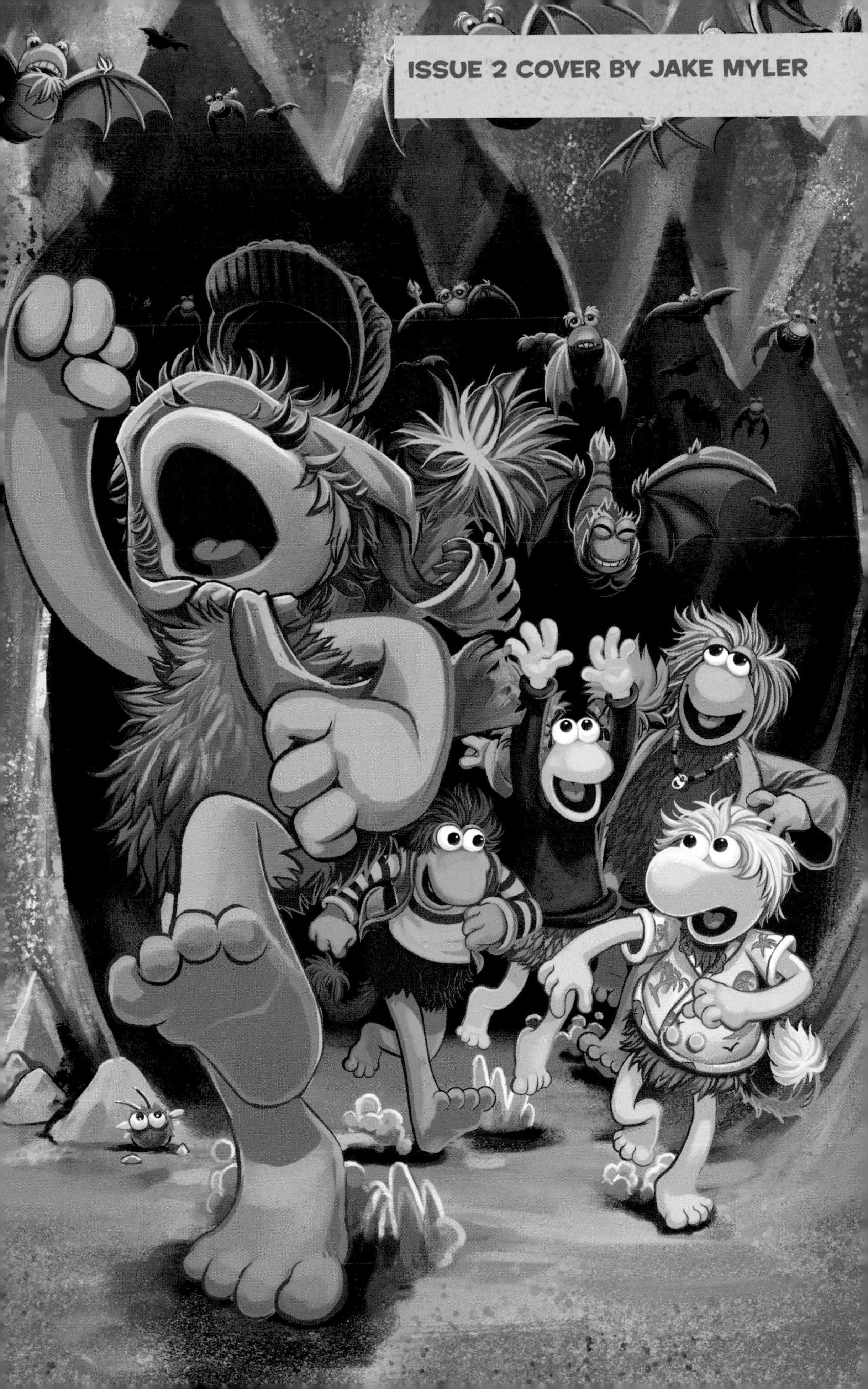

ISSUE 2 COVER BY JAKE MYLER

ISSUE 3 COVER BY JAKE MYLER

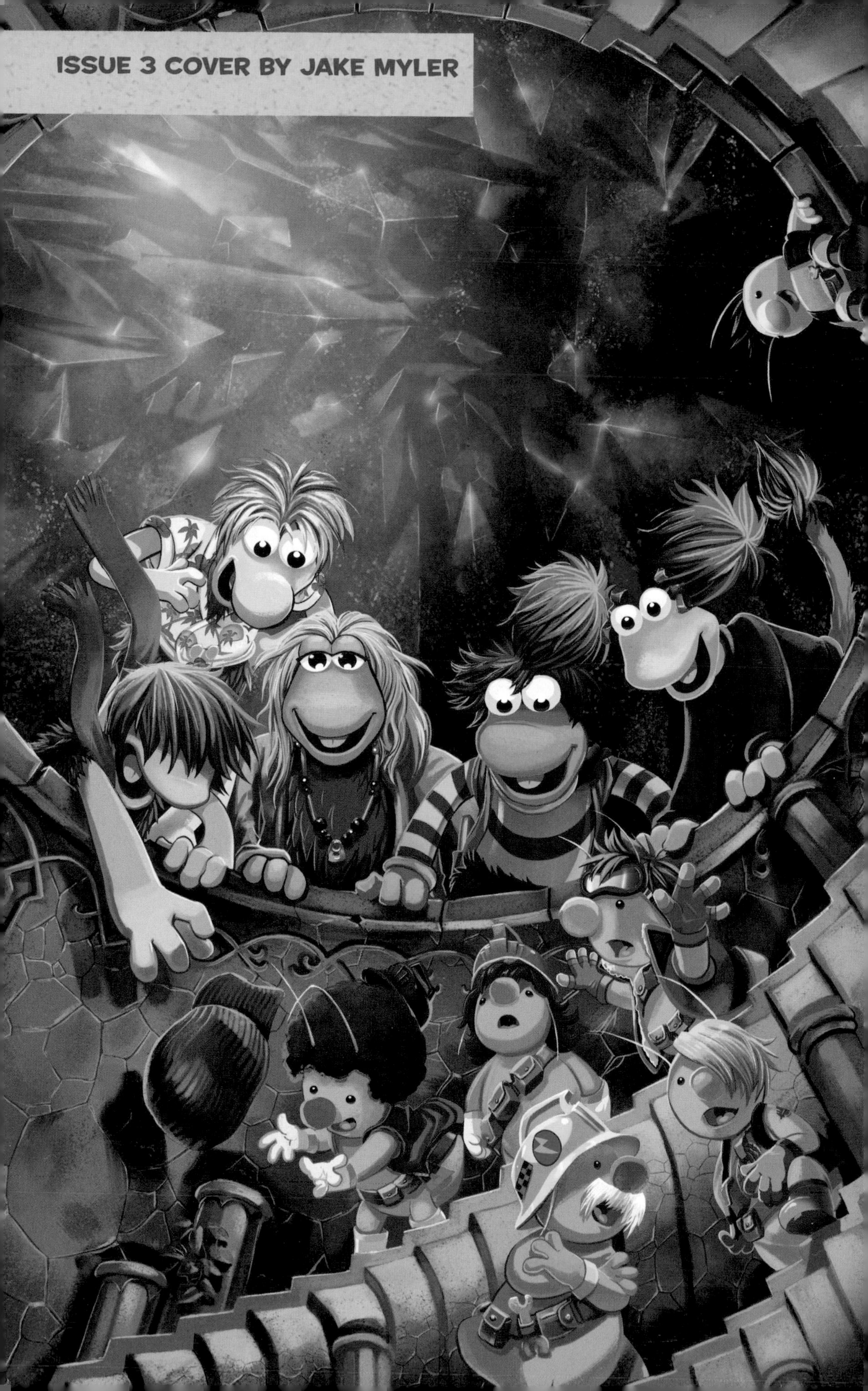

ISSUE 4 COVER BY JAKE MYLER

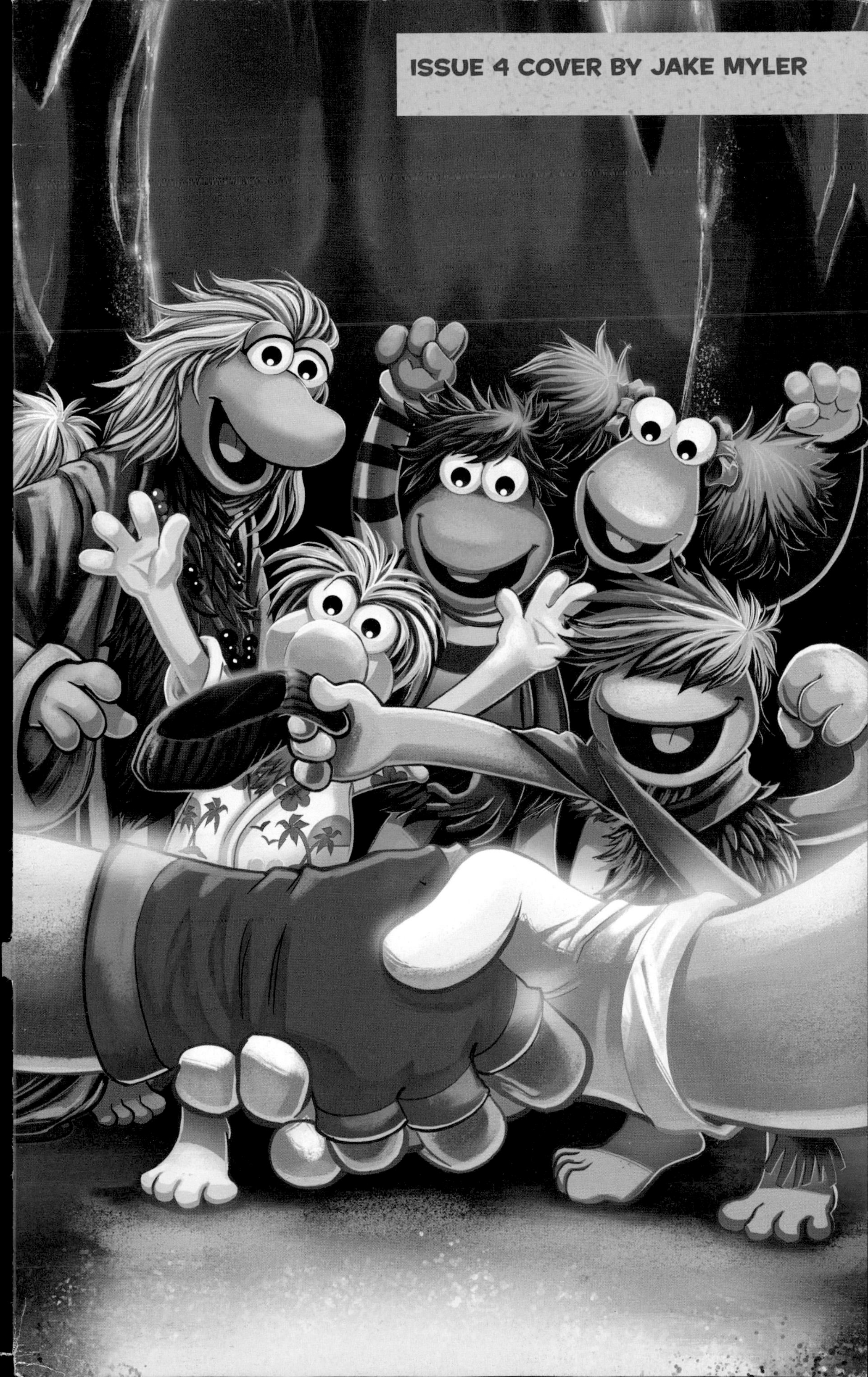

ABOUT THE AUTHORS
KATE LETH & JAKE MYLER

KATE LETH IS A WRITER AND ILLUSTRATOR! SHE IS THE AUTHOR OF TWO *ADVENTURE TIME* BOOKS: *BITTER SWEETS* AND *SEEING RED*. SHE HAS WRITTEN FOR *BRAVEST WARRIORS* AND *EDWARD SCISSORHANDS*, AS WELL AS PLENTY OF HER OWN COMICS ON THE INTERNET AND BEYOND! HER FAVOURITE FRAGGLE IS RED.

HOPELESSLY IN LOVE WITH COFFEE AND DESPISING SUNLIGHT, IT MAKES PERFECT SENSE THAT JAKE MYLER SETTLED DOWN IN SEATTLE WASHINGTON. JAKE HAS ILLUSTRATED THE GRAPHIC NOVELS *ORPHAN BLADE* AS WELL AS *UNDERTOWN*. HE HAS ALSO WORKED AS A COVER ARTIST, PENCILLER, AND COLORIST FOR MANY DISNEY, PIXAR, AND JIM HENSON PROPERTIES. HE ALSO HOPES ONE DAY TO BECOME A SPELUNKER, EXPLORE CAVES AND FIND AN ENTRANCE TO FRAGGLE ROCK. BUT FOR NOW IS HAPPY WITH DRINKING COFFEE AND MAKING COMICS. YOU CAN FIND HIM ON TWITTER AT @LAZESUMMERSTONE.